An action-pac... featuring high-... CIA operatives, ... smugglers, unknown murderers, and sunken treasures plundered from the deep.

"*Jon Coon has hatched a tense plot involving drug smuggling, murder, and wreck piracy in Bermuda waters. He weaves into the story much fascinating Bermuda maritime history and...portrays the controversy between wreck hunting and archaeological digs. The resulting story is both tense and informative, a very creditable first novel by an author who knows the diving world.*"
—Stan Waterman, winner of five Emmy Awards for underwater filmmaking

"*Jon Coon has provided us with an archaeological subterfuge having all the elements of an exciting underwater thriller. The plot twists and turns through a series of adventures that both divers and nondivers will thoroughly enjoy.*"
—R. Duncan Mathewson III, archaeologist for Mel Fisher's hunt for the treasure galleon *Atocha*, author of *Treasure of the Atocha*

THIE F OF THE DEEP

A NOVEL BY
JON COON

AQUA QUEST PUBLICATIONS, INC. ■ NEW YORK

This is a work of fiction. Characters, institutions and organizations in this work are either the product of the author's imagination or, if real, used ficticiously without any intent to describe their actual conduct.

Library of Congress Cataloging-in-Publication Data

Coon, Jon, 1944-
    Thief of the deep : a novel / by Jon Coon.
      p.   cm.
    ISBN 0-9623389-9-0 : $11.95
    I. Title.
PS3553.0577T48 1993
813'.54—dc20   93-16853
                                                  CIP

Cover illustration: Copyright © 1993 by Darrell Sweet
Cover type: Dan Smith

Printed in the United States
10 9 8 7 6 5 4 3 2 1

Distributed to book stores by Publishers Group West
1-800-788-3123

For Marsha and Keith O'Daniel
For adventures shared and yet to come,
For encouragement and laughter and love

For my wife, Rachel, and cat, Clementine
For support, encouragement and patience

ACKNOWLEDGEMENTS

For Tony and Josie Bliss, for believing in Thief and the hundreds of hours it's taken to bring these pages together. Thank you.

My sincere thanks to the following for their patient help and encouragement: Joe Ashley, research, Forman University; Pete Hamilton, Randall Made Knives; Dr. Edward Harris, Director, Bermuda Maritime Museum; Jay Jeffries, submersible engineering; Henry Keats, U-boats; Lorene Mayo, Archives, Smithsonian; Keith O'Daniel, computer and legal consultant; Margaret Potts, Bermuda Biological Station for Research; Captain Ralph Richardson and crew, submarine *Enterprise*; Paul and Janet Slaughter, Dive Bermuda; Professor Gordon Watts, archaeologist, East Carolina University; Doug Whitland, National Firearms Museum; Ralph Wilbanks, archaeologist, magnetometer technology; Joe Young, Division of Armed Forces History, Smithsonian; staff, Bermuda Public Library and Archives; students, 1992 East Carolina University Graduate Archaeological Field School, Bermuda; members, Bermuda Sub-Aqua Club.

For readers with red pencils which are much shorter now: B.C. "Arch" Archibald, Joe Bereswill, Mike Berry, Ione Brown, Al Hornsby, Marsha and Keith O'Daniel, Margaret Potts, Paul and Janet Slaughter, Bob Tallent, Gordon Watts and Ralph Wilbanks.

THIEF OF THE
DEEP

PROLOGUE

Bermuda: July

Debbie Holiday fought hard to clear her pounding head and tried desperately to shake off the fog of sleep threatening to engulf her. She panted hard, but still couldn't satisfy her brain's primal scream for oxygen. The submarine's scrubbers had failed nine hours ago when depth charges shattered the stern compartment's acrylic dome sending the boat plunging four hundred feet to the edge of the Bermuda trench. Now the air was foul with smoke from shorted circuits and burned wiring. Carbon dioxide levels were rising and oxygen was dangerously low.

The flashing red lights of the oxygen monitor alarm cast a morbid hue across Jason Richardson's battered, bleeding face. There were no visible signs that the renegade archaeologist was still alive, so Debbie pulled herself up to the helm seat where he lay unconscious. She reached over and checked his carotid pulse. The beat was weak and erratic, and her fingers came away warm and sticky with fresh blood from his soaked dressings. She took the last package from the first aid kit and struggled to open the thin sterile envelope. She was gasping for breath, her head was spinning, and she felt nauseous. She dropped to her knees by the chair. Her eyes closed and the dressing slipped from her hand, forgotten.

Now she was drifting, flying over patches of colorful coral with the ease and grace of a gull. But her tranquility was short-lived. Suddenly she was falling, past the edge of the shallow reef, down the splendor of the coral wall, beyond the warmth of the light. The water turned dark and with it came great black fish with glowing eyes, dagger teeth and neon markings. They moved around her as if she were part of a bizarre kaleidoscope of benthic monsters.

She watched them with detached fascination. Then a bright light—painful and violent—split the velvet darkness. She raised her arm to shield her eyes as a ghostly apparition descended toward her. Silhouetted in the painful brightness, it shimmered black with long webbed feet and great protuberances hanging from its mouth. The creature came to rest, kneeling on the acrylic dome above her like a huge winged gargoyle. A massive black hand pressed against the dome. She drew back, terrified.

In the glaring halogen lights of the research sub Doc Holiday saw his daughter, Debbie, lying beside the console seat holding Jason Richardson, her arm covering her eyes. Doc drew his long-bladed Randall from its leg sheath and pounded on the dome with its butt. Debbie remained motionless. He pounded harder and swore at Richardson into the mouthpiece of his closed-circuit recirculator. "You son-of-a-bitch, if you're not dead yet, you're going to wish you were."

Doc turned toward the research sub and signaled the captain to cut the lights. Then he pointed the beam of his dive light into the cabin, but away from Debbie's eyes, and pounded on the dome again. This time she lowered her arm, raised her head and stared up at him before collapsing back into her anoxic stupor.

Thank God she's alive, Doc thought, and his heart beat faster and momentarily tears blurred his vision.

He quickly checked the wrist display of the Westinghouse MK XVII closed-circuit, mixed-gas recirculator. The glowing green light told him it was functioning perfectly. With no noisy exhaust bubbles, only the gentle plop, plop of the large diaphragm reminded him of its presence.

Tom and Mike, carrying olive drab dry packs, landed

beside him. Pointing to Debbie, Tom held up the civilian diver OK? sign. Doc hesitated before responding.

I wonder how OK you can be, he asked himself, when you're about to trap yourself inside a disabled sub, not sure you've got enough air for the hours of decompression you'll need before the oversized coffin gets exhumed to the surface by a lunatic drug dealer just waiting for the chance to take you off the tax rolls?

He looked back down at his daughter, fighting for her life only inches away beyond his grasp, and he knew there was only one answer to Tom's question. He gave a military thumbs up and said to himself, "Damn right we're OK, Tom. Things at four hundred feet have never been better. Let's rock and roll."

CHAPTER

1

Bermuda: May

A thin fragment of emerald green metal, which Tom
Morrison recognized as copper bottom sheathing, protruded from the sand at the base of the coral wall. Tom motioned to Debbie Holiday, his diving partner, to come and
look. She swam to his side with slow graceful kicks, looked
and merely nodded. She had seen plenty of bottom sheathing in Bermuda—there were so many old wreck sites. Tom
fanned the sand away, exposing more of the metal. It had
the dull, reddish hue of pure copper, not the copper-zinc
alloy called Muntz metal used after 1850. This ship had to
have been built or resheathed sometime between 1770 and
1850.

They swam along the reef ledge and found more of the
green metal. Tom fanned the sand again, and this time was
rewarded with two musket balls and an unused gun flint. Now
Debbie was interested. Finding the flint suggested a date
earlier than 1830 when percussion caps came into use and
most flintlocks were converted. He put the flint in his buoyancy compensator pocket and took Debbie's hand. She smiled
and they continued exploring. The water was warm, clear
and shallow. They had swum one hundred fifty yards from
the rest of the group. A quick check of their pressure gauges

showed their tanks were still half full.

Tom pointed forward and they continued along the ledge. For fifteen or twenty yards there was no more evidence of the wreck, then Debbie saw the heavily encrusted muzzle of a large cannon protruding from the coral. It was iron with a three-inch bore. They dropped to the bottom for a closer look, and Tom pointed to the outlines of a second and third also encased in the reef. Tom fanned the sand again, uncovering large timbers with protruding brass spikes. As they crossed over the top of the narrow reef to the sand on the other side, Debbie's eyes opened wide in amazement.

Before them was a large sand patch the size of a tennis court. Coral walls ringed it, and the gentle surge waved purple sea fans hypnotically back and forth. But it was the large bronze cannons laying exposed in the sand that caught their attention. Wooden timbers, pieces of rigging, brass fittings and black glass bottles covered the bottom. She was a newly discovered wreck, but no virgin. Craters pockmarked the sand, testifying that someone had recently worked on the site with prop wash diverters called blasters by salvage divers.

Tom and Debbie swam cautiously to the sand. It was as if they were trespassing in a castle courtyard half-expecting the guards to suddenly appear and arrest them. A large stingray lifted out of the sand, startling them before it gracefully moved away. They dropped gently down beside the largest crater. Debbie checked her computer; they were now at sixty feet.

At the crater bottom were six-foot long, narrow wooden crates. Tom pulled at the planks and the water-logged wood broke easily. The crate contained long, thin rolls of heavy fabric like burlap impregnated with heavy grease. He was surprised at the weight as he lifted one of them, then he guessed what it contained. Carefully, he removed the protective swaddling. As it fell away it revealed a flintlock in excellent condition. The heavy grease had protected even the dark wooden stock. He handed it to Debbie and picked up another.

Captain Paul Singleton sat on the fly bridge of the *Mermaid*, his 38-foot wooden, twin-diesel charter boat. He removed his dark glasses and squinted across the calm western sea into the late afternoon sun. He was a solid man in his early fifties, darkly tanned with short, sandy blond hair and an easy smile that came from the confidence of knowing and doing one's job well. He was looking for the bubbles of his last two divers.

Tom and Debbie were not late, not really. They were just the last ones up. She was the daughter of one of his best friends and the thought that anything might happen to her, well, that was a thought he wouldn't allow. She was a good diver, an instructor in fact. There was no need to worry, so where the hell are they? He continued to scan the horizon, shading his eyes with his salt-stained Atlanta Braves ball cap, a gift from her father.

"They're on the safety bar, Captain," yelled Matt, his tow-headed young deckhand and divemaster. "Should be up soon."

Where could they have been that he missed them coming back? Paul wondered. They were certainly not west of the wreck he had anchored on. Well, they were back. Debbie could take care of herself. What was that tall, dark-headed boy's name again—her computer genius from NASA? Paul's memory lapse angered him. Was it only recently he couldn't remember names, or had he always been this bad?

Paul went down the varnished mahogany ladder to the deck to greet them, and to satisfy his curiosity. The richly oiled teak deck was strewn with scuba gear and he gave Matt a scowl. Matt understood and encouraged the customers to stow their equipment for the ride back to the Dockyard.

Debbie was first up the ladder. She was a swimmer with a lean, strong body. She wore her light brown hair short, and she had her mother's good looks and green eyes, frequently full of the devil. As a child she laughed more than she spoke. She was lucky to look like her mother, Paul chuckled to himself. Her father, Dr. John Holiday, a large, raw-boned ex-SEAL wouldn't have won any beauty contests. Matt hurried to help her out of her tank and to make certain neither it nor her weight belt dropped on the teak.

She quickly grabbed a towel and called over to Paul. "Come see what we've found. You won't believe it. It's the best wreck I've ever seen." Her eyes were wide and flashing with excitement.

She stepped back onto the dive platform, took the flint-locks from Tom, and handed them up to Paul and Matt. Paul stared at the gun in amazement. In thirty years of diving, he had never seen anything made of iron come out of the water as well preserved as these guns.

Tom Morrison pounded his desk, and swore in anger and disbelief. It was late and he was the only engineer working in the old NASA computer complex. Bob, the aging security guard, was on his rounds so only the wooden floors, high plaster walls and gray government furniture could hear his curses, and they remained indifferent. The room was dark except for the low lamp on his desk and the green glow of the computer screen. Morrison pushed back his chair and shook his head. Early last year he had discovered how to link his computer to the Navy satellites used for tracking subma-rines and locating downed aircraft. The satellite saw every-thing. It could tell you every time a whale passed gas, how much and what color. So why couldn't it find that wreck? He thumbed through the pages of the worn spiral notebook, found three more wrecks close to the new one, and fed in their coordinates.

The screen immediately showed, as it had a hundred times before, the infrared wreck images in sequence, and with support data. Then he reentered the GPS coordinates of the new site. Nothing, just an empty coral bottom in sixty feet of gin-clear Bermuda water. It was impossible, but there it was. Either the satellite was going blind or the computer was lying.

CHAPTER

2

Atlanta, Georgia: May

The old black Ford Bronco was a rusted friend. The seats were wide and comfortable, good for the many long dive trips Doc Holiday's family had made from Atlanta to Florida—to the small beach house and the panhandle that would always be home. The seats smelled like saltwater and there was a little rust where dive gear had drained. Had the carpet been any color other than black, the stains of chain saws, outboard motors, fish boxes, bait, tackle and the hair of a monster black lab named Buttons would have rendered it undesirable for contact with most life forms, especially human.

Then there was the sand—sand in the carpet, sand under the seats, sand in the glove box. Soft white sugar-fine sand was in everything, and there wasn't a vacuum made that could get it all out. Not that Doc had tried. He believed sand was a problem only if you hadn't learned to appreciate it. He liked sand and had once cultivated a pair of deck shoes until they contained samples of it from five oceans. It was a nice ecumenical mix. But just as they were reaching their salty prime, his young wife, Nancy, pitched them and got him new ones. It was a sad moment.

The loss of his favorite shoes was compounded by the

cruel realization that men and women are different. Nancy was his best friend, his wife, and the mother of his child. But she was never able to look at some things he valued and appreciate them nearly as much as he did—like the old Harley in the shed out back.

He was alone now. Nancy had died suddenly two years ago and his daughter, Debbie, was a Navy ensign stationed in Bermuda. As usual, he hadn't heard from her for a while. They didn't talk on the phone much; it was too hard to mesh busy schedules. But they did write, usually exchanging computer disks.

Even Buttons was gone. She'd died in her sleep last year at the foot of his bed. He wondered if it was because her job was done. She had helped raise Debbie while he was away, still in the Navy, and watched over the girls and their tiny house. Buttons had not liked the move to Atlanta. She missed the beach, and Nancy and Debbie. The morning she died he had cried, driven her to Florida and buried her by the lagoon in the shade of her favorite live oak.

That was the last time he had been to the beach house. When he finished caring for Buttons, he locked the doors and drove straight back to Atlanta. He would go again, but not yet—not soon.

Camping gear, a tackle box full of bass lures and two good graphite rods with Ambassador reels waited in the back of the truck. He was going to the lake this weekend. Lake Lanier was less than two hours away and he would spend the weekend grading papers and fishing. Finals were nearly over but the big bass were still in the shallows due to the late spring. It was too good to miss. There was a Bass Masters emblem on the rear window next to the "Go Navy" bumper sticker which was above the "Desert Storm" sticker, and across from a faded smiling red seal sitting on the letters USN.

The brakes squeaked a little as he turned into the Georgia State University parking lot. The sticker on his front bumper proved that the Bronco actually belonged in a faculty parking space, and even though he had completed his Ph.D. in English literature ten years ago—the year they bought the Bronco—he still had a hard time with the vision of himself as Dr. John Holiday. "Doc" Holiday, as he had been called in the Navy, fit because of his rating as a hospital corpsman with dive teams. But as much as he loved teaching, and loved early American literature and its history, Dr. Holiday in a coat and tie was never quite the same person as Doc Holiday in shorts and sand-filled, battered, paint-splattered deck shoes.

However, it was a coat-and-tie day so he wheeled the paid-for, ten-year old, unwashed, unpolished Bronco into his space between a gleaming beamer and an immaculate Mercedes. Wonder where they carry the fish boxes and the firewood, he thought and laughed. He gathered his books and student folders from the passenger seat, left his gym bag and headed to the office.

His office was not large, and appeared even smaller because of abundant memorabilia, unopened mail, and organized stacks of student themes. Overflowing bookcases lined two walls. In back of the modest metal desk was a table piled with journals, reference works and bass boat catalogs. Maggie, the department secretary, had left yesterday's mail on his chair, the only remaining unoccupied space. On top of the pile was an envelope with stamps of tall ships under full sail. Debbie had finally written.

He put the things he was carrying on the floor, cleared off the chair, sat and opened the envelope. It contained two photographs and a computer disk. He turned on his computer, put the keyboard in his lap, and studied the photographs while he waited. The photos were of Debbie, Paul and a young man he didn't recognize. He was a reasonably tall, athletic-looking fellow in his late twenties with a short military haircut and with his arm around Debbie. They were on board the *Mermaid*, holding two flintlock rifles.

When the computer was ready, he inserted the disk and pulled up the directory. There was only one file, titled "Hi Dad". He called it up and waited. The letter read:

Dear Dad,

Thanks a million for the great laptop and the software. What a great birthday surprise! I've really missed the old one you and mom gave me for college and still can't believe it was stolen. Things on the base are great;

you are going to love it here. The satellite survey and tracking is really interesting. We watch over submarines, ours and everyone else's.

I followed your advice and went to a Bermuda Sub-Aqua Club meeting. Your friends Paul and Janet are still very active, still have the dive store at the Dockyard, and best of all, still run the Mermaid for charters. They invited me to work with them and teach. I want to keep my rating active and this will be the perfect way.

The freshly scrubbed preppie in the photos is Tom Morrison from NASA. We've gone out a few times. We found a wonderful new wreck with cannon, saber hilts and crates of these old flintlocks. Can you believe the condition they are in? They were packed in some kind of heavy cloth and grease which protected them. Paul was so excited. He says this could be the most important archaeological discovery since Edmund Downing found the Sea Venture in 1958.

Someone has been working the site and Paul is trying to find out who. He doesn't think they have a permit, and if not, he will claim it for the Maritime Museum at the Dockyard and the club will start work real soon. So hurry up and get here. This is just what you need. I'm up for Lieutenant j.g. If I get it we'll celebrate and I'll buy. If not we'll still celebrate and you buy. What else is new? Thanks again for the computer. I won't let this one get away. More later. Hurry up and get here. This is going to be a great summer.

Love,
  Debbie

He smiled, turned off his computer and studied the photos again. She seemed happy, her green eyes flashing with excitement and looking very much like her mother. The ocean in the background appeared calm and inviting. He turned the chair around and stared at the photos on the "love me" wall. There were dive shots from all over the world—some of UDT and SEAL teams, some of dive classes he had taught and instructors he had trained. Debbie was in one of those.

She had been the outstanding candidate at her instructor evaluation.

In one photo, three faces stared back through scuba masks. Debbie was on his right and Nancy on his left. "Two years," he said softly. "My Lord, how can it be?" He breathed deeply and closed his eyes. There were parts of him that had not yet healed and he wondered if they ever would.

Turning the chair back to the desk, he picked up a theme paper from the top of one of the ungraded piles. The title page announced, "The Influence of Quaker Theology on the Philosophy of Ralph Waldo Emerson" by Mark Danvers. He looked back at the photos of Debbie and at the ocean behind her. Then he opened the paper and reached for a red pencil.

At six-thirty, the parking spaces on either side of the Bronco were empty. There was a squealing of tires in the parking garage as a glaring red, mid-sized, king cab pick-up turned the corner just a little too fast. A roll bar with four lights on top was mounted to the frame. Dive flags trimmed the vanity license plates which read "Sheri". The bumper sticker on the right side of the rear plate announced "Divers Do It Deeper", while the one on the left asked "Gone Down Lately?"

Twenty-seven year old Sheri Benson opened the door and bounced to the pavement. She was a tall, strikingly attractive, short-haired blond, perhaps a bit muscular from running and regular workouts, but she filled her pink-striped running shorts and matching tank top well. She brought her hands up to her breasts and swore softly. This was not the first time she had forgotten to step down rather than bounce.

She pushed her seat forward, and pulled out a heavy pink dive bag and a soft briefcase. As she crossed the street she saw Mark Danvers's new black Jeep with gold wheels and trim turn into the parking garage. She smiled and went into the pool building.

It was the fourth night of class. Mark Danvers, a grad student from Boston, was her divemaster and teaching assistant. They'd met last year on the archaeological field trip to

Bermuda. This year they were going back, and Sheri would be the trip leader which was reason enough for half the single male population of Georgia to want to go.

The lectures had gone well and now they were on the pool bottom practicing buoyancy control skills. Only one student was still having problems. She and Mark had nicknamed him "Buffalo" Bob because of his linebacker size and his penchant for ramming, kicking or landing on other students while remaining totally oblivious to the problems he left in his wake. Most of the other students were now able to hover nearly motionless, but Bob was still over-controlling and either roaring to the surface or crashing like an anchor to the bottom. But Sheri was confident that with a little more practice, even Bob could master this important skill.

"Remember the slides of the beautiful Bermuda reefs?" she said when the drill was complete and they were all standing in the shallow end. "The only way to protect those reefs is to never touch the coral. And the only way to do that is to have absolute control of your buoyancy. So this skill is very, very important. You did well and you'll be great divers."

Next was buddy breathing, an air sharing skill handy in out-of-air situations. She demonstrated on the surface and then in shallow water before dividing the group into donors and out-of-air dummies to have them try it.

Bob and his girlfriend, Karen, were the last to submerge and the first to break to the surface. She came up coughing.

"Now what's wrong?" Bob demanded in an accusative and condescending tone.

"I exhaled all my air waiting for you to give me the regulator and when you finally got around to it, your hand was covering the purge button so I couldn't clear it or get any air."

"I didn't cover anything. You just don't know what you're doing. I had it right."

Mark was closest to them and moved in. "Hi, everything OK?" he asked with a smile.

"Yeah, sure, she had another problem and I was straightening her out," Bob answered. Karen gave him a killing look behind his back. Sheri surfaced just in time to catch his comment and correctly sized up the situation.

"Bob," she said putting her hand on his shoulder, "why don't you practice with me a while and we'll let Mark work with Karen?"

"That's a great idea," Karen said a bit too quickly and then turned to face Mark.

Sheri moved Bob into position on her left. "Come on, Bob, you be the dummy," she said before they submerged.

"OK, Karen, what position do you want?" asked Mark.

"On top," Karen said with a suggestive smile. She was delighted when she saw him blush and moved to his right into the donor position. Underwater, she took two breaths and offered him the regulator.

He waited until he saw her exhalation bubbles, and when they came he accepted the regulator and continued the cycle. As they swam to the end of the pool, she moved in tight against him. He felt her hand slide from the small of his back to his posterior anatomy. When he rolled his shoulders so he could to look into her mask, a burst of bubbles came from her regulator. She was laughing. It was then they ran into the side of the pool.

They surfaced and Mark inflated both their buoyancy control jackets.

"Is watching where we're going part of this skill?" she asked.

"Guess one of us needs to concentrate on navigation."

"You lead, I'll follow, as long as you go where I want...."

"Karen, aren't you done yet?" Bob shouted from the other end of the pool.

"We haven't even started," she said softly enough for only Mark to hear. She pulled her hand from his and started to swim away, but then stopped.

"Well, come on, Mark. You can still swim, can't you?" Karen teased. "Or do you need some time by yourself?"

Before Mark could answer, she pulled him close, pulled the regulator from his mouth and resumed the exercise. When they reached the shallow end, she patted his rear again and was gone before he could say a word.

Sheri swam into the shallows and surfaced beside him. "Do you need a rescue?" she asked.

"I just might," he said with hesitation. "Are they coming

to Bermuda?"

"They're on the list. Shall I tell them to stay home, or can you handle it?"

"No, no, I'll be fine. But she's something—a barracuda with lipstick."

"Let's start wrapping up. After they're gone we can work on your divemaster skills or the rescue skills. Then I want to do some laps."

Karen really got to him in a hurry, Sheri thought. She tilted her head to the side and studied him for a moment as if coming to a decision. He was watching Karen climb the ladder at the far end of the pool and failed to notice Sheri's scrutiny. Karen's long blond hair came below her tiny waist. She tugged at her suit a bit at both top and bottom, then turned and looked back at Mark with a smile as if she had felt his eyes undressing her.

Sheri was jealous of that look. She moved over to Mark and touched his shoulder. He jumped. She laughed. "I want to warm up in the shower. Can you finish up here? Save our rigs and I'll be right back."

"Sure," he answered. "I'll get everything put away."

Sheri entered the shower as Karen was turning off the water. "You're lucky to be an instructor," Karen said wrapping her hair in a towel. "I bet you have some really great times. The guys are great and the water is such a turn on. Is it like that on trips too? I can't wait."

"The trips are even better. Just wait till we get to Bermuda, you'll see." Sheri stepped under the steaming shower with her suit on. She tried not to stare at Karen's breasts, but they were gorgeous, full and firm. She hoped her new ones looked as good. She was glad she had kept her suit on. She didn't want Karen to see her scars. Karen enjoyed being admired and she smiled before Sheri looked away. Sheri let the hot water warm her neck and shoulders, and shifted her thoughts to Mark. She hoped she hadn't waited too long.

He was waiting alone in the pool when she returned. "Did you lock up?" she asked.

"Yes, we are finally alone," he said laughing.

"OK, "she said, "why don't we start with rescue skills? You're doing pretty well with the divemaster stuff. Let's do an unconscious, non-breathing victim. Bring me up, simulate mouth-to-mouth while removing my equipment and swim me to the shallow end. Remember to ventilate every five seconds and count out loud—it's easier to concentrate. Ready?"

"I stay ready."

"Like in the corner with Karen? You looked plenty ready." But she was underwater when she said it and the words came innocently to the surface in her bubbles. She lay waiting on the bottom face down, arms floating outstretched. She was still warm from the shower and it was time to have some fun.

Mark was thinking of Karen as he swam. There was certainly no doubt of her intent, or was there? How could she stand being with Bob? If he closed his eyes he could almost still feel her beside him, pulling him to her and exploring his body. He shook his head to clear his mind. He was nearly to Sheri. Perhaps he could talk this over with her when they finished the skills. He began his descent.

Mark landed beside Sheri and reached under her to start the lift. When he touched her she took his hand and guided it inside her buoyancy control jacket to her breast. She held his hand there and slowly rolled to face him.

Doc passed some of the scuba students in the parking garage as he went to the Bronco to get his gym bag. He noticed the red pick-up next to his Ford and wondered what kind of girl would drive a truck with those bumper stickers. Times have changed. He shook his head and headed to the pool.

This was his favorite time to swim. The pool would be empty, dark and quiet. He would swim a mile or more. No sprints, nothing fancy, just a soul-flushing steady six-count crawl with polished racing turns and endurance to spare. He had his own key to the pool from one of the coaches he took fishing. To get it he had promised not to drown and not to sue the school if he did.

The locker room lights were still on. Scuba class must have run longer tonight. He hadn't taught for several years now and missed it. Someday he would have to get his rating current again. He hung his clothes in a locker, put on the old black suit and went to the pool. He stopped short when he realized there were divers on the bottom of the deep end. So much for tranquil solitude, he thought.

Storm clouds of bubbles billowed to the surface, and then a woman's tank suit was carried up in the tornado. The refraction bent the images, but he could see two naked divers wrapped in each other gliding gracefully along the bottom. He stepped back from the pool's edge. They don't teach that skill in beginning classes—nice buoyancy control, he chuckled while turning back toward the locker room. Let them have their fun. He would swim another night.

Sheri was on her back with her eyes closed as Mark guided them across the bottom. She was still breathing hard and lost in the moment. The look on Mark's face when she turned to him had been perfect. It had taken "Mr. Ready" only a second to accept her invitation and within an instant they were out of their suits. The exercise had been a complete academic success. She had accomplished all her teaching objectives and he had clearly demonstrated mastery of the skill. Now she closed her eyes and drifted, weightless, feeling only his warmth, his breathing and the power of his rhythmic dolphin kick.

Then a voice deep within her called her back from the dream. She tried to ignore it, but found her eyes open and staring up through the water at the distorted image of a man standing on the deck. She pulled Mark closer, and together they came to the surface. They arrived at the side of the pool too late to get a clear look at the face of the big, dark-haired man going into the locker room. But as he pulled open the door, Sheri thought she saw a red tattoo on his left arm. She was right. It was a smiling red seal.

CHAPTER
3

Bermuda: Wednesday, ten days later

Tom had been awake most of the night. He had given up trying to sleep and was now in his favorite chair, a creaky old white wicker rocker. He stared out the open window at the millions of stars in the clear night sky, gripped the arms of the rocker tightly, and rocked and creaked with great determination. Angry and concerned about his discovery, he needed to talk to his boss and mentor, Bill Roberts, the station director. But opening that discussion meant admitting he'd been using NASA computers and Navy satellites to bootleg wreck locations, and that confession could cost him his security clearance and his job.

It had taken college, a master's degree in computer science, two years of applications, interviews and waiting to get this job. He hadn't wanted just any job with NASA. He had gone after this one, here in Bermuda, and he intended to stay forever. Now, not only might he lose his career and Bermuda, he could lose Debbie as well. Not that much had happened yet, but she was everything on his shopping list—bright, beautiful, athletic and a great diver. She was the one he'd waited for...well, sort of waited. Yes, she was the one alright.

The chair continued to creak. It would be daylight soon

and he was still undecided. He could keep quiet about the whole thing. But what if there were more to this than just a computer glitch or another hacker trying to hide one wreck site? What if someone had found a way to access the satellite network and alter the data? The odds of that happening were a million to one, but what if that were the case? Could he take that chance? No, not even to save his butt. There was no easy way out. He knew what he had to do. He'd tell Debbie tomorrow and Bill Roberts the minute Roberts returned. He left the chair and went back to the bedroom. There was still another sleepless hour till dawn. The rocker continued rocking momentarily without him.

North Georgia: Wednesday

Sheri opened her eyes and stared at the ceiling of the tent. It was a cool morning in the north Georgia mountains. She snuggled down into the double sleeping bag against Mark Danvers who still slept soundly. The last three weeks had been wonderful. Mark was not only as diligent and kind as a boy scout, he was not trying to run her life as most men had. She knew he still thought about Karen, but since Karen was still with Bob, Sheri considered her more an irritation than a real threat.

They had laughed several times about being caught in the pool. Nothing had come of it, but still they wondered who it had been and how much he might have seen.

They were at the rock quarry beneath the tall Georgia pines to do Advanced and Rescue training for the group going to Bermuda. The navigation and underwater naturalist dives yesterday and the night dive last night had gone very well. The students, most of them from the city, had especially liked the campfire and cookout. It was so easy to be a kid again at a campfire. Soon they were telling ghost stories and then the more experienced divers started on their sea stories and dive adventures. They went around the circle telling of their most exciting dives. Sheri told about her first encounter with a moray eel.

It had been on her first night dive in the Florida Keys.

She was with her instructor looking for lobster under the low coral ledges on Molasses Reef. Suddenly a large green moray moved into her light. She came a foot off the bottom, banging her head on the ledge above. Her instructor calmed her by taking her hand, and then guided the offending light out of the eel's eyes. They waited for a moment and, no longer blinded, the five-foot long eel came cautiously forward displaying an impressive set of dental work.

It was only later Sheri learned that eels have to constantly open and close their mouths to force water through their gills. The eel was not threatening her. It was only breathing. Sheri was very frightened but she followed the direction of her instructor and held her open hand to the eel. As the eel came closer they saw the end of a stainless steel fishing leader hanging from its mouth. It took every bit of guts Sheri had not to pull her hand away. Slowly, the wounded eel came to her and in a heartbreaking moment laid its head in her open hand. The hook was swallowed well beyond its gullet, and the steel fishing leader had cut deeply into its jaw muscles and broken several teeth. It was obvious the eel could not feed and was starving. There was nothing she could do. There was silence around the campfire when she finished the story.

She looked at her watch and then quickly pulled her arm back into the warm sleeping bag. She smiled, rolled closer to Mark and slid her cold hand down his warm stomach. It was still early.

Bermuda: Wednesday evening

Tom met Debbie late that afternoon at the Naval Station Annex Computer Command Center near Somerset. Debbie climbed on the back of his Honda scooter and they were on their way to the Wednesday night British Sub-Aqua Club meeting on the north side of Hamilton. They followed the narrow winding road, flanked at times with stretches of high stone walls, and at other times with ocean views framed in tropical flowers and manicured gardens. They crossed the world's smallest drawbridge, which opens just wide enough for the mast of a modestly-sized sailboat, to the ferry landing at Somerset. The ferry arrived on time and after loading the scooter on board, they went out on the bow deck where they could talk in private. As the boat crossed the emerald bay to Hamilton, he told her of his discovery and his suspicions. A chill swept through her as she got the implication of his story. "I didn't mean any harm, Debbie, I swear," Tom finished. "I just wanted to find some new wrecks and the satellite was the perfect way to do it. I have a top secret clearance so I wasn't even doing anything illegal."

"But if someone else has bootlegged their way onto the network," Debbie said, "he could do a lot of damage. He could access the locations of our subs and compromise their security. I'd say that's plenty serious. He might even be able to use our satellite net as a targeting system."

"I don't think so," he answered. "Why would an enemy hide a shipwreck? Besides, I don't want to get anyone else involved until I can talk to Bill Roberts. He'll be back in two weeks. After all, he is the station director and we owe it to him not to create an international incident over something that could be nothing at all."

"You could be right," Debbie agreed. I'll do whatever I can to help, but we have to tell my boss. The Navy needs to know about this."

"I know, but can't we try to figure something out first? What if it's nothing? I don't want to lose my job over nothing, don't you see? At least give me a couple days and help me if you can. Please?"

"Well, I could run some checks and see if any of the Navy files have been altered. That wouldn't take long. And, we could change the security codes and try to lock your guy out. We do that occasionally anyway. Can you get me into your command?"

"With your clearance? Are you kidding?" he laughed. "They'll probably offer to hire you on the spot. Just don't go after my job. At least not yet. And there's something else we might try. If we had coordinates of other wreck sites, we could check them against the computer's data and see if this site is unique, or if other sites are being withheld as well."

"I think we need to talk to Paul about this. He and my dad have been friends for years. He knows as much about wrecks here as anyone in Bermuda. If we ask him I'm sure he'll help us."

The scooter ride to the clubhouse took about fifteen minutes. It was a dark, old stone building on the side of a hill above a sandy beach and a sparkling, shallow lagoon which the club used for training. The members had built submerged platforms and when students were ready, they could be led from the platforms directly to the lush coral reef which teemed with parrot fish, Bermuda chubs, yellowtail snappers and wrasses.

Inside, the building had low ceilings, dark paneling, and large trophy cabinets displaying silver cups awarded to the best individual clubs within the British Sub-Aqua Club network. There were several classrooms, locker rooms, equipment storage and compressor areas, and a large lounge area complete with a well-stocked bar.

Wednesdays were club nights and the evenings began with student training dives in the lagoon. After the dives and hot showers the students were served dinner from the bar-b-que. And then at the bell, it was off to class for lectures. After classes the bell rang again, this time for the opening of the bar and the beginning of the social hours. It was no wonder, Debbie thought, that there was often a two-year waiting list for membership and classes. This place was the most fun on the island.

Paul Singleton was teaching so they could not get him alone until the social hour was well underway. Debbie asked him to walk down the path with them to the lagoon.

"You said you wanted to talk in private," Paul said after the amenities were exchanged, and they were far enough down the path to be alone. "This is as private as it gets. Are you and this young gentleman getting married or something? If that's the case, lad, I should warn you I've known this little hurricane for quite awhile, and if you get in her track you best have a lee cove to shelter in or your hull'll be on bottom for sure!"

"Very salty, captain," responded Debbie. "No, we're not getting married. This is more serious than that. Tom discovered something about the wreck we found two weeks ago. We need your help."

Tom told the story. Even though he left out the national security implications and stuck to wrecks, Paul recognized the grave possibilities immediately.

"Sir, you know a great deal about the wrecks here," Tom concluded. "If we could get enough Loran or GPS coordinates on known sites, enough to really cover the island, and compare those to the charts we make from the satellite data, we could determine if what I stumbled onto is a single instance, perhaps some glitch in the computer or, well, who knows?"

Paul scratched his chin for a moment before answering, "Well now, that story sets the hair up on the back of your neck, doesn't it? I'll help you, of course. But there are hundreds of wrecks out there and I've got coordinates on fifty, maybe seventy-five. And, gettin' that information from the locals won't be easy. You see, most of 'em have spent their whole lives trying to make a living from what they know about the sea. It's a hard life and they don't share—not with strangers."

Tom looked at Debbie for a moment, his face blank, then his eyes brightened and the usually present boyish smile returned.

"Here's my plan," Tom began. "Tell the divers and fishermen, or anyone else who can help us, the truth. We'll tell them we know someone is using very sophisticated equipment to locate and clean out the last of the wrecks. That will hurt everyone, even the fishermen, when those habitats are disturbed. Tell them we plan to do the most comprehensive charts ever done on the island—a sort of inventory to protect what's left. We can solve the riddle of the satellite and at the same time learn more about what's left in these waters than anyone has ever known. And that's the only way any of it will ever be saved."

"Might work. Although I'm still not sure how many of 'em will trust us. But I've got an idea. My wife, Janet, taught a good bunch of their kids at the high school. If she talks to those kids and to their parents, we might have a better chance. All we need are one or two of the old families on our side and the rest will follow. It's the way things work here. Alright, start making those satellite charts and we'll give her a go.

How's that sound to you, Debbie?"

"Great! I knew we could count on you. Dad gave me a new laptop computer for my birthday. We can use it to record the data and make our own charts. But what about security? Most of this stuff is probably classified. We don't need to get court-martialed trying to be good guys."

"No one sees our charts until Bill Roberts gets back. If he says no, we scrap the whole thing. Fair enough?" Tom answered.

"OK with me. But I'm still going to run the checks we discussed, first thing tomorrow."

"Just wait till your old dad hears about this, Debbie," Paul chuckled. "He'll be washing dishes to get on our boat! I'll have him haulin' tanks, scrapin' boat bottoms and beggin' for the privilege of bein' our deckhand. It'll be simply lovely."

Debbie was cold on the scooter ride back to the Hamilton Ferry Terminal. Once on the ferry it was warmer, but she sat close to Tom holding his hand and trying to warm up. She was tired, and was content not to talk. She liked Tom, but she worried about what he was getting her into.

Tom Morrison's co-workers wondered about the love affair he was suddenly having with the Sat Nav computer. But because Bill Roberts was still in Texas and Tom had been there long enough to be trusted, no one worried enough to find out what Tom was up to. Most had met Debbie, and knew she was the bright young executive officer at the Navy's computer center. One of the NASA programmers suggested Tom was just using the computer to impress her and perhaps get himself laid. If it worked, more power to him. At least, then they could say their antiquated system was still good for something.

Tom showed her how he'd gotten into the satellite data bank and how he was able to locate the wrecks. She ran checks on the Navy's files and could find nothing that looked altered or tampered with. It seemed as though all their hacker had been able to access was a constantly updated bank of enhanced infrared reference photos from which the computer could break down ion density layers and analyze magnetic fields. That information could be used to locate anomalies in the earth's crust, dissimilar intrusions—junk which didn't belong, like old wrecks or new submarines. And there the path ended.

It was all very straightforward and most any half-bright kid could read the data. But when she tried to open the operating system files, she hit a stone wall. After several late nights of trying, she came to accept the obvious. Whoever hid that wreck had done it from inside the program. It was a very successful and sophisticated breach of the system's security. Not even the Navy could do what she now knew had been done.

Tom was having better luck. He spent his time building a data base of the computer's wreck sites. In order to change the computer data into something they could use on the boat, he wrote a program to translate the data into GPS, or Ground Positioning Satellite, coordinates. By Tuesday, Debbie was able to call a friend at the Naval Sub Tracking Center and arrange to use their chart printer. Reluctantly, she stuck to her agreement not to tell her boss what she was up to until Bill Roberts returned.

It was a cool evening on Tuesday and they had a long ride, so Tom borrowed a car. On their way to the Dockyard, they stopped at The Country Squire for some fresh wahoo. They were tired but excited by their accomplishments.

As they sat outside enjoying their dinner, Tom speculated about their find.

"Do you have any idea what salvage divers would pay for what we have?" Tom laughed. "If we ever wanted a get-rich-quick scheme, this would be it."

"I think you better be careful talking about what we've done, Tom. Don't forget for a minute how serious this could be. Have you had any luck finding out who wrote the NASA satellite data program?"

"No, not yet, but I'm sure Bill Roberts will know. He knows all the brains in D.C. It was probably some of those guys."

Debbie worried that with the new charts in hand, Tom was becoming more interested in treasure hunting than in solving the security problem. But the dinner was excellent and when they finished, they drove to a hilltop and watched the brilliant reds and fiery orange of the sun setting on the calm sea.

She was in a much better mood as they drove the winding coast road to the historic Royal Naval Dockyard. Set on twenty-five acres, the old fortress had served as the central power base for the Royal Navy in the Americas and the West Indies for a century and a half.

"What's that spooky-looking place up there on the hill?" Debbie asked as they came through the narrow stone gate of the Royal Naval Dockyard.

"The Commissioner's House," Tom answered. From atop the highest hill, the Commissioner's House, made of native Bermuda stone and cast iron beams and trusses, stood dominating the fortress. "This whole place is spooky to me. It was built with convict labor—nine thousand of them—in the early 1800's. The workers were treated like slaves and lived on stinking old hulks anchored over there," he said, pointing across the marina toward the bay. They passed the Clock Tower Warehouse, now converted to a mini-mall for tourists, and Debbie pointed to the seawall on their right.

"Is that the new tourist sub?" Debbie asked.

"That's her, the *Enterprise*. Got here about two years ago. Don't know how much it costs to go out on her but it must be fun," he answered.

"I bet Paul will know. I'd love to go out on her."

They drove around the marina with its neatly trimmed grounds and flags snapping in the sea breeze, past the boatyard, and circled around the Maritime Museum's high stone walls. They stopped in front of a row of two-story stone apartments which were once officers' quarters with walled courtyards and now served as restaurants and shops. A dive flag flew from a jack staff in the corner yard. Captain Paul Singleton was sitting in an aging rocker reading through half-frame glasses. His teacup sat on the air cleaner of a rusting red engine beside the chair, and a scruffy orange cat was curled at his feet. He looked up over the rims of his glasses and smiled when they came through the gate.

"Come on in, welcome aboard and all that nautical stuff."

He stood and came to the gate to meet them. Paul led them across the oak floor of the small showroom into the kitchen which served as a combination office, workroom and class-room. A massive oak table, out of place in the small room, was covered with charts and scattered notebooks. Lead diving weights and brass spikes held down the corners of charts. Paul set about clearing a spot for Debbie's computer and asked, "Well now, what kind of luck have you two had? Were you able to make the satellite charts?"

"You won't believe it," Tom answered. "Debbie plotted over four hundred anomalies."

"Four hundred! We'll be diving for years! Great work, Debbie. And just look at this stuff," he said pointing to the piles of clutter in the tiny kitchen. The well-used charts were covered with compass plot lines leading to multiple sites. "Janet tells me there's more coming. She's done a wonderful job. It seems there are a lot of folks interested in saving what's left of Bermuda's wrecks and in finding out what might still be out there.

"All my life I've wanted to do this," Paul continued. "To go out and find wonderful pieces of history. I don't need to be rich. I do what I want and have what I need, so I'm rich enough now. But wouldn't it be wonderful to build a really grand wreck museum here, spend our time exploring the wrecks, learning their stories and sharing the experience? That's what the best of life is: knowing your passion and being able to share it. Alright then, enough of this philoso-phizing. What do we do first?"

They set up the laptop. Tom took a stack of old charts and set to work converting the GPS conversions as Debbie entered them into the data base. Paul hovered over both of them, asking questions and studying Debbie's charts.

"Most all the wrecks I know are here," Paul said. "Here by Southwest Breaker is the *Mari Celeste*, the *L'Herminie* from 1839, and that other one, the little wreck Teddy Tucker found and worked six or eight years ago. This one here should be the *Virginia Merchant*. Went down in 1661, taking supplies to Jamestown, Virginia. I think those college kids from Georgia are going to work her for the museum this summer. Teddy found her and also this one, the *Eagle*. Both were owned by

the Virginia Company in England and went down about the
same time. This here by the light tower is that Portuguese
slaver that went down in 1543. I think she was worked by the
Smithsonian back in the sixties. Mendel Peterson would have
been on that one. Sorry I've never met him...."

They worked until midnight when the men took a break
and went out into the front courtyard to get some air. The
night was still and clear. The stars were thick in the sky, thick
as beach sand and seen as they may only be seen from a remote island or a ship far at sea.

"Captain," Tom began, "there's something about your
shop that surprises me. Most shops in the States are filled
with artifacts. With as many years as you've been diving here,
I'd expect you'd have quite a collection. Wouldn't it be good
for business to display a few things?"

"There's truth enough in that, Tom. Yes, there's a reason
we don't collect or display artifacts in the store. Here the
government claims ownership of all wrecks. Now, not everyone respects that claim, but for the most part it's been a workable arrangement. If you find a wreck you want to work, you
go to the Receiver of Wrecks and apply for a salvage lease.
The government has a look at what you bring up, buys what
it wants and you keep the rest. Then you sell what you've
found so you can afford to work your next site. There's not
much gold or silver, but you find a piece here and there. So
rich folks get some pretty trinkets, and if you're feeling gen-
erous or you want the publicity, you put things in a museum
like the one here in the Dockyard. So in theory, at least everyone wins: the salvor, the museum, the island's historians
and writers. Hell, even the tourists.

"Unfortunately, the truth is, the government doesn't pay
as well as the black market so very little of what's found is
ever shown to them. Once it comes to the surface it's gone,
that's all. And everyone else loses, because one day there
won't be anymore new sites and the old men who were afraid
to keep records about what they'd found won't be here anymore. We'll never know what's been lost or hear the stories
those artifacts might have told..." he trailed off lost in
thought. Tom waited for him to continue.

"So what's the answer?" Paul finally asked. "Leave the

stuff buried on the bottom and it may stay lost forever, or bring it up and sell it to the government? There's so very little money for conservation or display so it could sit in a warehouse forever.

"Then to make matters worse, a few months ago the government hired a new archaeologist. At first he argued that no one should be allowed on any of the wrecks unless they worked for him. He wasn't powerful enough to put the commercial salvage divers out of business, so he focused on charter boats and tourists.

"We're trying hard to work with him because we know that it's not our beautiful reefs that make Bermuda a grand dive spot. Here, the attraction is the wrecks and all their history. Nothing more.

"If we can't dive the wrecks, it will hurt us all—dive operations, hotels, restaurants, everybody. So, Tom, even when we do find things I worry about bringing them up. Unless it's something so special that we can raise the money ourselves to conserve it and properly display it, I'd rather have exciting things for my divers to see on the bottom than a shop full of trinkets, or a museum storehouse full of decaying junk."

"I think I understand," Tom said.

"Look at it this way," Paul exclaimed. "It's the same as shooting fish you can't eat. So we take a strong stand against souvenir hunting. Our divers are told not to bring anything up. If they do and our captains see it, back over the side it goes, or they are given the opportunity to make a 'gift' to the museum. Like the old flintlocks you and Debbie found. They were so beautiful when they came out of the water, but without proper care they'll be nothing but rust in just a few months, so I took them straight to Lisa in the museum conservation lab. She knows what to do, but it takes equipment, time and money. In the meantime, they're safe in a storage tank.

"We had a good working relationship with the last archaeologist, and the club did most of the work on the sites he was interested in. I certainly hope this new man, Dr. Richardson, won't make things too hard for us. We'll just have to wait and see."

Debbie found them in the courtyard. "Guys, I've had all
the fun I can stand for one night. I got a hundred and seventy entered and plotted, but there are so many more. If it's
alright, I'd like to leave everything set up here...Oh look, is
that sub getting underway?" As they watched, the white submarine was being towed away from the dock, and was heading out of the marina and into the bay.

"I've always been fascinated with submarines. I'd love to
go out in that one someday," she said looking at Tom with
her smiling green eyes.

"Sounds like an opportunity for some young man to win
your favor," Tom said. "Now if we can determine how much
favor he might win, I could ask around and see if there's any
interest."

"Tom Morrison, you are a jerk. And just for the record, if
ever on your best day you were fortunate enough...my favor,
euphemistically speaking, is a lot more than you could
handle! Now take me home, you dog! I'll get my own sub
ride and just see if I invite you." With that, she pounded on
his chest and winked at the captain.

CHAPTER 4

Georgia: The next weekend

Mark Danvers led his group of divers down the float line to the "wreck" on the bottom of the quarry. Over the past three years, the dive team had used old beams and timbers from the quarry's buildings to create a mock-up of a seventeenth century hull. It was now an underwater classroom for tadpole archaeologists. The float line was tied to the stern at the keelson, or centerline, and a fiberglass measuring tape ran forward to the bow providing a reference for the survey teams.

In addition to the timbers, anchors of various styles and vintages, old iron farm tools and glass bottles were added to the wreck site for the divers to draw and identify. For added interest there were four cannons cast from concrete, and a busty mermaid once the pedestal of a bird bath.

The divers needed their best buoyancy control to hover above the bottom silt so as not to destroy the already limited visibility. This meant moving weight belts high on the waist, and swimming and working in a fins up, head down attitude. Bob was the first to lose control and crash into the bottom raising a huge cloud of silt. Mark just shook his head and laughed.

It would take most of the weekend to measure, survey

and map the site. As the visibility grew worse because of diver activity, a new skill began to develop—the ability to visualize and remember objects which could only be felt or seen an inch at a time. Before long, they would be able to describe even unfamiliar farm machinery in detail, and relocate their finds using compass navigation, reference points, touch and intuition.

Mark had an uncanny ability to work in dark, murky water. He'd gained a sort of sixth sense like that of the blind, a sense of personal space which, if trusted, let him reach out and touch objects before he'd actually seen them.

After their orientation dive, which gave the students a general feeling for the site, the team set to work constructing a grid using yellow rebar rods and nylon cord. They laid out the pattern with PVC pipe templates, and then leveled the lines and established grade elevations with their depth gauges. This greatly simplified getting the depth perspective of timbers and "wreckage", and enabled Sheri to do three-dimensional drawings.

One other skill awaited the students. They would use underwater metal detectors to survey a mud flat planted with objects. Finding the targets was the easy part, but then they had to map the locations accurately enough so that another team, again working in near zero visibility, could relocate the same targets. To accomplish this, the students established center points called datum points with the yellow rods. A compass ring, made from a hula hoop, was placed around the rod and correctly oriented. Then one team member swam circles with a metal detector while holding a measured line tethered to the rod. His teammate remained at the center point and tended the line. They recorded both compass bearing and distance for each target found.

Bob and Karen were the first to return to the surface and take their slates full of drawings and numbers to Sheri. She listened patiently as they tried to decipher the notes they'd made underwater which now made little sense.

"I think you did well for your first dive," Sheri said tactfully, "especially if you learned what a slow and difficult process this is. Get comfortable and make a sketch of what you remember. Next dive, don't try to do so much. If you learn the techniques under these conditions, it will be a snap in clear, warm water."

"Give me that clear, warm water right now," Karen said. "Crawling around in the mud isn't my idea of a great time. So, if it's like this in Bermuda, Sheri, you're in for a long swim home." Karen laughed as she pulled off her wet suit jacket and looked over the table at Sheri's drawing.

"Nope! That's cheating. You can't look until you've finished your section," Sheri said.

"But cheating is a woman's prerogative, like changing hair color or adding a little padding," Karen said batting her eyelashes. "Don't deprive me of my civil liberties and greatest joys."

The hot summer day passed quickly. The "wreck" was shallow enough that the divers could spend several hours at their tasks. It was nearly dark when they finished cleanup from the evening meal and cleared up the tables to plan for the next day's work. Sheri spread out her drawings and showed them how she had used their information to construct large overviews of the site.

They gathered round, laughing and pointing at the drawings. It was the first time they could see the wreck more with their eyes than with their finger tips and they were enthusiastic.

"So that's what that hole in the big timber was, a mast step?"

"And those right-angle pieces that look like bent branches, those are braces for beams? What did you say they are called again, hanging knees?"

"And they support the beams and connect them to the frames?"

"And the wooden pegs they used instead of nails are treenails or trunnels? Oh yes, I remember now. That's all in our book."

After the din abated, Sheri talked them through the drawings, explaining the construction. Then they listed the projects yet to be completed. Mark made the team assignments and collected log books so that the record of the day's training could be made official by an instructor's signature.

It had been a good day. The newest divers had accomplished tasks far beyond their own expectations, and the more experienced ones had discovered there was still plenty to learn. Sheri knew she had done her job well, and when this last training weekend was over, they would be ready for their great Bermuda adventure.

As the sun sank slowly into the mountains, the team gathered at the campfire for their last night together until the trip.

"Did you see the look on Kit's face when that big catfish spooked up near the bow?"

"See her face? Hell, I couldn't even see her ass. Not even in that hot pink wet suit! It might have fallen off for all I could see....Kit, come here, we're worried about your ass...has it fallen off?"

"Why don't you come over here and check for yourself, Charlie? You might get to see a June moon."

The laughter and stories would last as long as the intentionally limited beer supply. Most had spent hours in the water, and tomorrow would be another full day followed by the three-hour drive back to Atlanta. Soon they were headed for the tents. It was a warm night and the flaps and windows were open for ventilation. In their tent, Sheri and Mark talked about the progress the students had made, laughed again about the catfish and about Bob crashing into the silt. They were soon both asleep.

Three hours later, Mark was awakened by the pressure of his full bladder. He looked out through the screen and watched heat lightning flashing in the night sky far away. It was overcast and muggy. He got up quietly hoping not to wake Sheri, and headed to one of the portable toilets. He walked down the trail past the main beach area. He thought he heard someone talking from the water, but the urgency of his mission caused him to delay investigating. On the way back he walked toward the beach.

"Karen, come on, I need some sleep," he heard Bob grumble. "Quit fooling around and let's go to bed. Alright, if you're going to stay in the water, I'm going back to the tent. Watch out for snakes. Good night."

Mark stepped back into the darkness of the trees until Bob passed him and then walked down to the beach.

Karen was swimming on her back in the shallow water. She was gorgeously nude. Just at the moment he was praying for more lightning, it flashed across the northeastern sky. In the brightness Karen saw him standing in the trees.

"Mark? Is that you? What are you doing?" She dropped into the water to conceal herself.

"Sorry, I didn't mean to scare you. I was just on my way back from the can. I heard Bob talking." He walked down to the water's edge. Karen came closer to him but remained submerged.

"It was too hot to sleep. Bob wouldn't come in the water. Say, I'm mad at you. You've never called me."

"Oh, I wanted to, Karen, but things have been really busy with the end of the semester, and getting ready for the trip and all."

"Yes, and didn't you forget to mention you and Sheri? Well...?"

"Yeah, that too."

"That's what you should have said in the first place, Mark. I don't mind that you're with somebody else, just be honest, that's all. Want to swim?" she asked, lifting high enough out of the water to expose her breasts.

"Aren't you afraid that Bob might come back?"

"Are you? And what if he did? You're not afraid of him, are you? Anyway, it would just simplify things." A gentle rain started to fall. "Too late—missed your chance. I'm getting cold. Next time don't hesitate. Women like men who go after what they want. Get my towel. It's on that bush," she said pointing.

Mark fetched the towel, and when he returned Karen was standing near the water's edge waiting for him. His arm slowly raised to hand her the towel. She took his hand and pulled him into the ankle deep water. She put the towel around his back pulling him close, and kissed him deeply. As his hands came up to her breasts she pushed him away and said, "That was just to give you something to think about. Now go home and don't wear your wet shoes into Sheri's tent."

Mark squished his way back up the trail. Sheri was awake when he got to the tent. "You're wet."

"I had to go to the can and it's raining. Sorry to wake you."

"Oh."

Bermuda

Only twenty more to go. Debbie's back ached from another six hours at the computer. It was late again. She hadn't gotten a decent night's sleep since this whole thing started. She stretched and twisted her shoulders forward and back, but it didn't help. Where the devil had Paul and Tom taken off to now? It was time for a break. She pushed the hard ladder-back chair away from the cluttered oak table, stood, stretched again and walked out through the store to the courtyard overlooking the boat basin. Both cars were in their spaces so Debbie assumed they were off snooping around the Dockyard again.

Tom Morrison was the most curious person she had ever met. He wanted to see everything, and the past few nights that had included everything under her clothes. It was becoming a problem. At least he respected her and he had a sense of humor. That was probably his most charming attribute. Whatever she thought was missing in the way of stability, reliability and maturity—all the things she admired in her father—she had to concede that Tom was fun. And as long as he was willing to play by her rules perhaps fun was OK. But not tonight. She was tired and wanted to get back to the base. Where could they have gone?

She went into the classroom, found a large cardboard box of fins and placed it near the only comfortably padded chair in the shop. The fin box made an acceptable ottoman. She put her feet up and in a moment was asleep.

Paul had taken Tom to the Keep, a small boat basin with high secure walls and an iron gate closing the small arched entrance. During the Dockyard's years of disuse, the Keep had been filled with debris and trash. When the first major restoration projects began, it was discovered that the Keep contained two hundred years worth of old bottles, glass ink wells, and other diver "treasures." From that point, getting volunteers to help empty it was no problem.

The men were enjoying a bottle-diving frenzy with masks and snorkels and hadn't noticed the passing time. They returned to the shop with their treasures to find the doors locked, the lights on and Debbie sleeping soundly inside. As Paul unlocked the door, she awoke and glared at them through blood-shot eyes.

"This better be good or you two turkeys are about to get plucked," she said.

"Does that mean we're in trouble?" Tom asked.

"Do whales defecate in salty water?"

The next day at the base was a tough one for Debbie. She had difficulty concentrating and had to rewrite one simple program three times to get it right. When the day was finally over, she went back to her apartment in the officer's quarters, collapsed on the bed in her uniform and slept for two glorious hours. She was still out when Tom's call from the lobby awakened her. She quickly changed to shorts and a light sweatshirt, and went down to meet him.

Tom was excited. "I talked to Paul today. He has the new GPS and depth recorder on the boat and we can start diving this weekend. I can't wait. This is going to be the best."

He had the borrowed car again. Good, she thought, scooters are fun but scary at night and it would have been a long, cold ride to the dive shop.

It took her less than an hour to finish constructing the data bank on Paul's wreck sites. As she had hoped, the computer at the Naval Annex would be available and they could print the second chart. She began the sorting process between the two data bases and in a few moments had what they spent the last three weeks working for: a list of wrecks known to exist but not recognized by the NASA satellite computer system.

The list was rather disappointing. There were only nineteen sites. But on the other hand, there were nearly two hundred sites known to the computer and unknown to Captain Paul Singleton. There would indeed be some exciting new discoveries.

"I'm not so sure we should dive these other sites, the ones from NASA. I feel like we sort of stole the information and we shouldn't," Debbie teased and winked at Paul.

Tom missed the wink and exclaimed in panic, "Debbie, are you crazy? This is the opportunity of a lifetime. What's going on with you today?"

Paul picked up her line and with a serious face said, "You know that's been bothering me too. I think I'd feel a lot better if we just turned this whole thing over to the Navy or the Marine Police."

Tom's face flushed as he struggled for a comeback. Debbie looked at Paul and they both laughed.

"Just kidding, Tom. But to be on the safe side you should probably buy us dinner," she said.

"Great idea," Paul agreed. "I'll call the restaurant at Somerset Bridge and see if they've got fresh wahoo."

That will teach him not to go off diving while I'm breaking my back, she thought smiling to herself. On the drive to the restaurant, her thoughts drifted back to her first visit there years ago with her parents. She recalled the many hours she'd spent in the hotel's hot tub with a slightly older scuba instructor. It had been quite a vacation. She wondered what had ever happened to Mike.

"What time do you want to go out Saturday?" Tom asked Paul between bites of fresh wahoo.

"Got a morning charter...should get back to the Dockyard a little after lunch...we'll need to load fresh tanks, the camera and buoys before we can go back out. Want to spend the night if the weather's good?"

Debbie quickly responded, "I'd love to do a night dive. I'll bring my camera."

"That's it! Alright, Debbie, a night dive it is."

CHAPTER

5

Atlanta

Sheri walked into the dive store expecting to see Bill, the owner, but there was no one there. She guessed he was back in the equipment room and loudly called his name. She was her usual perky self and wore her favorite pink running shorts and tank top. Bill had kidded her about really needing running shoes if she came in wearing that outfit again. Never one to shrink from a challenge, she wore it today without a bra.

"Sheri, that you? I'm on the phone and Randy's gone to the bank. Watch the front for a couple minutes and catch that other line if it rings. Be right out, thanks." She wanted a new lightweight wet suit for Bermuda. She looked over the suits on the rack, found nothing that excited her, and went behind the desk to look through the catalogs. A hot pink and teal number had just caught her eye when through the window she noticed an old black Bronco pull in beside her truck.

Doc stepped down from the Bronco and smiled at the flashy red pick-up. Sheri didn't look up for a moment and when she did was startled to see a large, lean, middle-aged man with salt-and-pepper hair looking down at the catalog. Or was he? She looked down and realized her loose tank top was offering him more of a view than she was comfortable with. She quickly sat back in the chair and closed the catalog.

"Hi, I'm Sheri Benson. I'm filling in for Bill and Randy for a few minutes. What brought you in today?" There was something about him that looked familiar. He was comfortably dressed and stood straight and poised. Other than the thin scar which ran across the left side of his neck he was quite good looking, even for an older man.

"Is that your truck outside? Wish my old Bronco looked that good," Doc said.

"It belonged to my ex. He missed a few payments so now I drive a truck. I get some strange looks, but it's great for hauling scuba gear. Have we met?"

"Don't think so. I'm John Holiday. I need to look at masks, fins and snorkels, and perhaps a BC and regulator. Oh, and also a dive bag. Guess I really need new everything. I bet you can help me."

"Great, let's start with masks. There are some super new low volume ones over here. Sounds like you're getting ready for a dive trip. Where are you headed?"

"Bermuda. My daughter's in the Navy there and I'm going for the summer."

"Really? I'm going too, in a couple of weeks with a student archaeological team from Georgia State. Maybe we'll see each other." She realized that sounded a bit forward and told herself to shut-up before she dug the hole any deeper. She took a silicone mask from the shelf and put it to her face. She handed it to him and as she did the tank top scooped open again. She recovered awkwardly and cursed herself for not having worn a bra.

"These new silicone ones, ah...masks, are really wonderful." Crap, she thought, why don't I just ask him if he'd mind if I take off my top and be done with it?

Doc smiled as he took the mask and tried it. It was too small. "Very nice, but do you have something larger?" he asked innocently.

"Larger?" she flushed red. "Larger? Oh, do you mean like the old buckets with windows in the sides? I think you'll be happier if you stick to a low profile. Here, try this one." She handed him another. This time she held her top in place as she moved toward him.

Again, Doc's face was too broad for the mask and he handed it back.

"I'm afraid that won't do either. Why don't we ask Bill if he has any of those old buckets left? I think that's what it's going to take for me to get a good fit. Is he here?"

She was ready to retreat in total defeat. Where the hell was Bill? She hoped that if she ever saw John Holiday again, she'd be wearing a big chicken costume and be totally unrecognizable.

"Yeah, he's on the phone in back. I'll find him. Why don't you look at snorkels and I'll check on your bucket? Have you tried these new ones with the exhaust in the bottom and the baffle on top? They are the easiest to clear of any I've ever used." She left him standing with the snorkel in his hand and went toward the back of the small store.

Doc held up the strange-looking snorkel at eye level and rotated it. He shook his head, first in amazement at the design and then in shock at the price. He put it back on the shelf and looked for something like the simple J-shaped tube with which he had trained and was most comfortable. Debbie had warned him that he was in for a shock. He'd agreed it was time to update the black, horse-collar style buoyancy compensator and ten-year-old regulator. But opening his old dive bag had been like walking into a room full of old friends. Leaving them behind was painful enough, but there were limits....Next she would have him in a lime green wet suit with coral pink accents....Perhaps he would come back when Bill had more time....Cute little instructor though. Wonder who she was with in the pool.

"Doc? Doc Holiday, is that you? Man it's great to see you," Bill said as he hurried out. He grabbed Doc's hand and pounded him on the back. "Where the hell you been keeping yourself? Sheri come back out here. I want you to meet one of the first SEAL's. Best damn diver I was ever in the water with. He could free dive deeper than any man I ever saw. Son of a gun, Doc, it's great to see you again. What can we do to help you?"

Sheri came out wearing a sweatshirt twice her size and a

chagrined face. "You were a SEAL? Now I'm really embarrassed. Guess you can wear whatever kind of mask you want. I'm used to students who haven't..."

"Gotten any bad habits yet?" Doc interrupted her with a laugh. "That's OK, I'm sure there have been lots of improvements since my day and I'd appreciate your helping me get up to speed."

Bill found Doc's mask and set it on the counter. He noticed that Sheri was quite taken with the professor. It came out more in the intensity with which she looked at him than in what she said. It was as if she were trying to count the neurons in his brain. Bill was certain he'd be answering a barrage of questions the moment Doc left.

Bermuda

On Saturday, Debbie and Tom arrived at the Dockyard boat basin just after noon. Paul's wife, Janet, was in the dive shop and Paul was still on the boat with his morning charter. There were tourists and regular customers crowded into the small store. Janet was swamped.

"What can I do to help?" Debbie asked.

"Could you find me something cold to drink? Paul called on the radio. He'll be in about one or one-thirty."

Debbie went to the corner store for cold drinks and Tom went into the tiny office in the back of the store. Paul had been working on the new charts. The wreck sites not acknowledged by the satellite computer were circled in red. The nineteen sites were scattered around the island, but Paul had divided them into clusters. Tom noticed that twelve of the sites were in deep water, at least too deep to work in scuba.

"This must be quite a project you are starting on, Debbie. I haven't seen Paul so excited in years," Janet said and thanked her for the drink. "I think he really wants to find something before your dad gets here—just to rub it in. Did Paul tell you that Captain Marley's daughter is bringing in his old charts and some of them belonged to his great-grandfather? She was one of my students. There will be lots of history on those charts. Her grandfather was a wrecker and probably his father too. If they kept good records, who knows what you'll find?"

Debbie winced as a psychosomatic arrow struck her lower back. The thought of returning to that hard-bottom, straight-backed chair was almost more than she could tolerate, but she kept her thoughts to herself. "You certainly are the hero of this story, Janet, for gathering all this information. I'll be glad when this satellite business is over and we can concentrate on the fun of exploring these new sites."

"What did you say about satellites?" Janet asked.

Tom came in from the office. "I just got Paul on the radio. He's pulling into the boat basin and wants us to give him a hand."

"Go ahead, you two. We'll talk later, Debbie. I sure want to hear the rest of this story."

Paul skillfully brought the *Mermaid* into the slip. The boat was his pride, and although over twenty years old, she was spotless. As the boat turned to back into the slip, Debbie noticed that the hand-carved, busty, green-tailed sea temptress adorning the stern wore new paint and looked more alluring than ever. The boatload of divers were all shouting and laughing as they packed their gear.

"Afternoon, Debbie, Tom. Lend a hand with those stern lines, will you? You missed some great divin' this mornin'. These folks got to see bronze cannon and reefs like they don't have back home. Isn't that right, you tube suckers?" Paul was on the fly bridge and putting on his best sea dog accent for the tourists. "We'll need to fill these tanks, Tom; Matt will give you a hand."

Tom took two of the tanks and lugged them around a strangely converted grocery cart on his way to the shop.

"Do you think we should tell him that's a tank cart, Debbie, or just let him haul all those on his back?"

"You're just like my Dad...rotten to the core, Captain. No, don't tell him. Let's see how many trips he makes before he figures it out." Debbie gave Paul a hug and said, "I know this is going to be fun. I wish Dad were here to be in on the start."

On his second trip, Matt told Tom about the tank cart and they filled the tanks and got all the equipment on board.

The boat pulled away from the marina and headed west towards Chub Cut.

Paul had set a block on the gin pole to feed the magnetometer cable through. Tom picked up the operating manual and scanned the first few paragraphs. At the end of the cable was the "fish", a sensor tube about eighteen inches long. The fish, or transducer, would be trailed behind the boat below the surface and just far enough back to get it away from any interference caused by the engines.

Reading further, he learned that a magnetometer is much more than a sophisticated metal detector. It measures changes in the magnetic field of the earth's crust and will show even older wrecks containing little ferrous metal, although a high density of iron certainly makes the job a lot easier.

Once the *Mermaid* passed through the narrow channel at Chub Cut, Paul put Debbie at the fly bridge helm and used the GPS to plot a course to the first dive site. Then he went below, explained what Tom's job would be, and showed him how to hook up the magnetometer and camera.

Nearly an hour passed before Debbie yelled, "We're getting close. Get ready." In a few moments, the alarm sounded and Tom threw the first flag float. The float's anchor line played out smoothly and Paul hurried back up the bridge ladder to watch the recording Fathometer. It showed one hundred seventy-two feet and a flat sloping bottom. No sign of a wreck.

"We'll circle the buoy a couple times to see what we pick up on the Fathometer before we start with the mag. We just might get lucky and see fish over the site or something sticking up down there." Paul slowly navigated in expanding circles out from the flag. Tom waited with the second flag. Debbie watched the instruments. No one spoke.

"There, there! See that point?" Paul yelled. "Could be a mast or a piece of rigging. Tom, throw another buoy. Quick, now."

The second flag went over the side and Paul put the *Mermaid* into a tight turn to make another pass. Nothing. "All right, let's try once more." He brought the boat back in close to the first buoy and started the slow circling again.

There was no breeze and the sea was flat calm. It was

suddenly muggy. Debbie realized her shirt was damp and removed it. She adjusted her bikini top and looked back at the instruments. Paul's eyes never left the Fathometer. Again the tiny spires appeared on the chart paper.

"Yes, that's it. That's what we saw before. Debbie, mark the reading...let's get a look with the camera. Tom, put over another flag and we'll triangulate...I'm sure we've got something worth seeing down there."

When the flags were out, Paul shut off the engines and went down to help Tom with the camera.

"Too bad we don't have one we can monitor on deck," said Paul, "but this will do. These video cameras can almost see in the dark. Now, all you have to do is rotate this knob clockwise and she's on. See the little red light...that's it. Now wait until we're back in position then put her over slow and easy. Ready? Here we go."

Back on the fly bridge, Paul started the diesels again and stood over Debbie's shoulder giving her driving lessons. "At slow speed, Debbie, steer by using the throttles and gearshifts, not the wheel. That's right, that's it," he said. "Ahead a little more on the port engine. See how easy it is? We'll push forward and the current will push back and we should be able to sit right here between the buoys. OK, let's come about now, forward on port, reverse on starboard. Easy, easy, now stop the swing by reversing what you just did: reverse port, forward starboard, just for a moment. There, now all stop. Good job, you'll be ready for super tankers before the summer's over. Now all you have to do to hold us is ease forward on one engine or both, just like that...and keep your eyes on those flags."

When he was confident she had the feel of the boat, Paul dropped back down the ladder to help Tom. Together they lowered the camera housing over the side. Paul stood behind Tom and fed him the line as the weight pulled the rig to the bottom. "On bottom. Yes, that's it. How high do you want to back off?" Tom asked.

"Let's come up at least six or eight feet." Paul took a large clothes pin out of his pocket and attached it to the line. "This will give you a good reference point."

"Pretty clever."

"It's our only camera, and we want to bring it back alive."

"Yes, sir, no problem."

"Good, now you hold her steady while I make a couple of passes. Then we'll get a look at what's down there. I'll call down the changes in depth and you adjust the line. I'm going to lose ten pounds just going up and down that ladder. That should make Janet happy."

Tom braced himself against the strain of the line. The weight had to be heavy enough to keep the camera pointed at the bottom while the boat was moving. Paul was right; this would be a good day's work. Sweat ran into his eyes and down his arms.

"All right, Tom, stand by. We'll be ready in a minute."

"Now what we want, Debbie, is to track our position and the time as we make these passes, so that as we look at the tape we will be able to come back to the right place. Take that notebook and write our start time, the course plotter readings and the depth. Then do it again every minute. We should be able to match that up to the tape just fine. Ready, Tom? Here we go."

The *Mermaid* moved slowly forward and the strain on the line increased. Tom shifted his stance. It took both hands to hold the line. He shifted his stance again and tried to shake the sweat from his brow. Already his back was aching. This was more than he'd bargained for.

Paul watched the electronics and the buoys, and said nothing other than to call the depth changes down to Tom. Debbie watched the Fathometer and GPS and wrote the coordinates in the notebook. This was the most intense she had ever seen Paul. He was like a surgeon, she imagined, or an airline pilot landing in a storm. She and Tom were parts of the equipment now, and were expected to perform and not break his concentration. The time went slowly.

They made two five-minute passes over the site and the Fathometer lines were flat—nothing to suggest a wreck. Then on the third pass, the marker jumped, showing a protrusion up from the bottom with fish over the top. "There, that's what we want. That would make a fisherman happy. Mark this spot, Debbie. We'll go real slow here. How long has the camera been down?"

"Sixteen minutes."

"I bet it feels more like sixteen hours to Tom. How are you doing, Tom? Your back broken yet?" Paul shouted. "Can you hold on for a little bit longer?"

"I'm doing just fine, sir," Tom shouted back.

"Not by the look on your face, son," Paul said softly. "Debbie, let me know when we are at twenty minutes and I'll help him pull her up. We can't kill him on the first site."

They continued on the same course barely moving forward until Debbie said, "That's it. That's twenty minutes."

"Well, shiver me timbers, child, let's pull up the camera and go to the movies. Take the helm and keep us going forward on this heading. Don't use reverse and don't run over the buoys. I know you can do it, matey. You've got the blood ye have, arrrrr."

"Aye, aye, Captain Long John, whatever you say, sir."

"Hold on, Tom, help is on the way."

Paul took the forward position, and with some grunting and groaning they brought in the camera. "You did well, Tom. Perhaps we can figure a better way to do this. Now let's see what we got. Debbie, kill the engines, break out the rum, a double ration for all hands. On second thought, better make that iced tea. We still have a couple of hours of light and Tom can't wait to do this again, can you, lad?"

Paul carefully dried the housing and then his hands. He set the housing on the galley table, opened it and removed the camera. He surmised correctly that the crew could stand no more of his sea dog humor so he connected the coax cables from the camera to the VCR, grabbed the iced tea pitcher from the fridge and filled two glasses. He toasted them, quickly downed the pitcher's remainder, and set about mixing a refill. The monitor was mounted on the bulkhead that separated the forward V berth from the main cabin. Debbie sat in the dinette, her notebook open and her watch resting beside it. Tom slid in beside her. The tea pitcher full again, Paul leaned against the galley counter.

The tape began with a shot of the deck of the *Mermaid* and Paul's instructions to Tom. Then it went over the side and the audio picked up the chug of the diesels. When the camera finally started down, there was silence; all that could be seen was the line and the weight fifteen feet below. A cloud of silt rose as the weight landed. The camera followed but stopped well short of striking bottom. "Good job, Tom."

The light and visibility were good and the image clear. There was a slight distraction caused by the gently rolling boat bringing the camera inches nearer and then farther from the bottom.

"That would be a real joy to watch in a heavy sea."

"Right you are, Debbie."

"Well, where's the wreck?" broke in Tom. "The bottom is pretty but that's not what I broke my back to see."

"It should start at about sixteen minutes," Debbie replied. "Should we fast-forward the tape?"

"No," Paul said. "Just to be on the safe side we need to watch it all."

Small fish came and went. An occasional crab and even a lobster came to look at the weight or run from it. Then at fourteen minutes, they saw the first pieces of wreckage.

"Look, there's a cannon, and another," Paul said. He was leaning toward the monitor and nearly spilled his tea. "Look at the size of those timbers, and there's the keelson. It must be eighteen inches wide. Why aren't those timbers covered or grown over? They look as if someone has vacuumed them clean. And where's the ballast stone? Shouldn't there be ballast? There are two more cannons. They're broken. Probably carried in the bilge for ballast. But why have the stones been removed?

"This must be the bow rising up off the bottom. Look out!" he shouted as if he were riding inside the camera housing. Debbie giggled at his excitement and Tom smiled. Paul realized they were enjoying his narration and justified himself by saying, "Well look, the camera weight almost got caught in those planks. Look at all the yellowtail snapper and the Bermuda chub. Those must be the fish we saw on the Fathometer. See the big barracuda? Look, there's a pile of ballast stone and they look clean. Oh, oh, we're off the wreck. Oh, there's some bottom sheathing. Is it copper or lead? Can't tell? Neither can I."

The rest of the tape was ocean bottom with no wreckage. Paul let it play to the end and then removed it from the VCR.

"We'll save this so we can see it again. I'm certain of one thing, that wreck is no virgin. Someone has worked her hard, and by the size of those guns and timbers my guess is she was a real find."

"But who, Paul? Who could work her that deep? As clean as the frames and planks are, it sure looks to me like the work was done very recently and with more than hand tools. Wouldn't you have heard about a major salvage operation?"

"Yes, Debbie, I'd have heard something, that's for sure. This is very strange. And, this one's the second wreck which has been worked over that your satellite computer tried to hide, Tom. I'd say we're on to something here and I don't like the looks of it, not one bit. It's one thing to work a wreck in eighty feet. It's something completely different to pick the bones of one this clean in a hundred and eighty feet. No one on the island has the equipment to do this, except the Navy, and they have better things to do."

The afternoon sun was now low on the horizon. The sea remained calm with only an occasional low roller. There was hardly a breath of wind and it was still hot.

"I'm ready for a dive, or even just a swim. I need to cool off," Debbie said.

The captain inspected his crew. They looked tired and ready to mutiny. He abandoned the idea of working another site in favor of a good meal and a moonlight dive. He suggested to Tom that if they went back to the *Constellation* and the *Montana*, the site that inspired Peter Benchley's <u>The Deep</u>, they might see an ampule or two.

"I'd rather see the girl in the wet 'T' shirt if it's all the same to you," Mark answered, holding his hands in the giant breast position.

"Whatever fills your sails, mate. But we have only one likely candidate aboard and you'll have to try your silver tongue on her."

"The only way I could fill the shirt you're talking about is if I borrowed a pair of cannon balls, and you keep your silver tongue to yourself, Tom Morrison, you chauvinist pervert."

They picked up the buoys and Paul pointed the *Mermaid* northeast for the short run to the two wrecks. The sun was close to slipping into the western sea when they got there and Tom tied up to the mooring buoy. Debbie called that their sandwiches were ready, and they ate on deck while watching a spectacular sunset. Paul turned on the radio and found some 40's big band dance music. No one hurried.

"It does cast a spell, doesn't it?" Debbie said as the sun touched the horizon.

"Yes, a powerful one," Paul answered. "I could never understand how your father could live inland the way he loved being at sea. He must really enjoy Atlanta or teaching or something to give this up. Either that, or something about him has changed. Does he ever talk about it?"

"Not really, and I doubt that it was intentional. He wanted to teach and when he finished his graduate work in Florida, the best offer was in Atlanta. I think it just happened."

Debbie was ready to get wet. It would be good to wash away the heat of the day—to rest and relax in the warm ocean. And night diving was special in Bermuda. She noticed that Tom was taking longer than usual with his equipment.

"Anything I can do to help?" she asked.

"Have you done a lot of night diving?" Tom responded.

"A lot in Florida, only a couple here. How about you?"

"Not many. Is there anything special to remember?"

A new night diver, she thought and smiled. "Not much different except the lights. Make your hand signals with the lights, and don't shine yours in my eyes or the eyes of any critter you want to get close to. That's about it. Oh, remember to move only into your light. As long as you do that you'll always be looking where you're going and go slow. There will be creatures out that we don't get to see during the day: octopus and moray eels, and perhaps small sharks. Ready?"

"Guess so."

They checked each other's air, compared watches, and turned on the lights. Debbie jumped in first. She moved away from the stern to give Tom room, and when he was in they gave each other OK's. She took the camera from Paul and they swam forward to the mooring line.

The evening sea was warm but refreshing. There was still a little light, enough to see the reef and pick a spot before darkness enveloped them. She led Tom over a coral ledge to the *Constellation*. It was going to be a perfect dive.

CHAPTER

6

The *Constellation* was perhaps the last of the great four-masted schooners in the freight-hauling trade. In the summer of 1943, her decks were piled with drums of roofing tar and hundreds of cement bags. Her holds were filled with medical supplies, construction tiles, clothing, electronics and seven hundred cases of Scotch. The cargo was needed in La Guira, Venezuela, which had just experienced a devastating earthquake.

Shortly after leaving New York, her steam-driven bilge pumps failed, and when the weather got rough she began taking on water. Capt. Howard Neaves made a desperate run for Bermuda while the crew struggled to keep the heavily-laden schooner seaworthy. Ironically, they were in sight of the island, waiting for the pilot boat to guide them in, when a strong current pushed the ship over a shallow reef, ripping open her hull.

She's still there, in fifteen feet of water, resting nearly on top of a Civil War blockade runner, the *Montana*. Most of her cargo was abandoned. The Navy, however, managed to save all seven hundred cases of the Scotch.

Tom, hoping to find a medicine ampule, headed immediately to the bow where some of the cement bags still remained stacked. He found a likely hole and started sifting through the sand. Only after he was at work did he remember to look back and signal to Debbie that he intended to stay there and search. She was more interested in getting good pictures than in grubbing through the wreck, but she stayed close by looking around for photo subjects.

Debbie had done enough night diving to know that sunset is a special time on a reef. Day creatures become nervous as the night hunters come out. They scurry to find safe refuge. Schools swim tighter and stragglers swim faster. Parrotfish find soft sponges to sleep in and envelop themselves with a protective mucus cocoon. Turtles wedge themselves under reef ledges and small reef fish cluster in tiny crevices or tight caves.

The night hunters—lobsters, moray eels and sharks —move into the open. The reef becomes their turf. Some hunt in pairs and set ambushes, seeking out the careless and the unsuspecting. They are fast and ruthless.

Debbie found a sand patch from which she could still see Tom's light. Near a fallen stack of cement bags, she saw a small hole in the sand about three inches in diameter and neatly ringed with empty sea shells. She let all the air out of her buoyancy jacket, knelt by a cement bag and watched the hole.

Could this octopus already be out for the evening? She knew the octopus, called a rock scuttle by Bermudians, is the most curious and perhaps the most interesting animal on the reef. It is fast, smart and able to change colors to match its mood: red for anger, white for fright, brown for the normal day at the office. She edged forward and moved one of the shells about two inches. A single tentacle came up immediately like a periscope, went directly to the shell and put it back in its original position. Then the arm withdrew.

Debbie smiled and sat on the cement bag. She began tapping on her strobe's hard plastic lens with her fingernail. Tap, tap...tap, tap...the creature's baseball-sized head came up cautiously. Tap, tap...two arms came out in Debbie's direction. Tap, tap...the octopus was out of the hole and scooted to a rock near her feet. An arm came slowly forward and tested her fin. She remained motionless. Soon the arm came over the top of her wet suit boot and touched her bare leg.

She jumped slightly and the arm withdrew, but not too

far. She regained her composure and the arm returned to her leg. The octopus waited. Debbie began tapping again. She concentrated on remaining still as the octopus moved up her bare skin and began exploring the camera and strobe in her lap. She tapped again on the lens and it wrapped an arm around her finger. Its skin was silky smooth. Content only for a moment, however, the octopus decided to explore more of his warm, soft new friend.

Debbie sat very still as the small creature moved from her lap to the space between her buoyancy jacket and her stomach. Then the tentacles reached her bikini top. She could no longer see it because of her mask, but she could feel the soft pressure of its suction cups exploring beneath her jacket. When a tentacle found her right breast, she didn't jump as she had at the first touch.

She brought her hand up slowly and tried to encourage the creature to go to her hand. Wrong move. Intimidated by the hand, the octopus secured its position.

Well, sir, she thought, if we're going to be this intimate, you could at least tell me your name. She removed her hand but the octopus held on. Slowly she picked up her light from the cement bag and started making crosses through the dark water towards Tom. If he would just pull his head out of the wreck for a moment, we might get some great photos, she thought.

Tom, however, was thoroughly engrossed. The slow sweeping motions of his hand swirled the water, washing away a layer of sand. Each swirl exposed new treasures. There were hundreds of bottle fragments in the small area. His light played off the glass fragments, and the reflections danced and sparkled. There were octagon-shaped tiles for bathroom floors. There were bases of stemmed wine glasses, handles from white navy-style coffee cups, large pieces of red glass from cheap water pitchers. And occasionally there were tube-shaped fragments of thin, clear glass—fragments of the delicate medicine ampules. In several dives on this wreck, Tom had found many fragments, but never an unbroken ampule. He looked with diligence, totally absorbed, and missed Debbie's signal.

She was sure the small creature clinging to her was not a

threat, even though she knew its bird-like beak could inflict a nasty bite if it felt threatened. For the moment it was quite content, securely entwined in her suit and peeking out from between the panels of her buoyancy control jacket. However, patience is not an octopus virtue and soon, like a hyperactive child with eight arms, an exploring tentacle came up and touched her regulator. Debbie was still signaling to Tom and was startled by the tug which nearly pulled the regulator from her mouth. The octopus tugged again, and though she was laughing, she held the regulator firmly with her teeth. Her laughter broke the seal of her mask and it began flooding. She continued to signal Tom.

In the beam of his light, Tom saw the end of a glass tube about three-eighths inch diameter. Only half of it was exposed, but he recognized what it was immediately and gently lifted it from its fifty-year-old resting place. The ampule was full of an amber liquid. He was thrilled. He'd found his first unbroken ampule. As he backed out of the hole to show it to Debbie, he saw her light cutting through the darkness with cross-shaped sweeps. He had totally forgotten her—so much for the same-ocean buddy system. What if she were in trouble?

He swam hard to reach her, and when he dropped to the sand by her side he could hardly believe his eyes. She was sitting on a cement bag with a flooded mask, laughing while an octopus played tug-of-war with her regulator as if it were desperate to buddy breathe. He didn't know what to do first—rescue her or take her picture. As he reached forward to get her camera, the octopus saw him and darted back inside her jacket. Debbie quickly cleared her mask and opened the jacket so he could see the octopus.

Tom moved in for a close-up and squeezed the shutter release. The startled little creature turned white with fear from the blinding flash. Tom advanced the film and moved closer. He snapped the second picture just as the octopus darted to Debbie's shoulder still clutching the bikini top.

"Enough is enough!" Debbie shouted through her regulator and grabbed the creature gently. She held it out to the camera with one hand and covered herself with the other. Tom took another photo. Again frightened by the strobe, the creature blasted itself from her hand and jetted away into the darkness.

Debbie quickly pulled the top of her suit back into place and then checked her air. She had slightly less than half a tank. She checked Tom's gauge and saw he was down to a third. They had at least fifteen minutes left on the bottom. She pointed in the direction of the paddle wheels and machinery of the *Montana*. As they swam towards the old blockade runner, Tom took her hand and gave a gentle squeeze. She returned it and they swam hand in hand.

The *Montana*'s bow lay on its side. The deck plates had long since fallen from the beams, which now gave the impression of large vertical windows. Tom motioned Debbie to go inside and pose for him. She looked in cautiously with her light, then moved into the empty frame and waited. Tom adjusted the focus of the Nikonos and took the first picture. Then he signaled her to open her buoyancy jacket. She pulled back the jacket's panels and arched her back. Tom came in closer and shot again. He applauded and gestured to her to remove her bikini top. She teased him as if she intended to, but then shook her head and swam out to his side. She took the camera and directed Tom inside the window. Debbie looked down to check the camera and when she lifted it, Tom's naked posterior filled the viewfinder.

You're hopeless, she laughed to herself as she snapped the picture. They swam back towards the anchor. When they found it, Tom removed his regulator and motioned Debbie to do the same. He kissed her gently at first, pulling her closer and cautiously moving one hand up to her breast. Instead of pushing him away as he had imagined she would, she put her hand over his and squeezed gently. It was a long kiss and the first time she had welcomed his advances. When breathing became more demanding than passion, they parted and recovered their regulators. She touched his face gently and then signaled to ascend.

Paul was waiting on deck and lifted their tanks and weight belts on board. As Debbie came up the ladder, he couldn't help noticing that the top of her suit was askew.

"How was the dive?" he asked with a smile before turning away to give her a chance to correct the problem.

"Just great," Tom answered from the ladder. "An octopus

fell in love with Debbie and tried to steal her suit. I found an ampule and we got some great pictures." Tom climbed in and helped stow their gear.

"Glad you enjoyed it; I nearly fell asleep on watch. We've got an early morning. I'll take the forward berth—good breeze with the hatch open. Looks like a good night to sleep on deck. Sheets and blankets are in the locker, and the dinette cushions make a good mattress. Well, good night. Don't howl at the moon too long."

After Paul had gone below, Debbie moved up behind Tom as he was putting their regulators away. "When I was a kid in Florida," she said softly, "we lived on the water and I loved to swim. The only problem was I hated swimming suits, and the minute I got away from my mom I'd be out of my suit and gone. She'd swat my tail when she caught me, but I did it anyway. I must have been about three or four then—funny how things stay with you." She put her arms around Tom's neck and pulled him close.

"My mother isn't here and I want to swim. But only if you promise to behave. We can't afford any surprises...you know what I mean. You must promise, OK?"

He put his arms around her and said, "Sure, whatever you say." He was grinning from ear to ear.

Debbie dropped the towel she was wrapped in and uncoiled the life line from its bracket on the transom. She threw the life ring out and secured the line to a cleat. Tom watched her eagerly as she stepped onto the dive platform and gracefully shed first the top and then the bottom of her suit. He reached to touch her, but she effortlessly sprang high into a dive and was gone. She surfaced by the life ring and called to him, "Hurry, it's wonderful."

"It sure as hell is," he said to himself. "In fact, it's the closest thing to perfect I've ever seen." He nearly fell in trying to stand on one foot while getting out of his suit.

Debbie laughed softly. "Come on, Tom, I know you can do it." Finally, he was in the water beside her.

"For a minute there I thought you were worried about parrotfish or something," she teased.

"Parrotfish?" he repeated with a worried look. "The ones with the big beaks that bite through coral?"

"Yeah, parrotfish. The ones that sleep in sponges at night."

"I knew that," he said with a look of relief before pulling her into a long kiss. She let go of the ring, wrapped her arms around him, and they sank beneath the surface.

Paul awoke well before sunrise. From the bow he could hear waves slapping against the hull, which told him the wind had increased. He got up to check the position of the boat and the mooring lines. He saw that Tom and Debbie had taken his advice and were asleep on the main deck. Debbie was nestled against Tom. They were still naked.

Wonder what Doc will make of this, Paul said to himself. The *Mermaid* was riding comfortably and the star-filled sky was cloudless. There was only a slight summer breeze coming up the Gulf Stream from the southern islands. After making sure the mooring lines were secure, he went back to his berth.

Debbie heard the cabin door close. She shook Tom gently and kissed him. He awoke with a snort.

"We need to get dressed," she whispered. "And thanks for keeping your promise," she continued after he rolled towards her. "I'm sorry we can't now, but we will."

"Don't get up yet," he said as she started to sit up. "Stay a little longer." She relaxed and put her head on his chest.

It was early dawn when Debbie opened her eyes again. The smell of fresh coffee, eggs and bacon was making her hungry. Paul was in the galley whipping up breakfast while Tom worked on setting up the electronics. She found herself wrapped modestly and comfortably in a sheet. Their cushions had been pulled far enough apart to give the appearance of separate twin beds. She smiled at Tom and he winked back. It was going to be a great day.

They were underway an hour after sunrise. The next site was to the north in relatively deep water—at least too deep for scuba. Paul used the GPS to set his course and calculated they had an hour and thirty minutes running time at their present speed. Debbie brought him a third cup of coffee and sat beside him on the fly bridge, smiling to herself and looking into the water. Both started to speak at the same time and Debbie began laughing.

"I like your laugh, child," he said. "It reminds me of your mother, full of the devil. Always made you wonder what she'd been up to. Are you having a good time?"

"Oh yes, I'm very happy," she said and gave him a hug to prove it.

When they were clear of the dangerous shallow reef near the *Constellation* and the *Montana*, Paul showed her the course the GPS had plotted and asked her to take the wheel. Then he climbed down the bridge ladder to the main deck and called Tom to join him in the cabin. He pulled their chart from the overhead rack and spread it out on the high-gloss mahogany table. It was not yet nine, but it was already getting hot, and sweat dropped from his forehead as he leaned over the chart.

"This one's over two hundred feet deep," he said, pointing out the site to Tom. "I don't know what the bottom's like out there, so you'll have to be on your toes just like yesterday. You up for it?"

"You bet."

"Good, lad. We'll be there in about an hour. Relax till then," he said and patted Tom on the back. He put a fresh tape in the camera, carefully checked the O-ring seals and closed the housing. After securing it to the down line, he headed back to the bridge and slid into the seat beside Debbie.

Tom was tired. He set a folding chair in the shade, got comfortable and let his thoughts return to last night with Debbie. She was unbelievable. With a contented smile, he drifted off to sleep while thinking about her.

"Buoy, Tom, throw the buoy!" Paul was shouting.

Tom lurched forward out of the chair, grabbed a buoy and heaved it over the stern.

It rotated rapidly as the line spun off and the weight headed down into the deep, clear water. The first one marked the GPS location. The *Mermaid* began slow, expanding circles out from the buoy as Paul searched the flat bottom with the Fathometer. After forty-five minutes with no luck, he decided to try the magnetometer.

"We don't have a headset cable long enough to reach the fly bridge, so Debbie will come down here with you," Paul told Tom. "We'll do the rest just like we did with the camera —should be no problem."

Debbie got set up and they began the first pass. They completed the run, but the mag remained silent. He brought the boat back into position, waited for the screen to stabilize and began the second line. Nothing. They continued the process for nearly an hour and were now seventy-five yards west of the buoy.

"Far enough," Paul finally said. "Let's move to the east side."

"Buoy," Debbie shouted just as they passed the float flag heading east. She jerked the headset off and looked for the volume control. Tom quickly got the second buoy over and started hauling in the heavy cable of the magnetometer.

"Hold on," Paul shouted down from the bridge. "Let's make a couple more runs before we bring in the transducer."

"Right," Tom agreed as he let the cable play back out over the stern. Paul lined up on the buoys and made a slow pass. He looked back at Debbie frequently, waiting for her to shout.

"There it is," she called out as the transducer crossed the spot again.

"Good girl. Now let's go perpendicular and see how wide it is."

They determined the site to be at least thirty yards wide. It took only a few minutes to bring up the mag and lower the video camera over the side. Paul brought the *Mermaid* slowly back and forth across the site. At the end of the twenty-minute tape, they brought up the camera. From the very beginning of the tape there was wreckage.

"Holy cow!" Tom said. "Look at those onion bottles. I saw some for sale in the Clock Tower gift shop for five hundred bucks each. There must be twenty or thirty right there."

"At least," Paul confirmed. "And there's a cannon. Look, you can see dolphins, the lifting eyes. It's got to be bronze."

"Has to be—it looks like new," Tom said enthusiastically. "What's that worth? Twenty to thirty thousand?"

"That's the right neighborhood," Paul answered.

"Really?" Debbie gasped. "Thirty thousand dollars each... well, don't look now but there are two more just like it. You mean there's a hundred thousand dollars down there just waiting for us to pick it up? No wonder someone wants to keep these wrecks a secret."

Paul laughed, "That's right, girl. You've got the picture. It looks like all the wood is either covered or gone, but you can bet no one has been here before or those onion bottles would all be gone. Looks like we beat them this time. I wish there was some way we could spare this wreck. At least until we learn who she was and what her story is," he continued.

"Yes," Debbie agreed. "Could the Maritime Museum help us?"

"Perhaps, but once word gets out, even the museum would be hard-pressed to protect this one. Wrecking's still in the blood here. I remember hearing the story of people rushing to the church door in the middle of Sunday services when the watch reported a ship had just struck the reef. Story goes the preacher shouted at them to stop, came down from the pulpit and gave 'em bloody hell. But as he talked, he was walking towards that door himself. When he got there, he said something like, 'Now that we've got a fair start, what are you waiting for?' And he led his congregation down the hill at full gallop.

"No, I'm afraid the only way to protect this one may be to keep quiet about it until we can get the right team and the right equipment together at the museum to do a proper job of it. This is a major project. We'll need a chamber on site, mixed gas and a big barge to work from. I doubt if there's even the proper equipment available anywhere in Bermuda."

"Yes, there is," Debbie said. "It belongs to the men who raped the site we were on yesterday. And you can bet this one's on their list too. We have to stop them."

"Right you are, Debbie. And with information like this," he said, holding up the tape, "We'll find these thieves and stop them for good. And we'll have Tom here to thank." He gave Tom a hearty slap on the back.

They were soon underway again heading to the next site. Paul was finishing his third pitcher of tea when the GPS alarm sounded and Tom threw a buoy. The *Mermaid* circled the buoy, and in short order the Fathometer showed spikes jutting up from the bottom indicating fish. Paul called for another buoy and continued the search. Then the Fathometer showed the sides of a hull and a deck house sitting upright in one hundred and sixty feet.

Paul was astounded. "She's fully intact! Look at this, Debbie," he said, pointing to the chart paper. "You don't see many this clear. There's the wheelhouse and the mast. The top of the wheelhouse is forty-five feet off the bottom. How could Tom's computer miss something like this? That's a steel hull, two hundred fifty feet long if she's an inch."

"What have we got, Paul?" Tom yelled from the deck.

"I'm not exactly sure, but she's tight into the reef. I don't want to risk dropping the camera. How do you feel about making a decompression dive?"

"No problem. Let's go."

"Do you want Debbie to dive with you?"

"Of course. Why not?"

Paul hesitated for a moment. "No reason," he answered. "Get another buoy ready. We'll drop this one right down her stack."

When everything was in place, they gathered in the stern and Paul began the briefing. "This should be an easy dive. You go down the anchor line to the deck, and remember to turn on the camera!"

They both laughed as he continued, "Take a quick spin about the deck and the wheelhouse. Try to tell if we're the first to find her, or if she's been dived before.

"Check the holds. If the hatches are still sealed, you may have to go in through the lower compartments. Tom, you take the camera, and Debbie, you are the safety and divemaster. If it looks too dangerous, stay out. Tom, you follow her lead."

"I'll have my hands full with the camera," Tom said when they were standing on the dive platform ready to jump. "Will you watch our time and depth, and give me a tap on the shoulder now and then so I'll know you're still with me?"

"Don't worry, I'll be right beside you," she laughed and started to put the regulator in her mouth.

"This should be great. What do you suppose is down

there?"

She held her regulator and answered while making a grab at his stomach, "Have you read <u>Beast</u>?"

He caught her arm and pulled her close. She struggled to free herself, gave up and kissed him, but he wouldn't let go.

"Come on, Tom, time to get your mind out of bed and into this dive," she whispered. "We're not alone here."

Paul was watching from the fly bridge and laughing. "Come on, let's get ready. There's probably a fortune down there just waiting for you."

"Or a big, purple critter with long arms and an insatiable appetite for neoprene. Is that ammonia I smell, or have you had an accident?" she teased, pulling on her mask. Then she put the regulator in her mouth and jumped.

CHAPTER

7

Fifty feet down the anchor line, they could see the stack and rigging rising from the wreck below. They dropped further and the entire superstructure emerged. It was a coastal freighter, like the *Hermes*, a popular dive off the south shore. They could see deck winches, booms and clutter including a clothesline from which laundry had been hung when the ship plunged to the bottom. Debbie pointed to a pair of men's briefs waving like a pennant from a steel shroud supporting the short mast.

Forward of the deckhouse, they saw two large cargo hatches, their timber and canvas covers collapsed under the weight of a fallen deck boom. They watched a blue and gold filefish come up from the hold, cross the deck and disappear over the rail, chased by a blue sergeant major. At one hundred feet they stopped, and Tom turned on the camera and panned the wreck. Debbie checked their air gauges. They exchanged OK signals and continued the descent.

The anchor had caught in the stern deck railing and Tom made a mental note that he would need to free it on the way back. They let go of the anchor line and dropped to the starboard catwalk outside the wheelhouse. Debbie checked her computer—one hundred and twenty feet.

She began to feel a bit dizzy and her air tasted slightly thick. She recognized the symptoms as a mild case of nitrogen narcosis and held on to the rail until her head began to clear. Tom swam into the wheelhouse and began the search. There was clutter everywhere—comic books with sexy covers, navigation charts, dirty dishes and brown coffee mugs. Two M16 rifles and a short-barreled shotgun had fallen from a wall rack and lay in a pile by the radios.

Nowhere did he see anything that looked like a ship's log. He heard a sharp rapping behind him and turned to see Debbie pounding on the hatch frame with a saucepan. She pointed to her watch and motioned for him to hurry. Time was important if they wanted to avoid long decompression.

He pushed open the door of the officers' stateroom and flooded the cabin with his dive light. Suddenly, an arm swung in front of his face from the ceiling. He jerked backwards and fell into the door frame.

He took quick deep breaths and pulled himself up. Slowly, he looked back up with the camera and the light. Floating on the ceiling was a partially-eaten, bloated body in blue jeans and a Grateful Dead T-shirt. A portion of the skull was missing.

He stared, transfixed in morbid fascination. Three heavy gold chains, two with large gold coins, dangled from the puffy neck. Strapped to a bony wrist was a gold Rolex with a jeweled bezel. The body was rocking gently, set in motion when he opened the door. Tom looked at the bulging eyes and swallowed hard; it was not a pretty sight.

Debbie tapped him on the back and he jumped again. He quickly pointed his light to the floor and guided her out of the wheelhouse. Back on the catwalk, they compared pressure gauges and checked the time. They were nine minutes into the dive and had two-thirds of their air left. Tom lifted himself over the catwalk railing, trimmed his buoyancy and dropped to the main deck. Debbie cleared her mask and followed.

As she swam down after Tom, her narcosis increased. Now her head was really buzzing. When they landed on the deck, her computer read one hundred and forty-two feet. She tried to read the slate on which she had recorded their dive plan, but it made no sense. Which profile were they to use? Why was she carrying the lift bag and collection bag full of line?

They were in the way and she tugged to get them off her belt. Tom came to her side and gave her an "OK?" signal. She wobbled her hand and pointed to the problem bags. They looked fine to Tom, but then he looked carefully into her eyes. Something was wrong: her eyes looked glazed, her face worried and confused. He guessed she was narked, and took the offending bags and hung them on his belt. Holding her hand, they moved up to the forward hold.

The opening through the crushed timbers and canvas, which had once sealed the hold, left barely enough space for him to drop through. It would be easier to go alone and get a quick look, but Debbie was in no condition to be left alone. He checked their air and signaled they were going down. Awkwardly holding her hand, his light and the camera, Tom deflated their BCs and they dropped into the darkness. It was a short drop—the hold was nearly full.

They had landed on stacked rows of marijuana bales wrapped in heavy burlap and black plastic. As he panned the hold with the dive light and camera, Debbie suddenly bolted towards the opening above. He dropped the camera and pulled her back down. He felt her trembling. He shook her and looked into her mask asking, "What?" She squeezed his hand tightly and pointed her light towards the corner behind them. Its beam revealed another badly-decomposed body.

Most of its face was gone and a small fish retreated into the skull to avoid the glare of the light. It was time to go. Tom grabbed the camera, took a quick shot of the second body and gathering Debbie under his arm, started up.

Tom pushed her through the opening first. When he tried to follow her, the lift bags on his belt caught on the edge of the hatch. He struggled to free them, and when Debbie turned to see if he was following, he anxiously pointed to the bags. She released the snap hook and got him clear, but the bags dropped into the hold. There was no going back for them now. He pointed up to the wheelhouse and they began their ascent. At the wheelhouse, Tom started swimming across to the anchor line with the camera. He still had to clear the anchor.

At one hundred and twenty feet, Debbie's head began to

clear and she realized she was alone. She looked down and saw Tom sitting on the stern, using the strength of his legs to pull the anchor free. Huge bursts of bubbles thundered from his regulator as he strained against the steady pull of the *Mermaid*. In a moment, the anchor was clear and he headed up the line.

Her computer said their bottom time was twenty-one minutes and she had a fourth of her air remaining. Tom's submersible pressure gauge was into the red—he was nearly out of air. Debbie handed him her spare regulator so he could share air from her tank. Way above them, they could see the *Mermaid* with a spare tank hanging beneath the hull.

As they continued coming up, the computer's ascent rate monitor alarm began beeping angrily. They slowed down until it was silent. When they finally reached the spare tank, Debbie's pressure gauge was also in the red.

Tom grabbed one of the spare tank's regulators and handed Debbie the other. He took several slow, deep breaths and gave her an "OK?". She smiled and returned the signal. Paul watched them on the line then jumped into the water with mask and fins. He took the camera and the lights, and returned to the dive platform. Tom took a small slate from his BC and wrote, "Tons of grass—two bodies. Film at eleven. We're OK." and signaled Paul down again. Paul's eyes got big as he read the slate. By the time their decompression was finished, Tom's heart rate was back to normal.

They broke the surface and Debbie started talking the second the regulator was out of her mouth. "Did you see the fish swim into that guy's skull? When I saw that I was so scared I could have walked on water. Tom saved me. I was headed for the surface like a trident missile. Thanks, Tom, I owe you one."

"You're welcome, and thank you for getting me unhooked from that hatch," he answered.

"Sounds like you two make a pretty good team," Paul said as he lifted their tanks into the boat.

Debbie was the first out. As she turned back to help Tom, she stared at him as if seeing him for the first time. They were indeed a good team, she thought.

Perhaps everything would be alright after all, Bill Roberts told himself as he stepped out of the shower early that Monday morning. Texas had been tiring and certainly not any vacation. It was good to see the old gang at A&M, especially Ben Travis, his brother-in-law and oldest friend. Roberts needed someone to talk to and Travis was the only person he could really trust.

Robert was in his mid-fifties, balding and a little paunchy, but he worked out and kept it mostly under control. He enjoyed sailing and athletics, and when he had the opportunity to come to Bermuda ten years ago as the NASA station commander, he had jumped at the chance. It was the opportunity to get out of the constant confrontations of agency politics and still be a key player—the perfect combination; and a great place to raise his family away from all the consumerism and problems of life in Texas or Florida, or, God forbid, Washington, D.C.

He glanced at the mirror, tightened his stomach and shook his head. Too much southern cooking, he thought. Exercise could fix that; too bad it wouldn't fix the bald spot as well. He smelled coffee, finished dressing and went down to the kitchen. His wife, Petra, a heavy-set blonde, wore her starched nurse's uniform, and poured his coffee. Fruit, cereal and a fresh homemade oat bran muffin were waiting on the table.

"I'll take a cup with me. I want to stop at the marina and check on the boat—make sure Charlie and his boys got that bright work refinished."

"I know, I know. It's right here, just like every day for the past ten years. You think because you're away for two weeks you have to retrain me?" she chided with a smile. "Don't forget your bran muffin. I'm having lunch with Papa."

"Be careful," Bill cautioned. "What will happen to us if anyone finds him here? It will certainly be the end of everything. Just be careful, that's all."

He finished the cereal, wrapped the muffin in a napkin and grabbed the coffee mug. He kissed her goodbye, came out of the pink stucco house with the spotless white stucco roof, and climbed in the hatch-back Toyota. He had less than a ten-minute ride through Georgetown to the marina where he kept his 40-foot sailboat, *Liebchen*. Having made sure the work on the boat met his demanding standards, he then drove the few remaining blocks to his office. Tom Morrison and Ensign Debbie Holiday were waiting for him.

He greeted them with a broad smile and his usual banalities about it being another perfect day in paradise. They apologized for jumping him so early on his first day back, and explained their immediate need for a private meeting. He fumbled with the door key, his hands full of briefcase, coffee and oat bran muffin. Once in the sanctity of his office, he launched the muffin into the trash with a fifteen-foot one-handed set shot.

"Don't you ever tell Petra I did that. She read another article on cholesterol about a year ago and has been force-feeding me those things ever since. Can't stand 'em. They smell like something a horse should eat, or perhaps did eat. Now, what's your big story?"

Tom gave him a detailed report. "That's it so far," Tom concluded. "We intend to go back out next weekend and look at more of the sites. Paul is going to the Marine Police to tell the inspector about the drug boat, but that's all. I'm really glad you're back. I hope we did the right thing waiting to tell you. Debbie was really worried, but it didn't look like anything more than a hacker to me, somebody interested in wrecks..."

"One who knows an awful lot about computers," Debbie added.

"That's some story," Bill said, sinking into his big leather swivel chair. He set his briefcase on the desk and opened it to look for antacids. "You were right to keep this under wraps, Tom. It's probably not much, but Debbie's right. We certainly can't take any chances. Debbie, is that your chart?"

They spread the chart on his desk and Debbie pointed out the locations of their dives the past weekend. "Notice that all these sites are deep—deeper than sport divers should be going anyway—and they're all on the outer edge of the reef," she said. "Yet the first two have been extensively worked. It took lots of bottom time to strip that site, yet as far as we have learned, no one knows of anybody even diving out there,

much less staying long enough to really work it."

"That is a mystery, isn't it? But my primary concerns are why our computer won't show it to us, and what damage may have been done to our security. The rest is for the Marine Police to worry about," Bill told them. "I want to get started right away. Is there any chance that we could borrow you for a few days, Debbie? There are hundreds of files in that program. We'll have to check them all."

They quickly worked out the details and as soon as they were gone, Bill Roberts staggered to his private washroom, fell to his knees and vomited violently.

Inspector Ian Cord was tall—six-foot four inches—and middle-aged, but still solid at two hundred forty-five pounds. A Scot, he had answered an advert fifteen years ago for police officers with three years experience willing to move to Bermuda. During those years the gentle, quiet man had become the head of the Marine Police, and the inspecting officer of all dive boats and instructors on the island. He and Paul had been friends for several years. Now they sat in his office looking at the tape of the drug ship.

"What do you make of that, Ian? Look at the gold the killers left behind on that bloke. They certainly didn't do this for the money. Even if they were in a hell of a hurry, they could have easily had those gold chains and that Rolex. That's twenty thousand, easy."

"Right you are, unless they didn't have the stomach for it, or more likely, they were in a hell of a hurry. Look how well those bales are sealed," Ian said as he moved closer to the screen. "That stuff's as good as the day it went down. They can still dry it and sell it.

"Did your divers discover how she sank? That might tell us if it was done by her crew settling a score, like the one in Grand Cayman." Paul shook his head. "Maybe it was commando style," Ian continued, "to keep the balance of supply and demand from being upset by a newcomer. One way or the other, there is a lot of money down there and if any of their people saw you diving her, you could be in real danger. If you want to keep a weapon on the boat, I'll sign a permit for you. Might be a good idea. In the meantime, my lads will keep a close eye on her. This could be our opportunity to put those scum into early retirement. I'm sure they'll be back for this load, and soon."

"No guns, not on my boat, nor in my house, nor on Bermuda. I've had enough of guns to last my lifetime, you know that. Just call if I can help, but no guns!" Paul removed the tape from the VCR and put it in his briefcase.

"Oh, may I have that?" Ian asked. "I suppose we should keep it for evidence and I want the commissioner to see it."

"Certainly," Paul answered and gave him the tape. "I would like to have it back though. Haven't had a chance to make a copy."

"Right, right, of course," came the reply. "You be careful, Paul. See you, mate, and thanks for this. Don't have to tell you to keep this under your cap, but it would be good to warn your young divers as well."

Paul was troubled as he left the inspector's office. Ian's hatred of drug dealers was well known, and there was a third explanation possible for the sinking of the little freighter. What if an overly zealous marine inspector had boarded her and taken matters into his own hands?

That might explain the cargo and jewelry left on board. And now that someone else had discovered the wreck, the government could raise the cargo, dispose of it properly and no one would ever know...or, someone could dispose of the divers who found it and keep the millions for themselves. It was a point to ponder. He opened his small briefcase. In the bottom was the copy of the tape he had lied about not making. He felt somewhat more secure having it. He needed to see Debbie and Tom, and let Janet in on the game. "I wonder when Doc is coming. Soon I hope," he muttered under his breath.

On Tuesday night Paul met Tom and Debbie at his front door. "Come in, come in. Glad you're here." He led them into the house and offered beer. Janet looked in from the kitchen to announce that dinner would be ready shortly. Settling in the comfortable, nautical-style living room, Tom began telling him of their meeting with Bill Roberts. When he finished, Debbie added, "He wants to meet you as soon as possible, and he wants our charts, notes and the tapes for safekeeping."

"That's interesting. Ian wanted to keep the tape I showed him as well. Perhaps we should go into the video business and forget the rest," Paul laughed, but then got very quiet. "This drug business scares me. I've known Ian a long time. He's as good as there is, honest and trustworthy, but he's never gotten over the death of his brother. I don't know what he might do to avenge Brian's death. And I'm sure your Bill Roberts is every bit the friend you think he is, Tom, but I think we should take steps to protect ourselves just in case." Janet was now standing in the door listening.

"I've made copies of the tapes and we should keep duplicates of the charts. At least until we know more about who the players are."

"What about the rest of our dives?" Tom asked. "Bill thinks we should go as quickly as possible."

"I agree. We'll go Saturday as planned, when there'll be lots of other boats out there. We'll come back in Saturday night and go out again Sunday morning. You can stay here the weekend so we can get an early start."

It was late when the last bottle of wine was empty and the roast lamb a fading memory.

Tom took the South Shore Road back from Somerset towards St.George's. He pulled over into an observation parking spot and turned off the engine. Without saying a word, he gently pulled Debbie into a long kiss.

"I was afraid Paul wouldn't want to stay out overnight again, and can't say that I'd blame him...so I brought a blanket and towels just in case you might be interested in a swim."

"Just in case I might suggest it?"

"Right, just in case you might."

"And in your careful preparations for this unlikely event, did you happen to remember swimming suits?" she teased.

"If you are referring to Bermudian bathing costumes, golly gee, I'm afraid I forgot."

"You forgot! Wasn't that taking a lot for granted?"

"Yes, it was and I am ever so ashamed." He looked at the

center of the steering wheel with a long face, biting his lip to keep from laughing.

"Quite, and so you should be. And just where did you think we might go and perform this illegal act without being incarcerated and publicly brought to shame?"

"Just beyond the Southampton Princess is a lovely beach with several secluded coves. That might be an appropriate place."

"Well, why don't you drive us there just in case the mood should strike and I might suggest going for a dip?"

"Only if you think it might be a good idea. I would never be that presumptive," he said as he slipped his hand under her blouse.

"No, I'm sure you wouldn't," she answered as she began to undo the buttons. "But while you are considering the possibilities, why don't you drive? I'd hate to be arrested for indecent exposure before we get in the water." With that, she undid the rest of the buttons and unfastened the center clasp of her bra.

Tom found an appropriate spot and spread out the blanket. In no time, Debbie was out of her clothes and in the water, waiting. Through the night they made love, in the water and on the beach, and by the time pale light peeked from the eastern sky, Debbie knew she had found the person she wanted to spend the rest of her life with. The sun had risen when they pulled themselves apart and rushed back to the base.

They were both late for the meeting with Bill Roberts and Paul. Debbie was glowing and Tom looked exhausted. Paul guessed what had happened and smiled while looking at Roberts's office floor.

"Well, we didn't wait for you," Roberts said, "and the coffee is gone, so you'll just have to suffer, or beg Susan to make another pot. And if I looked as bad as you do, Tom, I'd beg." Tom did an about-face to find Susan, Bill's secretary, to barter all his worldly possessions if necessary for one cup of coffee. In the office, the conversation continued without him.

"Paul told me about your plan. It's a good one, especially with this drug business. I offered to give you some Navy boys for security, but Paul thinks that will just attract more attention and we're not ready to start answering questions yet."

"Also," Debbie added, "if it was someone on the base who has been playing with the computer and the satellite data, we don't want to tip our hand and blow the chance to catch him."

Tom came back in with four cups of coffee. "I had to settle for instant and sign over the use of my Honda on weekends, but this smells drinkable. What's the plan?"

They brought him up-to-date and Bill concluded by saying, "I want to know where you are every minute out there. I'll give you one of our radios with a scrambler and I want you to check in regularly. We'll have a helicopter and support team on standby.

"I want us all back here Monday morning, on time if possible." He gave Tom a glare with a raised eyebrow and then smiled. "Captain Singleton, thanks for coming. You're certainly to be commended for everything you've done. Good luck." He walked Paul to the door, and when he returned he said, "I've got good news. I told the Navy enough to cover us, and Washington is sending the program designer to help us. Should be here Monday. I was able to get him without mentioning what you were up to, Tom. You two might even get commendations before this is over. All I ask is that you take care of each other and try to get some sleep every other day or so. Now get out of here and get those reports finished."

Even as he scolded, his charming smile never ceased. Walking them to the door, he put his hand in the small of Debbie's back and said, "Little lady, if Tom ever wears out his welcome, I have a son in Texas who'd just love to meet you. So don't feel obligated to put up with any of his nonsense. If Texans know anything, it's how to care for a beautiful filly. You just let me know if there's ever anything I can do to prove it."

"Thank you, sir. So far, I can't say that I've had any reasons to complain. But if he doesn't hold up his end of the bargain, it's nice to know there are backup systems on standby."

"Yes, ma'am. That's what's made NASA great."

CHAPTER

8

Friday finally came, and after a long slow day Tom and Debbie drove the South Shore Road back towards Paul and Janet's. As they passed the turn to Horseshoe Bay where they had spent the night, Tom put his hand on her lap and asked if she wanted to stop for a swim.

"Oh, was it a swim you were thinking about?" she teased, raising his hand to her mouth and nibbling at his finger tips. "Ask me again Sunday night and we'll see."

They stopped at the Somerset Country Squire on Mangrove Bay for dinner. From their outdoor table overlooking the bay, they sat quietly admiring the immaculately cared for, brightly painted boats secure on their moorings. The anticipation of an exciting weekend of diving and two nights with Debbie was enough to have Tom wound tighter than usual, but there was something else on his mind tonight. She knew it and waited for him to speak.

"We haven't talked much since the night on the beach, about us, I mean, and the things that have happened. I wanted to let you know that I have never been as happy as when we're together...and, well, I know you had some reservations about us, and I..."

"I love you, Tom. Is that what you wanted to hear? I still have reservations about us, but I love you, and the rest will just have to work itself out. The good news is, we have lots of time, and we don't have to rush into anything." She smiled and looked directly into his eyes. She spoke slowly and comfortably. It was obvious she had given the matter a lot of thought. "Being lovers is one thing, being good enough friends for a more permanent relationship is a whole different issue...well, let's just take that a day at a time, but I do love you."

He took her hands and sighed deeply. "I love you too, Debbie. I have wanted to say it, but I needed to know if you felt the same way. I couldn't handle it if you didn't. I've never felt this way about anyone else, and I'm very, very happy."

They ate their wahoo slowly with lots of smiling and hand-holding, and sometimes soft, private laughter. When they finished, they drove to Paul's house where they would spend the night. They needed to get an early start in the morning.

"Why did you bring the laptop?" Tom asked as he unloaded the car.

"I want to keep it with us; it has all our data. We'll need it tomorrow to enter whatever information we get and cross-reference the sites. And I have to write to my dad tonight. There just wasn't time this week, and I feel like a real jerk when I don't write. He is so lonely and it won't take long, I promise."

"No problem. Tom and Debbie go to room. Tom watches Debbie write a letter and falls asleep. Got it."

"Not on your life, Diver Dan," she said. "No sleep for you until Debbie is a happy girl."

Paul had prepared separate bedrooms, but found Debbie's room empty when he knocked to awaken her in the early dawn. This is getting pretty serious, he thought. I hope Tom is ready to settle down because I'd bet the boat she's playing for keeps.

They were loaded and away from the dock before seven. The twin diesels ran smoothly and the air was refreshingly cool. Today they were headed northwest across the shallow flats beyond the wrecks of the *Eagle* and the *Aristo*.

Paul was alone on the fly bridge deep in thought. He was troubled by the drug wreck and his conversation with Inspector Ian Cord. He wondered again if Ian was involved. It's disgusting to think of the things a man will do for a million dollars, he thought with a cynical laugh. He carefully scanned the horizon.

Tom was down below trying to wake Debbie from her nap. Her foot protruded from the forepeak berth and he ran his thumbnail up her arch. "You were wonderful last night," he said. "Do you think they heard us?"

"The dead probably heard us, especially when you banged my head into the headboard. Now leave me alone. I need to sleep."

"Debbie, come on. You've slept nearly two hours. Get up and have some coffee."

"No, go away! I need to sleep." Debbie crawled further into the V berth and covered herself with pillows. Tom laughed and went out on deck.

The *Mermaid* cut easily through the shallow blue-green water. It was a perfect diving day: a nearly flat sea, a cloudless sky, and a gentle breeze from the southwest. Tom sat on the back deck, and enjoyed the muffled droning of the diesels and the freshness of the morning. They ran for almost an hour until Paul pulled back the throttles and called down from the fly bridge.

"We're nearly there and I need some relief. Come up and take the wheel, Tom. Did Debbie go back to sleep?" he asked.

"Yes, sir, she's in the V berth. She chased me out."

"I'm happy to see you two getting along so well. She's a real prize, Tom. You'll have your hands full with her, but if she's half the woman her mother was, you won't find one better. Keep you on your toes she will, but then I expect you can handle yourself." He looked over at Tom and smiled. "Janet and I are happy for you. Just wanted you to know. Here now, take the wheel and watch out for the coral heads. They can fool you."

"Interesting," Tom said to himself when Paul was below. "I think that means they heard us."

The squeak of the hand pump in the head woke Debbie, and when she finally peered out from under the pillows, she saw Paul in the galley pouring a mug of coffee. He brought it to her and sat on the edge of the berth.

"Are we there yet?" she asked like a ten-year old, all bleary-eyed.

"Yes, sleeping beauty, we're nearly there and we request the pleasure of your company. Wouldn't hurt to make some more coffee—that's the last of it. You might bring me a refill. The adventure of the sea awaits."

She stretched and moaned loudly before climbing out of the berth. Her mouth tasted like bilge slime and her head was splitting. She searched her purse for her toothbrush. She brushed twice, took aspirin, and downed half the mug. As she put the toothbrush and paste back, she noticed the disk with the letter to her father. Must get this in the mail Monday, she thought and tossed the open bag back into the dinette seat. The disk fell out onto the deck beneath the table.

Debbie changed into shorts and a tank top, put on sun screen and headed topside with a large mug of coffee. Paul was at the helm and Tom on the deck. They were in deeper water beyond the northern edge of the reef when the GPS alarm went off. Tom threw the first buoy and they began circling. They had gone no more than twenty yards when the Fathometer showed a likely target in a hundred forty feet of water.

"Buoy, Tom," came the call from the bridge, and another float with the attached flag and weight went over the side. "OK, now let's put the camera in."

Tom quickly got the camera over the side while Paul watched the compass and GPS, and ran the grid. Debbie kept track of the time and told him when to turn.

"We're getting pretty good at this," Paul said just before the camera weight snagged in the wreckage below.

The effect was immediate. Tom was nearly pulled overboard by the sudden strain on the camera line. His hands were burned as the line jerked through his grip. Debbie hurried down the bridge ladder to help.

"Tie a buoy on the line and throw it over," Paul yelled from the bridge. He was backing down the boat, but the line continued to play out. "That line's not strong enough to hold us. We'll lose the camera!"

Debbie grabbed the end of the line, tied a bowline knot in the eye of the buoy, and shouted to let go of the line. Tom did and fell back.

"What a sailor, what marlinespike seamanship! Did you

see her tie that bowline?" Tom teased as he tried to regain his composure.

"I thought you knew by now, Tom, PADI instructors can do anything," came the cocky reply. "Let's see your hands."

Debbie took out the first aid kit and dressed his wounds. Paul anchored the *Mermaid* near the buoy and hurried to the stern. "How 'bout a drink for the pain? There's a bottle of Gosling's in the cabin," he informed Tom.

"I'm fine. Debbie just likes playing doctor."

"You saved the camera, lad, and I appreciate it. Looks like it's my turn to dive. I'll bring back the line, then Debbie can pull up the camera after I get it free."

"I don't think you should dive alone. I'll come with you," Debbie said.

"Thanks, but I'll be fine. I'm looking forward to getting wet."

At first, all he could see was the line going down into blue darkness. He paused to clear his ears and remembered his days of helmet diving when, unable to reach his nose, he would have equalized on thought command only or by contorting his upper lip against the helmet ring to close his nostrils and facilitate the valsalva maneuver. Now, going down more slowly was the key. Finally, his left eustachian tube opened and he continued the descent.

At seventy feet, he could see the bottom. He followed the arch of the line and it led to a steel hull with deck guns. The hull was long and slender with straight, clean lines. There was a single stack up through the deck house like a paddle wheeler, but there were no side paddles. Steam power on a sailing hull—wonder if she's a blockade runner, Paul thought. Certainly later than 1850, perhaps even post-Civil War. He had never seen one in condition this good. Steel decks too...what a beauty! An island of smugglers, shipwrecks and treasures...no wonder I love Bermuda so much, he chuckled.

As he continued his descent, he could see the camera caught in a handrail on the starboard side of the bow. He untangled the camera and looked at his instrument console. Depth one twenty-five and plenty of air. The camera looked OK, but the red light was off which told him the tape was full. It took only a moment to clear the weight. When he gave the line three tugs, the camera headed rapidly towards the surface.

Paul decided to take a quick tour before going back up. He tried to see into the wheelhouse, but heavy encrustation blocked the view. He scraped away a spot of growth from one and peered in. In the faint light, he could see the brass ship's wheel and what could be brass in the debris on the floor. The steel wheelhouse door on the port side wouldn't budge so he swam to the starboard door. It too was steel and would not give. Then he noticed the glass missing from a stern window. The frame was tall and narrow. He pulled off his fins, shoved a boot through the frame and pushed. Whatever had blocked his entrance fell away in an explosion of silt. He waited for the worst of it to settle and then pulled himself up into the frame. It was a tight squeeze, but he got in. His bubbles striking the ceiling dislodged more sediment, greatly reducing the visibility. He added air to his BC and tried to stay off the deck, but it didn't help much. It was like being in a blizzard. He dropped to his knees and moved forward, searching with his hands. He felt straight metal edges and picked up the object with a knowing smile. It was a brass sextant. He swept forward again with his other hand, and grabbed a brass set of parallel rules and turned back towards the frame. Because of the stirred up sediment, the visibility was now less than a foot.

He could not see light in any direction. He paused and took several deep breaths. Again, he checked the instrument console. He could barely see the luminescent face of the air pressure gauge. He still had more than a third of his air. Plenty to get out and make a safe ascent.

He began feeling his way back towards the open frame. Suddenly, a light appeared through the haze. He went directly to it and found Tom waiting. Paul handed out his treasures and wriggled through the frame. Tom led him to the bow where he had tied an up line.

They came up slowly and stopped at twenty feet. Tom looked at his tables and signaled an eight-minute decompression stop. After completing the stop, they swam up to the lift bag at the surface. As Tom cut the line and rolled up the bag, Paul saw blood coming from the dressings on Tom's hands.

"I was happy to see that light, Tom. Thanks, lad, but your hands...the salt in those wounds must burn like crazy!" With buoyancy control jackets inflated, they swam on their backs towards the boat. They were now close to the *Mermaid* and there was no sign of Debbie. Paul was worried.

"Tom," he said softly, "drop down and wait under the boat until I come and get you. Give me your bag. Quiet now." Without a word, Tom slipped beneath the surface and Paul swam to the dive platform. He quietly removed his fins, placed them and the other things on the platform, and pulled himself up the ladder.

"Had a nice dive, Captain?" the long-haired, tattooed man in the deck chair said as Paul came up the ladder. Leveled at Paul was an HK MP5 submachine gun.

"Where's Debbie?" Paul demanded.

"She's alright, don't worry. We're just going to take a little trip. You behave now and we won't need to hurt anybody. Just take off your equipment and let's wait for your friend. Tom, isn't it? I'll tell you my name if you like, but then of course I'd have to kill you...so I don't think you want a formal introduction, do you, Captain? No, I didn't think so."

Paul remained silent. He wanted to know if they were on the boat alone, and he was wondering if he should have accepted Ian's offer of a weapon for the boat. A short-barreled Mossberg twelve-gauge combat magnum would feel right handy about now.

Tom saw the inflatable tied to the *Mermaid*'s starboard rail. The motor started and the little boat pulled away, circling about twenty yards out before stopping off her port side. Tom's hand went down for the knife on his leg. He pulled it from the scabbard and waited. He saw a diver roll into the water from the inflatable and start swimming towards him about twenty-five feet beneath the surface. As the diver came closer, Tom could see he was not wearing scuba. There were no exhaust bubbles coming from either his mouth or the large pack on his back. The diver stopped about thirty feet away and waved at Tom.

Tom had been prepared for a confrontation and was disarmed by the friendly gesture. Just as he waved back, his mask was ripped off and the regulator pulled from his mouth by an attacker at his back. An arm closed over his throat. Now the diver from the inflatable closed in, knife in hand. Tom reacted instantly. He rolled forward and with all his strength, dolphin-kicked towards the surface, ramming the head of his attacker into the bottom of the *Mermaid.* The arm at his throat relaxed enough for him to push it up and spin out. He led with his dive knife and cut through the intake hose on the right side of his opponent's mouthpiece. He grabbed the man's hair and pulled his head down smashing the attacker's mask with his knee. Blood flowed from the broken nose and cut face. The injured diver kicked away to the surface.

Tom turned back to look for the other diver and caught the glint of a knife from the side of his mask. He twisted away and slashed out in one motion. His knife went through the second man's arm and was pulled from his hand.

The wounded assailant switched his own knife to his good hand and moved in. Tom backed away, undid the waistband of his buoyancy jacket and slipped out of the jacket, holding the tank in front of him to fend off the attack. As the man swam closer, Tom turned off the air of his own tank. Keeping the butt of the tank facing the other man, Tom removed the first stage of the regulator from the tank and opened the BC strap. He kept the second stage in his mouth and his hands on the tank valve.

Alright, you bastard, I've got a little surprise for you. Come on, I can't hold my breath for....He didn't have time to finish the thought before the blade flashed towards him. Tom shoved the tank at the diver's face and opened the valve as fast as he could. The ocean exploded in bubbles. The tank rocketed from his hand, spinning wildly, and smashed into his assailant's face. Again the sea was red with blood.

His brain was screaming for air as he pulled himself out from under the hull and kicked to the surface. Beneath him, his unconscious opponent sank slowly to the bottom. He came as quietly to the surface as he could and gasped for air.

"Very impressive, my friend. But anymore of your cute tricks and I'll play some of my own on your little friends here."

The long-haired man was on the bow pointing the MP5 at Paul. "Now get your ass on this boat before you really piss me off."

Tom swam to the stern, pulled off his fins and came up the ladder. The inflatable was tied alongside and Debbie was lying on the floorboards, tied and gagged. A man with a broken nose and a bloody face glared at him from the stern.

"You OK?" Tom asked. She nodded. Then something hit him very hard.

CHAPTER

9

The gleaming new 19-foot bass boat, black with gold trim, worked its way slowly around the point. It was early morning on the lake and not yet as hot as the north Florida summer day promised to become. The big one hundred fifty horsepower motor was silent, and the only sounds were birds and the electric trolling motor's quiet hum. In the dream, Doc Holiday was back—back on the clear water of this nearly hidden lake, sitting on the bow seat of the first new boat he had ever owned. What a beauty!

In his hand was his favorite seven-foot bass rod with cork handle and he was making long, snagless casts with the old, red Ambassador reel, expertly working a plastic purple worm complete with fish perfume through the stumps and brush of the shallows. It was on this lake that he'd gotten hooked on the art and science of pursuing largemouth bass.

Twelve years ago—or was it fifteen?—he'd been off this point in his old aluminum boat, working a yellow spinner bait, or was it white? He'd caught and released two nice fish, or was it...it was two. He was working the lure fairly quickly and was just lifting it out, picking the spot for the next cast when in the corner of his eye, he saw a log come to life and rise from the bottom. Two ten-inch smallmouth had followed the bait back to the boat and this monster had been waiting beneath the boat. It was as long as a canoe paddle blade and its mouth looked large enough to swallow a football. That hog would go over eighteen pounds, would certainly be a citation and possibly a lake record. The monster took the second smallmouth in one gulp, rolled sideways to glare at Doc, and then sank back into the boat's shadow. It was using Doc's boat as an ambush point. Pretty smart, he'd thought. He remembered that defiant glare. It was a challenge—a challenge he would now answer.

With a long underarm cast, he dropped the giant-sized worm softly into the brush within inches of the bank, let it rest a few seconds, and then worked it slowly back over the branches and snags. He watched the blue-tinted line carefully. There was no pressure on the rod, no tug, no jerk, no gentle pull, but suddenly, the worm began to move on its own. From the near shore shallows, it was running quickly towards deep water off the point.

Doc brought the rod up waist-high and with a great tug set the hook. The stout seven-foot graphite rod bent double as the fish nearly pulled it from his hand. Line burned off the spool as he fought to tighten the drag. Too tight and the fish would snap it; not tight enough and the fish would strip the reel.

Suddenly, the line went slack. The fish had turned and was blasting towards the surface. It would try to throw the lure, and Doc's only chance was to keep the line tight and control the jump. The old, red reel screamed as he cranked in line. This must be the one, he thought. There couldn't be two this big in the same lake.

The fish exploded into the sunlight, larger than a mailbox with the front door open, large enough to fill a trophy wall. It arched its back and tossed its head violently from side to side. Doc kept the rod pointed down and the line taut. The largemouth fell back into the water with a smack that sounded like a hot cannon ball.

The fish broke the surface again, and again Doc was ready. The big bass was so strong it was actually pulling the boat. The lunker fought like a twenty-pound catfish. It showed no sign of tiring, and Doc could feel the strain on his arms and back as he fought to maneuver the fish close to the boat. His heart raced with excitement when he got the fish close enough to get a good look. This was the fish. The one you only get one shot at. While he held the rod high with his right hand, he reached for the fish with his left.

"Come to papa, come to papa...." As he brought the fish closer to the boat, he could see the worm on the outside of the bass's mouth. It was only lip-hooked. This was going to be touchy.

"Now!" He lifted the rod tip high and reached for the fish. He got a good grip on the monster's lower jaw and carefully lifted it into the boat.

The first time the phone rang, he didn't hear it. The second time, his dream began to melt. He looked from the boat into the bedroom trying to find the phone. When he did, the huge fish jumped again, planting the hook in Doc's hand and at the same time, leveraging itself free. With another flip it was over the side, back in the cool dark water and safely out of the dream. Doc swore and examined the hook embedded halfway through his palm. The phone rang again. This time, he found it and growled, "What?" at the receiver. His own voice startled him into reality and the hook melted away with the trophy fish.

"Doc, Doc? Is that you? This is Janet Singleton. Doc, are you there? Please answer. I need you."

She was crying. Doc was now fully awake. "Janet, it's me. It's alright. It's me. I was dreaming. What is it?"

"You must come right away. Paul should have been back hours ago. The Marine Police are out looking and the Navy has planes out too. The boat has vanished. Not a trace. Ian thinks drug smugglers may have them."

"Them?"

"Yes. Debbie and Tom were on the boat. They were diving those new sites on the chart they made from all the old logs and records."

"Yes," he answered, but it took a moment to recall Debbie's last letter from nearly two weeks ago. "Oh, that thing with the satellite and the computer. Yes, I remember. What about drug smugglers? Come back with that again."

"One of the wrecks they found was new, a small freighter full of marijuana. Didn't Debbie tell you? Ian thinks the smugglers may have seen them diving it and wanted to keep them quiet. Oh, please come as fast as you can, Doc. I'm so worried."

"I'll be on the first flight. I'll call you back as soon as I can get something confirmed. Is there someone with you?"

"Yes, Margaret is here. Just hurry, please."

"Alright, we'll find them. I'll call you right back," he reassured her.

The shock of what Janet told him had not yet hit. He found his reading glasses and the phone book. In a few minutes, he had booked a reservation on the earliest flight to Bermuda. He called Janet back and gave her the details. She would have someone meet him and bring him to her home. Doc was now awake enough to want coffee. He went to the kitchen, filled the machine and waited for it to brew. It was then that the shock wave hit.

"Oh Lord, don't let anything happen to Debbie." He could feel the words tear out pieces of his soul, and was stunned when he heard the anguish of his prayer fill the dark room.

He had to lean against the counter to hold himself up. The coffee brewed slowly. He sat motionless at the breakfast bar and waited. The LED on the microwave said 12:35. The coffee finished perking, but he did not get up from the chair. He sat in the darkness and silence for over an hour before he moved or spoke again. Tears were flowing freely down his face, but he made no sound. Slowly, fear and grief turned to anger and resolve.

"No one is going to take her before she's had her chance —no one," he told himself. His face hardened as he pounded his fist into the bar hard enough to rattle dishes in the cabinet above. "No one."

It had taken years for him to get over being a SEAL, learning to act from within the boundaries of socially acceptable behavior, and not to react with survival instincts honed to a razor's edge. He had learned that you can't reach down the throat of the English department head, rip out his heart and still expect to get tenure.

It had been years, but the feeling was still with him; the feeling that civilization was only a thin veneer, a crust that could shatter and fall away. If the right buttons were pushed, the persona that was the friendly, middle-aged English professor with the little house in old Decatur would burn away, and from its ashes a dark phoenix would arise—a killer, an animal not welcome in academic circles or quiet southern neighborhoods. And the civilized life he'd spent twenty years building would be exposed as a lie. Georgia State faculty members do not take ears, or booby trap villages, or creep barefooted through the jungle, hunting and killing other human beings. They don't. That is, until someone threatens their family. That's the button. Push it and you die.

He got up from the table, poured a large mug of the steaming black coffee and headed to the garage. Out from a locked storage closet came a large, green foot locker. On the top was a black beret. He had kept one set of Navy dress blues to be buried in.

"Just in case times get tough and you can't throw my carcass back out to sea where I belong," had been his joke with his wife, Nancy. The uniform was not what he was looking for.

The trunk had a false bottom. Beneath it was a lightweight Swedish K 9 mm submachine gun and three of the standard thirty-six round magazines. Beside the gun was a Randall Model 16 custom diving knife. Made to fit Doc's hand, the heavy 440B stainless steel, tooth-backed, seven-inch blade had carved him out of a sinking helicopter. The trio was completed by a Browning hi-power 9 mm semi-automatic hand gun and six magazines. He sat staring at the guns and wondered how to get them into Bermuda. He would be no help to Debbie if he were caught bringing a fully automatic weapon into a country that does not allow air rifles. He withdrew the knife from the brown leather case and held it up to the light to inspect the edge.

"Looks like it's you and me, old friend. I hope we still have what it takes," he muttered aloud almost like a prayer.

Before repacking the trunk, he also took some duPont number eight fuse-type blasting caps and three pencil detonators. Never know when fireworks will come in handy, he thought. He then pulled the new diving bag and boxes of new equipment from the workbench where they had been sitting since his trip to the dive shop. He examined the large diameter hose on the stabilizer jacket. In a moment, he had removed it and slipped the detonators and blasting caps inside the jacket. Too easy, he thought. X-ray will see them right away. He removed them and looked at the regulator hoses. "High-pressure hoses have stainless steel sheaths that block X-ray. Good." He removed the regulator from the case and walked over to the workbench.

Two hours later, he had hidden blasting caps, pencil detonators, short lengths of detonating cord and six capacitor-type timer/detonators securely in his diving equipment.

"You never know," he said and turned out the garage light.

He waited until after seven to call his friends Miriam and Steve Anderson. He told them there had been an accident and asked if Miriam could stop his mail and check the house.

He had debated making his next call almost from the moment Janet had awakened him. It was to a small government office in northern Virginia. It took a while for the phone to ring through to the duty officer and then to Col. Sandy Andrews's home.

"Sandy, this is Doc Holiday. Can you talk?"

"At seven on Sunday morning? Just barely. Yeah, go ahead. You talk, I'll listen. What's up?"

"I may need your help." He told the story and asked Sandy to find out what he could about drug runners in Bermuda.

"Anything you can get on the locals," Doc asked, "or the people she worked with would be a help. Start with the NASA Station Commander, Bill Roberts," he said reading from his notes. "Also, the head of their Marine Patrol, Ian Cord." He gave him Janet's number.

"I'll owe you for this, Sandy, and I don't like that. But this is Debbie's life and she's all I've got left. Whatever it takes, that's what I want. I haven't forgotten how to say thanks. When this is over..." his voice trailed off.

"Relax, Doc. You're not re-enlisting or selling your soul here. We'll help you any way we can. Just watch your ass. It's a new game out there; these guys kill for target practice—even their own. We can get you most anything you need through the Naval Air Station. I'll make a couple of calls and set it up. Go do your homework, then give me a call."

"Thanks, Sandy. It's been a long time. I didn't know..."

"No problem, man. Just be careful."

Doc checked his watch. He would need to leave soon. He called a cab and then looked at the Rolex again. Nancy had given it to him on their fifteenth anniversary. It was a gold and stainless submariner with a blue face. He went back into the study and opened the side drawer of his desk. He removed the square, green box the new watch had come in and removed an old, black-faced stainless submariner. It was the watch he'd worn on active duty. It had a custom silver band with two crests. On the right was a small smiling seal, on the other a caduceus, the symbol of the Navy hospital corps. Doc rotated the watch and waited. The second hand began to move. He hesitated for a moment, then took off the gold and stainless and put on the black-faced submariner, as if in the exchange he could take off twenty years as well. He turned off the lights and picked up his bags. The cab was in the driveway.

Sheri was exhausted when she got everyone on the plane. It was hot. Hauling all the equipment was a chore, and the constant questions had been almost more than she could tolerate and still be civil. She was very thankful to finally collapse into the aisle seat next to Mark.

"Do I need a passport to get into Bermuda?" Mark teased. She turned in mock rage and circled his throat with her hands.

"The next time you ask me that, you won't need a passport. You'll need a toe tag. I'll strangle you and ship you home in a bag full of smelly wet suits."

"Hey, look," he said pulling her hands from his throat. "Isn't that Dr. Holiday?"

"Yes, that's him," she answered.

"Man, he looks terrible; like he's been on a two-week drunk. Our finals couldn't have been that bad. I wonder what's wrong."

Doc was wearing a rumpled, summer-weight khaki field jacket over a faded blue cotton shirt and jeans. An Atlanta Braves baseball cap covered his unkempt hair. He had not shaved and it showed. As he came down the aisle, he removed

dark sunglasses revealing very bloodshot eyes.
"You're right, he looks like shit."
Doc found his seat next to a young woman with a very
small baby and a four-year old girl. He smiled and after put-
ting his bag in the overhead compartment, took his seat.
"Where ya' goin'?" asked the child.
"To Bermuda."
"Why?"
"To visit my daughter and some friends." Doc looked at
the mother, hoping to be rescued from the child. The mother
only smiled.
"Why?" the child continued.
There was a gentle touch on Doc's shoulder. "Dr. Holiday?" He turned to see Sheri standing beside him. "There
are some empty seats back by us. We'd love to have you join
us, and the flight attendant says the flight is only half full."
There really are guardian angels, he thought, and accepted her invitation, bid goodbye to the mother and the
precocious child, got his carry-on bag and moved. He recognized Mark Danvers and said hello. The preflight announce-
ments began and soon the plane was pulling away from the
terminal. Doc sat quietly. He noticed Mark take Sheri's hand
as the engine noise increased and the plane started its take
off. She looked at Doc and explained, "I hate flying."
As soon as they were in the air, Doc put his sunglasses
back on and pulled the Braves baseball hat low over his eyes.
In a moment he was asleep.
He awoke startled and coiled, ready to strike. Sheri was
talking and gently shaking him. "Dr. Holiday, wake up. You're
dreaming. Please wake up."
He pulled himself back into consciousness. He was sweat-
ing even though it was quite cool. He had been back in the
Mekong Delta on the Bassac River in a sinking helicopter.
His head cleared and he saw Sheri anxiously looking at him.
She was shaking his shoulder and telling him it was alright.
"You were talking in your sleep. It wasn't pretty," she
smiled. "There are children here and I didn't want you to
get arrested."
"My daughter has been involved in some kind of acci-
dent. Their boat is missing. Guess I'm wound pretty tight.

Thanks for waking me," he said.

"If you feel like talking, I can stay...."

"Not much to talk about until we get there and I can find out what's really going on. But please, tell me about your archaeological project again."

She sat beside him and turned comfortably in the seat to face him. "There are fourteen of us. Nine girls...you should join us. The women are pretty sharp...." There was no hint of interest, but she continued, "We'll be working on the *Eagle* and the *Virginia Merchant.* Both were supply ships for the Virginia colonies that didn't make it. Fortunately, the colonies survived without them."

Interesting, Doc thought, but those wrecks have already been worked by the museum staff, the Bermuda Sub-Aqua Club and the Smithsonian. With all the wrecks available, why not use them on something new like the early nineteenth century site Debbie described? He said nothing.

"This year is going to be great. After this trip, we're going to Virginia to look at the early colonial sites around Williamsburg. We hope to find things that match, and then trace the origins to the original supply points in England. Doesn't it sound exciting?"

Doc was a bit skeptical of the value of tracing the origins of clay pipes and musket flints, but he nodded affirmatively anyway. He didn't want to dampen her enthusiasm or her kindness.

"Where will you be staying?"

"There's a new dorm and a new conservation lab on top of the hill by the Commissioner's House. We will be there. Two bathrooms for all of us and some scruffy sheep to keep us company. I haven't mentioned the sheep to anyone yet. Should be a nice surprise, don't you think? We could assign buddies."

"Sounds like a real adventure." He hadn't been listening.

"That's why they came. Sheep are just an added attraction." She realized she wasn't holding his attention and shifted the conversation. "You were a Navy SEAL, weren't you? Was that anything like the movie?"

His face hardened for a moment, then he said thoughtfully, "In my time it was a different kind of war. We couldn't just hop and pop, hit and run—we lived there twenty-four hours a day, months on end. You got to see the enemy as more than a target. He had a family just like you. Unconventional warfare, that was our business. I never found anything very conventional about war. Limited objectives—bomb 'em with roses, all the euphemisms we use to protect our delicate sensitivities from what war really is—it's all crap. War is about killing and watching people you care about get killed. It's about widows and orphans, and legs gone above the knee. It's about lies and greed, beefing up the economy and...I'm sorry....You didn't need to hear all that."

"My father was killed there," Sheri told him. "He was Special Forces. I never knew him, but I think I understand what you're saying. What did you do?"

At least she wasn't looking at him as if he were a lunatic —that helped. He pulled his head together quickly and answered, "I was a hospital corpsman, a medic, and I dabbled in explosives."

Poor kid, he thought. She lost her old man and I'm dumping on her for asking a simple question. She didn't deserve that. He was studying her now, noticing the athletic legs and full bust line. He liked her short hair, not too short but practical, light brown, and highlighted by pool chlorine and sun. She wore white cotton shorts and a blouse that looked starched, this time with a bra. He thought her watch was too large, too masculine. It had a wide band and lots of buttons on the sides, almost the size and weight of his Rolex. And then there was her smile. She had good teeth, not Hollywood-perfect but well formed and healthy. Her turned-up nose was definitely Scandinavian, and the eyes, pale blue and bright, had the openness and enthusiasm of a mid-westerner. Then he realized he was not talking. He was just staring and she was smiling back, a sort of understanding, compassionate, maternal smile.

He shook it off and continued, "...because the teams were small, there was lots of cross training. You never knew who was actually going to show up for work and so we had to be prepared to finish...would you mind if we put this on hold? It just doesn't fit now." Sheri put her hand gently on his.

"You'll find her, Doc. I know you will. If there's anything I can do, I'll be up there on the hill with the sheep and all. Just come find me. And when you find her, I want to meet her. Promise you'll bring her to the lab?" Doc looked hesitant. "Positive attitude, Doc. Promise you'll bring her, safe and sound."

"Yes, yes, I will."

"That's better. Now I should check on Mark and the rest of the group. We'll be there soon." She gave his arm a squeeze and crossed the aisle to her seat.

"What was that all about?" Mark asked.

"His daughter is missing, some kind of accident. He's in bad shape. Did you fill out your forms for immigration and customs?"

CHAPTER

10

Inspector Ian Cord was waiting for Doc just beyond the customs tables. Janet had insisted that they'd met at a Bermuda Sub-Aqua Club meeting several years earlier, but Ian didn't remember, so Janet found a photo of the professor and his beautiful wife taken on the *Mermaid* several years earlier. The years have not been kind, Ian observed as he identified the bedraggled professor among the crowd of arriving tourists and then looked again at the photo. He watched as Doc approached the customs tables with his suitcase and large dive bag.

Why the dive bag? Ian thought. He's not on vacation. Doc lifted the bag and the suitcase onto the table as Ian approached. The customs inspector asked him to open them both. Ian held out his hand in greeting and said hello. Doc shook his hand, returned the greeting and looked back towards the dive bag. The customs inspector lifted the buoyancy control jacket and looked beneath it.

"That's fine, sir. Enjoy your stay in Bermuda." Doc closed the dive bag and Ian lifted it from the table.

"My car is out front. Nice dive bag."

Doc followed him to the car in silence. They stored the bags in the back and Doc instinctively went towards the right side of the car. Ian chuckled and asked if Doc wanted to drive. Doc smiled, shook his head and walked back to the passenger side on the left.

"Welcome back to Bermuda, Dr. Holiday. I'm very sorry about your daughter," Ian began as they drove towards Long Bird Bridge which joins St. George's to Hamilton. "We've had our boats out since Janet called at nine-thirty last evening. We were out there in less than an hour. The Navy has two planes still searching. So far, nothing: no fires, no floating debris. Another vessel reported seeing the *Mermaid* at anchor at sundown and everything looked normal."

"What do you think happened, Inspector?"

"Paul came to my office Monday with some underwater video they had taken of a small coastal freighter. There were two bodies with little fish swimming in and out of the bullet holes in their skulls. The hold was full of marijuana bales. My guess is that someone has been watching that wreck, waiting for the right night to slip out and unload her. Then along comes Paul, your daughter and the lad from NASA. They find the wreck, and now someone has millions of dollars at risk. What do you think happened?"

"The *Mermaid* disappears to protect the secret. Doesn't look good, does it?"

"No, I'm afraid not. I hate to have to say this, but if your daughter is still alive and they have her...well, you understand. I'm sorry."

"So where do we start? What have your street people got?"

"That's the reason I wanted to come to meet you, Doctor. Janet told me a bit about you. I know that if this were my daughter, that new dive bag wouldn't be full of scuba gear. I'd be ready to go to war to get her back. And if our situation were reversed, you'd be wasting your breath trying to tell me to stay out of this and let the local yokels do their job.

"So even though that's exactly what I should say, I won't. It will be a lot easier for me to keep an eye on you if you're working with us, not playing cowboy off on your own. Am I on track so far?"

"I'm listening," Doc responded.

"Right. Now, what's the best thing you can do to help?"

"Our best lead is that wreck. With that much money at stake, someone's going to come looking for it."

Ian hesitated a moment, debating, then having made a

decision continued, "There's another possibility. Paul made a video tape of other sites. Apparently, someone with high-tech diving gear has been illegally working some new sites. Did you know about that?"

"Yes, my daughter mentioned it."

"I don't know if it fits, or how," the inspector continued. "But anyone that has anything to do with wrecks here is always connected to the Dockyard. Mind you, I'm not accusing anyone, but the staff up there is new and I'll wager a pint that if wrecks are part of this, someone up there on the hill knows something—someone who's not bloody likely going to tell me."

"There's a group of young, would-be archaeologists from the university where I teach moving into the Dockyard today. I might be able to join them."

"That could work. But we mustn't put any of those lovely children in harm's way. If you see anything, call me. I'll get you one of our small portable radios. The Navy will help, and we'll get some fishing boats and start watching the reefs tonight. It would certainly help if we could find those charts your daughter made. Right now, we've got nothing. Also, your daughter's commanding officer wants to meet with you as soon as possible. I'll take you this afternoon, but you need to see Janet first."

"How's she taking this?" asked Doc.

"She's a fighter. She knows the chances, but she's holding her own. Now tell me, what's in the dive bag—atomic warheads? Or are you shipping those in later?"

"Tomorrow."

"Yes, I see, and what's in the bag?" he demanded again.

"Not much. Guns are illegal in Bermuda."

"They are, and don't you forget it or I'll have you packing in an hour. You are only to observe and call us."

"Sure."

"One other thing. I think you should use another name. If word gets out up there who you are, you won't learn anything and you could be at risk as well. I don't want to have to go looking for you too. I don't have that many men. Pick a name and I'll get you some identification."

"Hemingway and Hawthorne are a bit presumptive. How

about Harrington? That's innocuous enough, and I won't have to worry about changing ID tags on my equipment."

"Fine. Harrington it is. I guess we should let you keep the Doctor if you are going to be with the university crew. Give me your passport and driver's license. I'll have new ones for you tomorrow and a credit card or two as well."

"Very efficient. I'm impressed."

"We do our best."

Bermuda was as beautiful as Doc remembered it. The narrow winding road to Somerset Village took them past magnificent coves and bays, aqua and coral-colored houses with white-stepped stucco roofs guttered to catch precious rain water.

Margaret, an old friend keeping Janet company, met them at the door, greeting Doc with a hug. Ian brought in the bags, looking at the dive bag with curiosity as he carried it in. Doc smiled and took it from him.

"I'm so glad you're here," Janet began. "I'm afraid for them, John. I wish Paul had stayed out of this whole mess."

"He did what he thought needed to be done," Ian said. "It's a man's way, Janet. Don't fault him for that. You wouldn't expect less, not from Paul."

"Ian," Doc said, "I want to wait until morning to go to the base. I'm sure the C.O. will understand. Is there anything we can do this afternoon? I certainly want to get a look at that freighter."

"Nothing we can do until we find those charts. It's a big, deep ocean out there," he said with a half smile. "It could take weeks without those charts. I'll pick you up about nine if that suits. Afternoon, ladies, Doctor. G'day."

As soon as he was gone, Doc turned to Janet. "OK, now I want to hear this whole story—every detail from the very beginning." He went to his suitcase for a notebook and sat across from her on the couch. Janet told him as much of the story as she knew, while Doc filled several pages with notes.

"Do you know anything more about the charts or list of wrecks they put together?"

"No. All I know was that it had something to do with a satellite and a computer. Paul said the computer might have been hiding information, and that by locating these wrecks they would know. Then they found the drug wreck. Also, Paul was concerned about Ian and the drug wreck. I think he was afraid Ian might have had a hand in the sinking. Ian's brother was killed by a smuggler. It changed Ian. There were rumors that he beat a drug dealer they caught. It made the papers."

"So the inspector has a dark side—that's good to know. How about Debbie's computer? That might help."

"I think she took everything with her on the boat. Everything except the tapes."

"Tapes?"

"Video tapes of the wreck sites. I have them here."

"Good. At least we have somewhere to start."

They spent the next two hours watching the tapes. Doc made notes at a rapid pace. He caught glimpses of Debbie as Tom was lowering the camera over the side. In the tape of the freighter, he laughed as Debbie banged the saucepan and motioned for Tom to hurry. The camera had also caught her face as she bolted in the hold of the freighter. The final shots were of the body in the hold, permanently resting on the bales like a sultan on a satin divan in his harem.

"Who says you can't take it with you?" Doc said cynically.

"That's what Paul said," Janet remarked as she went into the kitchen to fix iced tea.

"They used the remote camera so those early sites must have been deep. And yet some of them have been extensively worked." Turning to Margaret, Doc asked, "Who on the island has the equipment to do that?"

"No one that I know of, not even at the Biological Research Station," Margaret answered him.

"Are you still working there?"

"Yes, I love it."

"Any problem getting me some things from their lab?"

"Depends on what you want."

"Picric or nitric acid, nitromethane, ethyl alcohol, fifty pounds of ammonium nitrate—crushed prills would be best—and aluminum powder. You know, simple things. Just don't drop the bottles. Also, we'll need a plumbing supply house and a boat—a good fast one like a Whaler or a big inflatable. I don't suppose Paul has any assault rifles, machine guns, or old handguns? No, I remember how much he hated them. Not so strange considering how often he got shot at, I guess. Have to wonder about going empty-handed though. Especially if he was worried."

Margaret stared at him, speechless and wide-eyed, then she gave him a huge hug.

"Are there any other resources you will need for your diplomatic negotiations, Dr. Holiday, besides boats, bombs, and automatic weapons?" Janet asked from the doorway. She had her hands on her hips and was glaring at him. She detested violence, and it was hard to imagine this kind of thing had happened to her family, especially in Bermuda. But it had, and now was the time to face reality, not flounder in anger and denial.

Doc waited for the reality to sink in. He watched her face change and knew that she was now hardened for what might come. Then he said, "I need to go to the Dockyard. Is there a scooter here?"

"I remember patching you up the last time you rented a scooter. Margaret will drive you."

When they were alone in the car, Doc asked her, "How's Janet holding up?"

"I don't think it's hit her yet, that he might not be coming home. I can stay with her for a few days. Paul and Janet are well thought of at the Bio station. No one will mind if I take emergency leave for a day or two."

They parked Margaret's car by the dive store and walked through the courtyard to the entrance of the old fortress. The drawbridge had been replaced by a permanent bridge, but the moat and heavy wooden doors remained. The doors were still open. They went in and told the attendant they were going up to the hostel and the archaeological lab. They followed the steep road from the gate up the hill and across a large lawn to the hostel. Several people were sitting at picnic tables in the shade of the porch. A sign beside the door of the large, white stucco building identified it as The Institute of Maritime History and Archaeology Hostel. Not seeing Sheri among them, Doc asked an attractive, long-haired blonde where she was and introduced himself as Dr. Harrington.

"She's in a meeting upstairs in the office above the lab.

I'll take you if you like. I'm Karen."

"Thanks, we know where it is," Margaret answered with her British accent, establishing herself as a non-tourist. They turned back towards the lab.

"Watch out for the sheep shit," Karen called after them. "It's everywhere."

"Charming child," Margaret said quietly. "So you're Dr. Harrington now, are you?"

"Ian's idea. Probably a good one for now."

"Thank's for letting me in on it."

"Sorry," he said as they pulled open the high iron gate and crossed the cement courtyard to the conservation lab. The conservatory was a new, two-story block building. Displays covered the work tables and it smelled of damp concrete and interesting chemicals.

"There's a photo studio and darkroom in the back," Margaret said as they went up the stairs. At the end of the second floor was the conservator's large office. Doc knocked and called Sheri's name. In a moment she came to the door. "Doctor..."

"Harrington," Doc said loudly. "Sheri, may I see you for just a moment please? It's very important."

"Of course." She closed the door behind her and asked with a concerned look, "Is everything alright? Have you found your daughter?"

"No, that's why we need to talk. If you were serious about helping, it looks as if there is something you could do, something very important. May we go somewhere and talk?"

They walked across the yard to the battlement overlooking the ocean. The sun was low and bright in the western sky. "Sheri, this is Margaret, an old friend," Doc introduced the two women and began, "Here's the story: the police believe that my daughter and two friends were kidnapped or killed by drug dealers. The only way to find out what really happened is to catch these guys. Debbie and her friends found a sunken freighter full of drugs. It's right out there somewhere," he said, pointing northwest, "and the smugglers will be back for it. I want to be here when that happens and I need someplace to wait where I won't attract any attention —by the way, I am using the name Harrington while I'm here.

Your group would be perfect and I might even be able to give you a hand. I haven't forgotten how to dive, and I could help with the boats and equipment."

"There's more, isn't there? More you're not telling me. What is it? I deserve to know it all."

"You're right, there is more. Someone with very sophisticated diving equipment has been cleaning out some virgin sites. That may not be connected to my daughter's disappearance, but until we know for sure, the Marine Police are worried about your group. Inspector Ian Cord, head of the Marine Police, suggested I stay here with you. Who else besides Mark knows why I'm here?"

"Only Mark, and he's completely trustworthy."

"Good."

"Alright, I'll tell Lisa, the lab director, and Dr. Richardson, the new museum director, that you were sent by the school to write about our project. They like good publicity and that will give you freedom to come and go."

"Sheri," Margaret said, "it's very important that Doc not be identified as Debbie's father. We have no idea whom we can trust, even Lisa."

Sheri studied him for a moment. "Doctor," she said, her head tilted and her arms folded across her chest, "this had better be what you say it is or I'll go right to the Chair of your department at State. This program is too important to me to be playing games."

"You're a smart girl, Sheri," Doc answered. "I'll set up a meeting with Inspector Cord if you want, or you may call him right now before we do anything, and he'll verify what I've told you. I've got his number on this card." Doc handed her the card from his wallet and waited.

She examined the card. It looked legitimate enough and the doctor certainly sounded sincere. "OK, I'll get you a bunk in the hostel. How do you feel about sheep?"

"I think I'm burned to the end of my fuse," he said to Margaret when they were back in the car. "You got any ideas?"

"Yes. You need food and rest. You look like hell."

That night Doc collapsed into the guest room bed. Margaret was staying over in the room across the hall. She came into his room after a gentle knock at the door.

"Doc, I just wanted to say I am really glad you are here. And if there is anything..."

"I know I can count on you, Margaret. There is one thing more you can do."

"What is it? Anything."

"Pray." She nodded, left the room and quietly closed the door.

Doc repeated a single thought again and again for what felt like hours until he fell asleep. "Debbie, wherever you are, I love you. Be strong. I'll find you. Be strong. I love you."

Margaret thought she heard him talking in his sleep. But when she got up to check, he was quiet.

When Doc awoke, it was to the smell of a Bermuda-style breakfast of coffee, fresh banana bread, fruits and cereals. He was starving as he joined Janet and Margaret at the table. His shave and shower had helped, but he did not look rested. Inspector Cord walked in just as they were finishing.

"Any news, Inspector?"

"Afraid not, but I haven't gotten the Navy radar reports yet. We'll talk to them at the base. How 'bout you?"

"It looks like Dr. Harrington has joined the archaeological team in residence at the Dockyard, and with luck will be living on the north reef looking for twenty-seven varieties of clay pipes by nightfall. Did you get me that radio?"

"Yes, it's in the car. The other things will be ready this afternoon. I guess we should be off. These Navy chaps are terribly punctual."

First they went to the Naval Air Station and received a briefing from a Commander Kingsly, Debbie's C.O. The commander was very professional, concerned, sympathetic and not very encouraging.

Next on the list was NASA Station Director Bill Roberts.

"Gentlemen, please come in. Dr. Holiday, it's good to meet you. I'm so sorry this has happened. Debbie was looking forward so much to your being here this summer. Those two kids are like part of my family. Inspector, you've got to catch the slime who did this and string 'em up by their privates. That's what we'd have done in Texas in the old days, by God. That's what they deserve...."

"Sir, we have a few questions," Doc cut short Roberts's tirade.

"Of course, anything, anything," the director said.

"My daughter wrote about a wreck she and Tom found. She said the computer here refused to recognize it. They were trying to find out why. Is there anything you can tell me about that?"

"Yes, of course. It's true there was a glitch in one of the reporting and mapping programs. It was leaving out some geophysical magnetic anomalies that I suppose could be wreck sites. If you had heard from Debbie last week, she would have told you that we found the problem and corrected it. Her work, in fact, was brilliant. We were lucky to have her on loan from the Navy this past week. In the process, they may have found some new sites. Tom had a real passion about those wrecks, you know.

"They were real excited and invited me to go with them last weekend. Unfortunately, my wife had made other plans, or perhaps that wasn't so unfortunate after all. Certainly you don't think that had anything to do with their disappearance? That was nothing more than a software problem. No, I agree with Inspector Cord. It was those drug smugglers—no doubt."

"Debbie said that she was constructing some charts. Is it possible any of them or her notes are here? They might help us narrow down the search for the drug boat."

"I'd be happy for you to see everything she was working on, Dr. Holiday. Unfortunately, I believe she had everything with her. There was nothing relating to that project left here, but you're certainly welcome to look."

"Thank you. I'd like to see her living quarters as quickly as possible. Could you arrange that with the Navy this morning, please?"

"Of course, and anything else we can do for you, just name it, Doctor. Would you care for some coffee while I make the calls?"

Doc and the inspector sat quietly waiting for Roberts to return. He's lying through his teeth, Doc thought. But why? What has he got to hide? Do you kidnap or kill over a software problem or even over wreck sites? I doubt it. Could he be in on the drugs? That's a possibility...but it will have to wait until we get Debbie back. The freighter is still our best shot.

Roberts returned with a coffee tray. Doc and Ian both noticed that his hands were shaking as he poured the coffee. Roberts caught their glance and said, "I'm sorry, I've never been good with things like this. I cared about those kids, that's all. Stay and finish your coffee. My secretary will let you know when your escort arrives. Now, please excuse me." With that, he was gone.

Their escort didn't arrive for twenty minutes. "What do you make of that?" Ian asked when they were alone outside.

"Is there anyway you can keep him from leaving the island?" Doc answered.

The marine drove them to the B.O.Q. The old, pink two-story Bachelor Officers Quarters overlooked the tennis courts and had the feeling of a college dorm. The building was built by the Air Force and the rooms were designed with one head for each two rooms. When the Navy took possession after the war, it was decided that half a head was not suitable for naval personnel and the result was suites, strangely divided by large bathrooms. The furnishings were comfortable by military standards, and each room came with a television and VCR. The young lance corporal led them to Debbie's suite and opened the door.

The door was unlocked and as it swung open they saw clothing and books strewn everywhere. In the center of the floor was a duplicate of the large photo of Debbie, Nancy and Doc that hung in his office. The glass and frame were smashed and the sight of it sent a chill through Doc. Ian put a hand on his shoulder to steady him.

"They're after the charts, aren't they?" Ian asked.

"Yes. Get someone to Janet's right now. That's the next place they'll look." Doc knelt and retrieved the photo from the debris. "Any problem if I take this?"

"No, sir, but please wait. I'll get security over here on the double."

"Tell them to dust for prints and get photos," Ian said. "Come on, Doc, let's make that call."

Ian used his radio to place the call and send officers to

Janet's. There was no answer on her phone.

"Had they planned to go out this morning?"

"Yes, which means they could be coming home to a nasty surprise. Let's go."

CHAPTER
11

They arrived too late. The house looked like a bomb had gone off in the living room. Neither Janet nor Margaret was there.

"Get your team to work, and perhaps we can start cleaning up before they get back." Doc went to his room to check the dive bag. The diving equipment was dumped on the floor. At first glance, it appeared that everything was still there. He picked up the bag and opened the double lining on the side. From it he removed his knife.

"Custom Randall?" Ian asked.

"Yes."

"Beauty. Glad they didn't find it."

They heard a scream from the living room. "I think Janet's home," Doc said.

Margaret tried to calm her but to no avail. "I hope they come back and I get my hands on them. There won't be enough left for shark chum. How could they do this? This is my home! Doc, find them and hurt them. Hurt them for me. This is a bloody outrage!" she said as tears of anger rolled down her face.

The students were gathered at the dining room picnic tables, note pads ready. Dr. Jason Richardson stood to begin the first lecture. Karen looked him over with a hungry eye. Tan and lean, dressed in military tan shirt and shorts, he looked preppie, prosperous and professional.

There's definite potential here, she thought. Bob took her hand as if reading her mind. She looked at him innocently and smiled. He was getting too smart for his own good.

Richardson waited for the group to quiet down and then, with theatrical polish and dramatic flair, delivered his lines from memory.

"Boatswain!

"Here, Master, What cheer?

"Good, speak to the mariners; fall to the yarely, or we run ourselves aground. Bestir, Bestir!

"Good Boatswain have care, Where's the master? Play the men.

"I pray now, keep below.

"Where is the master, Bos'n?

"Do you not hear him? You mar our labor. Keep your cabins; you do assist the storm.

"Nay, good, be patient.

"When the sea is. Hence! What cares these roarers for the name of King? To cabin! Silence! Trouble us not!"

His eyes flashed with enthusiasm. He moved around the tables as he spun the yarn. His audience, taken completely by surprise, was spellbound.

"Good, yet remember whom thou hast aboard.

"None that I love more than myself. You are a counselor: if you can command these elements to silence and work the peace of the present, we will not hand a rope more; use your authority. If you cannot, give thanks you have lived so long, and make yourself ready in your cabin for the mischance of the hour, if it so hap. Cheerly, good hearts! Out of the way, I say!

"I have great comfort from this fellow: methinks he hath no drowning mark upon him; his complexion is perfect gallows. Stand fast, good Fate, to his hanging! Make the rope of his destiny our cable, for our own doth little advantage. If he be not born to be hanged, our case is miserable.

"Down with the topmast! Yare! Lower, lower! Bring her to try with main course! A plague upon this howling! They are louder than the weather or our office...Yet again? What do you here? Shall we give o'er and drown? Have you a mind to sink?

"A pox on your throat, you bawling, blasphemous, incharitable dog!

"Work you then.

"Hang, cur, hang, you whoreson, insolent noisemaker! We are less afraid to be drowned than thou art.

"I'll warrant him for drowning, though the ship were no stronger than a nutshell and as leaky as an unstanched wench.

"Lay her ahold, ahold! Set her two courses! Off to sea again! Lay her off!

"All lost! To prayers, to prayers! All lost!

"What, must our mouths be cold?

"The King and the Prince are at prayers. Let's assist them, for our case is as theirs.

"I am out of patience.

"We are merely cheated of our lives by drunkards. This wide-chopped rascal...would thou mightst lie drowning...The washing of ten tides!

"He'll be hanged yet, though every drop of water swear against it. And gape at wid'st to glut him...Mercy on us! We split! We split! Farewell, my wife and children! Farewell, brother! We split, we split, we split!

"Let's all sink with the King.

"Let's take leave of him.

"Now would I give a thousand furlongs of sea for an acre of barren ground—long heath, brown furze, anything. The wills above be done, but I would fain die a dry death."

Richardson paused. It took a moment for them to be released from his spell, then they applauded heartily.

"Thanks for your indulgence. I'm sure you recognized the opening scene of Shakespeare's <u>The Tempest</u>—my favorite of his works. He got the idea for the play from the sinking of the 300-ton vessel, *Sea Venture,* in 1609 right here in Bermuda. In fact, it was that sinking which was responsible for the colonization of the island and the beginning of our written history. You will read that the *Sea Venture* was the flagship of Sir George Somers and was part of a fleet carrying supplies to the Virginia colony at Jamestown. Towards the end of your month with us, we will arrange for you to dive the wreck.

"The two sites we have chosen for you to research and explore have much in common with the *Sea Venture*. The *Virginia Merchant* and the *Eagle* were also supply ships bound for Virginia that wrecked only fifty years after the sinking of the *Sea Venture*. In fact, the wreck of the *Virginia Merchant* was one of the bloodiest in Bermuda history. The storm was so violent that the ship was driven up and over the south shore cliffs, and her bow smashed into a house near the present-day site of the Sonesta Beach Hotel. One of her cannons is on display there now.

"One hundred and seventy lives were lost. Legend holds that her ghosts can be heard crying in the howl of the wind when big storms blow in from the south.

"The violent storms and dangerous reefs of Bermuda have given the island a unique reputation. Spaniards visiting the island even before the wreck of the *Sea Venture* thought they heard devils in the woods and called the place the 'Island of Devils'. Charming, don't you think?

"All of us have heard of the mysteries of the Bermuda Triangle, which I won't even attempt to explain. We will leave that to novelists.

"But Bermuda is in fact a unique and special place. Because of the unusual double ring of reefs, there is more nautical history here than any place in the Americas. Or at least there should be. We have ships from every epoch: Spanish galleons, British men-of-war, colonial merchants, pirates, Revolutionary War smugglers, and many prizes captured in the War of 1812. The raid on Washington and Baltimore was launched from Bermuda. And Francis Scott Key wrote 'The Star Spangled Banner' while the guns of Admiral Sir George Cockburn were shelling Fort McKinley. You can read the first-hand British accounts of the battle in the Royal Gazette at the library in Hamilton.

"There are Civil War blockade runners and World War II Liberty ships, or at least ships of the same design. In the deep waters beyond the reef lie vessels torpedoed by German U-boats, and there may be a U-boat or two out there as well. The tracking of the Russian nuclear submarine that gave Tom

Clancy the idea for his <u>Hunt for Red October</u> was conducted from the Naval Station Annex here, and she may rest off our shores. The entire history of the development of North America lies in these waters. Or at least it did.

"Unfortunately, much of that history has vanished forever into private collections. There are those who place a higher value on selfish gain than on preserving a once-in-a-lifetime opportunity for learning, and passing that learning on to our children. They rob the graves of our ancestors; they steal our history; they steal our heritage. It is our moral and civic responsibility to take back what has been stolen and to stop them. The wreck sites we dive are sacred ground, hallowed by the blood of those who died there. They must be treated with respect and disturbed only to bring forth that which will honor the memory of those lost souls. We must preserve their legend and legacy for the future. That is what you will learn to do during your stay with us."

Again, Richardson paused and relaxed the grasp with which he held them. Most were leaning forward, faces drawn, hanging on every polished word. He owned them now and he knew it.

"There will be five critical parts of your learning experience with us: first, we will concentrate on research technique. You will become old friends with LeFroy's <u>Bermuda Memorials</u> and with the Royal Gazette, which goes back to the mid-eighteenth century. In addition to our sources, you will use the National Archives in the Government Building in Hamilton. We will give you several projects from different time frames. In the last week, you will present your work.

"Next, there is field technique. I know that Sheri and Mark have done an excellent job of preparing you, and I have heard the stories about your work in the quarry. Now is your opportunity to make them look good and I know you will do a magnificent job. Let me assure you our diving conditions are just a bit better here.

"The third part is learning conservation technique. We are fortunate to have Lisa Bower with us from the U.K. Lisa is a first-rate conservationist and is in charge of our new lab. You could not ask for a more qualified or helpful instructor.

"And fourth, you will prepare a report of publication

quality. The Maritime Museum now publishes The Journal of Marine History, and we will publish your report so that our members and supporters can keep tabs on how we are spending their money. So again, give it your best shot.

"Finally, as guests and representatives of the Institute of Maritime History and Archaeology, we expect that you will become involved in our campaign for ethical conservation of Bermuda wreck sites. The implications of this involvement are twofold: first, you will not remove any object or artifact from any site without the permission of the dive supervisor, and anything brought to the surface is the property of the museum. You will be dismissed from the project immediately for any violation of this rule.

"Second, we are involved in an educational and political campaign to stop private collection from all wreck sites. I encourage you to become involved in that campaign. We will give you specifics in the weeks to come.

"I welcome you to Bermuda as our esteemed guests. As director of the program and the museum, my door is always open for your questions, or to help with any special problems," he said, looking directly at Karen. "Please don't hesitate to call. That's all I have for now. I want to turn you over to Lisa who will brief you on the first assignments. Have a wonderful stay. We are delighted that you're here." Again the students applauded. Richardson made his exit while Lisa passed handouts around.

"Here is a reading list of resources we want you to become familiar with," she began. "I recommend Zuill's <u>The Story of Bermuda and Her People</u> as a good introductory history. It is available at the museum bookstore in paperback."

Mark and Sheri were at the back of the room. "That guy Dr. Richardson is really sharp, isn't he?" Mark said.

"Yeah. He's a real class act, that's for sure. Not bad looking either," she responded.

When Doc returned from his run, the women were still busy cleaning. He'd done six easy eight-minute miles. Time to stretch and try to put the pieces together. It was hot and he was soaked, but he felt his best since Janet's call had ruined his fishing.

"You can help too, Doc," Janet said after he showered and changed to faded green shorts and a Divers Alert Network T-shirt. "All those books go back in that case. Be careful of the broken glass."

"What did you find out about a boat?" he asked.

"We borrowed a twenty-foot Boston Whaler with a big engine," Margaret answered. "It belongs to a member of the dive club and you must promise to take care of it."

"Wonderful. And what about the shopping?"

"The lab had most everything you wanted, and the hardware had the ammonium nitrate fertilizer and the pipe. What are you going to do with the nitromethane and the ethylene diamine?"

"THE WHAT?" demanded Janet who taught chemistry. "John Holiday, I know you need to do whatever it is you are going to do, but do you have to do it here? Nitromethane? Do you know what that will do if it goes off? At least those bloody bastards left me a roof over my head. Now you, my friend, are going to blow that away too. Can't you do that at the shop, please?"

"Well, which question shall I answer first? How 'bout 'What could it do?' When we add the ethylene diamine to sensitize it, the alumina to add oxygen, and the nitrate for consumable bulk, it should have a detonating velocity of about nine thousand meters per second. I would prefer C-5 or C-7, but RDX is much harder to make. We won't need any of this if I can get what I want from the States, but I'm not sure my source will deliver, so we haven't much choice.

"Last question: 'Can we do it at the shop?' We can do it at the Hamilton Library if that will make you happy. Getting caught might be rather interesting to explain. 'Pardon me, sir, why are you making explosives in the library?' 'Because they don't have any I can check out....' 'Pardon me sir, why are you making bombs in the dive shop?' 'Because they sold the last one on Tuesday.' Any more questions, or can I get to work?"

"I'm sorry, go ahead," Janet said. "But are you sure you know what you are doing with that stuff?"

"You know," Doc said, "you've got a point; it's been a

while. You might want to leave and come back in a few hours just to see if the place is still standing. Do you have a first year chemistry book anywhere? Do you add acid to water, or water to acid?"

"Doc Holiday is the perfect name for you, John. I'm sure you are just as much an outlaw as your great-grandfather or whoever it was. No, you're probably worse. Come on, Margaret. Let's get out of here before he blows us all to kingdom come. We'll bring you back some dinner, although you don't deserve it. Goodbye."

"Thank you, Janet. I love you too."

Doc worked quickly, sealing the pipe containers and drilling ports for the detonators. He was nearly finished when there was a knock at the door. It was Inspector Cord. Doc took a moment to dust himself off and wash his hands. On the way to the door, he sniffed his shirt and realized it was permeated with chemical smells. He pulled off the shirt, threw it behind a chair, then answered the door.

"Hello, Ian, any news?" Doc stood blocking the doorway.

"No, I'm sorry. Nothing yet. I've brought your papers, including a driver's license. And I've arranged for a car. Can't have you out on a scooter terrorizing the locals. Say, what is that smell?"

"Must be the cleaning solvents Janet used on the carpet."

"Right. Thought it was familiar. Well, my lads will drop off the car in a bit. You going to the Dockyard then? Interesting smell. I remember it from somewhere...can't quite place it though."

"Thanks for the car. I'm waiting for a phone call from the States, then I'll move out. Wish I could join you on the boat tonight. It will be good to be back on the water again."

"There will be plenty of time for that, mate. Just stay by your radio. We'll pick you up quick if anything happens."

The phone rang. Ian waved goodbye and Doc went in to answer it.

"Hello, may I speak to Dr. John Holiday please?"

"Sandy, this is Doc. Go ahead."

"Any word on Debbie and your friends?"

"Nothing yet. Hope you're having better luck."

"Let's start with the inspector, Ian Cord. Looks straight

arrow to us. Good record. Some special assignments with our D.E.A. Lost a partner in '86 on a drug bust. Been pretty aggressive since. Has given them good leads on runners and mules. Currently working with international task force on something big. We'll get more when their offices open tomorrow."

"I heard that partner may have been his brother. You might check that out. What about Roberts?"

"Interesting fellow. Educated at Texas A&M. Ph.D. in computer science with a secondary work in physical oceanography and history. Strong interest in scuba, sailing and archaeology. Spent summers working on archaeological digs with their institute in Greece and Turkey. Let's see...looks like he was really going places in NASA. Developed their current software for tracking satellites and interpreting satellite data.

"Could have had a shot at division chief or even director in Houston, but had problems dealing with the politics and stress. He was hospitalized for exhaustion and an anxiety attack in '78 and again the next year. Put in for the station director job in Bermuda and moved in '80. No more problems, but any chance of major promotion very slight. Still is a heavy hitter with their computer design boys. Has made several trips to trouble shoot for them. Four or five back to Houston and D.C. in the last two years. Wife, Petra. Two kids, sons, both at A&M. Looks like one just graduated. What else do you want?"

"Any history with drugs, substance abuse of any kind?"

"Not in this file but I can ask."

"Good, and try to get a financial statement. He's in this, I'm sure of it. I want to know why and how and who's pulling his strings. The next time you call, I'll be at the Institute of Maritime History and Archaeology. The a.k.a. is Harrington. Dr. John Harrington. Tell them you are a relative and I'll return the call from a safe phone. Thanks, Sandy. I owe you."

"You're welcome, buddy. Now about that care package, everything's a go. Everything but explosives over five megatons, and heavy artillery. Just let me know what you need."

Doc picked up his note pad and started reading down the list. He was just hanging up the phone when the women returned.

"Is it safe?" Janet asked.

"Good question," was his terse reply.

As Doc drove to the Dockyard, he thought back over the conversation with Sandy. If Roberts had designed the computer software, he shouldn't have needed help to debug it. But involving Tom and Debbie was an excellent way to control their activities and limit whom they would talk to. Much in the way Ian had involved him. Was Roberts using the satellites to collect wreck data and passing it along to someone else? It was certainly a possibility. But that still didn't add up to kidnapping and perhaps murder. Was Roberts connected to the drugs? That was the question. Assume that he was. Could he be made to talk? Probably not without putting Debbie in much greater danger, if she was still alive. No, the best plan was to watch Roberts closely and see where he might lead them. Nervous frogs don't sit still for long.

And what about the "something big" Ian was involved in? Could the freighter be part of that? Could the *Mermaid* have disappeared because what they had found would implicate the inspector? Perhaps an act of revenge for the loss of a partner? Wouldn't that be an ironic twist? How far would the big Scot go for a million bucks, or to avenge a murdered brother?

Doc's mind raced with questions as he drove the small car past the entrance to Horseshoe Bay where Tom and Debbie had spent the night. He pulled into an overlook and got out. I've always loved this place, he thought. Who would have believed coming back could be such a nightmare? "Stop, breathe and think before you act," he remembered from teaching scuba rescue courses. The teacher needs to pay attention to the lesson. He sat down on the grass and watched the sea roll for nearly an hour. His mind rested and clearer, he got back in the car and continued the drive to the Dockyard.

It was after dinner and the students were sitting around in the lounge area of the large room that contained the kitchen, dining room/classroom, several old refrigerators covered with stickers from dive clubs all over the world, and a few well-worn chairs and couches. Some were watching a video of past projects while others talked or read. A single door led into the first bunk room where ten double bunk beds and several Navy-style lockers were lined up against the wall. A single door at the rear of this room led to an identical room, furnished in the same sparse manner for the women. It had a side door leading out to the two small bathrooms and laundry deck.

Doc parked outside the gate and carried his bags up the long hill and across the sheep-embellished lawn. Mark and Sheri were sitting at one of the picnic tables on the porch by the front door. Mark recognized him and got up to lend a hand.

"Dr. Holiday, it is great to see you...."

"Dr. Harrington, Mark, please. At least for now. How are you?"

"Fine, sir. I'm really sorry to hear about your daughter."

Thank you, Mr. Completely Trustworthy, Doc thought and stopped.

"Mark, my daughter's life may still be saved. The reason I'm here is part of a police plan that requires my identity to remain secret, especially my identity as Debbie's father. Now, who else is aware of who I really am?"

"Oh, no one, sir. Only Sheri and me."

"That's Sheri and I, Mark. The nominative case is...sorry, never mind."

"Yes, sir, that's what I meant. I guess it's hard being an English teacher, always having to think about what you're saying, huh?"

"Yes, at times it's hard. Alright, let's go in. And please try to remember, Dr. Harrington. Got it?"

"Yes, sir."

Doc was hoping he would not encounter any more of his students. He was lucky. For the ones who just passed him in the halls, Harrington was a name as easily forgotten as Holiday. He was introduced all around. After storing his clothing and equipment, he joined Sheri and Mark at the outside table. They were alone and spoke quietly.

"Things may start happening very soon. I'm going back

to the base in the morning and then I'll be here. When do we start diving?"

"I didn't know you were a diver, Doctor. That's great," Mark interrupted. "I just finished my divemaster. Are you PADI certified?"

"Yes, Mark, I'm PADI."

"You missed a great orientation lecture this morning by the director, Dr. Jason Richardson," Mark continued. "I'm not sure when the diving starts. We'll probably find out at the briefing in the morning. They have a lot of research they want us to do before we see the site. The staff is all new since last summer. Looks like they are going to be much more demanding. Oh, one other rule is lights out at eleven. And the lower gates are locked, but we'll try to get you a key. That will be easier than climbing the rampart walls. No sneaking out for a beer, even if there were anywhere to go," Mark chattered on.

Doc looked at Sheri and wondered if she could rescue him again, the way she had saved him from the inquisitive four-year old on the plane. Her smile told him she had read his thoughts precisely.

"What are you?" Mark continued.

"I beg your pardon, Mark?"

"You know, what level of certification?"

"I was a Course Director, an Instructor Trainer, but that was a few years ago."

"Wow, that's great. I want to be an instructor. Perhaps you could help me?"

"I don't do the training anymore, but I'll get you going in the right direction. Whenever you're ready, just let me know."

"That's great! Thanks."

"Thank me after you are certified. It isn't easy, you know."

"Oh."

Someone called "Lights out," and they went inside. Sheri still had not spoken, but when they left the table she touched his arm gently and smiled again. He understood.

Doc dreaded going to bed. The nightmares last night were worse. Wounded kids in the river, calling out to him, just beyond his reach. And he'd seen Debbie. She kept appearing and disappearing behind stone walls, like in a music video. She didn't speak and he couldn't find her. His dream changed and he found himself as a doctoral candidate again, defending his thesis. His committee members couldn't agree and kept changing the rules. It was a perfect Catch-22 and he knew it would never end. It was better not to sleep.

He took a short Navy shower. The sign on the mirror said "Please help conserve water," and he remembered that water was a precious commodity in Bermuda. At least the water was hot.

There was moonlight in the lounge area. He got a cold drink from a refrigerator, found a book and settled into a comfortable chair to read. He adjusted the lamp so it wouldn't shine into the bunk room.

He was awakened by Sheri about an hour later. This time he was swimming, trying to get Mac Johnson out of a bamboo cage in the Rung Sat river. The cage was drifting and sinking slowly. When he pulled himself back into reality, Sheri was kneeling beside him with her hand on his shoulder.

"What have you got against sleep?" she asked softly.

"Not a thing, except that my subconscious keeps trying to kill me. I had the same trouble after my third deployment. Funny, the nightmares didn't start until I came home. Did I wake the whole house?"

"No, I don't think anyone heard but me. I was thirsty." She sat on the floor beside his chair. She was wearing a long T-shirt and she tucked it beneath her. "What was it like—combat I mean?"

"It was a job. Good days and bad days, lots of rain. Hours of boredom, punctuated by moments of unadulterated terror is the way someone said it. Your adrenalin pump got a lot of exercise, that's for sure. Hunting, or being hunted does that.

"Samuel Johnson said something like 'Nothing helps a man straighten out his priorities like the certain knowledge that he will be hanged in a fortnight.' We were young and we played hard; we didn't want to miss anything. The war was a momentary inconvenience, or a golden opportunity, 'the best of times or the worst of times' depending on your attitude.

"It wasn't so bad until I met Nancy, then I wanted to get

home real bad. It was dangerous to let yourself be distracted with that kind of thinking. But I was in love. What else was there to think about?" he said and was quiet.

"It's hot back there," she said, nodding towards the bunk room. "At least there's a breeze in here. Mind if I stay for a while?"

"I'd like that, but you should sleep."

She moved to a couch and he remained in the sagging, overstuffed chair. "Thanks for listening to Mark," she said. "Sometimes he chatters like a blue jay at a tom cat. I think it is because he's really impressed by you." She curled up facing him and tried to stretch the shirt into a blanket. In a moment she was asleep. He watched her and thought about Debbie. As she slept, she pulled up into a fetal position as if she were cold. He got a light blanket from his bed, covered her and returned to his vigil. He took out his notebook and tried to make sense of all that had happened.

"I'm an idiot," he said when his subconscious woke him at a little after five. When Sheri woke up an hour later, he was gone.

Inspector Cord sat on the bridge of the old fishing trawler and waited for sunrise and the men who would relieve him. The night had been cool and clear. A slight chop had rolled the boat just enough to make staying awake difficult, and he was finishing the second large pot of coffee.

After a while, the orange flashing of the radar screen had a hypnotic effect, and it took concentration to notice slight changes, especially near the coastline. It was no wonder, Ian thought, that large ships hit small ones in the night. Wood and fiberglass hulls are nearly invisible on the screen. And then it's too late to slow or turn a vessel displacing thousands of tons. He remembered a tanker coming into port with a large mast and stays hanging from the starboard anchor. The crew, of course, claimed no knowledge of the obviously fatal collision.

His portable radio crackled him back to attention. "Marine Patrol One, Marine Patrol One, this is Doc, this is Doc. Over."

"Go ahead, Doc. This is One. Over."

"Meet me at the base at Roberts's office, quick as you can, Ian. I know how to find the *Mermaid*. Over."

"Right, Doc. There's nothing happening out here. I'm on the way. Out."

The eastern sky was showing the first light, a pale pink, but it was enough to see the coral heads. He pulled the anchor and navigated between them carefully until he was safely in the flats. He watched so carefully that he missed a tiny blip on the radar screen coming out of the town cut at St. George's and heading towards open sea beyond Gibbs Hill Light. The 40-foot ketch *Liebchen*, with freshly refinished bright work, was putting out. The frog had jumped—Bill Roberts was on the run.

"I'm sorry, sir. He worked late and then we followed him home. We didn't know he had left until the guard at the marina called this morning. His boat was gone, but he hadn't signed it out. We checked at the house and he wasn't there." The young marine was standing at full attention, eyes locked straight ahead, not daring even to glance at the fuming inspector.

"That's all, Corporal. Dismissed," snapped the duty officer.

"Sir, yes, sir," came the reply, followed by a crisp about-face.

"We really didn't have grounds to stop him anyway. It's his boat," said Mike Berry, the starched and pressed lieutenant in charge of security. "What do you want him for, Inspector?"

"We believe he is involved with the disappearance of Ensign Debbie Holiday and a NASA engineer, Tom Morrison. If not directly involved, he certainly has information about their disappearance," Ian answered.

"Lieutenant Berry, come and take a look at this," came an urgent call from the computer room next to Roberts's office. "He wiped out the main frame. Even the operational systems are dead. Come and look." They went into the room to stare at a blank screen.

"So much for using the satellite to find the *Mermaid*," Doc said, pounding the desk. The startled technician jerked backward, wide-eyed. "How long until you get it up again? It could be really important."

"We may need help from the States, and Wash-ington's going to be pissed. This could take days, even a couple of weeks," the technician answered. "Even then, Dr. Roberts designed the whole system including the backups. Who knows what's left of any of it?"

"Unless we get our hands on Roberts," Doc said. "Certainly you have enough for a warrant now, Ian. Let's get out there and find him. He couldn't have gotten far. Get a chopper and let's go."

"You got it," said the lieutenant. "I'll call the flight deck and get us a ride. We don't need a warrant to ask him about that computer. We can worry about the rest later. Let's go."

They were in the air within minutes.

"The flight deck gave us four radar targets, three to the south, one west," Lt. Berry said. "Which way do we go first?"

"Head south, towards the Bahamas," Doc suggested. "It's a shorter run—easier to hide."

"South it is, gentlemen," the pilot called back.

"That boat should make eight knots or so in this air. If he left at midnight, he couldn't have made more than fifty or sixty miles," Doc said. "This shouldn't take long."

"There's one, a 40-foot ketch, right? That's it!" exclaimed Lt. Berry.

"I think that's a schooner, Lieutenant," Doc corrected. "See the gaff at the top of the main...that's the big sail in the rear...that's a schooner. Let's take a look at that one towards the west."

Ian laughed at Doc's humor. "Dry bastard, aren't you now? Give the lad a break. How should he know the difference between a schooner and a ketch? His Navy uses engines, you know."

"Two points for Ian," Doc laughed.

The helicopter made a low pass over the second boat. "That's it. Now, where's Roberts?" The boat was on a port tack trailing a small dinghy. The self-steering arm was set at the helm and she was making good time, but the cockpit was empty.

"I don't like the looks of this," Ian said.

"Take us lower," Doc shouted.

"What are you up to, Doc?"

"Going for a swim. Care to join me?"

"Don't be a bloody cowboy. I'll send out a boat."

"I want this guy now, not next week. There may still be time to save him from a Viking funeral if that's his plan. Lieutenant, ask the pilot to take us in on the port just off the bow. Use the rotor blast to back wind the sails. I'll have a look and bring her back to the marina. You guys stick around until we're on board, OK?"

"No problem. I'll go with you if you want," Berry answered.

"You can help more by covering us from up here, thanks. Besides, we can't have you polluting the ocean with all that starch," Doc said as he emptied his pockets and handed over the contents.

"Anytime, gents," the pilot called back.

"Are you coming, Inspector?"

"Of course. I have to protect you bloody tourists. I presume you know how to sail that rig?"

"My Navy had sails, remember?" Doc said as he jumped.

"Bloody cowboy," Ian shouted as he followed.

CHAPTER

12

C lass began sharply at eight after the morning kitchen crew finished cleanup and coffee pots were perking again. Lisa Bower, the conservation lab director, began her presentation with a charming British accent. Sheri sat near the window watching for Doc. Why in the world would he have gone out in the middle of the night?

"And so before you actually dive the wreck site of the *Eagle*, we want you to have some background on how we know what is known about seventeenth century ship construction, and give you some expectation of what's left after a ship's been on the bottom for two hundred years.

"We can divide the sources of our information into three sections. First are the few remaining written records. The three best known are <u>Architectura Navalis</u> by Joseph Furttenbach, written in 1629. Next is <u>Architectura Navalis Mercatoria</u> by the Swedish master, Fredrik Henrik af Chapman, written in 1768. Finally, there is the French masterpiece <u>Souvenirs de Marine,</u> which contains scaled drawings of vessels from many nations. It was written in 1884 by Vice-Admiral Edmond Paris—good name for a Frenchman, don't you agree? If you happen to have any first editions of these volumes at home in the attic that you would like to contribute, I'm sure Dr. Richardson would be happy to talk to you about never having to pay taxes again.

"We are fortunate to have reprints of the Furttenbach book, which is of great interest because there were no blueprints as we think of them used in the seventeenth century. But there were formulae for the relationship of length, width and draft. Knowing those formulae lets us extrapolate hull dimensions even when little of the hull remains. In the case of the *Sea Venture* which you remember went down in 1609, fifty-one feet of keel remains, and the project archaeologist, Allen Wingwood, established the length of the vessel at twenty-two point nine meters, or seventy-five feet for those of you not fortunate enough to be raised on the metric system. This obviously leads to our second source of information: the archaeological sites themselves.

"We know a great bit about what to expect on the *Eagle* because of what was found on the careful excavation of the *Sea Venture*. For example, would you expect to see fine Ming porcelain? There was some on board the *Sea Venture*.

"The final major source of information comes from the old ship models, some of which are amazingly historically accurate. The British Admiralty collection is a wonderful resource, especially for military vessels. Scale models were built to be used by shipwrights as construction guides, much as a construction superintendent uses his blueprints today.

"There's an excellent new resource available to you in our library. That is the work by naval historical writer and consultant Brian Lavery on the colonial merchantman, *Susan Constant*. Does anyone recognize that name?" Lisa looked around at the group.

"No? Well, she was the vessel which carried colonists of the first permanent American settlement, not to Cape Cod, but to Jamestown, Virginia.

"She arrived in 1607, thirteen years ahead of the *Mayflower*. Captain John Smith was a passenger. My guess is that she was very much like the *Eagle*, between one hundred and a hundred thirty tons, about fifty-five feet long and twenty-two feet wide, the size of a good dive boat, yet the *Susan Constant* carried seventy-one people. Can you imagine? At any rate, you'll find this book to be a helpful tool in your research, especially for comparing the sizes of structural members and for getting an idea of what the rigging was like."

"Comparing structural members sounds like fun," Karen whispered to the girls closest to her. There was a burst of laughter and then silence as they realized Lisa was blushing. She recovered quickly and continued, "As part of your learning experience this summer, we hope to expose you to enough ship construction history to make identifying the age and perhaps even understanding the style of a wreck easier. There are some easy-to-remember dates that you should add to your field notebooks.

"Let's start with antifouling protection. In tropical waters, shipworms could destroy an unprotected vessel in two years or less. Prior to the advent of iron hulls in 1860—the *HMS Warrior*, later stationed here in Bermuda, was one of the first —and bottom paints sometime later, there were three types of antifouling protection. First was lead sheathing which goes back to the Phoenicians or earlier, but wasn't commonly used in the western world.

"Copper sheathing was tried after 1760, about the time Lloyds of London went into business. But because of electrolytic reactions between the copper and the iron fastenings, which dissolved the iron, copper sheathing was not standard practice until the introduction of copper-zinc alloy hull fastenings and spikes in 1783. Prior to that, hulls were usually coated with tar and hair and then covered with thin sacrificial planking. Lavery suggests the use of elm, and this, he says, was covered with 'a mixture of train oil, rosin and brimstone, giving a white finish.'"

Sheri watched Mark taking notes as fast as he could write. She looked down at her blank page and then back at Mark. This was his life and it had been hers as well until last night. Now all she could do was wonder what had happened to Dr. Holiday. As she looked at Mark, she could not remember what had attracted her so strongly to him, or why she had put so much energy into pulling him into a relationship.

And what about Dr. John Holiday/Harrington? What could this vulnerable, intellectual old warrior, so emotionally distressed and exhausted, hope to accomplish against drug smugglers and killers? Did he have any chance at all?

The wash from the helicopter's rotor blades drove the salt spray into Doc's eyes which burned like crazy. He dove beneath the surface and stroked powerfully to the stern of the *Liebchen*. He surfaced, pulled down the swim ladder, climbed aboard and quickly removed the self-steering arm and slacked the jibs, main and mizzen of the Bermuda rig. The helicopter pulled away, relieving the gale force winds. With the sails luffing and snapping in the air, he looked for Ian. The inspector had landed badly and had the wind knocked from him. He was coughing and swimming awkwardly towards the dinghy. Doc threw him a life ring, pulled him to the ladder and said, "Never go when you can throw."

There was no sign of Roberts in the main cabin, so Doc checked the forepeak and head. On the salon table was a hand-addressed envelope to "Dear Petra".

"Here's a letter to his wife," Doc said as he came back into the cockpit. "No body. He beat us. He knows where Debbie is and he beat us. Check the cabin while I get us headed back." He brought the boat about to a starboard tack and tightened down the sheets.

"Son-of-a-bitch beat us!" There were tears of frustration and anger in his eyes as he pushed the boat back towards the island. The bow smashed hard into the choppy sea, sending spray showering over the deck. Ian came up the cabin ladder shaking his head. There was nothing left below that would lead them to Roberts.

When he saw the look on Doc's face, Ian knew the best course was to keep quiet and let Doc work it out. He sat in the cockpit behind the helm, holding on for life itself, sputtering in the spray of waves breaking over the bow, while Doc stood at the wheel and held her on a broad reach. He pounded the boat through the swells with a vengeance.

It was mid-afternoon when they reached the marina, secured the *Liebchen* and drove to the Roberts's home. Lt. Berry was waiting outside. They went in together.

Mrs. Roberts was composed as she heard of her husband's disappearance. She opened the letter and read aloud.

> *Dearest Petra,*
> *I am so sorry to leave you like this. We have had a*

good life together and I could not stand the pain of watching it be destroyed. What began as such a grand plan has become an evil scheme in the hands of evil men. I could not be a part, or see my work used to aid them. For your own safety, I suggest you leave the island immediately.

My love always. Please try to explain to the boys.

Bill

"What's this all about, Mrs. Roberts? What was this grand plan?" Ian asked.

Doc excused himself to find a bathroom. He went down the short hall and looked quickly into the master bedroom. There was a large suitcase hurriedly shoved under the bed full of her clothing. Doc returned to the living room. Mrs. Roberts was crying and telling Ian that she knew little of her husband's work, and why he would have taken his life when they were so happy.

Doc waited for a pause and then said in a soft and gentle voice, "Mrs. Roberts, I have only one question, and I want you to think about the answer very carefully. Do angels brush their teeth?" He waited and watched her demeanor change from wounded kitten to snarling mountain cat. "Where's your husband's toothbrush, Mrs. Roberts?" Doc asked in a more authoritative tone.

"My husband had nothing to do with the disappearance of Debbie Holiday or Tom Morrison," she hissed. "But because of their curiosity, his career and our future are ruined. I am sorry for the loss, but don't expect me to help you. I wouldn't, even if I could. That's all I have to say, Inspector. Now either arrest me or leave."

"I'm afraid we'll have to arrest you, Mrs. Roberts," Ian said.

Lt. Berry's radio crackled to life. The young lieutenant stepped out of the room and when he returned, he motioned Doc to join him outside.

"There's a message for you, Doctor. A very large crate's arrived from the States. It was on a special military flight with a Special Forces escort from Ft. Bragg. They need you to sign for it. Mind telling me how you rate special delivery from the army?" Berry asked with a perplexed look.

The museum had two dive boats: the first, a 21-foot Privateer with a Volvo inboard/outboard and the second, a smaller center console outboard. Sheri rode in the Privateer and ran last-minute equipment checks. They were on the way north to the *Eagle* wreck site. The boat was crowded, even with some divers riding on the bow. She would work on cutting down the amount of equipment they carried; only the bare essentials from here on.

The excitement of the dive had occupied Sheri's mind for the afternoon. She was tired of the mornings in the classroom although the lectures were the best she had heard. Now that they were diving, she was in charge again and that made her happy.

This was to be an orientation dive. The divers would be sent out in pairs to sketch and measure the site, and get an overview of the surrounding reef. Lisa had given Sheri the map drawn by the Bermuda Sub-Aqua Club in 1984.

After the hour-long boat ride, the captain found the wreck and carefully set the anchor in a large sand patch. By the time the boat was anchored, most of the divers were already suited up. Sheri completed the briefing and they were quickly in the water.

Lisa watched with interest. She noted how well Sheri's divers were able to work close to the bottom, maintaining a head-down attitude which kept them from kicking up the sand or damaging the coral. Unusual ability for new divers, she thought.

She made a slow circle of the group and found Sheri hovering above the sand, sketching a cannon. Lisa indicated her approval of the students and looked at Sheri's drawing. It was excellent. Mark approached with his video camera. He had begun his special assignment to produce a video documentary of the project. Lisa was pleased. It was going to be a productive month.

Sheri finished her sketch and took a quick tour of the shallow reef. It was flourishing with almost no dead coral.

She would insist that during the uncovering of the timbers, great care be taken to protect the corals from falling sand. If they used venturi water dredges, the discharge would be kept low near the bottom.

The dive lasted over fifty minutes. As soon as they were up and logbooks were filled in, Sheri began the first of many composite drawings on her large, white board. The wreck lay in two large sand patches. She studied the team's sketches and used a yardstick and navigator's parallel rules to maintain the correct proportions and perspective. The most noteworthy discoveries were the five cannons: two in the larger southern sand patch and three embedded in the reef. There were also piles of ballast stone and some red fire bricks from the galley stoves. One of the divers brought her a rifle flint from a ballast pile. Sheri immediately gave it to Lisa and apologized.

"Don't worry. It's OK as long as they bring the things to us. They're so enthusiastic this is bound to happen. They're doing a great job. I'm thinking we're going to need a second project to hold their interest. I'll talk to Jason about it and let you know."

The students were excited by the dive and the finding of the cannons. Bob and Karen were arguing about Bob's landing on the coral, and two girls were flirting with the young boat captain, a grad student from the U.K. They found his British accent intriguing and his tan, lean body a prize worth competing for. That they were young, pretty and in bikinis was certainly enough to hold his interest.

When her work was finished on deck, Sheri climbed up to the bow and tried to get comfortable. She sat quietly on a bench, watching the choppy, shallow bay and the overcast sky, and worried about Doc.

From his second-story window in the old Commissioner's House, Jason Richardson glanced away from his easel and saw a large, middle-aged man walking across the lawn to the hostel. The man's clothing had been wind- dried on his body. His hair was unkempt and he was sunburned.

"Tourists never learn," he laughed with superiority. Then

Richardson realized this sunburnt, rumpled man must be the elusive Dr. Harrington. Anxious to meet the doctor and exchange academic banter, he left his large office and headed down to the hostel to indulge his curiosity.

Richardson entered the hostel and called out to Dr. Harrington. There was no answer. He went to the back door and heard water running in a shower. He would wait. He walked through the two bunk rooms. The women's room was strewn with clothing. Richardson was attracted to a black lace bra hanging from a bed post and as he reached for it, an authoritative voice said, "May I help you?" Doc was standing in the men's quarters wrapped in a towel.

Embarrassed to be caught off guard, Richardson came quickly out of the women's area and held out his hand to Doc. Doc kept a cool expression and waited. "I am Dr. Richardson. Please call me Jason. You must be Dr. Harrington from Georgia State. I have been hoping to meet you."

Doc did not change his stone-like expression, choosing to hold Richardson at bay. There was something about the lithe, glib, undergraduate-looking young man that caused Doc to be cautious.

Then Richardson saw the tattoo.

"Isn't that a US Navy SEAL tattoo? You must have been on submarines. I've always been fascinated by them. My grandfather was the captain of a German U-boat—that's 'U-boot' in German. He worked with the German divers; I bet you would enjoy seeing the old movies. I've got them on video. I was told you'll be writing about this project. We're certainly glad to get some good PR, especially when grant-writing time comes. Guess the students won't be back for a while. This would be a good time for us to get started. I'll put on fresh coffee if you'd like. No offense, but you look like you could use a cup. You'll need background on me and the history of this spooky old place, of course. Regular or decaffeinated?" He finally paused for breath.

"Regular."

"Wonderful. See you in a few minutes then?"

"Fine," Doc said, maintaining eye contact. Jason backed around him and hurried out the door. Doc stood shaking his head. He was in no mood for the exchange of idle pleasantries with a flake like Richardson, but he remembered what Ian had said about the Dockyard and thought perhaps he could learn something. Anything that could give a sense of direction to his search would help—anything.

He finished dressing and climbed the double flight of stairs to the top floor of the Commissioner's House. The door at the top was open and Jason welcomed him in. The room was more of a large loft studio and library than an office. The ceiling was high and the original plaster had been removed to expose the beams. There were improvised plank and brick bookcases, and a wide plank-floor. The room was filled with art. Several canvases were stacked in the corner by Jason's easel, most of which were female torsos, nude and well done. The painting Jason was working on now, however, had started with a face with the torso only sketched in. Jason was working from a photo which Doc recognized as Karen, and saw her student application file and those of the other girls sitting on a side table. It didn't take much to get the general drift of what Jason was up to.

The portrait, however, was excellent. Doc nodded in appreciation as Jason continued to paint. Doc poured coffee and looked over the rest of the loft. There were some excellent antiques, a Napoleon desk of mahogany or cherry, some Empire chests and tables, sea chests and navigational equipment. There were also a number of high quality bronze statues, mostly female nudes from classical Greek to art deco.

"I've always liked nudes," Jason began, "especially the art deco pieces from the twenties. The butterfly girls and water nymphs are just exquisite, don't you agree?"

Doc nodded.

"I suppose at my age, one is expected to have outgrown a fascination with breasts—to be able to look a braless woman in the eye first, and carry on a conversation without letting your eyes fall. But so far, I'm afraid I must delightfully report I've yet to attain that level of sophistication."

Doc laughed.

Encouraged, Jason continued, "Have you ever considered all the possibilities? Not just size and cleavage, or the lack thereof, but the subtle things—the softness of skin that's never seen sunlight, the size of the areola and how it changes color, the sensitivity of a nipple and how much pleasure or pain it can take. And then there's the nipple orientation, which could be plotted like the orbit of a moon around its mother planet." Jason demonstrated with his hands. "Straight forward, turned up like a Swedish nose, in, out, down when they're used up and tired, symmetrical, divergent...as many variables as there are women. The quest for perfection, or even the search for a definition of it, could be endless. Consider, Doctor, would you know the perfect boob if it marched right into your life today?

"Perhaps that will be my contribution to humanity, to end forever the anxiety caused by our lack of definition of true perfection. After all, we can never really appreciate that which we don't understand, or can we?

"Anyway, welcome to my primary cultural deposit—a land of unlimited imagination and little else." His gold Rolex caught the glint of the afternoon sun as he swung his arm across the length and breadth of his domain.

"Looks like there's ample evidence of the imagination's transition from abstract to tangible here," Doc responded. "Some of these pieces are magnificent. And I trust that watch you're wearing didn't come from a cereal box." Doc remembered the gold Rolex in the video of the drug wreck and wondered.

"Most of it belongs to the museum," Jason said and slid his sleeve back over the watch. "Archaeologists travel light, unencumbered by the accoutrements of wealth, or the comforts of it...at least for now. I've acquired a few trinkets, but they're superficial, like the watch. They're not the tip of an iceberg—unfortunately, they're the whole damn glacier. How about you...made your fortune teaching English lit?"

"Hardly," Doc answered. "But we all make choices." He was looking at several photos on the Napoleon desk. One was of a young German officer with his wife and two young girls. "That your grandfather?"

"Ah, yes, the captain. The old wolf used to scare me to death. Still does if the truth were known. Brilliant, cold-blooded, decorated for sinking an allied convoy. They never got off a shot and most were unarmed. I have the battle tapes. He was an engineer, a weapons designer. At the end of the war he was working on an engine that would run on hydrogen extracted from salt water. This country would have given anything for it. Imagine an engine fueled by earth's most abundant resource and its only exhaust emission would be pure oxygen. What would you think that's worth?"

"Probably a bit more than teachers or archaeologists make."

"That's what he thought," Jason answered with a ring of irony in his voice. "That's what all of us thought," he said mostly to himself.

The diving equipment had been rinsed and stored in the locker by the Keep, the small boat basin behind the high wall near the diving museum. The students came exuberantly up the hill to the hostel. The first dive had been a grand success and they were all excited to begin the dig in earnest. Doc was stretched out on a couch and sat up when they came in.

"You jerk," Sheri shouted at him. "I've been worried about you all day, and here you are with your butt on the couch, sacked out without a care in the world." The room got suddenly quiet. The words were out and she was shocked that they had come from her. She had no intention of attacking him, not that way.

"I'm sorry," she said, in control again. "Are you alright?"

Before Doc could answer, Mark charged in, oblivious. "Hey, Doc. Man, you missed a great dive today! We found the wreck. Cannon and everything, ballast, firebrick, everything. Well, I'm starved." He turned to the group and shouted, "What's the plan for dinner? I'm so hungry I could eat a sheep."

"The plan is, it's your turn to cook," Karen said, reading from the schedule. "Come on, I'll teach you how to boil water."

"Careful, Mark. Once the water's boiling, she'll put you in it," one of the other girls chided.

"Oh," Karen quipped. "Now you've spoiled the surprise. I've been trying to get Mark in hot water for a long time. Come on, Mark, bring those great buns in here and let's make-a some-a pasta the old-a fashioned way." Cheers came from the group. Mark hung his head and followed her like a lamb to the stew pot.

Doc led Sheri out to the porch. Another couple was there, so they walked across the yard to a large gun emplacement overlooking the ocean.

"Sorry if I worried you," he began. "When I woke up this morning, my subconscious was telling me that the NASA computer could find the *Mermaid*, the boat Debbie was on. If we compared the data the day before and the day after, there should be one new wreck and that would be the *Mermaid*. But I got there too late." She heard the discouragement in his voice as he told her the rest of the story and what the technician had said about fixing the computer.

"The thing I don't understand is why. Unless Roberts was protecting the location of the drug boat. But he knew that Paul had already gone to Inspector Cord with that information. There has to be something else, but what? What else was he hiding that was worth sacrificing his career for? I'm stuck and time is on their side. The longer this drags on, the less chance there is of finding Debbie." He took her hand and looked at her. "Will you go to the Sub-Aqua Club meeting tomorrow night for me? I'd be recognized, but you just might hear something. We might get lucky."

"Sure, but I still believe what I told you on the plane, Doc. You'll find her and bring her back, OK? I know it. But please, don't leave me like that again. I care..." She didn't finish the thought verbally, but squeezed his hand and leaned against his arm. He got the message.

Karen's spaghetti was a huge success for which Mark tried to take credit. However, he was no match for her deadly quick wit, and the more he tried to defend himself, the more she bombarded him with full broadsides. The result was rowdy entertainment for the diners and a new image for Mark—one he would spend the rest of the month trying to overcome.

Sheri was preoccupied with Doc and plans for the next dive. She was glad Mark was taking it in stride and even enjoying himself. They were still at the table when the phone rang. It was for Dr. Harrington.

"Hello, Doc? This is Sandy. Things are happening; here's

the number. Call me back quick as you can." Doc put down the phone and returned to the table beside Sheri.

"I have to get to a phone and then pick up some things at the base. We could get a beer."

"I'll get my purse." She told Mark she was leaving and walked beside Doc down the hill. Mark watched her go out the door and didn't like what he was feeling. Karen added to his discomfort by commenting that it looked as if Sheri had found someone her own age to play with. Mark laughed and swatted her tail with a dish towel.

"I'm going to take a shower," Mark said as soon as the dishes were done.

"Remember to wash behind your ears. I'm going to check," Karen teased.

She left the kitchen, walked through the men's bunk room on the way to her own and saw Bob still in his clothes, sleeping soundly. Why wait? she said to herself with a smile and grabbed her towel. Without hesitation, she marched into the men's bathroom where Mark was in the shower. She hung her clothes on the wall peg and pulled open the curtain.

"Ear check," she said and laughed at his startled expression. "You're in hot water now, Mark. Let's see if you're a big enough boy to handle it." She kissed him just long enough and then said, "Oh, yes," as she pulled the shower curtain closed behind them.

"Sandy? Thanks for the call. What have you got?"

"We just got something you need to know. First a little background: in '86 some South American recreational chemical suppliers had a little convention in Bermuda. They came to strengthen their market share, so to speak. Your Inspector Cord and his men got a tip, probably from a competitor, and as you heard, during the negotiations Inspector Cord lost his partner, a rookie named Brian Cord, his kid brother. Now apparently your freighter full of grass was the property of that same South American investment group, and no one is saying how it got to the bottom. Rumor has it, however, that top management commodity speculators in Medellín, sent down an executive memo: 'Don't come home without that cargo or appropriate payment.' So, you can expect the players to be highly motivated, with incentive at least equal to that of ancient Mayan basketball players.

"The head of the South American trade delegation is an experienced dealer named Esteban Maldias. Should you have the bad fortune to cross his trail, you'll recognize him instantly by the absence of his left ear and eye, and other particularly distinctive scarring. D.E.A. believes Señor Maldias was the perpetrator in the death of Brian Cord.

"It's a good possibility that Maldias's brother was on the freighter your kids found. Add that to the fact that Maldias finds body parts hard to amortize and holds the inspector responsible for what we might refer to as his loss of face, and you've got one pissed off *vaquero*. You copy?"

"I get your drift. Now give it to me straight. Maldias is on his way here, right?"

"Right, any minute now. He's got a 300-foot freighter just like the last one, and probably his own yacht, a floating fortress he calls the *Rose*. They should be just off the coast. Doc, don't make me sorry I'm telling you this. Take my advice and sit this one out. I doubt that it has anything to do with Debbie and you'll be in way over your head. I'm only telling you so you can keep out of the way. Oh, your care package should be there by now. Have you picked it up yet?"

"Tonight, thanks. And thanks for the warning, but you know I can't sit this out. Not if there's a chance they took Debbie. Also, Bill Roberts is missing. He faked a suicide this morning. My guess is that he's still on the island, so tell your men to keep an eye out for him. Second, get me a file on Dr. Jason Richardson and look for any relationship to Roberts through the university. Probably a long shot. Roberts is twenty years older, but right now I'm grasping at straws. Call me the minute you get anything. And thanks."

"Just remember our motto, 'We're from the government...'" Sandy joked, but Doc noticed a slight change in his voice.

What was it? Something I said? Doc wondered but quickly answered, "'We do 'em all and the easy ones twice.' Yes, I remember."

Doc's second call was to Lt. Berry. He told Mike what

he'd just learned and asked him to check it out. Mike called Aerial Recon. They had already been monitoring a large freighter holding with a second, smaller vessel seventy-five miles northwest. Aerial Recon would bring photos in the morning.

"Call me the minute they move, Mike. I may need a head start on Ian. Any problem?"

"Up to you, Doc. Just let me know how we can help."

He looked recharged and focused when he returned to the car. Sheri demanded to know what he had heard.

"It's started. This may not get me any closer to Debbie, but I can't afford to ignore it. There is one thing. Be careful of Inspector Cord. I'm not so sure we can trust him. Don't let him pump you for information."

"Nobody pumps me until at least the third date."

"I'm so relieved."

CHAPTER

13

When they got to the Naval Station hangar, Sheri looked at the crate and asked Doc, "What's in it?"

"A scooter, diving equipment, navigation equipment for the boat, a hand-held sonar and some other toys. We're going to have to unpack this. I'll get the tool box." They worked together for half an hour opening the boxes. The last box had a crushed red bow on the top. Doc laughed and looked at the note.

Please forget where these came from when you get arrested, and don't call us. Keep your head down and good luck.
—Sandy

The box was a military ammo can with a cam-locking top. Doc opened the seal and removed the lid. Inside was a Smith & Wesson 10 mm handgun with silencer and an HK MP5 submachine gun with spare magazines and plenty of ammunition.

"Paul wouldn't like this," Doc said, looking around the hangar to see if anyone was watching. He then lifted the gun from the box. "He believes if they can keep guns off the island, that will somehow keep the bad guys away too. Wonder what he thinks now."

"He could be right, you know. Guns haven't helped Atlanta, or Chicago or D.C. or..."

"It's not the gun, it's the...Never mind, we don't have time for this now. Help me get this stuff to the car. If it eases the pangs of your liberal heart, it would suit me just fine if we didn't have to use any of these, but I was a Boy Scout and they taught me to be prepared, that's all."

"Are you serious about not using those guns? I thought you were really into this macho stuff. And I'm not a liberal, not the way you meant it. We all learned to shoot on my grandfather's farm. That was different."

He drove the South Shore Road back to the Dockyard. When they reached the Sonesta Beach Hotel, he turned down the long winding drive and parked by the lagoon. "How 'bout that beer?" he asked.

"Sure."

They sat out on the large deck overlooking the water. The dive store boat rode at comfortable anchor on the glass-flat water of the protected cove. Stars peeked through the mostly clouded sky.

They had been sitting quietly when Sheri said, "Since my dad was killed in Vietnam—I've had a hard time with the military stuff. Part of me wants to know what it was like, as if I could know him. The other part is just scared."

"Your father missed a lot not knowing you. I'm sure he'd be very proud."

"Somebody told Mom it was God's will. That was the last time we went to church. You ever wonder about that, like now, with Debbie?"

"Of course. I think He intended good, but it's up to us to make it happen. If we can't fail, then we can never know what it is to win. It's that old business of free will and growing in His image enough to find our own way."

"I like that. It sounds kind of like Emerson's writing about being guided by the inner light, and being totally responsible for yourself. I think he got that from the Quakers..."

"And Mark got that excellent final paper from you. I wondered how he had improved so much in such a short time. You write very well. There was good thinking in that paper, better than a lot of the grad student stuff I see."

"I didn't write it. Not all of it at least. All I did was help him think it through and proofread a little."

They remained silent a while longer. He was still holding her hand when they got up and walked down to the cove.

"I'm sorry about your father. Anytime you want to talk about it, it's OK. I'll tell you as much as I can." He stopped to look deeply into her eyes and squeezed her hand. She squeezed back. She thought he was going to kiss her. She wanted him to, but he hesitated and they continued walking.

"I hate this kind of business. It's why I got out of the Navy. I wanted peace and security, and to be able to believe in what I was doing. It didn't compute, what we were doing over there. The only thing that made sense was that someone had figured out how to make a buck by sending us to Nam, and after a while I didn't want to play anymore."

"But you stayed for three deployments?"

"Because the kids needed me. I thought I could keep some of them alive and perhaps I did. Then when I got back, there was the Cuban thing—training in the Everglades to get Castro and retake Cuba. I had Cuban friends. I thought they were right. That's how I got involved with Sandy and his intra-agency task force. What a mistake that was."

"Perhaps, but don't you see...?"

"See what?" Doc asked.

"Life has a reason. Debbie doesn't need an accountant, or a pilot, or a even an English professor to save her. She needs you—you, with everything you learned in Vietnam and in the Everglades. Most of us wouldn't have a chance in a crisis like this. You do. And it's because of what you've learned along the way. Life was preparing you for this, and it wasn't a mistake. Things don't work that way, you'll see."

He pondered this silently, then simply looked at her and said, "Thanks." He pulled her to him and kissed her on the forehead.

"That was a little girl kiss, Doc. I want you to kiss me, but not like that." He looked down into her eyes, then lifted her easily to his eye level and held her without straining.

"When this is over, if you want to explore what we might be, I'll make time for that. But if I get lost in you now, that won't help Debbie. Right now little girl kisses are the best I can do."

She was surprised by his strength and his gentleness. She put her arms around his neck and put her head against his forehead. A middle-aged philosopher with an MP5 sub-machine gun...would he be the best thing that ever happened to her, or the biggest disaster?

Morning came painfully. Sheri let the short, hot shower pound her brain out of its stuporous state. Wearing shorts and a "Save the Manatee" T-shirt from a benefit she had helped organize in Atlanta, she came to the dining room picnic tables. Karen slid into the seat beside her.

"Had a late night with the old Doc, babe? Like a long swim on a lonely beach? I think you have a story to tell and like I want to hear it."

"What I need this morning is more coffee and a little mercy, babe, and none of your valley girl routine. Even though there's no story, I'm sure you'll come up with something. Just make it good, something with a little class, OK?"

"You got it, honey, and even though you're being tacky-tacky, you look so bad I'm going to get you coffee."

There's something wrong with this picture, Sheri thought as Karen left the table. Charity and kindness don't take up a lot of space on her personality pie chart. What's she up to?

Doc came in the back door, got a breakfast plate and sat across the table from her.

"Morning. Thanks for last night," he whispered as he sat down. "I finished nearly everything on the boat this morning. That Whaler's a great boat. I've got to call Ian and the Naval Base and then we are ready. If our friends from down south do try to join us during this little blow, the reception party is ready. Not much left to do now but wait. What's on the schedule here?"

"We start classes in the conservation lab and if we can't get the boats out to dive, I imagine there'll be more lectures this afternoon. Did you sleep, or did you work all night on that boat?"

"I slept on the couch a bit this morning. How are you?"

Mark plopped down beside her and interrupted, "Didn't

hear you come in, Sheri."

"She helped me at the Naval Station until late," Doc said.
Mark ignored Doc and continued, "I thought we were
going to town. I missed you."

"Sorry, another time, OK?"

"Yeah, sure. How 'bout tonight?"

"Sorry, I have a meeting in town."

"Fine. Well, let me know when you can work me into your
busy schedule. Until then I suppose I'll just have to amuse
myself the best I can. See you in the lab." He angrily pushed
away from the table and left the room.

"If that was my fault, I'm sorry," Doc remarked.

"It's been coming," Sheri answered. "I haven't given him
much time lately."

"Can't say that I blame him for being frustrated. I sure
wouldn't want to miss my alone time with you either."

"You passed up your chance last night—lover's moon,
inviting water, willing woman. I just hope you're worth all
the trouble, Dr. Hollingsworth."

"The name is Harrington, John Harrington."

"Right. I'll try to remember." She leaned closer and whispered, "But if you expect me to remember, you'll need to do
a little better than last night. Hurry up and find Debbie so
we can start having some fun. Just be careful, please." She
squeezed his hand under the table and slipped away without
giving him a chance to respond. Now I've blown it, she
thought. He'll probably run like hell and I'll be stuck raising
Mark.

The day passed quickly as the storm clouds rolled over
the island. Heavy rains fell for short intervals, followed by
moments of wind and sunlight, followed by more rain. In
the early afternoon, Lt. Berry called to let Doc know that the
two boats were underway towards the island. They would arrive late that night.

In the conservation lab, Lisa had set up samples of her
work and walked the students from table to table. She explained the basics of wax displacement for wood conservation, the use of reagents to remove coral encrustation from
metals, and the use of X-ray to reveal the original form of
iron artifacts transformed by salt and time into unrecogniz-

able masses of oxides. The lab had experimented with displacement-casting techniques to recreate the form of ancient objects, using epoxy resins to replace the lost iron. On display was an ornate Spanish sword with an elaborate hilt. Only the weight betrayed its secret.

Two cannons were being treated by electrolysis in large wooden tanks on the floor. "This is a common technique," she explained, "for reversing the oxygen reduction of metals in salt water. A DC power source is used to pull salt ions to a stainless steel anode and away from the artifact. The process is very slow but effective. After iron objects have been treated and washed to remove the electrolyte, they are bathed in tannic acid which bonds with the metal and creates a protective coating."

On the table, several eighteenth and nineteenth century silver coins were being treated in the same manner. Karen moved away from Bob and when she got close enough to Mark, whispered, "Don't you think those would look great on a long gold chain around my neck?"

"Sure, which one would you like?" Mark asked naively.

"All of them, silly," she replied. "Wasn't I worth it?"

Jason Richardson watched Karen admiring the coins from the lab doorway and homed in like a heat-seeking missile.

"So you like the Spanish coins?" he asked.

"Of course. All smart girls like money, and old money is the best kind," she said before turning to identify the speaker.

"I suppose so," laughed Richardson. "You'll have to come and see the coins we keep in the safe. We have some beautiful ones that would make such elegant necklaces. I'd love to show them to you."

His eyes hardly left her tight T-shirt as he spoke. She watched him in amusement and thought, what a jerk, to come on to me like this....What the hell, he's asking for it.

Jason was wearing the same tight khaki shorts and starched shirt open to mid-chest. There was a heavy gold chain around his neck from which a gold coin, a Spanish doubloon, hung in a masterfully crafted bezel.

She reached into his shirt and fondled the coin, drawing him closer as she did. She put a hand on her hip, pushed her breasts towards him and in her best breathy Mae West, vamped, "Thanks, Doc. I'd just love to come up and see you sometime." The other students laughed. Karen was up to her tricks again and Dr. Richardson wasn't doing much better than Mark had in the kitchen last night.

Caught at his own game, Richardson was embarrassed. He blushed and tried to back away. She held on to the coin and shook her tail at him. The laughter and his embarrassment increased. But Bob wasn't laughing. He grabbed Karen's arm and marched her out the door.

"Why are you always screwing around? Everyone can see right through that damn shirt, and that guy's the director. How do you think I feel when you act like a tramp?"

"Let go of me!" she cried. "You're breaking my arm!"

Mark followed them out. "Let her go, Bob. Don't hurt her. Richardson started it; she was only putting him in his place."

"Screw you."

It was the wrong thing to say, especially with his hands full. Mark sucker-punched him twice in the lower ribs before he could get his hands free to defend himself. As he was going down Karen kicked him in the groin, adding insult to injury. He doubled over and dropped like a sack of potatoes.

"Geez, Karen..." Mark said.

"He was hurting me," she cried. "I hate him! He's self-centered and he thinks he owns me, always telling me what to do. Well, not any more. Take me to the hostel. I have a headache and I want to be alone for a while."

"Sure." He put his arm around her waist and they walked across the courtyard.

"Shit," Bob moaned. He was still down holding his crotch.

"So that's what this morning was about," Sheri said as she knelt to check on Bob. "Guess I won't have to worry about Mark anymore."

Doc knelt beside her to help Bob up. "What did you say?" he asked.

"I said I think Mark's been studying ornithology and has discovered a new species: a blonde-frosted, great-breasted, gold digger."

"What?" Bob asked, still doubled up in pain.

"I said it looks like you're going to be taking cold showers for a while, Bob. But don't worry, it's for the best. Your mother wouldn't have liked her, trust me," Sheri said. It didn't sound comforting.

"Shit," Bob moaned again as they helped him back to the lab.

Doc bit the side of his lip to keep from laughing.

Sheri caught the ferry to Hamilton at a little past six. She saw Lisa and Dr. Richardson come on board and she waved to them. They came to sit beside her. Dr. Richardson immediately began to flatter her on the performance of her team. She answered his questions about the group, about Mark and then Karen. His interest in Karen was obvious. Lisa looked out the window disapprovingly as he continued. Would she go out with him? he wanted to know. Sheri wanted to tell him Karen would go out with a Shetland pony if she thought it had money, but she held her tongue and was proud of herself for that. Lisa gave Sheri a knowing look and rolled her eyes. Sheri acknowledged the look with a nod.

Richardson began asking questions about Doc. At first they were general, relating to his academic background. Then he wanted to know about his military background and when he joined the dive team. She hated to lie, but she did. She told him Doc and been with them from the beginning and she couldn't understand why his papers hadn't been included in the original package she sent in March. He pushed for more. She remembered what Doc had told her that first day at the rampart and wondered, could Richardson be involved? Why so many questions? She felt very uncomfortable. Lisa sensed it and came to her rescue. They left Jason and went in search of soft drinks.

"Sometimes he can be a real ass, Sheri. Don't feel at all obligated to get information for him. And for God's sake, don't set him up with Karen. If you have any influence over her, tell her not to get involved with him. Not that she needs our help. But by the look she gave him this morning, I thought she might take him down on that table and let us all watch and post scores or something. She might be the first woman he's ever met more outrageous than he is." They laughed, paid for their drinks and went back to their seats.

The aging coastal freighter *Marguerite* pushed ahead through the squall. The captain, a middle-aged, wiry little Colombian named Raul, strained to see beyond the vessel's bow. It was impossible. The Loran C told him they were on course fifty-five miles northwest of Bermuda. Occasionally, he would check the radar to confirm the location of the other boat. The elegant little yacht was keeping an easy pace beside the stodgy freighter.

At the yacht's helm was a tall, ugly man, painfully scarred from an exploding flare that had cost him his left eye and ear. It had not always been so for Esteban Maldias. He had come to the drug trade a handsome young adventurer. His early successes had given him fame and fortune in Colombia, with beautiful señoritas from Medellín to Cartagena at his beck and call. Now the sight of him sent children running in fright, and the girls in his bed had to be well-paid.

Maldias loved his boat, so much so that he rarely allowed anyone in the teak-appointed wheelhouse except to relieve him for brief periods of sleep. The 130-foot, steel-hulled yacht, with an aluminum superstructure and triple turbo diesels was his greatest prize, and his home. He called her *The Rose of Colombia*. She was custom-built and heavily armed, and had outrun and outgunned more than one D.E.A. or U.S. Coast Guard vessel. On her stern the *Rose* carried two cigarette boats and a small Bell helicopter. The cigarettes were also custom-built and had pedestals for machine guns fore and aft.

Maldias had two reasons for living. The first was to kill Inspector Ian Cord. He knew his mother would never forgive him for the death of her youngest son, but killing the inspector would restore honor to her and to his family. It was the right thing to do.

Second, he had to recover the two hundred bales of plastic-wrapped marijuana and forty keys of Colombian cocaine that had been entrusted to his family for transport, and had gone down on his brother's boat. From the moment it was learned the cargo was still intact, he had become responsible for salvaging it.

Preparation had taken too long, but he knew it was still there and he couldn't go home without it. It was the second shipment his family had lost. There would not be a third. Business was business.

As he stared into the darkness, he remembered his last trip to Bermuda in 1986 and the loss of the first consignment. He and his crew had laid a trap for the Marine Police. It was to have been a hard lesson in minding one's own business. His men would lay low and when the Marine Police boarded, they would kill them all. Those who followed would remember and the lesson would not have to be repeated. But one of his crew, a terrified boy, started shooting too soon, giving the inspector a split second to pull away. The police boat fired back and Maldias's brave crew ran for cover.

Three of his men were killed before he could turn the freighter and ram the disabled police boat, killing a young officer and leaving the other two adrift. Inspector Cord had grabbed a flare pistol as he dove clear of the oncoming disaster. He swam away, surfaced and fired. It was sheer luck and nothing else. The white phosphorus flare punched through the wheelhouse window and exploded. Maldias remembered only the blinding flash and the terrible pain. He was blown into the water and the phosphorus continued to burn away the tissues of his handsome face. His little brother dove after him and kept him afloat until the deserting crew picked them up in a launch. They abandoned the freighter, stole a sailboat from Hamilton Harbor and made for the Bahamas.

They kept the sailboat's two women alive for a while, but became bored with them and eventually threw them overboard to join their husbands. He remembered the redhead. How sad that she had not wanted to live badly enough to stop that infernal whining.

He had stayed stoned for days because of the pain. By the time they returned to Colombia, it was too late to save the eye and most of the left side of his face. Now he wore the scars like a mask, one that brought fear and power, and rekindled his hatred each time he looked in the mirror. Only when Ian Cord dies—staring into his horrible mask—would Maldias submit to reconstructive surgery to remove it.

He glared into the night from the wheelhouse of the *Rose.* His hatred burned through the darkness like a laser beaming from the empty socket of that missing eye. Tomorrow he would have his revenge, restore the honor of his family and recover his lost fortune.

Doc stood staring at the Naval Air Station control tower's radar screen. It was set on a hundred-mile scan. A block of rain squalls covered the screen. The operator showed him the satellite images from the Naval Oceanographic Command and explained, "This won't move past us for twenty-four hours—might hang on for thirty-six, sir. It's a pretty good-sized low pressure system, and the worst of it will be tonight, when the warm and cold air masses converge. I wouldn't want to be out there when it starts to blow."

"You really think he will try to work in weather like this?" Lt. Berry asked.

"What are his choices?" Doc answered. "In clear weather, an air strike could take him out in thirty seconds. Those bales are worth millions, enough justification for him to hire top divers. And we have to assume that his intelligence network is good enough to have found the wreck for him, or he wouldn't be here. He can have those bales up in no time. Inspector Cord, on the other hand, is going to have a hell of a time in his small boats. Heard from him yet?"

"Not yet."

"He has something up his sleeve, count on it. All I need is a two- or three-hour head start. But when I call, I would appreciate seeing the entire Sixth Fleet on the horizon."

"We'll be there, just like in the movies."

"What's the latest ETA for the freighter?"

"At present course and speed, about 0100, sir," the operator reported.

Doc wanted to say to the enlisted technician who had called him "sir" something original like "don't call me 'sir,' I work for a living," but he looked at all the gold braid in the tower and thought better of it.

"Thanks, Airman. Well, Lieutenant, I'll see you in a few hours. I'll stick close to the radio on the way out and try to give you a call as soon as I'm sure what we've got.

"Thanks again for you help, Mike. If this is something other than what we expect, only one of us will look like an idiot, and it won't be the Navy. I'll have a better chance getting to Maldias on my own, especially if Ian is planning a warm reception."

"Who you trying to convince?" Mike laughed cryptically.

"Right."

Margaret was angry at herself. Her new business suit had gotten soaked just running from the car into the clubhouse, and her shoes were probably ruined. She was the club's training officer for this term. In the locker room she removed her wet clothing, dried off, and pulled on a club sweatshirt and shorts. A pair of rubber beach sandals completed her ensemble and she was ready to help out behind the bar.

Back in the clubhouse lounge area, she greeted Lisa and Dr. Richardson as old friends and introduced herself to Sheri. "What a blow," she said. "*Virginia Merchant*'s ghosts will be howling tonight."

Water dropped from Sheri's hair as she removed her hooded sailing jacket. She declined the towel Margaret offered her.

"Janet won't be here," Margaret continued. "She rang me to keep an eye out for you. I'll introduce you about, and you're welcome to sit in on the lectures if you like. Is this your first trip to Bermuda?"

As usual, the clubhouse was crowded and noisy. The bar would not open until after classes, but soft drinks were in abundance. Sheri was pleased by the lack of cigarette smoke and the friendliness of the members. Soon she was surrounded by interested men, and found herself repeating the story of her reason for coming to the island and her work in Georgia like a broken record.

Margaret, heeding Doc's instructions, watched for divers who had been on the boat the day of the discovery of the wreck that started Tom's computer investigation. She also watched Lisa and Dr. Richardson. If there had been anything between them, as had been rumored, either it had ended, or they were certainly good at keeping it private. Lisa was with other friends, leaving Richardson to fend for himself. Sheri was invited to go diving on every wreck in Bermuda, especially if she was willing to model for the photographers. She enjoyed the attention and collected names and numbers. No one had mentioned Paul to Sheri, but Margaret was getting questions about Janet and what had been learned. The room continued to fill as more drenched club members poured through the door. It was becoming harder to hear, and standing room was now a valuable commodity. It reminded Sheri of a fraternity house party and she liked it, even with all the noise.

Margaret spotted a friend who had been on the discovery dive with Debbie and Tom. She moved through the crowd towards him. On the way, she caught Sheri's eye and motioned her to come. Dressed in shorts and pull-over, Dave Younger was well known to the club. A Canadian and a well-paid manager for an oil company storage dock, he had a large dive boat and had led several of the club's most successful archaeological projects. He was also known to have an eye for attractive female dive companions.

He greeted Margaret with a kiss and asked about Janet. They were good friends and had served as club officers together.

"This is a terrible thing. I still can't believe it. Especially not Paul. To just vanish without a bloody trace. Is Ian Cord here? I want to find out what they've learned."

"Haven't seen him yet, but I imagine he will pop in about the time the bar opens."

"Right you are."

Sheri joined them and Margaret made the introductions. One look at her golden tan, short blonde hair and athletic figure was all it took to gain his full attention.

"You're an instructor then? At that university in Atlanta? I like Atlanta, but where do you dive?" He asked if she had seen the lagoon where the club conducted training. She had not. He offered to give her a guided tour providing the rain had stopped. They worked their way to the front door, but it was still pouring so they just stood at the entrance and talked.

Sheri wanted to know about Paul, and he told her the story of his disappearance and their last dive together. He'd gone back to the site the American kids had found to do a quick survey with Paul. He said the wreck promised to be among the most productive he had seen.

"Have you collected many artifacts?" she asked him.

Laughing, he told her of a bottle collection more extensive than the museum's at the Dockyard, and coins and spikes from over thirty wrecks. "Of course I'll give them all to the museum someday," he explained. "If I wanted to climb the corporate ladder, I would have left the island years ago. It's the diving that keeps me here. I go two or three times a week and most weekends." Flashing his best smile, he asked Sheri, "Can I show you some lovely wrecks?" but she did not respond.

They huddled in the doorway looking out at the expansive lawn. When lightning flashed, Sheri could see luxuriant trees and tropical flowering plants. A jungle-like closeness pervaded the night air as tree frogs sang melodiously.

"It's so beautiful and lush, not like the Dockyard," she observed.

"Yes. It belonged to the Navy for the admiral of the island. Over there on the point are tunnels leading to the water and some old gun placements cut in the rock. Not good to explore in the dark without torches, especially when the stone is wet, but still worthwhile. There was a large cannon at the top of the hill, but it's out at the Dockyard now."

"Would you tell Lisa and Dr. Richardson about that wreck you found with Paul? We are looking for another site to dive besides the *Eagle*, and that one sounds really exciting...."

"You don't understand much about Bermuda, miss," he interrupted her. "Richardson can keep us from diving any wreck he wants, despite who found her. This one is really special and I'm not bloody eager to give her up. But I'll be happy to take you. We could go this weekend if the weather lightens up."

Sheri pushed harder. "How 'bout a joint project between your club and our team? We could dive together and Lisa could help with the conservation. If there's as much down there as you say, you'll have tons of rotting iron to conserve. There are probably beautiful things that will be lost without X-rays and good conservation. Come on, we'll have a great time, and you'll love the rest of the girls on our team."

He knew she was right about conserving the iron. All of it would be lost without Lisa and her lab. The flintlocks he'd recovered were now soaking in his bathtub, and he knew that had to be a short-term arrangement. Finally, diving with Sheri and her team wouldn't be bad either. It was logical and so he agreed. Now he had to sell Richardson on the idea.

It began to blow hard rain again. They ducked back through the doorway, and Sheri took him by the hand to find Lisa and Richardson.

"There's Ian Cord talking to Margaret. Come, I'll introduce you," Dave said. But as they got closer, it was obvious Margaret and Ian were arguing.

The inspector was still wearing his official yellow foul-weather gear. Margaret was shaking her head, and her expression was not pleasant. Sheri couldn't hear what they were saying until she was right behind them.

"All this time and nothing? Come on, Ian. This is Paul we're talking about, not some rummy falling off a pier."

"Bloody hell, Margaret. We are doing everything we can. The boat is gone without as much as a grease spot. We've searched half the bloody ocean. My lads have been putting in all their off time looking for them. Bobby hasn't been home since last Sunday; he's been sleeping on the boat. Now don't give me hell about this. Give me an idea, a lead, anything."

Dave heard enough. They spotted Lisa and threaded their way across the room. Dave repeated the story of the wreck with crates of flintlock rifles and Lisa listened wide-eyed.

"I've never heard anything about a wreck like that," she said when he finished. "It would be perfect for us. We'd love to work it with you. And don't worry, Dave, we'll be fair about the artifacts. The museum doesn't have to have everything. Jason will be thrilled."

Jason wasn't thrilled. He was stunned. "I've heard about this wreck. The man who owns the charter boat in the Dockyard told me about her and filed papers, but they're still on my desk. Now he's missing. The museum cannot get involved until we know what's happened to him. Besides, that would be a major project and it's not in our budget."

Lisa could tell he was nervous. His voice went up half an octave the way it always did when he was under the gun, and his eyes were flashing from side to side, looking for a way out.

"Lisa," he continued, "I'm surprised that you'd suggest risking such a valuable wreck to students and amateurs. It is obvious that only trained professionals should be allowed on that site." His face was flushed and he tried to conceal his shaking hands behind his back. The room had gotten deathly quiet and all eyes were on him.

"Now, Jason Richardson, you listen to me," Lisa began. Her back was arched, she was on her toes, and there was fire in her eyes. "This is the best opportunity we've had at a site that's not been picked clean. I don't know what's wrong with you. If I have to, I'll go to the Board with this."

"That won't be necessary, Lisa," Dave interrupted, stepping in front of her like a shield. "I'm on the Board and my company was the largest contributor last year. We can get down to business right here.

"Dr. Richardson, my name's on that application right beside Paul's and I'm certain Janet will approve. The club has ample funds for a project like this and if necessary, we can use my boat. If this wreck turns out to be half what I think it is, it could be as important as the *Sea Venture* or the *Mary Rose*. I'm sure whatever additional funding we might need can be arranged.

"And another thing, this club has been supporting and carrying out most of the decent site work on this island for years before you got here. If we're not professional enough for you, you may need to start looking for other sources of funding and volunteer labor. Now, as one of the people who found that wreck, as a Board member and representative of your largest financial supporter, I suggest you find a way to make this work. I'll come around in the morning for an answer. Is eight too early for you government chaps, or would nine be better?"

Jason was gutted. He stumbled back against a chair and nearly fell into it. "Eight...eight will be fine," he stammered and pushed his way out through the crowd.

"I'd better go talk to him," Lisa said. "What an ass he is sometimes. Thank's, Dave. If this costs me my job, it will have been worth it just to have seen someone finally put him in his place. But be careful. He'll remember tonight. Sheri, you'd best lay low for a day or so. He's going to need a bit of time to get over this one." She gave Sheri a hug, got her coat and followed Jason out into the rain.

Margaret came to Sheri's side and said, "When you're ready, I'll take you. I heard something."

"Perhaps we should go now." She turned and thanked Dave. "I hope we get to dive together soon. You'll like our team and they'll appreciate what you've done for us. I've got to go now. Thanks again."

Margaret gathered her wet clothes and they ran to her car. "One of my students has been out on his father's fishing boat for the past three days," she informed Sheri. "He said he saw another fishing boat searching yesterday west of Daniel's Head, beyond Chub Cut. Tell Doc the fishing boat left a large buoy with a radar reflector and some kind of transmitter out there. I don't know what that means, but it could be important."

"I'll tell him, thanks. I saw you talking to Inspector Cord. Did he leave? I didn't get to meet him."

"He got a radio message and left like a tommycat with his tail caught under a rocking chair. Doc should know that also."

The hard, driving rain had begun again and it was slow going to the Dockyard. Margaret dropped Sheri at the hill below the hostel. She tightened down her hood and ran up the hill.

There was a note from Doc asking her to come down to the dive store.

"Not until I get dry clothes, coffee and something to eat," she muttered to herself. She hung her wet things, put on a warm, royal blue fleece set and went to the kitchen. Bob was already sleeping. Mark and Karen were sitting in the lounge area with a couple of other night owls. Sheri poured herself coffee, then told them about the club meeting and asked that they warn the others about Richardson. She also told them about the exciting new wreck. When she went back to the kitchen area to fix herself a sandwich, Karen followed her.

"Did Dr. Richardson ask about me?" she asked quietly.

"Yes. He asked, panted and drooled. You certainly got his attention this morning, honey, and everyone else's too," Sheri said, turning to face Karen and touching her arm gently. "It's none of my business who you pick for playmates, Karen, but this guy is bad news. I'd be pretty careful."

"He sure is cute and I bet he's rich too. Did you see that gold coin he wears? I bet it's worth a fortune."

"I bet it's a copy."

"No, it couldn't be. He's a doctor."

"OK, whatever you say, but please, be careful."

When Karen returned to the couch beside Mark, he asked what her conversation with Sheri had been about. "Just girl talk, nothing important. Why don't we go take a shower?" she added in a whisper.

Sheri found the bottoms to her foul-weather gear and her high-top deck boots, then made more coffee and sandwiches. She imagined Doc would be working on the boat and waiting for a call from the base. First she went looking for the boat. It had been moved to the boat basin by the repair yard's marine railway. She walked past it twice before recognizing it. He had used a dark plastic tarp to cover it like a kayak. The tarp was sealed to the hull with heavy tape and supported by a lumber frame. The beautiful, new Whaler now looked like an ugly, black turtle. How could he have done such a thing? How would he explain to the owner?

Doc was in the dive shop. He was wearing a strange-looking, thin black wet suit with lots of zippers and large pockets. A black beret covered his salt-and-pepper hair.

"You look like something out of a bad Japanese movie," she laughed when she found him. "Where are you going dressed like that?"

"The ships Sandy told me about are getting here tonight." He took the sandwiches and coffee, and continued, "I've left an envelope for you on Paul's desk. You won't need to open it unless...well, you know, unless. I don't have a will and if Debbie isn't found..." He paused and looked at her, then continued. "There are a couple of small houses, one in Stone Mountain and another in Pensacola—the diving's not bad there. Anyway, do whatever you want with them. I trust you, and there really isn't anyone...."

"Doc, I don't want..."

"Please, Sheri, don't...I'll be back by breakfast. The letter's to tie up loose ends, that's all. Now, what did you learn tonight?"

She quickly told him about the evening's events, Richardson's strange behavior and Margaret's story of the fisherman and the buoy.

Doc got up and went to the table where he had spread a chart. "That would put them out here somewhere. If we run west until we hit deep water—one hundred feet or so—we should find them. We'll check with the Navy. They should be able to guide us right in, even in this weather. That helps a lot, thanks."

"You're going with the inspector or Lieutenant Berry, aren't you?" Sheri asked him. "I thought the inspector would already be here. He left the club in an awful hurry."

"This is a one idiot job. More than that would attract too much attention. Besides, I'm still not sure which team some of the key players are on. If I go alone, I won't need eyes in the back of my head," Doc said as he studied the chart. "Don't worry, I'll find out what I need to know and be out of there before they can sneeze."

"That's ridiculous! You won't have a chance, not in this storm."

"The storm will protect me, just like they think it's going to protect them. This is my only chance, and I've been in a little rough water before."

"You and the *Titanic* and the *Andrea Doria*, Doc, come on. This is dumb." Her tone was angry.

"Thank's for the coffee and the help, but now it's time for you to go. Good night." He pointed her towards the door.

"You're right. It's past time for me to go and one idiot is more than enough for this job. Have fun with your little boat and all your little toys," she said. But he didn't soften. She shook her head, put on her hood and slammed the shop door on her way back out into the rain. She was off balance and confused. It was over, she told herself. He was going out in the storm alone to kill himself. She might even be in love with him and it was over.

"Bullshit!" she shouted to the dark sky. She stepped out from under the dive shop's porch, tightened her hood and ran to the boat basin.

Less than an hour later, Doc was standing at the Whaler's helm, heading out of the boat basin. He went north of the Dockyard and then northwest of Daniel's Head towards Chub Cut. Beneath the shelter of the ugly tarp, the yellow glow of the Fathometer, the orange flash of the small radar, and the green LED of the Sat Nav system gave support to Doc's chart work and dead reckoning. He was about to cross one of the most dangerous reefs in the world, at night, in a driving rain with gale force winds.

I wonder, Sheri thought in her hiding place in the bow, if this counts as our second date or our third? She sat quietly, listening to the rain and waiting. She wouldn't let him know she was on board until it was too late for him to turn back. This was dumb, major league dumb, and she knew it, but someone else could tie up the loose ends.

CHAPTER

14

The little boat pitched violently in the choppy water. Doc went cautiously at first, testing the boat, and then slowly increased speed. The lights of the Dockyard were soon swallowed by the storm and he concentrated on the radar and the GPS. He compared the scrolling numbers to the turning points he'd memorized and eased the big Mercury forward. Finding Chub Cut in this sea, even with all the new toys, was still going to be tough. As he rounded the point heading west, he was hit by the full force of the storm. Waves broke over the bow and slammed the side, sending a shudder through the boat. Keeping his balance at the helm and the Whaler on course was a real challenge, but as the waves crashed and the water rolled off the back of his improvised canopy, he knew he would win. He looked into the face of the storm, laughed and pushed the throttle forward. It was good to be home.

From her hiding place beneath the tarp, Sheri couldn't see the swells coming so she remained tense and braced. Her muscles ached and her head pounded. She was terrified by the beating the boat was taking, and clenched her jaws to keep from screaming as the waves lifted the hull on one crest only to slam it into the next trough. Like a grave digger throwing dirt on a coffin, the waves came one after the other to break completely over the hull.

Each time, the boat shuddered as it recovered. In the moment of relative calm that followed, she thought she heard Doc laughing. It was a loud, gutsy laugh, almost as if it were Neptune scoffing at her misery. Then the next wave lifted her completely off the deck and slammed her down again, knocking the wind out of her. As she gasped for breath, she heard the Mercury growl; Doc was pushing the boat even harder.

She was scared, wet, cold, battered, bruised and shaking, and she'd only been in the boat an hour. Doc was a complete madman—a lunatic, a cowboy—and she loved him. She pulled her knees up tighter and tried to comfort herself in philosophic monologue. Emerson would be proud of her. She was following her inner light—this was where she belonged. It was her moment, the adventure of her lifetime.

It took an hour of pounding to cross the flats. Doc pushed the boat hard until the GPS told him he was close to Chub Cut. Then he pulled the throttle back and listened. He still couldn't see more than ten feet in front of the boat, but he could hear the roar of breaking surf. He checked the power tilt on the big Merc by bringing the engine up until he could hear the prop cavitate. After lowering it again, he ran parallel to the breakers, trying to find the cut or a break in the surf line. He found a spot and waited. He could barely make out the white of crashing waves as he counted...five, six, seven, one, two. He watched and counted again. Then satisfied this was his best shot, he climbed the next roller at a forty-five degree angle and quickly straightened into the next. He dropped in the trough until he could see coral heads below. He hit the tilt switch and got the Merc up before they hit. He braced himself, but the landing was anti-climactic—the sea set the Whaler high and dry on the coral as gently as a dowager nestling a gold-rimmed tea cup back in its saucer.

He heard the next wave before he saw it. It was a wall of thundering white, towering over the boat.

"OH SHIT!" he shouted and dropped behind the console. He grabbed the wheel, took a deep breath and braced himself. The roar was deafening. Sheri had never heard anything with that much raw power. She screamed in terror as it crashed over the tarp, crushing it. Doc fought to stay in the boat. Tons of water ripped the new electronic units from their mounting brackets and snatched away heavy gear bags like small cobbles tumbling down a raging river bed. The Whaler was completely flooded, but its foam-filled hull popped up again. Doc quickly pushed the throttle forward until the battered boat lunged off the reef into open sea.

The swells were larger now and farther apart but no longer breaking. Doc knew the boat was still in great danger of flipping or rolling until he could drain the excess water. His only salvation was the Merc—as long as it ran, he had some control. And so far it hadn't missed a beat.

Sheri pushed her head up out of the water and gasped for air. She felt dizzy and sick. Her head ached and she could feel a wound in her hairline. She had to push the tarp up to make enough air space to breathe. She rose to her knees, but as the boat took a roll, she lost her footing and screamed for Doc's help.

Doc heard her, but couldn't take his hands off the wheel nor his eyes off the bow. Another big swell was coming and if the Whaler broached, they would be in real trouble. He felt the bow rise and increased the power. Although the boat floundered badly as the wave passed, it remained upright. Sheri screamed again. She had to get out from under the heavy tarp.

The swell passed and Doc shouted back to Sheri. There was no answer. He crawled over the console, slit the tarp with his Randall and pulled Sheri out of the wreckage before the next swell came.

"What the hell are you..." he began, but the next wave was upon them and it nearly rolled the boat.

"I'm sorry," she said crying. "I was so afraid for you. I couldn't let you do this alone, no matter what. I wanted to be with you."

"Well, congratulations! Here you are. We've got to dump this water. Find the scuppers...see if you can tell if the water's going out or coming in."

"What's a scupper?" she asked.

"The drains in the deck. Are you OK?" He held a hand out to her and pulled her to him while keeping the other on the wheel and watching for the next wave. It came and passed before he could really look at her.

"I got hit in the head."

"We can fix that. Find those drains, see if they're plugged or something. Hurry! We aren't out of this yet."

He increased the power and caught the next swell just about right—at a slight angle.

"I can't tell if the water is coming in or going out," Sheri yelled from the stern.

"Then we'll have to plug them and bail. I'll go over the side. Find some rags, then take the wheel." He grabbed a white plastic trash bucket and cut a hole in the bottom. He pulled line from a rescue bag secured to the helm, tied the bucket off and threw it off the port side.

He told her to idle the engine to test his makeshift sea anchor. It seemed to work and hold the bow into the swells. In any case, it would have to do. He pulled off his jacket and zipped up the sides of his sleeveless wet suit, pulling it snug. "Get the mask, fins and boots out of the dive bag."

Sheri pushed aside the submerged tarp, fished out the dive bag and handed it to Doc. A brief look of shock passed over her face as she saw the tattoo on his right arm.

"You ass...you never told me you saw us in the pool that night."

"I wasn't sure it was you."

"You knew."

"I was fairly sure, yes. Why bring it up now?"

"The tattoo. I saw the tattoo as you were leaving. I didn't see your face."

"Now you know why the seal is smiling."

Another swell rolled the boat dangerously and they were thrown against the console. Doc helped her up and she held herself against him for a moment.

"You sure know how to show a girl a great time, Doc. Now get us out of here." This time she kissed him and laughed. There was blood on the side of her face from the wound. Doc saw a small bleeder pumping spurts from the wound. He told her to get the first aid kit and put a pressure dressing on it until he could find the super glue. For a moment she took him seriously. Then he held onto a line and did a back roll into the water.

The sea was warmer than the rain, he noticed, as he quickly stuffed rags into the two drains and then climbed back up the short ladder.

"Let's empty a couple of those packs to bail with...please," he shouted as he pulled his jacket back on to break the wind. It took half an hour of hand-bailing along with both electric bilge pumps to bring the deck back above the outside waterline. Doc jumped back in the water and removed the plugs. Now the scuppers were working as intended.

Sheri held the wheel while Doc propped the tarp frame up and tried to hold it together with duct tape. The boat was riding well with the sea anchor, so he had Sheri lay back on the bags and he set a dive light by her head.

"Scalp wounds always bleed a lot," he said with quiet reassurance. "We'll tie that off and stop it. Just relax. Be finished in a minute."

She was shivering and that made the delicate job harder, but he finally tied off the tiny vessel with chromate suture. He then took strands of her hair and tied them across the wound pulling it closed.

"Try not to get this wet for a couple days and it will be fine," he said and they both laughed. "Let's get you out of those wet clothes. I have a heavy wool sweater here somewhere."

She pulled off the soaked jacket and sweatshirt while he found the dry bag with the sweater and a towel. She dried herself and as she stretched up to pull on the sweater, she caught Doc staring at her with a smile.

"See something you like?" she teased and smiled back. "They're the best Northside Hospital has to offer." Her breasts were firm and full with no sag. The thin scars were still pink.

"You are beautiful, Sheri. You didn't need surgery for that, but you got your money's worth. Don't take them back."

"Glad you approve. Thanks for the sweater."

He looked at the old, black-faced Rolex. "It's four. We've lost nearly two hours. I need to be on board that freighter before dawn."

He studied the chart with the dive light and plotted a course. Without the electronics, he would have to rely on dead reckoning. The sea was rolling from the southwest and moving northeast. As he set a westerly course, they were running nearly abeam to the sea. The swells were further apart now and easier to climb. He guessed the big ones at twelve to fifteen feet.

It was slow going, but the rain softened to an irritating drizzle. At four-thirty the outline of the freighter appeared out of the darkness. He quickly cut back the engine and called Sheri to the helm.

"It's show time," he said almost in a whisper.

Sheri kept the bow into the swells while he ducked beneath the tarp and sorted through the remains of his equipment. He pulled on a light wet suit jacket and covered his face with black grease paint. Then he carried the tank, the drypac with the explosives, and the scooter to the stern.

"Once I'm over the side, take the boat back towards the reef. They'll still be able to see you," he said with a determined grin, "but by then, they'll have plenty of other things to worry about. If anyone comes after you, just slip back over the reef and run like hell. Nothing of any size will be able to follow you—just remember to bring the motor up. And don't use the radio until I call you on channel twenty-two. Remember, you'll have to change back to sixteen to talk to the base or to the Navy boats.

"And I want you to keep the Smith & Wesson. Just point and start pulling the trigger. It works like a double-action on the first round and after that it's semi-auto. There are more magazines in the bag. This is the last thing: if you haven't heard from me by dawn, go home and wait. There won't be any way you can help and I can always swim back—it's with the current. I'll get there, so don't wait. Just go, OK?"

"I promise. But I'm so scared. Isn't there another way?"

He thought for a moment while he tightened a harness strap and then said, "Sure. We can go back now, but is that what you risked your neck for? To give up before the real fun starts? What if Debbie is on one of those boats—what then?"

"I know, but..."

"You'll be fine. Just remember to do what I've told you, and one other thing...thanks. I'd never have asked anyone to come along, but there's no one I'd rather have out here than you."

"Do you mean it, really?"

"Well, with the possible exception of SEAL Team 2, you bet I do." She laughed, then he lifted her to her toes and kissed her.

"Oh," she said when he eased her back down, "That was a big girl kiss."

Doc brought the Whaler within a mile of the freighter. Beyond it, he could faintly see the ghostly white outline of a second vessel. Both were at anchor, rolling heavily with the big swells. He eased himself over the side, and Sheri handed him the scooter and the green rubber drypac. He hung the scooter on a tag line and snapped the connectors of the drypac to his chest harness.

In the faint glow of the compass mounted on the scooter, Doc found the correct bearing. He squeezed the trigger in the scooter handle and it responded with a strong pull towards the waiting target. He had dropped down to fifteen feet, a good depth to conserve air. From a habit he developed a long time ago, he prayed, "Lord, forgive the years and give me strength. And if you can't help me, for goodness sake, watch over that girl. Thanks. Amen."

He estimated his speed at two knots. It should be a thirty-minute run.

Sheri eased the Whaler through the big swells in a giant arc away from the freighter and towards the island. She fought back tears of fright and anger, and concentrated on the boat and the compass. Doc had told her to wait before calling the Naval Station. She would wait, but not a second longer than first light. The rain had stopped and they were running out of darkness.

"Hurry, Doc, hurry and come back to me. I'm so scared." She was shaking again and this time it wasn't from the cold.

There was life aboard the *Rose*. Esteban Maldias put down the small cup of thick, dark coffee and picked up the radio mike. He called the captain of the freighter and yelled at him to get the crew on deck and the divers ready. Rotund

Captain Juan had been seasick most of the night as had most of his landlubber crew. Three hours ago, he'd begged Maldias for a few hours rest because his crew was too sick and exhausted to risk diving. Maldias was furious but he consented. Better to let them rest a few hours and let the angry sea wear herself out. Now they had rested. The weather was improving and he would tolerate no more delays. It was time to get the job done.

Juan rubbed his face to try to clear the heaviness from his head. The sea had been howling at him and beating him all night. He felt exhausted and hungover. This was his last trip, he told himself, as he had several times before. This time he would save the money. This time he would marry the mother of his two children and build them a real house in Cartagena and never go to sea again. This time he would really do it. He called the cook to wake the crew and lay back on his pillow.

Back on the *Rose*, Maldias's crew were coming out on deck. He wanted the cigarette boats in the water and the gun crews on watch. If the weather cleared enough for the Marine Police or the Navy to fly, it could be trouble and he wanted to be ready. He ordered his pilot to preflight the small Bell helicopter. He would use it to watch the island for boats or planes coming their way. Many of his own crew were still seasick. But from experience, they knew better than to let Maldias see any sign of weakness.

Those who could eat grabbed whatever they could find in the galley and ran to their stations on deck. The *Rose* was rolling in heavy swells and launching the boats would be dangerous.

Doc surfaced to check his position. He was about two hundred yards from the freighter's bow. There were still no signs of life. He slipped back beneath the waves and the scooter pulled him on his way.

Lt. Mike Berry pounded his fist on the dash of the twenty-year old, 38-foot, jet-driven Swift. "Why the hell doesn't he call?" he exclaimed. They were maintaining radar contact with the freighter and the *Rose* but keeping well out of sight. "It will be light soon and he should have been on board an hour ago."

In the rough sea, it was difficult to track the position of small boats, but they had a radar fix on the Whaler's position due east of the larger boats.

"Wonder who he got to go with him. Probably one of Paul Singleton's friends. Some of those guys are ex-British military and can handle themselves," Berry said, mostly to himself.

He had pulled Doc's service record before agreeing to help. It was full of decorations for special ops. Two long deployments in Vietnam and volunteered for a third—a helo crash kept him from finishing it. Two silver stars, one bronze and two purple hearts. Not bad. He had refused a commission and stayed enlisted. Berry had a hard time with that one. Something to ask Doc about over a cold beer someday.

Doc could hear the sound of an engine—probably a generator—and knew he was close. He told himself to be patient, squeezed the scooter's trigger again and in an instant was under the hull of the freighter. He went under far enough to find the keel and then headed forward towards the anchor chain. The bow was rising and falling at least fifteen feet, jerking the chain violently. He steered clear of it and dropped to twenty feet to escape the worst of the surge. It took him only a minute to get ready. Pulling a stainless steel bicycle cable from his BC pocket, he swam cautiously to the side of the anchor chain. His timing was good. He caught the chain and ran one end of the cable through a chain link and hung the scooter from it. Then he attached his weight belt, tank and regulator. As he rode the chain up and down, he took a long breath from the regulator and then turned off the tank. He began a slow exhale and started his free ascent. The green rubber drypac was heavy and even without the weight belt, he had to kick hard to reach the surface.

Twenty years and a few pounds ago, he would have climbed the chain. Tonight, that was out of the question.

From his pac, he got a folding aluminum grapple with tape-wrapped hooks. He raised the launcher which looked like an oversized flare gun and fired. The grapple cleared the rail and caught. He deftly pulled the messenger line through the block at the grapple's base until the climbing line was rigged. When the bow dropped with the next big wave, he pulled the braided climbing line through an ascender and then through carabiners on his seat harness.

When the bow rose again, he rode it up like an elevator. As soon as it plunged down into the water, he pushed away and pulled in line as fast as he could. The bow rose again, the ascender held and he rode the crest to its height. By the next drop, he had leveraged himself above the waterline. Now he was ready to begin the inchworm climb up the side of the ship.

Through the binoculars Sheri could see men moving on the sleek, white yacht trying to rig the cigarette boats. But big swells were breaking over the heaving stern deck, and lines and davits were swinging out of control.

"Good, that will take them a while," she said. She had her hand on the radio mike, but still she waited.

Doc got an arm up over the edge of the rail and pulled himself up high enough to get a look at the deck. He could see lights and men moving in the galley. He caught his breath and planned his route to the engine room. There were only two deck winches and a couple of fuel drums for cover. He pulled up the pac, lowered it gently to the deck and hoisted himself aboard. As soon as he hit the deck, he picked up the pac and walked casually to the forward hatch.

"The runner's on first," he said softly and slipped through the engine room hatch.

Maldias was screaming over the radio at Captain Juan. What the hell was taking so long? He wanted action on deck and no one was moving. The captain had turned down the volume and was trying hard to go back to sleep. Lt. Berry listened to the message and laughed. His Spanish wasn't that good, but he caught the idea.

"That crew better get moving or there won't be any of them left to arrest!" Mike laughed. It was after five and there was a faint gray light in the eastern sky. The lieutenant switched channels and called his other boats. "Anyone heard from Inspector Cord? This is supposed to be his party and he's nowhere in sight."

Doc came down the ladder into the main hold. There were pallets of scuba tanks, two large portable compressors, boxes of new wet suits and large lift bags attached to reels. He found a box of dive lights, took one and headed back to the engine room. It didn't take long to find two six-inch diameter raw-water induction valves, and tape a charge and timer to each. He set the timers for fifteen minutes. He placed the next charge beneath the deck plating at the base of the hatch leading into the compartment.

"And the runner heads for second base," he told himself as he quietly moved out of the engine compartment and back into the forward hold. He found two bilge pump discharge lines, secured charges to their through-hull fittings and set the timers.

Hearing noises above, he dropped back into the darkness of the engine room. Men were coming down to unpack the crates of diving equipment. Doc slipped behind a compressor and then retreated through the engine room hatch. He went up the ladder and came out on the stern deck. It was empty. Still quiet, he thought, but too much light—no time to lose. He stepped boldly out on the deck and walked briskly to the wheelhouse ladder. Quickly climbing the ladder, he eased open the hatch to the companionway between the officer staterooms.

He paused to listen before trying the first door. It was unlocked. The compartment was dark and empty. He turned on a desk lamp and looked around the room. The absentee owner was a slob, but fortunately a big slob with clothing Doc's size. He stripped out of the diving harness and wet suit, wiped off the grease paint and borrowed the largest shirt and jeans. From the drypac, he laid out rolls of gray duct tape and bundles of long plastic electrical connectors. He removed the Randall from the harness and shoved the scabbard into the back of his pants under the shirt.

"Time to meet the captain," he said under his breath as he headed to the wheelhouse.

Even with the long blade of the Randall at his throat, the captain's behavior was unpredictably surly. Doc secured his prisoner's wrists and ankles with the electrical tie wraps, then pulled him to his knees and put another plastic band loosely around the short neck of the uncooperative man.

"How many men, Captain, do you have on board?" There was only silence until Doc tightened the neck band two clicks. Still silence. Click, click...the band drew tighter and the man's face began turning red. Doc waited patiently. The captain's resistance began to diminish as the onset of carotid sinus reflex told his brain that its oxygen supply was suddenly in question.

"Twenty-six...twenty-six. Take it off! I can't breathe," the corpulent man gasped.

"How many on the other boat?"

"Fifteen or twenty, I don't know. Take it off, please," he begged.

"Where is Señor Maldias?"

"On the *Rose*....Please, I can't breathe."

Doc held a small side cutter in front of the bulging eyes as a promise of liberation and continued, "Your guns, amigo. Where do you keep the guns?"

The man's face was turning purple. Doc used the cutters to remove the band. The captain gasped again and dropped to his knees and forehead.

"Come now, let's not waste time doing all that again," Doc said as he pulled him back to his knees.

"A locker here in the wheelhouse and another in the galley. But most of the men keep their own. You haven't a chance."

"Well, let's try to keep a positive attitude about that, shall we? Now, what are we going to do with you? Over the side? Cut your throat? Another band?"

"Please, señor, I have a family."

"Yes, so did I." Doc looked around the compartment and then pulled open the door to a small closet. "Don't real sailors call these hanging lockers?" he asked the captain while shoving him towards it. "Let's see if we can figure out why." He pushed the captain through the door, secured his hands to the clothes bar and covered his mouth with tape. "If you move, if you squeak, my men will gut you and feed you to the sharks. Do you understand?"

The round head nodded nervously. Doc closed the locker door and searched the wheelhouse. He found two rings of keys, a 9 mm Beretta and an old Greek sailor's hat which he put on. A glance at the Rolex bezel showed he had six minutes until the charges detonated.

Through the wheelhouse windows, he could see the dive teams preparing to enter the water. He counted ten divers. Half of them stood on a round platform as the crane operator lifted it out of the hold and swung it over the side. The divers began throwing weighted bundles of lift bags into the water and then jumped in after them. He wondered if this was the first group, or were more divers already in the water? In the semi-darkness and rough seas it was impossible to see bubbles. Better to assume these were the first. The crane operator retrieved the platform and the next team climbed aboard with fire hoses connected to two deck compressors. When the second group of divers were on the bottom and the hose reels stopped turning, the deck crew started the large compressors. A smile crossed Doc's lips. He remembered working with air lines from big compressors, and how tough it was to control them as air pressure turned them into writhing snakes, capable of crushing a man's skull with their heavy brass nozzles. He set his jaw and counted the men on the deck and in the hold.

Ten divers in the water and the captain in the locker— eleven who wouldn't be creeping up behind him. Fifteen remaining for him to creep up behind. He tried the captain's keys until he found the right one to open the wheelhouse gun cabinet. It contained eight M16s and two AK47s. Perhaps, Doc thought, a present from the Cubans. He grabbed an M16 and a handful of magazines, pulled the bolt back and chambered a round. Then he locked the steel doors and used the butt of the rifle to break off the key in the lock.

He dropped silently down the ladder to the galley and found four men willing to accept his gun-point invitation. He found the gun locker, took what he wanted and again smashed off the key. He marched the four to the captain's stateroom and locked them together with the plastic tie wraps. Then he waited, watching the Rolex's second hand sweep to twelve. He held his breath, then smiled when he felt the deck bounce as if it had been struck by a large hammer.

An instant later, the second pair of charges fired with the same muffled result. He guessed it would take one to two hours before the boat started sinking. Still plenty of time to save her, but she was crippled too badly to run. Third base, nearly home.

Within a minute, two terrified crewmen came running up the ladder shouting for the captain. They quickly joined their friends in bondage. Seventeen, Doc counted to himself. I wonder if the captain counted himself—probably not. Nine to go. Time to go hunting.

It was now light and the sun was breaking through the low clouds on the horizon. Doc watched the deck through the wheelhouse windows and switched the radio to Sheri's channel.

"Sheri, acknowledge."

"Oh, thank God! I've been so worried," came the reply.

"So far, so good. Tell Lieutenant Berry to hold tight, then you back off. Got it?"

"OK."

"Standby on this channel. Out."

Three men burst into the wheelhouse through the back hatchway. The first lunged at Doc, but met the flat palm of Doc's massive hand full force against his nose. He fell unconscious to the deck. The second pulled a handgun and fired as Doc dove and returned fire with the Beretta. Doc was hit in the leg, but his opponent went down with two in the chest and one neatly between the eyes. The third crewman ran down the ladder yelling. Doc swore at himself for letting him escape but was distracted by the hole in his leg. The wound was more a laceration than a puncture, tearing through muscle but with no bone injury, he noted clinically. However, it was bleeding badly and hurt like hell. He pulled a first aid kit from the bulkhead and as he watched the deck through the wheelhouse windows, quickly packed the wound with four-inch gauze bandages and wrapped it with elastic wrap.

He was fastening the pins to hold the dressing in place when a burst of heavy caliber rifle fire took out the wheelhouse windows.

"Some folks just can't take a joke," he said, and did a low crawl to the portside hatch and eased it open. A short burst hit the hatch and he pulled it closed.

He continued his low crawl to the rear hatch. A shadow crossed the passageway and he fired. There was a scream and the target dropped. Doc changed magazines in the Beretta and eased back into the wheelhouse for the M16.

The cigarette boats were swinging dangerously in their rigging and Maldias's men were struggling to launch them, but when the shooting started, things suddenly got easier. Maldias was shouting at them loudly from the *Rose's* bridge through a PA system. They got the first boat away with a crew of five armed with automatic weapons, and then turned their attention to the second one.

Just as the cigarette boat started towards the freighter, the sea became an obstacle course of huge yellow mushrooms as the big lift bags tied to two hundred-pound bales of marijuana burst to the surface. The helmsman turned to avoid them, but it was impossible. His props got tangled in the nylon webbing and heavy fabric, stopping the boat dead in the water twenty yards from the freighter. The deck gunner immediately opened fire on the wheelhouse.

Doc still hugged the deck as he watched heavy rounds punch through the bulkhead and destroy the radio. He rolled out of the line of fire, grabbing the bag with the last of his explosives, and crawled into the passageway between the staterooms.

When he reached the rear hatch, he gasped when he saw the body on the catwalk. It was a woman with short, dark hair like Debbie. He rolled her over and she moaned. She was young, attractive and dying. He took the .45 from her hand

and looked sadly into her eyes.

"*Padre?*" she asked, reaching towards him. Then she coughed blood and died. He touched her face gently and closed her eyes.

Doc crawled on the catwalk to the corner of the wheelhouse. He could see two more men on the bow behind the deck winches. A three-shot burst from Doc's M16 took down the first, and the second dropped behind the large winch. Doc fired at the base of the cable spool. The second man screamed and rolled out onto the deck.

It was quiet for a moment and he tried to remember the count. There should only be four left. Where were they? Either the captain had lied or he had miscounted.

Lift bags continued to pop to the surface and no one was collecting them. Then in the distance, Doc heard the popping startup of a helicopter. It soon became a droning roar as the Bell lifted clear of the small flight deck on the stern of the *Rose*. Maldias was at the controls with a shooter in the right seat.

Doc was exposed on the catwalk, so he hobbled down the ladder to the galley, pushing through the hatch just as the chopper made its first pass. It circled the freighter twice and then flew away to the east. He'll see the Whaler and know it's mine, Doc thought. Sheri won't have a chance.

He opened the galley door again and rounds slammed into the frame. He went out the back, down the engine room ladder and then forward into the hold.

The disabled cigarette's crew had paddled it towards the freighter. Two divers were cutting away the nylon webbing to clear the props while several others floated close by. The crane operator was nowhere in sight and the divers could not get back on board. Doc crawled along the deck to the point closest to the boat below. He removed two of the pipe bombs from the green bag. He tried to visualize the arc of the bombs as he counted. Five seconds to the water, he guessed, and set the first at ten seconds and hit the start button. He counted aloud, came off the deck on three and threw on five. He drew fire from the bow gunner, but was down before they got the range. He rolled down the deck behind the winch and set the second timer. The first bomb missed the boat, but went off just beneath it, cracking the hull, rupturing the fuel tank and killing several divers.

"Petrol, petrol!" the bow gunner screamed when he smelled the fuel, and he dove overboard. Doc punched in the numbers on the second timer, threw it and dropped back to the deck. His aim had improved. The gas fumes ignited with a terrible roar and the oxygen was pulled from his lungs.

The cigarette boat was engulfed in flames. Black smoke poured from it and the fumes of the burning polystyrene foam burned Doc's lungs. He covered his mouth and nose, and half-ran, half-crawled to the ladder. Scrambling into the hold, he found a scuba rig, grabbed the regulator and took several deep breaths.

The chopper was bearing down on the Whaler when Maldias heard the cigarette boat explode and saw the smoke and fire. He turned back towards the freighter as he yelled into the radio to get the second cigarette launched. In a moment, its engines were roaring, pushing the boat through the swells at nearly fifty miles an hour.

Sheri hit the button on the mike and called Lt. Berry again, but got no response. Where were the Navy boats? Doc had said they would be here, but the only 40-foot boat she could see was the cigarette, flying at her from one blast of spray to the next as it broke out of one swell and soared to another going airborne thirty feet between the crests. She turned the wheel hard over and ran east towards the edge of the reef.

The chopper slowly circled the freighter, surveying the disaster and looking for a target. Maldias saw the line hanging from the bow and was sure Ian Cord was there, waiting for him in the shadow of the hold or in one of the dark passageways. Rage pushed him on as he put the chopper in a steep bank and circled lower. He turned into the wind and set the Bell down between the compressors on the freighter's bow. His gunner stared at him in amazement as he shut the engine down. There wasn't room for a cockroach on that bow, much less a chopper. Before the rotor stopped turning, Maldias and his bodyguard jumped clear and moved towards the edge of the hold.

Doc came up through a small hatch from the chain locker, forward of the helicopter and behind the two men.

"Looking for me?" Doc asked in a pleasant voice. The bodyguard fired as he turned and Doc's three-shot burst blew him off the deck. Maldias put his gun over his head and did not turn.

"Who are you?" he asked without looking back.

"You took my daughter and two friends from a boat called the *Mermaid*. I want them back."

"I'm afraid I don't know anything about this."

"Throw the gun overboard," Doc demanded.

Maldias threw his Uzi over the side and turned slowly.

Sheri leaned on the throttle and the Whaler leaped forward, but she couldn't outrun the cigarette boat. She could, however, outturn him, but she was running out of room. The cigarette was crowding her towards the reef's edge and she couldn't find a safe place to cross it. The bow gunner opened fire at her and she dropped low, hiding behind the helm. Crouched behind the big Mercury and still trying to see the reef, she found herself nose to nose with the radio.

"Holy shit! I've been calling on the wrong channel." She punched in the new numbers and screamed, "Lieutenant Berry, Lieutenant Berry, help me!"

Berry had not waited. The three charcoal-black, jet-driven Swifts were screaming towards the freighter. As they got closer, Berry could see the cigarette nearly on top of the Whaler. He sent two boats towards the freighter and the white yacht while he ran full power after the cigarette boat.

"And where is Inspector Cord?" Maldias demanded. "We have some unfinished business."

"The only business you have is with me and that won't last long if you don't call in your boat. Get on your radio and do it now." Doc's leg was bleeding again and there was great pain in his face. Doc shook his head as if trying to force his eyes to focus.

He has only a little while, Maldias thought, and answered, "No, señor. If you want to see your daughter again, you call in those men and invite the inspector to join us. Otherwise, I go to my grave with honor and take her with me." He opened his left hand enough for Doc to see the small grenade with the pin removed.

Sheri screamed as several rounds exploded through the bow of the Whaler. She turned the boat sharply and then began to zig zag. Behind her she heard the deep-throated roar of twin-fifties as the Swift opened fire on the cigarette. The cigarette's deck gunner spun around to defend himself, and the boat came dangerously close to Sheri. She turned sharply to avoid the collision and as she did, she began squeezing off rounds from the Smith & Wesson until she had emptied it at the cigarette. Her stepfather had taught her well. The bow gunner clutched the wound in his chest and collapsed back into the cockpit. His friends threw him overboard and a replacement climbed to the gun.

Sheri pushed the Whaler full throttle alongside the edge of the reef. She was surfing the building crest of the swells and from her high vantage point, she could see the coral just inches below the surface. The cigarette boat opened fire again. She cut the wheel, and as she rose to the crest, she saw a break in the surf line—a narrow channel through the coral. She tried to surf the chute, but when she started bringing up the motor, the hull lost its tiller and the boat slammed into the shallow coral. The lower unit hit hard and the prop disintegrated. Sheri was pitched into the surf and the boat broached, filled and flipped before floating into calmer water.

The surf pulled Sheri down. She fought against it and against the weight of her heavy clothing. Frantically, she pulled off her rain boots and then struggled with the jacket zipper. Her brain was screaming for air when she finally clawed her way to the surface. She got only two half gasps before being pulled down again. The zipper finally gave way.

She stripped off the jacket and heavy wool sweater, and got back up for another breath. She dropped under long enough to pull off the bibbed rain pants and was finally able to stay up and swim.

The water deflecting back from the reef face created an undertow like a whirlpool turned sideways. It caught her again and pulled her down. But this time she was ready. Rather than fight it she would let it help her. The water pulled her down and away from the reef. When it brought her back up, she swam hard and got free of its endless wash cycle.

A loud explosion startled her. When she rose on the next swell, she could see the cigarette boat in flames. Beyond it was the sinister-looking black Swift, her potential salvation. She waved and screamed for help, but the swell passed and she dropped into the trough. She swam towards the next crest and when it lifted her up, she dolphin-kicked to get as high out of the water as she could, yelled and waved again. This time one of the crewmen pointed and waved back.

She saw the boat start towards her before the wave passed. When she saw the Swift from the next crest, black smoke was pouring from the engine compartment, and the boat was dead in the water. Sheri rolled on her side and swam towards it with smooth, measured strokes.

On board, Lt. Berry was covered with broken glass and blood oozed from his scalp and left arm. The gunners on the *Rose* had killed two of his men and disabled his boat. He climbed from the bridge to the bow gun. It was still functional. He reloaded and waited, but the *Rose* was now out of range and heading towards the freighter.

Doc stared at the grenade. "If you really think you can throw that thing faster than I can squeeze this trigger, have at it, asshole. You're a dead man if you try."

"Alive or dead, I still take you with me, señor," responded Maldias. "Let me get back in my helicopter and go. I will send your daughter to you, or you can come with me. You are bleeding badly. We have a good medic on my boat, trained by the U.S. Navy—the best."

"How do I know you have her, or that she is still alive?"

"Trust me, señor. I am a man of honor with children of my own. I would not lie about something as serious as a man's family."

Over Maldias's shoulder, Doc could see the white yacht approaching. "Where is my daughter?"

"She is on my boat. She is fine, you will see."

"What's my daughter's name?" Doc was fading, almost ready to drop.

Maldias glanced back quickly and saw the *Rose* approaching.

"I call her *la puta* and I gave her to my crew..." he began with a vicious smile. He threw the grenade at Doc and jumped over the side in one smooth motion. Doc got off a short reflex burst and then looked for the grenade. It bounced off the hatch combing back onto the deck. There was no time to reach it, so Doc threw himself backward into the hold as it exploded. It was a ten-foot drop to the steel deck. He landed on the boxes of diving equipment which broke his fall and nearly his back. He tried to move but only groaned in agony. His vision blurred as he faded into unconsciousness. Beneath the boxes, a foot of water sloshed across the hold. The freighter was sinking.

Maldias swam towards his yacht. The helmsman saw him but also saw the two Marine Police launches closing in.

"*Madre de Dios!*" the helmsman said and put the *Rose* into a power turn to run from the police boats. The turn put him on a collision course with the disabled Swift which Sheri had just boarded, her lack of clothing bringing smiles from the battered crew.

The helmsman considered avoiding the Swift, but there was no need. It would be three hundred tons of steel hull against plastic. Instead, he grinned and pushed the *Rose* to full throttle.

Lt. Berry was the first to realize the danger. He jumped to the bow, spun the twin fifties and opened fire. The gun crew on the *Rose* went down and Berry blew out the wheelhouse windows, but the big boat kept coming. Now the yacht was less than fifty yards away. Sheri dropped her blanket and grabbed a life jacket. She was at the rail, ready to jump, when she saw two jet streams of bubbles pass beneath her and fly towards the yacht.

The detonation had the crisp snap of a heavy caliber sporting rifle amplified hundreds of times and orange flame filled the sky. The *Rose* was blown nearly in half and sank straight to the bottom. The blast knocked Sheri into the water. She lost consciousness and bobbed like a lifeless orange cork in the Navy life jacket.

Lt. Berry pulled himself up in the wreckage of the Swift. There was burning debris and fire all around him. As he searched for Sheri, he saw the armada coming from the north. Two small Marine Police boats were in front, followed by fishing boats, trawlers, pleasure boats and even the harbor tugs. Inspector Cord had mobilized half the boats on the island. Bermuda had launched a private navy to fight the drug war at sea, only they were thirty minutes too late. Berry shook his head in amazement and then dove into the water to rescue Sheri.

C H A P T E R

15

The explosion of the *Rose* sent a shock wave through the water that hit Maldias like a kick in the groin. The blast was followed by a miniature tidal wave and from the crest of it, he could see the freighter listing and sinking, and the police boats closing fast. The lift bags and bales were everywhere. He clutched the nearest one and held on, gasping for breath. The lift bag bobbed in the swells and drifted away from the fires, oil and debris of the wrecks. Above the sound of the air compressors' diesels, he could hear the screams of the men trapped in the freighter's staterooms. Their deaths, Maldias thought, were no more than they deserved for their failure and betrayal. He vengefully willed the freighter to sink faster and cowered beneath the lift bag on his drifting bale. The current was carrying the bales slowly towards the reef; beyond lay the island.

The water in the hold, splashing over Doc, revived him. He awoke, choking and coughing. He had fierce pains in his leg and shoulder. The water level was three feet deep in the hold and the ship groaned mournfully as steel strained against the water's weight.

Doc washed the blood from his face, the salt burning his wounds. He raised himself up to look at his wounded leg.

His pants were soaked with blood. With the Randall, he cut away the pant leg and used the cloth to make a new dressing over the original bandage. He applied pressure until the bleeding stopped and then secured the dressing. The air compressors on the main deck were still running at a loud roar and the sound was painful. "Why doesn't someone shut those damned things off?" he said to himself. And just then, someone did. Were Maldias or his men back on board? Doc rolled off the box into the water and started looking for the M16. Again the salt burned his face wounds and eyes as he looked in the oily water. Finally, he found the weapon and moved to the cover of the forward part of the hold. Then from the deck, he heard Inspector Cord call one of his men.

"Get on the radio and get us oil barriers and pumps. Let's see if we can keep this bloody mess off the reef," Inspector Ian Cord said as he surveyed the damage before him in rage. Only one person could be responsible for this, he told himself. He would find that bloody cowboy, John Holiday, and the good doctor will soon regret ever having set foot on the beautiful island of Bermuda.

"Get someone below," Cord continued. "Close as many valves as you can. Let's see if we can keep her from sinking."

"Forget this tub," Doc shouted up from the hold. "Find Sheri and Maldias. Come down here and give me a hand. I can't climb."

Ian chambered a round in his short-barreled 12 gauge Mossberg and peered over the edge of the hold. Oh, we'll find them all right, he was thinking, but first I'm going to take one Holiday off the calendar.

His sergeant saw the acid look on Ian's face and put a calming hand on his shoulder. "Arrest the bastard, Ian, don't shoot 'im. Arrest 'im for pollutin'. This is going to be a real mess."

Two officers helped Doc up to the main deck. The prisoners from the staterooms were led down by two of Ian's volunteer army.

"Where are the others?" Ian demanded.

Doc sat on the winch frame holding his leg. Ian ignored the wound and waited. "There can't be many more than this,"

Doc answered. "I doubt that any of the divers survived. Maldias jumped overboard and was headed towards the white yacht. The grenade he threw took me out just about then. What happened to the yacht?"

"We didn't get close enough to find out. She exploded just as we arrived." Ian was softening. He moved closer and dropped down to examine Doc's wounded leg. "All we saw was one hell of a blast. Probably shook the windows in Hamilton."

"*Si, La Rosa*, she blow up, all *muerto*, all die," one of the prisoners said. "We watch through the porthole."

"Berry must have got her with one of the Swifts," Doc responded. "But how? With 3.5 rockets? Have you found Sheri? Is she OK?"

"Yes. The other boat has her on board. She's hurt—flash burns from the explosion, her eyes..."

"Oh no!" he said in shock. "Can you take me to her?"

"Of course," Ian said quietly. "Is there anyway to save this boat, and keep her fuel and oil destroying half the coral on South Shore?"

"Yes. Get scuba rigs from the hold and pillows from the crew's quarters. There were four small charges all on through-hull fittings in the engine room. Easier to find from outside the hull. I'll show you."

"You've shown me quite enough for one day. Just tell me where to look, and stay off that leg. From the grenade?" Ian asked.

"No, an inhospitable crewman. Can you imagine? There's a girl up behind the bridge. Any chance she's still alive? She thought I was her priest. Hell, I'm the one that shot her."

"We found the body—she didn't make it. That priest business...if it gets you off my island, give it some thought."

"We have to talk, Ian. There's a lot you didn't tell me. Like your brother and your private war with Maldias. I want some answers."

"Later...right now, we have to keep this scow from sinking and get you off that leg and down to the patrol boat with Sheri. She's worried about you, but for the life of me I can't imagine why." He laughed as he helped lift Doc to the crane's basket. "You're not allowed to bleed to death until you get my bill. Cleaning up this mess isn't coming out of my budget," Ian continued. "Did you learn anything about your daughter or Paul?"

"Maldias claimed she was on his yacht, but he was lying. I don't think he knew anything about it."

The freighter shuddered, groaned and shifted more to port. The prisoners screamed and ran towards the side. Ian shouted to his men to hurry with the diving equipment and pillows. They eased Doc unto the platform and Ian motioned for the operator to lower it down to the waiting patrol boat. Then he pulled the tank on over his uniform, grabbed mask and fins and jumped over the side.

Lt. Berry was waiting on the patrol boat with Sheri. He helped Doc out of the basket and to a bunk beside her. Sheri lay wrapped in a blanket with her eyes bandaged. Doc took her hand and pulled her close. She was crying.

"You're going to be fine," he said, trying to sound confident and praying he was right.

"You ass, I was so worried about you. How could you do this to me?"

"I'm sorry. Things got out of hand. I'm really sorry. But you will be alright, I promise."

"Damn right I will, and then I'm going to kick your butt," she laughed grimly. "What happened? Did we win? Did you find Debbie?"

Doc hesitated and Lt. Berry came to his rescue. "It was a hell of a fight, Doc. Did you see the yacht blow? She must have been carrying explosives—that was no low-order secondary. It sounded like cases of C-7. I've never seen anything like that."

"No, I missed it. If you're alright, Mike, Inspector Cord is under the freighter trying to fix the plumbing. I'll bet he could use another diver. There's scuba gear in the hold and pillows on deck. Be careful of the suction; it could pin you."

"I'm on it. See you later. Hell of a fight, Doc."

Maldias was now several hundred yards from the freighter, his floating bale drifting in a cluster with others. It was quiet now, beyond the noise of the boats. The morning sky was still overcast, but the water deep and clear. As he looked down, he saw two large, sleek gray bodies pass beneath him. The curious sharks had come. He watched in terror as they inspected the drifting bales. As the sharks turned and came closer, he pulled his legs up as tightly as he could and looked around him, fearing the small boats now beginning to collect the bales would find him. Sharks were bad, he thought, but letting Cord or the big commando win the final round would be worse. The sharks returned for another pass and Maldias choked back his screams.

Doc and Sheri lay on a mattress on the back deck of the patrol boat taking them to the Hamilton hospital. Doc's leg was freshly bandaged and elevated. Sheri nestled against his side with her head on his chest.

"What about Debbie?" Sheri asked again. "Did you find out anything that will help?"

"Nothing. Not a damned thing and I'm beginning to believe that's all we'll ever know."

"Don't even think it for a minute, Doc. We'll keep on looking. You have to find out what really happened. And she's OK. I'm just as sure of it as anything."

"I'm beginning to doubt...but, you're right. We won't quit until we find something." He hugged her.

"I shot one of them. They were trying to kill me. They were shooting at the lieutenant's boat and they almost ran me over. I shot the one at the bow gun and the others threw him overboard. Lieutenant Berry got there just in time, or they would have killed me. Then I wrecked the Whaler on the reef and I lost your sweater. I'm sorry."

Doc didn't answer for a moment. He was thinking of the dead girl with the .45 automatic.

"Did you hear me? I said I shot someone and killed him, and I lost your sweater—hope it wasn't a favorite."

"Yes, I heard. I'm sorry. Killing is..."

"Sorry? Hell, it was him or me, Doc, and I'm not sorry it was him! I was scared to death, but suddenly I was calm and steady, and I knew I could do it. When I saw him go down I wasn't scared anymore. I was just mad as hell and I wanted to

kill them all. I would have too, but then the boat hit the reef.
I wanted more—it was such a powerful feeling. I don't think
I'll ever feel helpless again."

Doc pulled her closer and kissed her. "I know." His voice
came from far away. He looked out across the water and saw
the dying girl asking if he were her priest, but this time she
had Debbie's face. A chill went through him and he kissed
Sheri again, holding her close. In the east, a ray of sunlight
broke through the clouds, and as they rounded the point
past the Dockyard, the sea lay calm.

Inspector Cord and Lt. Berry were successful in keeping
the freighter from sinking, but the cleanup of fuel and oil
from the *Rose* and the sunken cigarette boats would take days.
Barriers were anchored in place, and boats with skimmers
stood by to keep the constant stream of oil off the reef. The
freighter, with pillows stuffed in her plumbing, was towed to
the Dockyard. After a good cleaning, she would be an excellent candidate for an artificial reef.

There were almost two hundred floating bales of marijuana and not all were recovered by the police. Half of the
Colombian crew and nearly all the divers were unaccounted
for. Bodies continued to drift ashore for the next ten days.
Some were badly burned, some mauled by sharks. It was believed highly unlikely that any crewmen made it to shore alive.

The wire services picked up the story and it ran on the
front page of the local papers. It told of a joint operation
between the Bermuda Marine Police, the U.S. Navy, D.E.A.
and an unnamed international drug task force. There were
pictures of the freighter, the prisoners, the bales and the
bodies. Inspector Ian Cord made official statements and es-
timates of the street value of the captured cargo and thanked
the Navy for their support. Doc and Sheri were not mentioned.

Doc finished reading the story to Sheri and angrily threw
the paper at the corner trash can. "I don't want to be mentioned, that's not important. But telling the truth, that's im-

portant. There was nothing to hide out there. Why can't they tell the truth? They completely left out the *Rose*—not one word about the explosion, or that she was ever there. That's sloppy reporting. And worse, it makes a lie out of the story."

The hospital room was comfortable and designed for four. Doc shared it with an old Bermudian fisherman with whom he enjoyed exchanging sea stories. Doc was in bed with his leg elevated and an I.V. in his arm. His low hematocrit testified to significant blood loss, and the dextrose and water would stabilize the plasma volume while his body replaced the lost cells. Now he needed rest.

Sheri sat in the chair beside his bed. They had been in the hospital for two days. Her eyes were still bandaged and her face was peeling from the flash burn. Her eyes would remain covered for two more, then she might be released. If Doc's leg was healing without infection and if he promised to stay off it, he might be out in three.

There was a knock and a Navy captain stood in the open doorway.

"Dr. Holiday? I'm Chaplain Stone. May I come in?"

Doc welcomed him and introduced Sheri. The chaplain announced that services were planned for the three Navy men killed in the operation. Then he explained that he had been contacted by Tom Morrison's family regarding a memorial service. The family was flying in and the service would be Saturday morning.

"Your daughter, Debbie, was very well thought of on the base, and with your permission I'd like to make that a double service. Tom and Debbie were very close those last weeks. If you agree, I think it would be appropriate."

The chaplain's words hung in the air like summer thunder. Sheri stood from her chair and felt for Doc's hand. She could feel the pain of defeat and loss go through him. He exhaled deeply, and when he answered his voice came from that same far away place it had on the back of the patrol boat. Although she could not see his face, she knew there were tears in his eyes.

"Yes, that would be appropriate," Doc answered as Sheri sank back into her chair. "There are two hymns that were her favorites. I wonder, could..."

"Of course, and I'd like us to talk about her for a while. Is this a good time?"

The chaplain pulled over a chair, sat beside the bed and began asking questions about Debbie's childhood and her mother. Sheri heard the story of a happy girl—an achiever —growing up in Florida waters and wanting to be a sailor. Doc told the story with love and pride. He told of her becoming a scuba instructor and of the day she certified her first students. He told of her passion for sea creatures and the first time she swam with dolphins. He told of her sense of humor and the mischief she loved to create. He told about her growing up in their church, and how important that time had been for their family. Then he spoke about Nancy's death and how terrible that loss had been. Sheri held his hand, tightly wishing she could take some of his pain away.

"When Janet called," Doc said, his voice getting harder, "I swore nothing could take Debbie from me. I was so proud of her. She was all that I had left of our family. I was the old warrior who would charge in and bring her back. But all I did was get some good men killed. Sheri could have been killed. I was so arrogant...proud is the word. It was hubris... stupid, arrogant pride."

There was a long silence before the chaplain spoke.

"You were a SEAL, weren't you, John? Mike told me you were highly decorated. I was a lance corporal with the 3rd Marines and was in a fire fight or two. As I recall, in those days we didn't get paid to sit on our thumbs. You came out of your corner ready to fight for your daughter and if necessary, give your life for her. There is no disgrace in that."

"And it's not over yet," Inspector Cord said from the doorway. "You don't know that Debbie is dead, Doc. All you know is that we haven't found her yet. In the meantime you put a major drug dealer out of business and when we finish cleaning up that freighter, she's going to make a lovely new dive site. Perhaps we'll name her after you. 'Holiday Reef' has a nice ring, don't you think?" The inspector came in and stood by the foot of the bed. "So there's no time for lying in bed, feeling bloody sorry for yourself, mate. We didn't find Maldias's body, and the government of Bermuda wants you on the job. So does your government; someone named Colonel

Andrews sent his regards and has agreed to pay some of your bills. Seems they want Señor Maldias as much as we do. So get your ass out of that bed, Dr. Harrington. You have work to do." Ian saluted, winked, did a smart about-face and left the hospital room.

Sheri breathed deeply. "Thank you, Inspector Cord," she said under her breath. She felt as if a great weight had been lifted from the room. Doc looked to Chaplain Stone for guidance.

"Well, that changes things now, doesn't it?" the chaplain said. "He's right, John. There will always be time for funerals. But not while there's still a chance for those kids. Get your ass out of bed, Dr. Harrington, and go find them. There'll be no funerals in my chapel until we know for certain what's happened. I'll tell Tom's parents. And one other thing. I couldn't help overhearing what you said about the article in the paper. If you like, I'll ask some questions on my own. I'll let you know if I turn up anything interesting."

Chaplain Stone prayed with them before he left. Sheri thought it was one of the most beautiful prayers she had ever heard. He prayed as if talking to a dear and trusted friend, one from whom no secrets were kept and no embellishment necessary. It was a simple prayer. Debbie and Tom were lost and had to be found; we need something to go on. There was quiet confidence in the prayer as if there was no doubt in the good chaplain's mind that the prayer would be answered. God finds his lost and brings them home. That's the way it works. Amen.

Inspector Cord was back the next morning with Lt. Berry. The lieutenant brought flowers to Sheri from the Swift crew that had picked her up. He told her that three of them had volunteered to re-enlist if she'd repeat the performance. She laughed and asked what they were offering her.

"Say, do you know what scuba diving and bear hunting have in common?" Mike began when they entered Doc's room.

"No, but I'm afraid we're about to learn," Doc bit, knowing he was in for abuse.

"Well, this dive shop got a booster pump. You know, one of those jammers for topping off tanks—the kind that runs on air pressure."

"A Haskel."

"Right. Well, they weren't too hot at reading directions and they hooked the thing up backwards. No one realized the problem until they took a bunch of students to the pool."

"And?"

"Everything was going great until the instructor had the first bunch of students sit on the bottom to try their regulators for the first time."

"And?"

"Oh, no more than you'd expect. The suction in the tanks turned the students inside out and sucked them right up."

"And?"

"Well, that's why diving is like bear hunting—sometimes you get the air, sometimes the air gets you."

"That's really sick, Mike," Sheri groaned. "Yuck!"

"When will they release you?" Ian asked, shaking his head at Mike's awful joke.

"Tomorrow. Sunday morning at the latest."

Sheri was now seated by the bed. Ian commented on the attractiveness of the hospital attire and Mike added how much he liked her gown's open back. Sheri made a comment about paybacks then they settled down to business. Ian produced yellow pads and a portable tape recorder.

"What we need to do is reconstruct the fight and try to get every detail on paper and on tape, like a mission debrief," Ian told them. "We need it all, everything you can remember. I have Mike's report from the Navy. What we need now is what you two can add." He turned on the tape recorder and asked the questions in his notebook. They had been working for an hour when Dr. Richardson and Lisa appeared at the door.

It was an awkward moment. Ian broke the silence and quickly explained that Doc and Sheri had been kidnapped from the Dockyard by men stealing Doc's Boston Whaler. There had been a fight at sea and an explosion, the one described in the paper. Doc and Sheri were lucky to be alive. Now they were completing the police reports. And yes, the kidnappers had been caught.

"We can come back later. We were very worried about you both," Lisa said.

Richardson stared uneasily at the inspector and then said to Sheri, "We need you back in action right away so we can start on that new wreck site. Lisa convinced me you were right, and we're making a deal with the dive club to help us."

"We can't do it without you, Sheri," Lisa added enthusiastically. Jason looked around the room apprehensively, gave Lisa a nod and they quickly left.

Mike got up and closed the door, and Ian quickly brought them back on task. "So no one saw Maldias get on the yacht before it blew. And as far as we know, the Swift's twin-fifties were the only things being fired at the time of the explosion. So, lads, what sank the bloody yacht? The twin-fifties didn't. Mike was shooting at the wheelhouse, not the hull. None of the prisoners knew of anything on board that would have created that kind of high order secondary explosion. So again, what sank the bloody yacht? And where did Maldias go and how? I think we have some diving to do. We need some answers."

"You're not diving without me," Doc told Ian firmly. "Maldias said Debbie was on his yacht. I'm sure he was lying, but we have to find out. I'll be ready to dive by Monday. Put a charge on that scooter and I'm good as new."

"Monday it is then. Anything else?"

"Yes. How did the first freighter sink—the one Paul had the video of?" Doc asked.

"I don't know. That tape was the first any of us knew about it. But I think we should have a look. There might be a connection," Ian answered.

"Let's get a VCR in here and see that tape again. Also, check on Janet please, Ian. She was in bad shape Wednesday night."

"Right. Will do, Doc. See you Monday." Ian folded up his briefcase and went to the door.

"Sunday afternoon there is a service for the men we lost," Mike said. "Captain Stone asked me to invite you both. Tom Morrison's family has decided to postpone his service. The chaplain thought you'd want to know."

"Thanks, Mike. We'll be there. Stone is a good man."

"The best. Did you know he won a Congressional Medal of Honor in Nam? Refused to accept it. Said he was just doing the job and gave it back to the President. Made quite a ruckus. The Corps was not real pleased. Tried to keep it quiet. But ten years later, the Navy took him back as a chaplain and he made captain. No one can say that old man hasn't been there."

"What a great story," Sheri said.

"Somehow it doesn't surprise me," Doc observed. "He has a confidence that most never achieve. And it's not just from combat experience. You're right, Sheri. He is a great story."

"There was one other thing," Ian said from the door. "We found the fisherman who put the buoy on the freighter, but he's not talking—scared to death Maldias is still alive. I think he's right. Well, g'day. I'll pop 'round tomorrow."

When they had gone, Sheri reached out from her chair beside the bed for Doc's hand and sat in silence for a short while.

"You have that kind of confidence, the kind you said Chaplain Stone has."

"Not often, and certainly not lately. But thanks anyway."

Doc took the phone from the bedside table and placed a call to northern Virginia. "Hello, Sandy? Can you talk? Call me back." He gave the number and hung up.

"Why did you do that?" Sheri asked.

"He has a Watts line and can make certain this isn't a party line. Old habit."

In a moment, the phone rang.

"Thanks for the call back. Yes, I'm fine. Out of here in a day or so. What have you got on Roberts and Richardson?" He listened for a minute, and then his eyes narrowed and his face hardened.

"Any idea who? Of course not." He was turning red now. She could feel his arm trembling and she was afraid.

"Fine," he said with disgust. "Now what?"

After listening again for a minute, he said, "When? Right. Got it. Call me."

"What is it? What's wrong?" Sheri asked after he hung up

the phone.

"Someone's locked the files on Roberts and Richardson. All Sandy can get is name, rank and serial number. This stinks. We have to get out of here. Heal faster."

"I'll try."

"I hate this business!" he fumed, and slammed his fist into his open hand. "What's going on here?" he said as he ran his hand through his hair and looked at her in frustration. "Why would Washington protect Richardson and Roberts? I hate this business! I should have been a boat builder, or a scuba instructor, or..."

"Or an English professor?"

"Yes, heaven forbid, even an English professor."

CHAPTER

16

On Saturday Lt. Mike Berry arrived with a VCR and Ian's copy of the tape Tom had made of the dope-laden freighter. On the third viewing Doc stopped the tape at the first body in the wheelhouse stateroom.

"See those gold chains and the big coin around his neck?" he said. "Why would anyone leave those? They're worth at least twenty thousand and that watch is another ten thousand. It doesn't make sense."

"Describe them," Sheri asked in frustration, her eyes still bandaged.

"The largest coin looks like a gold doubloon set in a heavy ornate bezel with a chain that looks like it weighs five pounds —the kind of stuff you see in the Caymans or the Keys, but better."

"Dr. Richardson was wearing a coin like that in the lab Wednesday. Karen might recognize it...she got a real close look."

"Good. Maybe you can have your photo lab make some prints from this tape and we'll ask her. How 'bout it, Mike?"

"No problem. We can get them stat, as the hospital people say. Have you heard if they're kicking you out tomorrow, Sheri?"

"I won't know till the bandages come off in the morning," she answered. "It will be good to see again, but you know, it's amazing how much you adapt. I'm going to be a much better quarry diver now." They all laughed.

"Mike, can you get us a boat from special services tomorrow afternoon?" Doc asked. "There's a place by South West Breaker I want to dive with Sheri. Did any of my equipment survive?"

"Yes, I have it at the base and the boat is no problem. But are you sure you want to dive with that leg?" Mike answered hesitantly.

"Salt water heals everything, you know that. The swim will be good physical therapy. I'm getting stiff laying here."

A thin smile crossed Sheri's lips but she said nothing.

When Sheri's breakfast came the next morning, Doc was there to feed her and shortly afterward the nurse came to take off the bandages. She closed the blinds and began unwrapping the dressing. Even the low light hurt and it took several moments to see clearly, but the healing was complete. The nurse gave her a pair of very dark glasses and wished her well.

Doc left the crutches they had insisted he take in the closet, and leaning on Sheri, hobbled down the hospital steps to the police car Ian had sent to take them home.

At the memorial service, the familiar old Navy hymn brought tears to Doc's eyes. He knew the service was not for Debbie, but it was impossible not to think of her as he sang the words in a strong but sometimes cracking bass.

> *Eternal Father strong to save,*
> *Who's arm hath bound the restless wave,*
> *Oh hear us as we pray to thee*
> *For those in peril on the Sea.*

He had attended many memorial services, and there was a composite emotional drain as the faces of old ghosts—old friends and teammates—gathered about him. Like in his dreams, he found their presence disquieting, and chose to open his eyes for the remainder of Chaplain Stone's prayer rather than be visited by them. There was one thing though —Debbie's face had not been among them.

It was a service with a real sense of worship, the kind that left the congregation saying, "Surely the Lord is in this place." In the sermon, Chaplain Stone said that the promise of resurrection was the balm that healed the pain of losing loved ones. In the closing prayer, he prayed as he had done in the hospital room: in close conversation with a dear and trusted friend. He concluded the prayer with an appeal for the safety of Debbie, Tom and Paul, and lifted up their peril for God's special attention and care. Sheri reached for Doc's hand and held on to it.

Two hours after the service Doc and Sheri were in a small boat headed for South West Breaker. There was only a light chop on the afternoon sea, and they went slowly, enjoying the sun and talking to each other.

"We found this grotto when Debbie was a teenager," he told her. "She called it her chapel in the sea. You'll see why she loved to come here when we get inside."

They secured the boat to a permanent mooring buoy, geared up and followed the mooring line to the bottom. With the scooter pulling them both easily across the bottom, they crossed a large white sand patch. In a high coral wall on the north side was the entrance.

Getting in was a tight squeeze. Doc led the way through a dark passageway with the light. After thirty feet of tunnels, they crawled into the main room. Shafts of sunlight shone through openings in the cathedral ceiling and made columns of light to the fine, white sand floor twenty-five feet below. It had the texture of light filtered through priceless stained glass. The walls were festooned with purple encrusting corals and fire red sponges. It was indeed a chapel.

Appropriately, the low entrance compelled visitors to their knees and once inside, most were so awestruck by the quiet beauty that they remained kneeling. They were met by a pair of blue and gold queen angelfish, swimming like acolytes in close formation around the cavern. It was breathtaking.

Doc didn't know why he had come or what he expected

to find, but over the years he had learned to trust that quiet voice inside. As he knelt in the sand in the quiet beauty of this hidden place, he felt much of his anguish being lifted. There was no blinding flash or voice from beyond, but there was something: something that gave his soul a chance to catch its breath, something that renewed his bond to creation. Still on his knees, he gave thanks for whatever that something was.

He turned to Sheri. Her hands were folded, her face turned up towards the shafts of sunlight and her eyes were closed. It was hard to tell whether the radiance he saw there came from above or within. He waited and when she opened her eyes she reached out, took his hand and pulled herself against his shoulder. He wasn't sure how long they stayed that way, but when it was time to ascend he knew something special had happened.

Beyond the reef on the other side of the island, the *Mermaid* rested upright on the soft bottom. She was fully intact except for cuts in the exhaust and induction hoses. She had gone to the bottom quickly; an old wooden hull with heavy engines and a load of tanks and electronic equipment. She was down but not for the count.

A rusty, old hose clamp in the bilge that should have been replaced long ago, and would have been except for the difficulty in reaching it, finally gave way, sending a small stream of air and diesel fuel to the surface as if the old girl were reaching up for help.

Dr. Jason Richardson awoke early Monday morning and propped himself up on the satin pillows of the pre-Civil War, elaborately-carved John Henry Belter bed. Soft morning light filled the museum-like top floor room in the southeast corner of the Commissioner's House. From the high bed, he had a commanding view of Hamilton Harbor. He was fond of telling people that it was probably the best view on the island.

Many of the polished antiques in the room had been gifts

to the museum. Some were his own—more than he had led Doc to believe—like the bronze copies of Rodin sculptures of lovers in various impossible positions, the graceful French art deco bronze nudes and the matching bronze eagles perched atop an Elizabethan wardrobe. A small mirror lay on the Napoleon writing desk in the middle of the room and on it was a fine white powder. Beside it lay a small gold spoon and a golden razor blade.

He rubbed his eyes and picked up the gold Rolex with jeweled bezel from the night table. It showed 5:45. He turned to the tangle of long, blonde hair on the pillow beside him. He found the nape of Karen's neck and began kissing it gently as he moved into position behind her. She woke up as he entered her and she felt the soreness of last night's revelry. He was insatiable, or was it the inexhaustible supply of cocaine?

Another night of dreams had broken Doc's sleep into short bursts until he finally got up, moved to the couch and read until early dawn. He was coming out of the men's room when Karen came down the stairs from the back door of the Commissioner's House and crossed the concrete deck to the women's bathroom. She didn't look good, and as she passed him she stared at the ground. He had hoped to ask her about the coin, but evidently this was not the time.

At the boatyard after a shower and breakfast, Doc inspected the Whaler. His jury-rigged superstructure had been removed, and other than a few scrapes and dings and the bullet holes in the bow, the boat was in serviceable condition. He thought the bullet holes gave it character in a perverse sort of way. Some fiberglass and paint, and she'd be good as new—well, almost. The engine was not on the boat. He could see it through the workshop window, the power head up on a rack and the foot in pieces on a bench. Doc wondered if any of the thousands of dollars of electronics had survived. He'd have to wait for the rest of the world to get up to find out. Normal people, Sheri had informed him, slept more than three hours a night.

His leg felt better this morning. Swimming with fins had

helped, but he was still limping. Scrounging through a junk pile behind the workshop, he found a four-foot piece of inch-and-a-half spruce doweling and shortly had a usable cane. "Thoreau would approve," he chuckled as he limped back up the hill.

Karen came running past him on the road to the hostel. She was crying, and Mark, with an angry scowl, was running after her. When Doc got to the hostel, he joined Sheri at a table.

"She spent the night with Richardson," she explained. "Mark caught her coming back and gave her hell. Now she has the whole place in a furor. I warned her about Richardson. I knew there'd be trouble and I was right. Now her pride won't let her turn tail and run. Mark is furious and I guess she had it coming."

"Mark gave her hell? Does that mean something's been going on between them?"

"Guess so. Got any idea where I might find a replacement?"

"Mark will be hard to replace," he said, sounding very serious. "Have to think about that one," he paused and scratched his head. With a twinkle in his eyes, he leaned over and whispered, "I've got it! Bob might be just right. A great diver, and he's available," he answered without realizing the serious intent of her question.

"You can do better than that, Doc. You don't get a girl nearly killed, crippled and blinded, and then leave her hanging too. You need some coaching on those lines, pal." She was mad.

"Sheri, I was only..."

"It doesn't matter. I guess that really wasn't fair of me. Just forget it, OK?" She quickly left the table and dumped her dishes in the sink on the way out the door.

Doc sat shaking his head, angry at himself for missing the opportunity to give her the affirmation she sought.

"What's her problem?" one of the other girls asked.

"The guy she's in love with's a jerk," Doc answered and left the table.

"Aren't they all?" the worldly coed said to the empty chair.

The call he was expecting from Inspector Cord came

exactly on time. Ian wanted to dive the yacht and the freighter this morning. Could Doc leave the Dockyard earlier than planned? Doc was ready, but told Ian that he didn't think Sheri wanted to go. He headed to Somerset to meet the police boat.

Sheri sat waiting impatiently for the briefing on the new project to begin. She was angry with herself for pushing Doc, and angry with him for not giving the answer she wanted. She was angry with Karen for getting involved with Dr. Richardson, and angry with Mark for getting involved with Karen. Was this the trip she had looked forward to all last year? It seemed to be deteriorating like a delicate tropical fish losing its bright colors when taken from the water.

Dr. Richardson was his usual self in starched khaki. He was full of energy and in high spirits on this auspicious Monday. That was reason enough for Sheri, in her foul mood, not to like him. Mark sat alone in the back and Karen was nowhere to be seen. Lisa gave Sheri a welcome-back hug and sat down beside her.

Dr. Richardson moved to center stage and the day's performance began. On the lab table in front of him were several old guns, an assortment of musket balls and flints, and two encrusted muskets of undetermined origin.

"We're certainly happy to have Sheri and Dr. Harrington safely back from their nefarious adventures of last week. I presume Dr. Harrington will be joining us later?" His question hung in the air unanswered. Richardson stared at Sheri, realized she wasn't paying attention, then continued, "As you were told last week, you are about to be entrusted with an opportunity for which most graduate archaeologists would mortgage their souls—the chance to open the tomb of a nearly undisturbed nineteenth century sailing vessel. Unlike the *Eagle* site, I believe you will find enough material on this vessel to keep you engaged for several summers.

"We know little at present about the history of the vessel. She might be a wonderful thesis opportunity if you go on to graduate work. Therefore, be extremely precise in both your data collecting and note taking. We're very enthusiastic to begin this project and I hope you appreciate the great faith we, the staff of the institute, are placing in your integrity and ability, which is a reflection of our affection and respect for Sheri, and the outstanding training she provided you prior to your arrival."

"He's full of it today," Sheri whispered to Lisa.

"He's like that just after getting laid. Poor Karen, she can't possibly imagine what she has gotten herself into."

"Is this the voice of experience I hear?" Sheri laughed softly.

"Unfortunately. It happened when we worked together on San Salvador Island on the Columbus project. I thought he was really something, but I was a lot younger then in more ways than one." Lisa shook her head sorrowfully.

"And so," Richardson droned on, "in preparation for your endeavors, it is necessary to introduce you to the history and development of the type of weaponry you may encounter on the vessel. As we look then at the history of arms development in the late eighteenth and early nineteenth centuries, one weapon clearly dominates the scene. That was the India pattern, or short land pattern, Brown Bess, which was the backbone of the British soldier from 1760 to 1830. The museum is fortunate to have these two fine examples. Like most flintlocks of the period, the Brown Bess was styled after the French guns manufactured at Charlieville. But they were designed in the British tradition, a bit heavier and with a larger bore. The Brown Bess is a .75 caliber weapon with a 59-inch barrel, generally weighing ten pounds.

"Now let's compare the Brown Bess to the competition. The Americans were dependent on imports, mostly from Belgium and France, until the opening of the Springfield armory. This fine example was one of the first made there," he said, holding up another flintlock. "This weapon is a .69 caliber and a little lighter at nine point six pounds and has a 60-inch barrel. Most of the flintlocks of the late seventeen hundreds were smooth bore and had limited accuracy. The troops on both sides relied on fire power volume rather than long-range accuracy.

"A British Marine would have had a Brown Bess with a blackened finish, the navy model, and was expected to load and fire four rounds per minute. The American Springfield had somewhat of an advantage in that it was easier to load because of the smaller caliber and the cartridge design. Now let's look at what two hundred years in salt water can do to one of these weapons, and then explore what we can do to restore it."

Sheri saw Mark making notes at a furious pace. Again her notebook page was blank. She wished she had gone on the dive with Doc. He could certainly do a better job learning his lines or at least pretend a bit...no, that wasn't any good either. One of the reasons she respected him was his refusal to do just that: no games, no surprises. Two hours till lunch. The lecture was boring and she wanted to leave. Where the hell was Karen?

Ian looked happy for the first time in days. As they sat on the bow and waited for Mike, Ian told Doc that two of the prisoners—the freighter's top divers—had become conversational. The topic was: Let's make a deal. According to the story, they had been ordered by Maldias to recover two inflatable boats from the freighter's roof. The boat hulls were full of cocaine, the purest and best, of course. The divers had survived the battle, but because they had come up empty-handed they felt they were between a rock and a hard place. With the cocaine unaccounted for, they were terrified that if Maldias had survived, he would hunt them down, believing they had betrayed him. And then there was the cartel.

If the cartel believed they had helped Maldias escape with the coke, the divers wouldn't be safe, even in the belly of the biggest whale in the briny deep. Unfortunately, the informants knew nothing of Paul, Debbie or Tom.

"So what are you going to do?" Doc asked.

"Look for those inflatables, find them a bigger whale... hell, I don't know," the inspector said. "But this is what I do know. If they are telling the truth, someone is going to come looking for that coke. And when they do, we'll get another chance to put an end to this bloody game. And that makes me happy."

Lt. Berry parked his Jeep and came down the dock on

the double. He had a message in one hand and a gear bag on his shoulder.

"We may have something on the *Mermaid!*" he began excitedly. "The father of one of Janet Singleton's students, a fisherman, called her last night and told her about a small diesel slick just beyond the north rim of the reef. She called me trying to find you, Doc. We sent a chopper out at first light and he verified. Here are the GPS coordinates," he said, handing the paper to Doc.

"Get your gear aboard, mate, and let's go." Ian took the note from Doc and led the way to the wheelhouse. "It's about time we got a break."

The police launch headed for Chub Cut to go outside the reef and then north. Passing through the Cut, they sighted a large vessel with a bright orange hull and a crane on the stern.

"Who is she?" Doc asked.

"A research vessel from the States," Ian answered. "She has an international team on board, doing work on deep ocean current nutrients and sixgill sharks—bunch of lads from the Smithsonian or your National Geographic. Met them a couple years ago when they lost a Russian diver. Nice chaps. The crane handles their deep sub. Quite a toy, that thing is. Love to go down in it someday. Doubt that will ever happen though."

"You never know, Ian. Anything is possible."

The wind had picked up, creating a light chop, but the launch was heavy and cut through it well. In less than an hour, they were circling on location looking for the oil slick. The chop made it impossible to locate the exact source of the diesel fuel, although by now there was a good bit of it. It was being carried to the open sea to join the thousands of gallons of oil and fuel lost daily in the world's oceans.

"Hate to see that, but at least it's not going towards the reefs," Mike said.

"Not to ours, but to someone else's. Count on it," Ian corrected.

The sergeant manning the helm reported a target on the Fathometer and a buoy was thrown. After two passes, they confirmed the target and dropped anchor. The depth was ninety-two feet.

"You doing alright, Doc? Can I help?" Mike asked when he saw Doc just sitting and staring at his tank. Then Mike realized what could be waiting for them on the bottom. He sat down beside Doc and said, "You don't have to do this. We can check it out first. You can wait till the second dive." Mike looked at Ian for support. Ian was silent—it was up to Doc.

"Thanks, but it's OK. I'm sure she's not down there. But if she is, it's time to bring her home. Could you hand me the scooter when I'm in?" he said and picked up the tank. There was a determined set to his jaw. He was doing what had to be done, just as he had always done, and he wasn't going to back away now.

They hit the water in quick succession and were soon descending the anchor line. Thirty feet down, they could see the *Mermaid* glistening white against the sand bottom. She was resting upright on her keel and port chine. As they swam closer they could see no apparent damage.

Doc focused on the wreck. He refused to admit that Debbie might be aboard. When they got close enough to see the deck he breathed easier—there were no bodies anywhere in sight, so far.

The boat had been lucky considering the storm, Doc thought. Any closer to the reef and she'd have been toothpicks. The tanks, magnetometer, cables and dive bags were piled on the deck. The engine compartment hatches were open and the cabin door window was broken.

They dropped to the stern, and Ian signaled to Mike and Doc to wait. He took several deep breaths and then opened the cabin door, expecting the worst. He looked carefully in the main salon, but there were no bodies, not even a sign of a struggle. He dropped to his knees and looked again. In the beam of his dive light, he saw a computer disk on the deck beneath the galley table. He put it in his buoyancy compensator pocket and then swam to the forward berth. His stomach tightened when he saw the pile of blankets on the berth.

Mike waited patiently by the cabin door for Ian while Doc searched the dive bags on deck. Finding Debbie's bag, he opened it and pulled out an Ikelite dive light. The beam still shone brightly. He let all the air out of his BC and lowered himself into the open engine compartment between the two 671 Detroit diesels. He found the fuel leak fairly quickly and crawled out of the bilge and back to Debbie's gear bag. In her spares kit were long plastic electrical tie wraps, the kind Doc had found useful on the freighter. He stuck a half-dozen up his sleeve and swam back to the bilge. He couldn't reach the leaking fuel line with his tank on, so he slipped it off and then wedged himself in between the deck and the generator. Now he could reach the line and install the make-shift clamps. The leak stopped and he retrieved the tank.

He scanned the rest of the bilge and quickly discovered why the *Mermaid* had gone to the bottom. Her four-inch exhaust hoses and raw water induction lines had been cut. Easy enough to fix, he thought and checked his watch. They were eighteen minutes into the dive—time to head up.

As Ian approached the bunk, his instincts told him a body down this long would now be bloated and floating, not snuggled under blankets like a recalcitrant teenager on a Monday morning, but still....He raised the blanket and exhaled a sigh of relief—just pillows....He sorted through the pile and hit pay dirt beneath them—Debbie's laptop computer. Doc and Mike were waiting when he came out of the cabin with the computer. Doc gave a thumbs up, nodded approvingly and gave the signal for them to ascend.

Mike had rigged an ascent line with the lift bag and line Doc found in Tom's bag. They ascended slowly and after a safety stop at fifteen feet, climbed aboard the launch.

At Doc's suggestion, the computer and disk were put in a bucket of fresh water.

"I'm sure they were taken off the boat before she went down," Ian began, "and whatever clothing they had was taken with them. That's a good sign. Also, the computer was hidden under the pillows in the bow berth as if Debbie had heard or seen something and was trying to protect it."

"It has a hard drive," Doc said. "They're pretty well sealed in an aluminum housing. If we can save it, we might get a look at those maps they were working on and find out what this was really all about. I'd sure like to give it a try.

"Also, we should raise the *Mermaid*. She's still in good shape and Janet could at least sell her. Don't think they had much insurance. Do you have pumps and any of those lift bags left from the freighter?"

"Of course. I'll get on the radio. The stuff will be here by the time our surface interval is over. I'll ask them to bring lunch as well."

When Ian came back from the radio, Doc was working on a drawing of the *Mermaid* and explaining his plan to Mike. "The trick is to keep the tops of the lift bags just at her waterline so that they make a secure cradle for her and get her deck rails up good and high. The only hard part will be working lines under her hull and attaching the lift bags. We'll weave a makeshift net with the lines, tie in the bags, fill them and up she goes. Plug the through-hulls with rags, toss in the pumps and tow her home to the boatyard."

"Would that be the boatyard filling in the bullet holes in the Whaler you borrowed, Doctor?" Ian asked, staring at the deck.

"The same, Inspector. The one I'll be taking out a second mortgage to pay for. Thank you for reminding me."

"No problem, mate. Lieutenant Berry, never, never loan this man your boat. Terrible things happen to his boats. Things insurance companies don't like at all."

"Yes, Inspector. I've heard rumors to that effect."

Doc said something under his breath, smiled at them both and escaped into the cabin for coffee and a respite from the abuse. There sat Debbie's laptop in a trash can full of water. For several minutes, he sat transfixed by it and then a tear came to the corner of his eye. He folded his hands and closed his eyes.

Lt. Berry had started in for coffee but saw Doc through the cabin door window and decided to leave him to his thoughts. He rejoined the inspector. "What do you think the chances are of finding them?"

"Pretty slim, I'm afraid. I expected to find bodies on the boat or signs of a fight—bullet holes, shell casings, explosion, fire, something—but there was nothing. If Maldias had a hand in it, he would have taken Debbie and killed the Morrison lad and Paul on the spot. I know they were on some special project with Roberts, something to do with the NASA computers, but nothing this serious. I hope we can get something out of her computer."

"Yeah, this sure is hard on Doc. He was really something to take on Maldias's whole crew, and he almost got them all."

"Almost seldom counts," Doc said from behind Mike at the cabin door.

"Right on, mate," Ian said. "But if there is any truth to that cocaine story, they'll be back. And next time we'll get them. No doubt about it."

Esteban Maldias knew he was on his own. It would be far too dangerous to go to anyone in his small Bermuda network for help. So after drifting to the beach on the bale, he set about finding a hiding place. Once he had a base and a phone, he could get all the help he needed from the States, but for now he had best become a tourist, or risk becoming a permanent resident of the Dockyard prison.

His plan worked easily. He walked to the highway, waved down a cab and offered the driver five hundred dollars to do his shopping and find him a quiet little hotel—one where the staff knew enough to mind its own business. He carried gold credit cards in three different names and plenty of cash, so there was no problem. He had to keep a low profile and come up with a plan. The cocaine was the key. If he could find it before the cartel found him, he still had a chance.

Ian led the group, reinforced by two of his divers, down the buoy line. In short order the makeshift net was rigged under the *Mermaid*, the lift bags attached, and she was on her way to the surface. The expanding air poured from the open bottoms of the bags like a jet stream, and the boat arrived at the surface in a spectacular explosion of bubbles.

As the divers followed the *Mermaid* up, something caught Doc's eye several yards from the wreck. He signaled to Lt. Berry and pointed the nose of the scooter back down. Mike would wait. Doc stayed as high as he could and still keep the bottom in sight. As he distinguished the shape of a body lying on the bottom, he closed his eyes for a quick "Please God, don't let it be...." Small fish and crabs were at work on the

remains. It wore a black military-style wet suit, and a double
-hose mouthpiece floated above the mouth. The mask was
smashed into the face. Doc descended and examined it more
closely, then grabbed the harness and rolled the body over.
On its back was a Westinghouse MK XVII closed circuit
recirculator—standard issue for U.S. Navy SEALs and Underwater Demolition Teams.

He inflated the black horse-collar buoyancy compensator and sent the body to the surface. Oh shit, he thought.
what am I up against now? There was no civilian market for
these non-magnetic, all plastic units. What could Paul and
Debbie have stumbled into? No wonder Sandy was having a
hard time getting information. Doc's paranoia of all things
government swept over him like a black cloud and he swore
again. He watched the body accelerate towards the surface
and then began his own much slower ascent.

Lt. Berry was waiting on the anchor line at fifteen feet.
Doc checked the old Rolex and his dive tables and did an
eight-minute stop. When they broke the surface at the stern
of the police launch, they could hardly hear each other over
the roar of the water pumps emptying out the *Mermaid*. She
had been pulled alongside the starboard rail, resting comfortably in the cradle of lift bags. Her through-hull fittings
were stuffed with rags and soon she would be floating high
and dry. She was a welcome sight to Doc, a welcome old friend
in a lonely, confusing and dangerous world.

Doc told Ian about the body and Ian sent a boat to pick
it up. In a short while, it was wrapped in a tarp on the back
deck of the smaller launch.

"If it's alright with you," Doc asked Ian, "I want to take
that Westinghouse rig and try to trace it. As far as I know,
those anti-magnetic units were never released to civilians.
They were designed to get close to mines without setting them
off and the cost for scientific work would be prohibitive."

"I can have a chopper come and fly us in."

"No, thanks. I want to ride in with the *Mermaid*. See you
tonight. You might call Janet and ask if she wants to meet us
at the Dockyard."

It was dusk when they arrived. Janet and Margaret were
waiting at the dock. The return of the *Mermaid* was a joyful

event. The Bermuda Gazette ran the story with photos of the
crowd of Dockyard regulars welcoming her home. Janet announced the boat would be repaired and put back in charter
service, and a few of the other Dockyard store owners passed
a hat to begin the repair fund.

Esteban Maldias watched it all on the evening news in
his cozy little suite in St. George's. He saw the large man on
the deck of the *Mermaid* and recognized Doc immediately.
"Amigo, how good to see you again. We have a little unfinished business, you and me, no?" With that, Maldias smiled,
picked up the phone and placed a call to New York.

When she had finished filling tanks in the institute's dive
locker for the next day's dive, Sheri went looking for Doc.
She found him working in the dive shop. The long workbench was covered with electronics in various states of disas-
sembly, and the floor was cluttered with plastic pails full of
water. In one was Debbie's laptop computer. Beside the disconnected telephone were two yellow pads with pages of
barely legible notes. Through the glass in the door, she could
see Doc sitting on the floor removing the case from the MK
XVII mixed gas recirculator. He got up and let her in, and
with no more than a "Hi," pointed her to a chair and returned to the floor. At first she sat in silence and watched,
but was soon on the floor beside Doc. Without being asked,
he started teaching her about the rig.

"The originals were designed to be good for six hours at
a thousand feet, completely self-contained. They were developed in the late sixties to be used by NASA as life support for
the astronauts. It's simple technology really. This large do-
nut is the breathing canister with the scrubbing agent soda-
sorb, or baralyme. It removes the carbon dioxide. In the
center are these three BioMarine sensors—little fuel cells that
burn oxygen and make electricity. The more oxygen, the
more electricity, and so you have a very accurate way of monitoring the gas percentages in the system. The sensors aver-
age their readings and use the electricity to activate these

solenoids, adding oxygen or a dilutent, in this case helium, as required to maintain the partial pressures needed for the depth of the dive. This housing contains the micro-processor that controls the partial pressures according to changes in depth." He stopped and took her hand. "I'm really sorry about this morning, Sheri. You deserved better than that. Better than me. The timing is just a little tough and the people I care about most have not been surviving well lately."

"It was my fault. I was feeling pretty rough and I know you have much more to worry about than me. I'm sorry too, Doc. Can we just start over?"

"Sounds good. Want to learn all the secrets of closed circuit mixed gas? Swim for miles with no bubbles and disarm mines without getting blown to pieces?"

"What could it do in the pool at Georgia State?"

"Do you mean in the deep end with the doors locked?"

She moved closer and kissed him. She got up, locked the door, turned off the lights and pulled her tank top off. Soft light from the marina across the street filled the room. She returned to the floor and knelt beside Doc. "I love you. And I want whatever you can give. Just holding me will be enough. Please..."

Doc pulled her to him and stroked her hair. They were joined in a kiss when there was a loud knock on the door.

"Sorry, Doc, we need to talk," Ian called in. He had obviously seen them through the glass in the door.

"Damn it," Sheri said. "Where's my top?"

"They feel like they're both still here," Doc said with a low laugh.

"Not my boobs, asshole, my tank top. Don't turn on the light till we find it."

"It's on the counter by the door," Ian offered.

"Thanks, Inspector, it's nice to see you too."

"Certainly is my pleasure, miss."

She found the top, pulled it on and turned on the light. As she opened the door for the inspector, she did a formal curtsy and he returned the gesture with a deep bow.

Doc was still sitting on the floor laughing.

"Lose the grin, Doc. It isn't that funny," she said.

His laughter deepened as he pulled her to the floor beside him.

"I want to know," he asked her, "for future reference, when the usually pejorative noun, 'asshole' became a term of endearment?"

"Who said it ever had?"

"Well, if that's going to be all I ever get called, it had better be."

"We'll have to talk about that," she teased.

"Ian, have a seat. What brings you to our door at such an inopportune and totally awkward moment?"

"Obviously to protect this young lassie's innocence, and I can only hope I got here in time," he chuckled. "We may have a bit of important news," he continued in a more serious tone. "We got a fax back on the dental records of that boy you found—not military at all. He was a graduate student at Texas A&M."

"Any connection to Roberts?"

"Nothing yet. We'll know more tomorrow. How did you do?"

"Colonel Andrews is trying to trace the MK XVII; it will take a while. I decided not to send the computer to the States. The tech rep at their service center in New York thinks if we put the hard drive in a new machine, it just might work. The drive is in a tightly sealed aluminum case and if the gasket held, we might be able to retrieve all of Debbie's data. I ordered a new computer exactly the same as her old one. They'll ship it to a dealer in Hamilton by air tomorrow. He's sending some old-style, screw-together diskettes, so we might be able to read that disk as well, although Debbie probably backed it up on the hard drive." Then he added under his breath, "There goes my bass boat."

"What?"

"Nothing...not important."

"Will you be able to save any of Paul's electronics?"

"Let you know in a day or so. Looks like everything was off when the *Mermaid* went down, but these circuit boards don't like salt water. The boatyard will start on the engines tomorrow. She could be running in three or four days."

"Paul and Janet loved that boat. I'm glad we could bring her back for them," Ian said. "Let's dive again on Wednesday. I want to get a look at the yacht and the freighter. And put the bloody phone back on the hook so I don't have to drive across the island just to talk, although in this case, it was certainly worth the trip. Very nice getting to see you, miss. 'Night all."

Sheri threw a book at him as he ducked out the door.

"You might try the cabin on the *Mermaid*. The cushions are damp but at least there are curtains," he called back to them.

"Good night, Inspector. Don't trip on your nightstick," she called. "Come on, let's go to the hostel and get some sleep, Doc."

"Does that mean you have a headache?"

"You are my headache. No, it just means my storm of passion has been becalmed by the gentle wind of reason—at least for now."

"How poetic."

"And trite," she said. "Come on, let's go."

He locked the door behind them and put his arm around her. They walked by the *Mermaid* on their way to the hostel.

"She'd tell us if she could," he said wistfully. "That old boat has been a good friend, part of some great times."

"Some boats are just boats, but some have souls. I can tell she does. What graceful lines. And look at those teak decks and all that varnished mahogany. Somebody loved her a lot or that would have been covered with paint and forgotten—especially on a dive boat. She's beautiful."

"She is not the only one with great lines. I saw some pretty spectacular ones tonight."

"Thanks, Doc. It's nice to finally get your attention." She emphasized the "finally" with an elbow in the ribs.

"Come on! Let's go," she said as she began jogging up the hill.

Jason Richardson and Karen watched them from his chambers. She was posing nude in the window seat as Jason painted her by moonlight.

"Strange fellow that Dr. Harrington," he said. "Wonder what she sees in him?"

"Who cares? He's old."

"Tell me more about Mark. He's young."

"He's a wimp and a jerk. What else do you want to know?"

"Tell me about the two of you."

"You mean the two of us doing it, don't you?"

"Sure, what did you do?"

"Why don't you clean your brushes...let me get warm for a while and I might show you."

"What do you mean 'might'?" he laughed.

Later that night, Karen lay on the mauve satin sheets staring at the cracks in the old plaster ceiling while Jason slept. Her argument with Mark this morning had pushed her back into Richardson's ornate bed tonight. What right did Mark have to treat her the way he had? She was a free spirit, free to go where she wanted with whomever she wished. To hell with him! He was a puppy with nothing to offer. Jason could give her anything she wanted. The problem was, she didn't really like him. He used her like a commodity, like the cocaine. But he was her chance—her ticket. She would keep him happy whatever it took. In return she would have the life and the things she had always wanted. And what could Sheri possibly know, anyway? To hell with her too—to hell with all of them.

CHAPTER

17

As Sheri slid in beside Doc at the breakfast table, she said, "I wish you were coming with us, Doc. This dive is going to be something special—an almost virgin site loaded with weapons." She added in a whisper, "How can you pass up a shot at a virgin?"

"Probably wouldn't remember what to do," he answered.

"That had better not be your best shot or you're back in the doghouse. Try again."

"Right. How about 'Golly gee, honey, I'd give anything to go with you but I've got so much work at the office. My boss will kill me and I'll never get tenure if I don't get these papers graded.' Better?"

"Has possibilities. Keep working on it. What are you doing today?"

"Diving the freighter and the yacht. I want to know what sank that freighter and have a look at what's left of the yacht."

"There can't be much left after the explosion. I'll never forget that."

"Let you know tonight. Have fun today—sounds like a great wreck. Bring me back a musket ball or something."

"You know that's against the rules. Shame on you, Doc, asking me to steal valuable artifacts. Next you'll be trying to get in my shorts." She discreetly touched his hand under the table before sliding out from the picnic table bench and departed for the lab.

There were still containment barriers floating over the remains of the yacht as small amounts of diesel fuel and oil continued to ooze to the surface. The 40-foot police launch tied onto the buoy marking the freighter. Lt. Berry was stuck working on a pile of monthly reports, so the inspector and Doc would be diving without him.

"The cocaine," Ian said, "is supposed to be hidden inside two inflatable life boats. Let's do the deep part first. We'll look at the hull and then work our way back up to the wheelhouse."

"Good. I'll tie the extra tank on the buoy line in case we need it. This is Debbie's dive computer," Doc said as he handed it to the inspector. "It will give you a check on our bottom time and rate of ascent. Here is what the profile looks like from the tables. I've got it on the slates in case we get narked."

"Not you, mate."

"Bet on it. I haven't done anything this deep in years. Stay close...I may need someone to hold my hand."

"Sorry, you're not my type."

Doc did a back roll from the side of the launch and was quickly followed by Ian. They checked their equipment at the surface and one of the men on board handed down the scooter.

"Hang on to my tank, Ian. This scooter really saves air."

"You are getting soft, Doc."

"Not soft—old and smart. Come on."

Doc tied off the spare tank at fifteen feet. Ian grabbed his tank valve and the scooter pulled them down quickly. It was a bright day and the sunlight penetrated deeply into the water. They could see clearly over a hundred feet and had no trouble picking a landing spot on the roof of the wreck. They saw racks where the inflatables had been, but as they had been told, the racks were empty. They dropped below the deck and began to survey the hull. The freighter was a little over three hundred feet long, but with the scooter they covered the distance in no time. On the portside amidships they found two holes twenty feet apart just below the waterline. The holes were eight feet across and the metal was blown in, not out. The cause of the sinking had come from outside the hull, not a saboteur within. Doc steered the scooter towards the stern to survey the rest of the hull.

They were at one hundred fifty-five feet and Doc could feel it. The air was thick and heavy, and his head was buzzing. When they had completed the sweep around the stern, he pointed the scooter up towards the wheelhouse. Doc's head began to clear the moment they started up and he was fine by the time they set down on the wheelhouse roof. They quickly compared air pressure gauges and dropped to the catwalk outside the wheelhouse. The wreck was already attracting marine life. Several large grouper hovered around the wheelhouse, and in the distance Doc saw a large manta.

He remembered the bodies in Paul's tape and wondered what they would find inside. The body in the first stateroom was now face down on the deck, and the compartment was littered with the contents of drawers and the hanging locker. Ian lifted away the debris and rolled the body over. The gold watch, chains and coins in the video were gone. Ian scanned the compartment with an experienced eye and noticed a bullet embedded in the paneled wall. He extracted it with his dive knife and put it inside his wet suit sleeve.

The next cabin had also been ransacked. However, as Ian looked into the bunk frame, he saw a plastic bag half full of small flat leaves. He recognized them as coca leaves chewed by millions of South Americans. Ian put the bag in his buoyancy compensator pocket.

They checked their air and headed for the up line. Doc attached a small lift bag to the scooter and sent it up the line on a carabiner. They began slowly pulling themselves up the line. The dive computer tracked their ascent and flashed their first decompression stop.

Sheri looked in disbelief: their virgin site had been desecrated. There were large holes blown into the sand in a regular pattern over the site, and ship timbers were strewn everywhere. The remains of the ship had been devastated and even the coral near it was smashed and broken. Pieces of encrusted bottles and hardware were exposed in the broken coral. Dead soft corals were scattered over the site and the piles of ballast stone were displaced randomly. The glint of brass caught her eye and Sheri extracted a rifle butt plate from the sand. Beside it were several one-inch squares of stone which she recognized as rifle flints. She noted the location on her slate and in violation of all her training, put several in the pocket of her buoyancy compensator.

Lisa approached and Sheri showed her the butt plate and the flints, and then pointed to the plundered site. They were angry and disappointed as they swam back to the dive boat to tell Richardson and the others what they had seen.

Richardson went ballistic. He paced the deck and swore. When his tantrum eventually abated, he called them together at the stern.

"Here's the plan," he began. "Mark, get your video camera. I want good footage of Karen and me surveying the site. This has to be your best work because we are going for international television coverage. This is the work of commercial salvage divers, and this time we are going to put them out of business for good. Karen, honey, get out of that dive skin. Haven't you got a bikini? You are going to be on television so let's dedicate that beautiful body to science. What we need here is your deeply committed cleavage." The others laughed until they realized he wasn't kidding.

"Everyone else, listen closely. As soon as we are back aboard, Lisa and Sheri will get you started on a survey. I want as much material as we can get brought back to the lab. Don't worry about reconstruction or stratigraphy. Just get us a good representation of what's down there. Lisa, baby, make it happen. This could be the chance we needed. We may have lost a wreck, but the public relations potential here is unlimited. When this is over, we're going to own every site on the island and at least ten minutes of prime time. Let's go, people, it's show time."

"Lisa, baby?" She stood smoldering in his vapor trail. "That opportunistic, pompous, self-centered, lecherous, chauvinistic, cliche-spouting little shit. I didn't spend three years in grad school to be 'Lisa baby' to the likes of him. It's show time, my royal ass."

The twisted remains of the white steel yacht lay in two separate sections on the sea floor. The explosion had torn her completely in half and most of the midships section had simply vanished. Doc landed them on the stern and they began to explore the wreckage. Pieces of melted metal were everywhere. As with the freighter, the warp of the hull plate was concave, not convex, again suggesting the cause was external. But how? Who could have placed a charge of this magnitude on the hull of a moving vessel? There had to be another answer. The heat of the explosion had destroyed almost everything in the forward portion of the boat. They made another pass with the scooter and returned to the surface.

"Torpedoes? But how? From where?" Ian asked. They were on the fly bridge of the police launch with Ian at the helm. Doc stretched in the seat beside him and held a cup of steaming coffee.

"Haven't a clue," Doc answered, after blowing on the coffee to cool it. "But that's the only thing that makes sense. Start with the freighter. Someone put two fish in her side, boarded her, killed those two and let her sink without a whisper. Perhaps some of the crew escaped in the lifeboats—remember, the wheelhouse roof had no inflatables. I don't think this was an inside job unless they were working with a second vessel that had torpedoes."

"Bloody hell," Ian snorted. "We don't know anything more than when we started."

"Well, we do know someone got the gold jewelry from Maldias's brother, and none of Maldias's divers had the stuff."

"Right. Now who?"

"For a while I thought it was you," Doc said. "You were setting a trap for Maldias—an invitation to settle the score for your brother. How 'bout it?"

"I wish I could take credit, but we knew nothing about it until Paul came in with the tape. I swear...nothing."

"Then what's your relation to Colonel Sandy Andrews?"

Ian looked at him with surprise, nodded slowly and then

began, "When my brother, Brian, was killed I went to your D.E.A. for help to find Maldias. The colonel returned my call and said he was from a special agency task force and might be able to help. Last week he called to tell me Maldias had left Colombia and that they believed he was headed here. When you showed up, he called again to warn me about you...said you had the bad habit of not following orders and starting little wars. That true?"

"A vicious rumor totally unsupported by fact."

"Right. And I'm the next King of England. And what about you, how did you get involved?"

Doc stared out over the calm water, pulling the Atlanta Braves cap lower on his forehead. He folded his arms and answered slowly, "When I first got out of the Navy, I needed money for school. Sandy's outfit wanted someone to teach kitchen table explosives to Cuban exiles. So I went down to the Everglades and taught recreational use and manufacture of high explosives for a couple months. We were going to rescue Cuba from communism. Fair enough. Maybe this was one we could win. Then I was invited on some special ops in South America. I went once. And what I saw down there didn't hold with what we were being sold back home, so I decided I wanted no part of being a mercenary. I wasn't even sure what side we should have been on. Too much like Vietnam, you know. So I came back and worked in the oil fields, diving and designing explosive tools. Most of it was salvaging shut-down platforms and well heads. Worked some fires and when offshore work was slow, I took down bridges. I made enough in the summers to feed the family and go to school—no complaints."

"And now?"

"Find Debbie, buy a bass boat, write a book, go back to teaching in September—who knows? There is one thing though."

"Yes, what?"

"A ride on a submarine."

"Torpedoes and submarines, good thinking. But the *Enterprise*? She is for tourists," Ian said.

"So color me a tourist. She's the only sub I've seen on the island and we have to start somewhere."

"Good point. I'll ring them soon as we get back."

"I want to bring Sheri. OK?"

"No problem, mate. Tomorrow if possible."

As the launch headed towards Chub Cut, they again saw the bright orange research vessel on the horizon.

"Wonder what they are after out there?"

"A warm willin' lass and a tall cold glass, mate. Same as sailors everywhere. Out there wishin' they was here. When they get here they'll be wishin' they was there. My father was in the Merchant Marine. Most restless man I ever knew. Told me about Bermuda when I was a boy. Hoped I'd find him here one day. He may be back in Scotland looking for me. Who knows?"

"You have the soul of a poet, Ian."

"Aye, mate. It's in the Scottish blood. There were so few jobs at home that most of the men had to leave to support their families. What they took was a good education, a bad case of melancholy and wanderlust. It's a bad combination: means you're smart enough to know what you're leaving behind, and that leaving is the only way. So Scots go everywhere, and everywhere they go they're looking for what they left behind. 'Tis terrible sad; dreams of far off places full of happiness, which are really dreams of home. Only home the way you wish it was—peaceful times, love that doesn't hurt. I thought once it was like losing an arm or a leg and thinking, if I could just find it, I could put it back on and everything would be peaches. Good poetry, like your country songs. Good poetry, good ballads, but it's only dreams. That's why those South American lads are dead. Someone told them this was the easy way. 'Make this one trip and you're set for life.' You can bet no one told them the sad news: you can have as much as you want, but life—all of it—comes with a bloody payment book. The more you want, the higher the price. For most of us the payments are high. So high for just a little piece of the pie, it'll take all we'll ever hope to make and then some. Your Thoreau said it: 'lives of quiet desperation,' that's what's waiting for most. And we'd all like an easy way out, but in the end, mate, everyone pays the price. No one beats the bank."

Jason worked through the night on the script for his upcoming performance. Mark had indeed produced network-worthy footage. Now they would shoot commentary from the museum and show artifacts being conserved the right way in the lab. He would bury the salvors and rise from the ashes of their destruction a hero in the battle for historical conservation. Karen lay asleep on the satin sheets. The gold coin necklace he had given her tonight rested in the splendor of her "deeply committed cleavage". He chuckled at his own cleverness. She had played her part well, a useful and amusing toy.

On the desk before him lay catalogs of antique arms and duplicates of Naval records from both sides. He was onto a great story, one that would grab the interest and sympathy of a huge audience, and he was going to work all the angles. It was perfect.

Doc was stretched out on a couch in the lounge of the hostel with his arm over Sheri's shoulder as she sat on the floor. He had just finished massaging her neck and back while telling her about the day's discoveries.

"Torpedoes?" Sheri said. "You know that morning, just as I was jumping off the Navy boat, two trails—like bubbles or phosphorescence—went past me. It was like seeing dolphins swimming in the bow wake at night. You don't see the dolphins, just the jet streams they leave behind. That was just before the yacht blew up. Guess I'd forgotten it until now...I must have had other things on my mind...."

"You don't have any idea where they could have come from?"

"No, there were no other boats on the surface behind us—nothing."

"That may be the answer, Sheri—nothing on the surface. We're going to get a ride on that sub sooner than we thought. Can you get away for a few hours in the morning?"

"Sure. Lisa and Mark can cover for me. We'll be in the lab cleaning up the stuff we brought in today. That site is so sad, Doc. All that history gone. It was like discovering someone had robbed your parents' grave. Really, it was terrible.

That would have been a wonderful site for us to work...a lot of the hull was still intact. Now it's all torn to pieces."

"That's the wreck that started this whole thing. It's the one the NASA computer wouldn't acknowledge. Whoever the thief is, he must have known someone else had found the site, and he was in one hell of a hurry to take what he could and clear out."

"Sure, but we would have seen a boat out there working. It's less than a mile from the site of the *Eagle*. Wait a minute! What were we just talking about? What if the reason no one saw anything on the surface was that there was nothing on the surface to see? You're right. They must have been working out of a submarine."

"Of course," he agreed, "a lockout sub. And if they were really sophisticated, they'd have closed circuit recirculators so that there wouldn't even be bubbles on the surface. But what could they hope to find to justify the expense? All that for a treasure hunt? I doubt it—only governments spend money like that."

The crew of the *Enterprise* was waiting when Inspector Cord led his party aboard early the next morning. They were met by the Bermudian captain, a gold-braided, uniformed, middle-aged man named Johnston who welcomed them aboard and gave orders to get the boat underway. The sub would be towed to the dive site to save time and battery power. The tow boat—once an overpowered drug runner purchased at a government sale—snorted to life, carefully pulled the slack from the hawser and eased the sub away from the dock. An attractive attendant seated them, and after offering coffee and tea, began her briefing.

"The *Enterprise* is sixty-five feet long and a bit over twelve feet in diameter. There are two hatches, one on the forward deck and one in the sail. She operates on power stored in two hundred seventy-six batteries carried in a keel compartment and their weight gives the boat stability. There are two-inch thick, machined acrylic hemispheres in the bow and stern, and five-inch thick view ports line the sides. Air conditioners both cool our air and filter out carbon dioxide through the Dregger scrubbers. And an analog computer system monitors and maintains proper oxygen levels. The rated crush depth of the hull," she continued, "is eight hundred fifty feet, but in emergencies she could go deeper.

"Thrust and maneuverability are accomplished by ten thrusters operated by a single joystick. Ballast is controlled in the normal manner: tanks that are either flooded with water or blown dry with compressed air. The control console is much like that of a large aircraft and certainly as sophisticated. It is mostly digital/LED with green and red lights on all critical valve functions. There are several radios and a PA system for use by the tour narrator."

Captain Johnston had remained in the sail, piloting the sub with a remote joystick. Soon they were away from the pier and heading north across the flats towards the wreck site. The crew watched silently as Doc, Ian and Mike talked among themselves quietly.

The sub was spotless and extremely comfortable, but that was not what interested Doc. "Look at this flange, Mike. It would be the perfect place to add a bulkhead with a pressure bulkhead and a hatch. Once the bulkhead is in place, you have two separate pressure locks and you convert the stern compartment to a diver lock out. Now you'd have a self-contained, portable saturation diving system. All you'd need would be a generator to recharge the batteries. Use a ballast tank or two to carry a couple thousand gallons of diesel and you could go anywhere and stay for as long as you wanted. And," Doc continued, "if you added closed circuit diving equipment, there wouldn't even be bubbles to let anyone know you were down. Brilliant."

"You're right," Mike said and Ian nodded, "but this boat is in use everyday. They couldn't convert her back and forth every night."

"True. I don't think it's this sub we're after, but let's start asking questions and see if they can help us."

Jason was pleased with himself. He had called the Bermuda Sub-Aqua Club president, told the story of the pilfered site and asked for their immediate help. She responded by pulling together another dive team on Dave Younger's boat. They would work to save the remaining artifacts while the Georgia State students worked in the lab. If he was to be successful, Jason needed the political strength of the club plus enough artifacts to stir up outrage at what had been lost.

By lunchtime the next day, the cleaning tables in the back of the lab were covered with masses of oxide and clumps of encrustation recovered from the site. Some were marked for X-ray and would be wrapped in plastic and taken to the local hospital. Old bathtubs were used for wet storage and primary treatment. When the divers returned in late afternoon from their second trip, the tubs were piled high with artifacts.

It was not the slow and precise pace at which Lisa preferred to work. Already, enough material had been collected to keep several conservationists busy for weeks, even months. She had counted on Sheri and Mark, but both jumped ship in her hour of need—Sheri to the sub and Mark to a video production lab near the dive shop.

In spite of her efforts to catalog the materials and record the locations on the master site plot, she was certain most of the data she was getting was haphazard at best. She put Bob in charge and marched up the back stairs to Jason's office. She blew through the double doors like a tropical storm and found Jason and Karen working at a large table stacked high with historical references on the War of 1812. Karen was wearing tight shorts and a very open blouse. Around her neck was a heavy gold chain and a gold doubloon set in an elaborate bezel. Lisa knew the coin was worth at least ten thousand dollars.

She stared at it in disbelief and for a moment, forgot why she had come.

"Isn't it fabulous?" Karen asked, holding the coin for Lisa to see. "Jason gave it to me, but he said I can't wear it in public yet, not until we get the insurance papers and that could take a while. But I just love it."

"It's beautiful, congratulations." She was glaring at Jason as she spoke, wondering where he had gotten the coin. He avoided her stare by continuing to write.

"What do you want, Lisa? I'm busy."

"I want you in the lab. There is too much going on, too many pieces coming in. No one knows what they are doing, and Mark and Sheri are gone. If you want to ever be able to reconstruct the data, you need to be in the lab."

"I don't think that is the most important thing right now. Just concentrate on getting the best pieces in shape for X-ray so we'll know which casks to open. Store the rest for later. All I need now are the very best pieces for the network camera crew—nothing special. Museum grade will do."

"Museum grade? Nothing special? Have you lost your mind? It's a zoo down there and you want museum-grade work in two days?"

"Lisa, honey, you can do it. You're the best, that's why you're here and not grubbing on a dig in the Outback or South Africa. But if you can't do this for me..."

"What you are asking has nothing to do with archaeology or conservation, does it?"

"Not this time. This is much more important. This is the best chance we'll ever have to tell our side of the story, so we're stooping to show business to do it. So what? Be a realist, Lisa. Think of what's at stake. If need be, we have other pieces we can use. One Brown Bess looks just like another...a musket ball is a musket ball. This is going to work and you can do it. I'll come down after a bit, but you don't need me to..."

"You are certainly right about that. Put some clothes on, Karen. He's demented enough already. Don't bother coming down from your castle, Doctor...the bloody serfs will do just fine." She turned on her heel and blew back through the double doors.

"What a witch."

"No, not always. She's just jealous."

"Of me? That's nice. I like that."

"No, love, of me. Find me that copy of <u>The Man Who Burned the White House</u>, will you please? I want to check this reference on Admiral Cockburn."

The *Enterprise* was twenty minutes into the dive over the

freighter and Maldias's yacht. "Do you know what Maldias was wearing when he went over the side, Doc?" Ian asked.

"Yes. One of those fancy short-sleeved shirts with black embroidery and black slacks. Also a black leather vest and a shoulder holster. Oh, and that ten-pound, fancy gold Rolex with diamonds in the bezel."

"Like the one on the body in Tom's tape?"

"Yes, just like that."

"Is that what we are doing here, looking for bodies?" Captain Johnston asked.

"'Fraid so, Captain. We need to know how many of the bad guys got away, and at this depth we couldn't stay down long enough to do much in scuba," Mike answered.

"This sub is really something, Captain," Doc said. "Are there many more like her?"

"Now there are only two: this one and the one in Grand Cayman. But three were built. The third was in St. Thomas, but she disappeared mysteriously two years ago—stolen from her moorings. The story was that one of her crew took her out to give his girl a ride and went too deep. It's amazing that she's never been found. She was the first of the 65-footers...a terrible loss."

Bull, Doc thought. That boat is on this island working these wrecks and Lord knows what else. He exchanged glances with Ian and Mike. Pay dirt! Now all we have to do is find her.

The sub returned to the Dockyard in time for Doc to go into Hamilton and pick up the new laptop computer. When the clerk brought the box, Doc looked at the computer, then at the bill and remorsefully handed over his credit card.

Back in the dive shop, he placed it on the workbench and reached for a screw driver. Sheri was sitting in the corner reading <u>The Story of Bermuda and Her People</u> by Zuill, one of the books recommended by Lisa for general historical background.

As Doc was fumbling to get the tiny screws in place to install the hard disk from Debbie's computer, Sheri jumped to her feet in excitement. He dropped a screw and turned with a swear. The work was hard enough without distractions: his hands were large and thick, and his eyes were not good for work this close.

She tactfully ignored him. "Listen to this, listen to this: 'During World War II a captured German U-boat, the 505, was brought to Bermuda and used to train British and American submarine commanders in warfare games. They kept the existence of the U-boat a secret until the end of the war.' How could they have kept it a secret without a secret base to operate from? We have to find that base."

"Let me see."

"Look, there on page 173."

"Yes, that's the sub on display in Chicago. I'd forgotten that story. Get on the phone and call Ian. You found it, you should be the one to tell him. Call Mike Berry too. Let them get started asking questions. This could be really important," Doc said as he reached out and pulled her close.

"Doc, can I ask you something...something pretty personal?"

"Sure."

"Are you alright? Physically, I mean. You didn't get wounded in that helicopter crash..." She ran her finger down the thin scar on the side of his neck. "Do you know what I mean? Like that guy, Jake, in Hemingway's story?"

"What makes you think...? Oh, because we haven't..., I see. No, as far as I know I'm fine. After Nancy died, it was different. I...well it's hard to talk about it—guess I just lost interest."

"But it's not a physical thing?" she asked again.

"No, I don't think so."

"I'm so glad," she said and hugged him tighter.

He watched her for a moment, bewildered, trying to guess what was going through her mind, gave up and returned to the computer. When he had completed installing the hard drive in the new machine, he called over to Sheri.

"Here we go. Let's start with this floppy disk." He tried to load Debbie's word processing program, but was blocked by a security code. He thought for a moment then typed "Buttons," the name of Debbie's first puppy. The directory appeared on the screen. There was only one file, labeled "Dad." He pulled it up and began reading.

The letter described her growing relationship with Tom

Morrison, their diving with Paul looking for the new sites, and finally, the meeting with NASA station commander Bill Roberts, and his order that they keep the information confidential. The last paragraph gave the details of the cottage she had found for him and her desire for them to be together.

"It was Roberts. He led them right into it," Sheri said.

"Right, Sheri. He sure did. But what could he have been protecting that is worth all this? We still don't have all the pieces, that's for sure. Cross your fingers and let's see if anything survived on the hard drive."

He logged onto the internal hard drive and scrolled through the directory. There were several files labeled with numbers, and the extension "map". She had used the same security code, and in a minute Doc and Sheri were staring at columns of numbers with other codes they did not understand.

"All I know is that these are GPS coordinates. We're going to need help with the rest. And I think it's time to pay another visit to Mrs. Roberts. I'm sure she knew exactly what her husband was up to."

He paused a moment then added, "I hate to go to NASA or the Navy with this, but if the government is involved, this may be the way to smoke out some answers. I'm going to copy the files from this drive and if anything happens, you find someone to give them to. I don't know who, just someone."

It was well past midnight when they walked arm in arm up the hill to the hostel.

"I need to be here tomorrow. Lisa is having a fit with Richardson and all the stuff they brought in. He's serious about the television thing and has called a network press conference for Friday. Lisa says it's the most unprofessional thing she has ever seen and thinks he is off the deep end. She mentioned cocaine."

"Too bad. It will own him and he's the type—manic, compulsive, aggressive. The perfect user. What about Karen? Has she got enough sense to stay clear of the drugs?"

"I doubt it. She's never had much restraint. Anything for a good time—no limits, no boundaries."

"The person who stands for nothing will fall for anything."

"Sounds like a very wise Chinese proverb—or a good country song."

"Close enough, but I think it was Zig Ziggler."

"It's such a beautiful night," Sheri said wistfully. "Could we sit out on the ramparts awhile? I want to soak in the stars and watch the night sea before I go to sleep." She leaned on him and looked up with large, dreamy eyes.

"Well, it's past my bedtime."

"Come on, Doc, you aren't that old. Come on."

They walked the few yards to the rampart overlooking Daniel's Head and the calm western sea. In the far distance, they could see the lights of the research vessel and smaller fishing boats.

"Did you like being at sea for long stretches?" Sheri asked.

"Until I had a family...even after, I guess. Life is simple and uncomplicated out there. Things are what they appear and you can really fix most of the things that break. It's a good life."

They heard laughter from the water twenty yards below. In the moonlight they could see a naked couple splashing and playing in the clear shallow water.

"Can you tell who it is?"

"That's Karen's laugh," Sheri answered. "She's with Dr. Richardson. Oh look, they're having a good time now. The real fun starts when the laughing is over."

"Like in the deep end of State's pool?" he teased. "Come on, let them have some privacy. Let's go."

"No way. I want to watch. You need to see this too...maybe it will jog your memory."

"You can't see anything from up here. And my memory doesn't need jogging, thank you."

"Not from there you can't. Come over here."

She pulled him to the wall, but it was not the couple in the shallow water that got his attention.

"Sneri, do you have binoculars in the hostel?" he whispered.

"Well, listen to you. Binoculars are a bit much, Doc. What do you want to do, count the pimples on her butt..."

"Do you have binoculars? Get them now. Run! Now!" His commanding tone left no room for debate or delay. She ran across the courtyard and returned out of breath.

"This better be good, Doc."

He took the binoculars and quickly scanned to the north of Daniel's Head and a third of the way to the horizon.

"There it is. Look." He guided her until she found the source of his excitement.

"Doc, it's the same sub we were on this morning—the *Enterprise*. So what?"

"No. The *Enterprise* is in her slip across from the Clock Tower Warehouse. That's a real live ghost. That's the sub that disappeared in St. Thomas, and it came back to life just in time to save you from Maldias's yacht. Take a good look. I think we're going to be seeing her again real soon."

The sub headed through the cut into deeper water and submerged. As Doc turned to go, Sheri asked for the binoculars.

"Damn, wouldn't you know it!"

"What?" he asked.

"No pimples, not one."

They walked back to the hostel holding hands, and sat quietly at the picnic table looking at the night sky. "I have a proposition for you," Doc said after a while.

"Well, it's about time."

"You have to humor me with this, but it's really important. Do you remember the riddle of the sphinx: what creature walks on four legs, then two legs, then three?"

"Yes. The one that Oedipus answered correctly?"

"Very good. OK, I have a riddle for you and if you can come up with an answer that matches mine, you can choose the prize—within reason, of course. Want to play?"

"Let me see if I understand what you're almost saying. If I can figure out your riddle, I can have you, presuming that's what I'd choose, is that it? This is dumb, Doc, and not very romantic. I'm not so sure you qualify as the prize behind door number three."

"Then choose something else. It doesn't have to be that. I said you'll have to humor me. Come on, this will be fun," Doc insisted.

"OK, what's your riddle?"

"We just saw Dr. Richardson and Karen playing in the

surf. When you got here you were in a relationship with Mark, and he had a relationship with Karen, we think. And she'd been in a relationship with Bob, who is now spending a lot of time alone in the shower—cold, we presume. Now I want you to give this a lot of thought before you answer; the riddle is: what does sex mean?"

"What? There's no answer to that question...."

"Careful. If it has no meaning, it has no value; if it has no value, why do we spend so much time worrying about it?"

"You're serious about this, aren't you?"

"Yes, very."

"OK, if I play, how do I know that you'll play fair? That once I answer you won't change the answer or something?"

"No chance. I'll write my answer and lock it somewhere safe. When you are ready, we'll compare."

"Do I get more than one chance?"

"As many as you want."

"Before I agree to play," Sheri said, "you have to answer a question for me."

"If I can."

"Why? Why is it important to you to play this game?"

"It's a thinking game," Doc answered. "Thinking is a rare and valuable commodity. This will be a good way to get to know each other a little better, that's all. That OK?"

"I guess. OK, I'll think about it for a while. Let's get some sleep."

The next morning, Doc met Inspector Cord in Hamilton and they drove to the Naval Station to see Petra Roberts. "We've had her under surveillance," the inspector informed Doc. "No contact from her husband as far as we can tell. What have you found out?"

"I've got a pretty good idea now what happened to Debbie and Paul," Doc said. "If I'm right, Roberts set the kids up. I'm certain she knows more than she's telling us."

"Is this really necessary?" Mrs. Roberts began. She stood defiantly blocking her front door and demanded, "Couldn't you have asked your questions on the phone?"

"Yes, I suppose, but I wanted you to hear what I have to

say firsthand," Doc answered bluntly. "There are people's lives at stake and you can help them. That makes it worth the trip. May we come in, please?"

She hesitated, then reluctantly stepped aside and let them in. When they were seated in the spacious living room, Doc began, "Mrs. Roberts, your husband was responsible for the disappearance of my daughter and her friends. We know when, and we have a pretty good idea how. What I want to know is why. What have you heard from him?"

"Dr. Holiday, as far as I know my husband is dead. I have not heard anything since the morning he left and that was the note you brought me."

"Mrs. Roberts, what did your husband know about submarines?"

"How should I know..."

The phone rang and she excused herself to answer it. Doc immediately got up and began to examine the room. He could hear her talking in the kitchen. She watched him through the doorway as he looked over a collection of photographs on her baby grand.

When she realized that he might be listening, she began speaking in German. She smiled and turned her back on Doc, knowing she had locked him out of her private life. It was an arrogant smile.

Doc was holding a photograph from the piano when she returned to the room. "Mrs. Roberts, is this you with your father and sister?"

"Yes. Why do you ask?"

"Is your father still alive, Mrs. Roberts?"

"Yes, but what difference..."

"Where is he now, Mrs. Roberts?"

"That is none of your..."

"Answer his questions, Mrs. Roberts," Ian interrupted. "I hate to see you spend the night in jail."

"Now see here, you can't..."

"All I want is your father's name, Mrs. Roberts. Just his name, then we'll leave you alone. But if you don't give it to me, Ian will get a warrant, put you in jail and then we'll tear this beautiful home to pieces until I find what I'm looking for."

"You wouldn't..." She clenched her jaw to keep it from trembling.

Doc took two steps towards her. His eyes narrowed with anger. He towered over her, wondering if she could possibly be as stubborn as he. "I want his name, Mrs. Roberts, and I want it right now."

She continued to glare into his eyes, but when she looked away, he knew he'd won.

"It's Dr. Hans Behrmann," she said disdainfully and glared at the floor.

"Thank you, and where is Dr. Behrmann now?"

"He is in Germany. I haven't seen him in years. He has nothing to do with your daughter or any of this. He is a scientist and rarely travels."

"That's very interesting. That's enough for now, but we'll be back. When you hear from your husband, you'll remember to let Inspector Cord know, won't you?"

As soon as they were outside, Ian grabbed Doc by the arm and chided, "You were awfully hard on her, Doc. Now before I lose my badge, I want to know what the bloody hell that was about."

"Dr. Hans Behrmann was a U-boat commander and is Jason Richardson's grandfather. I recognized him from the photos Richardson had. Now, what if he stole that sub in St. Thomas and converted her? And what if it's here now, diving on those wrecks? What if Jason Richardson is in this up to his scrawny neck?"

"Where to now?" Ian asked as they walked to the car.

"Let's see if we can find anything about Captain Hans Behrmann at the Hamilton Library, then I'll take the ferry back to the Dockyard. I promised Sheri I would be back for the press conference this afternoon."

It didn't take long to find what Doc was looking for. Fortunately, they had several reference works on the history and construction of German subs. There were several mentions of Hans Behrmann: first as a young engineer and chemist, then as a highly decorated U-boat commander, and finally as the recipient of a commendation for leading a research team which developed a hydrogen peroxide-based fuel for the high command's new turbine engines.

"He was a busy lad, and apparently a brilliant one," Ian remarked. "I'll get our men to run a check on him. He certainly has all the qualifications to convert that stolen sub you saw last night. Do you think we should tell your Navy as well?"

"The recirculator that dead diver was wearing suggests we wouldn't be telling the Navy anything they don't already know. No, I think we'd better wait a bit longer before we tip our hand." His voice had the same distant quality Sheri had heard the day they lay wounded on the police launch. It was as if he were looking far away through time in the presence of old ghosts.

CHAPTER
18

Karen turned to Jason as he hung up the phone, "What language were you speaking?"

"German, love." Jason sounded distracted. He looked around his spacious office in a state of confusion and slumped into the leather chair behind the massive antique desk. He stared at the glass-front book cabinets and the beautiful oil paintings of graceful sailing vessels on emerald seas. On the corner of the desk was a bronze sculpture of a reclining mermaid. He grabbed the sculpture and nervously rubbed her upturned breasts with his thumb as if rubbing a lucky talisman. Then, he sat erect in the chair, smashed the bronze into the century-old finish of the desk and hurled the sculpture into the glass face of an antique cabinet. Karen screamed and looked at him in fear.

"Sit down and shut up. I'm alright. How much time before the television crews arrive?"

"An hour and a half."

"That's fine. And did you invite everyone to the party?"

"Yes, just like you said. The tables are set up. All we have to do is put out the junk in the refrigerators and we're ready. Is that still what you want?"

"Yes, yes, that's what I want. Now, I want you to go to the hostel and get the rest of your things. We are leaving on a little trip as soon as the party is over. Don't tell anyone, understand? You are going to love this trip. It will be a celebration party just for us."

"Will we be gone long?" she asked distrustfully.

"Only a week or so...don't worry. It will be great. Now go, and try to get your things without being seen. Hurry, Karen, and be happy. This is going to be a wonderful adventure."

She hesitated, but he smiled at her and waved her out of the room. She smiled back and as she turned to close the double doors, she saw him reach for the phone and say something in German.

Esteban Maldias sat on the bridge of his new 65-foot sportfisherman and smiled with satisfaction. The work he had ordered in the New Jersey boat yard—to add extra fuel tanks and to install sophisticated electronics—had been quickly accomplished.

The new boat performed majestically on the voyage to Bermuda, and the delivery crew never suspected they were bringing automatic weapons into the country. Now they were paid, the boat was his, and his own crew was beginning to arrive. So far he was confident he'd avoided the cartel's intelligence network, and there was no word of anyone, local or international, trying to sell large amounts of cocaine. That strengthened his belief that the rest of his drugs were still on the island. Now all he had to do was find them and he would—he had to.

When Inspector Cord got the phone message to call Immigration, he left the restaurant and went to the privacy of his car. The officer informed him that two suspicious men had just flown into Bermuda from New York. New York authorities believed one of them was a cousin of Maldias. Neither was carrying and they were not detained. Immigration further reported the arrival of a sleek, new 65-foot sportfisherman from New Jersey. The boat's delivery crew were flying home. At the customs desk, an agent overheard one of them laugh about the missing ear and the eye patch of the new owner. The comment was immediately passed on to the supervisor and relayed to the inspector.

Ian ordered his sergeant to call in all his off-duty men.
Then he called Lt. Berry at Naval Air Station Security.

"Mike, we've got a lead on Maldias. We're looking for a
big, white sportfisherman with Hispanics aboard, and we certainly would appreciate your help. Could you get your boats
out? Perhaps we can keep this snake from slithering off into
the tall grass again."

Doc took a rumpled herringbone sport coat from the
bottom of his bag and tried to shake the wrinkles out. It was
hopeless. He went instead to the locker and found a relatively clean shirt and his only tie. They would have to do.
The press conference was being held in the theater behind
the dive store. All the students were requested to attend the
party at the Commissioner's House afterwards.

Sheri and Lisa were acting as hostesses at the theater and
had already gone down the hill. Doc took his clothes and as
he headed to the men's shower, he saw Karen going in the
back entrance of the Commissioner's House. She was carrying two designer duffel bags. He wondered if he should warn
her about the trouble she was headed for, but decided he
could not risk Jason knowing about his suspicions. He shook
his head and told himself she was old enough to make her
own choices—for better or for worse.

"This one sure isn't for better," he said half aloud as he
finished dressing.

When he arrived, the small theater was filling up quickly.
Sheri had saved them seats in the back.

"This is quite a turnout. I had no idea he had this many
fans," Doc said.

Lisa leaned across Sheri and answered, "A lot of these
people are from the dive club and the historical society. The
front rows are for the press. Anything Jason does is a news
event here. The island is small and the museum is a real point
of pride, so this is important to them."

"And to him?"

"Are you kidding? He lives for this stuff. I've never seen
anyone like him. Watch how he turns on the charm for

them—he's a combination Errol Flynn and Mr. Wizard. They love him."

The house lights flickered, the room got quiet and Dr. Jason Richardson stepped up to center stage in front of the theater screen. There was a welcoming applause. He was starched and pressed in his best, and glowing with charm and confidence.

"Welcome, dear friends and supporters of the Maritime Museum. It is wonderful to see all of you again, and I very much appreciate your coming on such short notice to this very important meeting. The things I want to tell you about are so important that I have, as you can see, invited the journalists and television people to be with us, and you will shortly understand my reasons for doing so.

"All of us are aware that while the museum and the institute have been able to assemble an excellent representative collection of artifacts from the many wreck sites in our waters, the vast majority of valuable historical artifacts have disappeared into private collections through illegal sales and illegal pilfering and plundering of these, our irreplaceable time capsules of history.

"It is my sad duty today to report to you that we have discovered that the criminal activity of wreck site plundering may be at an all time high. In spite of the best efforts of our Marine Police and other enforcement agencies, new sites have been discovered and stripped of their history, their artifacts and their potential as valuable learning sites for archaeologists in training, such as the excellent group we currently have with us from Georgia State University. During the past two weeks, we have discovered a wreck site of unbelievable significance, which is my reason for calling you here today. In order to appreciate the potential value of this discovery, it is necessary to review a little history. We are fortunate to have saved the excellent presentation that once ran daily in this theater, 'The Attack on Washington'. Please pay careful attention—there will be a test. Thank you."

There was laughter at the comment about the test, for most had seen the multi-projector presentation many times. The film began and recounted the story of the War of 1812, an ill-fated war for the United States, brought on by the de-

sire to annex Canada. It began with a surprise attack on
Toronto. The town was burned and many lives were lost. Re-
taliation was slow in coming because the British were at war
with Napoleon. Eventually thousands of battle-seasoned
troops arrived in Bermuda to prepare for the attack that
would avenge the outrageous behavior of the treacherous
Americans.

Admiral Sir George Cockburn was chosen to lead the
operation. He had been a contemporary and shipmate of
Lord Nelson, and was highly qualified for the job. He as-
sembled a fleet of fifty warships, and in the fall of 1814 sailed
up the Chesapeake sweeping away everything in his path.
Warning came late to the ill-prepared White House. First Lady
Dolly Madison began packing. Her husband faltered with
indecision. While the town was in the midst of panic, the
over-confident President ordered that a victory dinner be
prepared for his returning troops. It was done, but moments
later he and Dolly fled in terror. The British came up the bay
and then up the Patuxent River. They made a short overland
march and took Washington from the rear, almost without
opposition.

The presentation continued with the story of Admiral
Cockburn's arrival at the abandoned White House in time to
enjoy the still-warm victory dinner. After eating, they burned
the magnificent structure and most of the other government
buildings including the National Armory and the Treasury
Building.

Word of the fall of Washington spread quickly, and the
troops at Baltimore were much better prepared when the
British attack came. They were able to hold the fort and se-
verely damage some of the British vessels. It was in the heat
of that battle that Francis Scott Key, observing from a small
vessel up river, penned the lines "Oh, say can you see, by the
dawn's early light, what so proudly we hailed at the twilight's
last gleaming..." as in the early light of dawn, he saw the
"bright stars and broad stripes" still waving proudly above
the fort. The British withdrew and their officers wrote glowing reports of their victory to the Admiralty in London and
the reports were printed in Bermuda's Royal Gazette.

Yes, the audience in the theater knew the story well because the Governor of Bermuda at the time was Admiral Cockburn's brother, and the plans for the attack and the assembly of the British fleet occurred in Bermuda. The audience waited and the house lights came back up. Dr. Richardson took the stage again.

"Dear friends, it is my sad responsibility to inform you that we have found one of the vessels which was returning to Bermuda from the August, 1814 attack on Washington and Baltimore. She was loaded with weapons from the American National Armory, and she may have even carried national treasures from the White House. Think about it...what could the troops have taken in that raid? What could have been on this vessel? Unfortunately, we will never know because the site has been stripped and destroyed by thieves. Yes, thieves —thieves of the deep, and they must be caught and punished. We must bring pressure on the government to stop this outrage once and for all.

"We have an excellent video tape of the site. After you have seen the tape, there is a display of the few remaining artifacts here on stage, and I will be happy to explain how we were able to use these pieces to determine the origin and history of the wreck. Thank you."

Mark's video tape was shown, and angry rumbles passed through the crowd as they saw the huge potholes and the timbers and ballast strewn across the site. It would be impossible to ever reconstruct the hull or do any in situ work. It was an outrage. Visions of rare art and personal possessions of past presidents passed through their minds. What would a sword from General Washington, or Thomas Jefferson's pistols be worth? What of the gifts given to the presidents by other heads of state? Could a price ever be put on the works of art that adorned the White House walls? And what about the original flintlocks from the Springfield, Massachusetts armory?

"You were wonderful, darling, just wonderful," Karen praised.

"Yes, I know," Jason said coldly. His hands were shaking as he removed the cap from a small vial, raised it to his nose and snorted the contents. He leaned back against the wall and waited for the rush. Karen looked to see if any of the others backstage had seen, and wiped the residue of white powder from Jason's nostrils.

The video was nearly over. He stood erect and looked her over carefully. She was dressed in khaki shorts with a matching safari-style shirt, quite form-fitting. He undid one of the buttons on her shirt and then a second. "Use what you have, baby. You are going to be on international television. This could be your big chance. Remember, don't talk. Just hold up the guns and smile; I'll do the rest. Here we go."

The audience applauded as Jason and Karen returned to the stage. On the tables around them, a large collection of flintlocks and handguns were in various stages of conservation. Also displayed were swords and shot of many sizes, and samples of the hull timbers. The screen lifted and Jason invited the cameramen forward. As Karen lifted the weapons, Jason explained how they fit as pieces in the puzzle.

Lisa watched in anger from her seat between Sheri and Mark. "He could have at least acknowledged our work," she leaned across Sheri to say to Doc. "I went without sleep for three days so he could put on this dog and pony show. He's got the bimbo up there and he won't even mention my name."

"Lisa, how did you ever get that many pieces ready for display? They are beautiful! Some of them look like they were never wet," Sheri said.

"I didn't. I don't know where he got them. Only three were done in our lab, but those Springfields must be from this site. I've never seen any others like them. They are priceless, but I didn't conserve them. We replaced the wooden stocks with heavy foam, but frankly, I have no idea how he restored the metal so completely. They look almost new."

Jason continued his briefing to the fascinated audience. "All of you are familiar with the technology of reverse electrolysis through which we reverse the flow of ions away from the artifact, and to some extent reconstitute the metal with ions from a sacrificial metal. In the lab, you have seen the transformers and the tanks for electrolyte baths. I have developed a way to greatly speed and enhance the process. It is based on accelerated ion bombardment of target metals. That is all I can tell you about it now. I will be publishing as soon as the patents are complete. This is the first public display of pieces conserved using my new process. It is very exciting. Look at the flawless restoration of the Springfield flintlock which Karen is holding. The work was accomplished in less than three days and it will last forever. Are there any questions?"

"Dr. Richardson, how can you be so certain of the identity of the wreck?" a reporter asked.

"Actually, it's quite simple. Flintlocks, nearly worldwide, were converted to percussion caplocks in 1832. The percussion cap was invented in 1830, so we know the wreck was not newer than that. Also, these Springfields were new and very well protected in their crates. Some wooden stocks even survived and you know how rare that is. Now, there is no place new ones in such large quantitiy could have come from except the National Armory. Next, there were British uniforms and arms aboard. We found buttons from uniforms of Royal Marines and from the 85th Regiment of the King's Light Infantry. They were the regiment with the highest casualties in the Washington raid.

"But there were no American buttons found, or any other American accoutrements—only these Springfield flintlocks. So put all the pieces together and then imagine the vessel, badly damaged, wallowing her way home from Baltimore. She's so heavy with cargo and perhaps leaking badly that she falls behind the rest of the fleet. When she's finally in sight of home, she gets caught in a squall and goes down, probably at night, or she would likely have been seen from shore. There are no survivors and she's not on the reef like most of our wrecks, so there she sits for a hundred and seventy years, waiting to tell someone her story, waiting for us to help her finally come home.

"The most important point here is that this is not a great discovery. Instead, this is a great tragedy for Bermuda, certainly for the United States and for the worldwide archaeological and historical community. Pillaging of historical wreck sites must be stopped. If that means restricting access to our wrecks to only the scientific community, so be it. We probably will never know who did the damage to the site you saw in the video, but their kind of vandalism must be stopped.

I'll be speaking to the Premier and to Parliament in a few days and I'm counting on your help."

The hall filled with cheers and applause. He waited, soaking in every decibel. Finally, it was quiet enough for him to finish. "Now, if there are no more questions, you are all invited into the courtyard for refreshments. I understand we will be on network news at seven this evening. Thank you for coming and remember, we need your support now more than ever."

"What do you think?" Sheri asked Doc as they walked into the courtyard. "What do you think of all that righteous indignation?"

"Like Mark Twain's line about the righteous indignation of a Christian with four aces? It works, except that guy was never a Christian. We've just seen the performance of a lifetime. He was the one who raided that site, and when you wanted to dive it with the dive club, he concocted this story to cover his trail. Now we have to prove it before recreational divers are locked out of every wreck in Bermuda. Come on, we need to find Ian."

They found Ian waiting for them at the hostel. "I didn't get here until the show was over. How did it go?" he asked. Doc and Sheri told him over coffee and sandwiches about Richardson's charade and its implications.

"I had a call from Immigration," Ian recounted. "One of Maldias's cousins will be visiting us for a few days, and there's a big, white sportfisherman just over from the States with a South American-looking crew. We're looking for it now. We haven't had a single bloody lead to Maldias, but he's here. I can feel it."

"Yes," Doc agreed. "And I'm just as sure Richardson is tied to his uncle Bill Roberts in the kidnapping. And both of them are working for Hans Behrmann, the U-boat captain, but we don't have enough to arrest Richardson. If we push him, Debbie might be more in danger."

"Aye, but if we don't," Ian said, "he could pull out any time and we'll be left with a hat and no rabbit. So what do we do?"

Doc took two deep breaths and slammed his fist into the table. "You're right. We'll turn up the heat as soon as his little party is over. We can't wait any longer."

"I've already asked Lieutenant Berry for his two boats. They should be on the way, and I'll get some of my lads on watch here. You stay on Richardson and I'll look for Maldias. Oh," Ian added, "I checked on Dr. Hans Behrmann with Immigration. His daughter was lying. He's been here several times in the last three years. Last year, he brought two other German-scientist types. This island is getting overrun with bloody doctors. The interesting thing is that your government is very anxious to talk with him—no explanation. We're not to arrest him or let him know we're interested—just call Washington. Very unusual."

"They must have been working on the other sub, the one that disappeared in St. Thomas. Keep on it, Ian. This gets more interesting by the minute."

"Right. See what you can find out at the party and try not to start anything without me, alright, mate? None of your cowboy crap now, or I swear I'll chain you to a light tower on the north reef and forget which one. You call me, right?"

"I will be there to make sure he does, Inspector. We won't go anywhere without you."

"Thank you, miss. It's nice to know there's at least one person here I can trust." He laughed, kissed Sheri, pounded Doc robustly on the back and was gone.

"OK," Doc said to Sheri. "Let's go. First we need to check the work on the Whaler and the *Mermaid* before we go to the party. I want something in the water ready to run if we need it in a hurry." They walked briskly down the hill and through the museum gates.

"Sheri," he said after they'd passed the dive shop, "if things start happening like last time, stay here and keep a low profile. I nearly got you killed and I couldn't live with that."

"Thanks for the thought, Doc, but someone has to look after you, and I still have a score to settle with those guys. You give me back that Smith & Wesson and I'll be just fine."

He looked at her, shook his head and laughed. "Dear Lord, what have I got on my conscience now? I've turned this sweet little Georgia peach into a one woman SEAL team."

"Georgia peach, my ass. Doc, no Georgia peach would put up with you for fifteen seconds, you sorry sack of horse pucky."

"Does this mean I'm demoted from bozo back to asshole?"

"Or worse, as soon as I can think of something worse. How dare you call me a peach. I'll kick your butt," she laughed while pounding his arm as they walked. Doc laughed with her, a deep solid laugh and he felt very good.

The Whaler was not ready. The lower unit parts had not yet arrived. But the *Mermaid* was ready for sea trials. The mechanic handed Doc the keys and said, "Check her out."

On board, there was still the strong smell from the salt-soaked cushions. Doc opened the cabin to air it and then opened the engine hatches. The bilge was spotless. All the filters had been changed and the engines drained, cleaned and refilled with oil. He checked the fuel lines. They had been bled and resealed. The Racor filters were free of water and the diesel was clear and clean. The exhaust hoses were new. She looked ready and eager to run.

He turned on the preheaters, waited and hit the ignition on the port engine. It started without hesitation as did the starboard. The oil pressure came quickly to the mark and the fuel gauges read full. Sheri dropped the bow lines while he freed the spring and stern lines. Slowly and carefully, he guided the boat out of the slip. As he steered her towards open water, he remembered how beautifully heavy wooden hulls respond to the helm and what a pleasure the *Mermaid* was to handle. Sheri finished coiling the lines and joined him on the bridge.

"She was Paul's life, this boat. We spent a lot of nights sitting on the stern, fishing and howling at the moon. I have been lucky to have good friends in my life, but not many like Paul."

"I'll look forward to meeting him, I hope in this lifetime."

"Well said."

They cruised slowly towards the boat basin entrance past the *Enterprise*. Captain Johnston was on the deck and waved as they went past. Sheri waved back and said, "They're such nice guys. I certainly hope they are not involved in any of this mess. I just can't imagine."

"I hope you're right."

"I've been thinking about your question about sex."

"And?"

"Besides the physical, it has a lot to do with communication, opening up the relationship, going for intimacy, right?"

"Of course. Keep going."

"So the physical part is not as important in your big picture, but does that mean it is not important at all?"

"Of course it's important. The issue is perspective...think about it. You're making good progress. I knew you would."

Doc brought the *Mermaid* through the basin entrance and into the bay. As they were going out, a spotless, new 65-foot sportfisherman was coming in. The man in the white yachting jacket and dark glasses at the helm was Esteban Maldias. The afternoon sun glaring from his windscreen kept Doc from seeing him clearly. But Doc had an uneasy feeling as he got a look at two of the crew.

"That's the boat Ian is looking for. And who do those guys remind you of?"

"Trouble, big trouble. Do we have a gun on board?" asked Sheri.

"No, and the radios don't work. We need to get back to the dock. Let's just circle out here a bit and keep an eye on those guys."

On board the sportfisherman, Maldias had gotten a good look at Doc and Sheri. He immediately left the fly bridge and climbed down to the cabin. He took an assault rifle from the hidden locker, chambered a round and sat behind the darkened glass of the cabin watching. His helmsman brought the boat neatly alongside the fuel pier.

"Can you see what they're doing?" Doc asked Sheri.

"No, I can't, but it doesn't look like anyone is at the fuel pump. No, wait, here comes the attendant. Maybe they are just getting fuel. Did you see Maldias?"

"I don't think so. There was so much glare I couldn't see much of anything. I should have gotten that damn police radio before we left the hostel. Let's go back. When we get tied up, you run to the hostel, get the radio and call Ian. Those guys are nuts bringing that boat in here, but you can bet they didn't come empty-handed. I'm going to the dive shop to get some things."

"I want to stay with you."

"If you are going to be in the Navy, you have to follow orders. I go to the dive shop and you go to the hostel. That's an order, got it?" His tone was stern.

Doc brought the *Mermaid* slowly back into the alley of their slip, neatly turned and backed into place. Not bad after five years, he thought. Sheri got the stern lines, and he secured the bow and spring line to the dock. She was off up the hill as he went the back way through the court of shops to the dive shop's rear entrance. He found the black bag under the tool bench with the Smith, two Berettas and several boxes of ammo. His Randall was on top of the ammo. He locked the dive shop, backtracked through the courtyard and went up the hill to the hostel. He was certain he was being watched by two men in the courtyard, but they made no effort to follow him through the museum gate.

When he was sure they were alone, Doc asked Sheri, "Did you get Ian?" He was still trying to catch his breath after running up the hill.

"His sergeant said they're on the way and we should sit tight. Ian will meet us up here."

"Good. I'd rather be down there, but we can't let Richardson get away while we're distracted with Maldias," he said as he opened the black bag.

The Berettas were smaller and easier to conceal than the Smith & Wesson. He put on a light windbreaker and stuck one of the Berettas in the back of his waist band. He dropped two extra magazines in the lining of his jacket and started to put the bag in his locker.

"Whoa, big fella, before you lock that, I hope you have something for me," Sheri said, standing beside him with an outstretched hand. He looked over his shoulder again to make sure no one was coming and gave her the Smith with two extra magazines.

"Leave it down here, locked in your locker," he told her. "There'd be no way to explain it without spooking Richardson. And you won't need it at the party."

"Then why are you carrying that one?"

"So that you don't need to. Now, lock it up and let's go."

They went from the hostel through the lab's courtyard up the back stairs of the Commissioner's House to Jason Richardson's spacious office and living quarters.

CHAPTER

19

Karen was playing hostess dressed in an elegant cocktail gown with a proudly plunging neckline. She greeted Doc and Sheri with hugs. The Spanish gold coin hung from a nautical-style, gold rope chain and nestled comfortably on her full breasts.

"Isn't this a beautiful dress?" she said, taking Sheri's arm. "Jason got it for me. He wanted me to wear a push-up bra. Wasn't that silly?"

"It certainly was," said Sheri in mock seriousness. Doc bent over to look carefully at the coin. He was sure it was the one in the video.

Sheri hit him with her elbow and pulled him away. "Come on, Doc, you've seen coins before. Just as nice as that one."

The students gathered excitedly around Jason's large television. Dr. Jason Richardson's press conference was the lead news item. First came a quick clip of him on the stage and then a cutaway to Karen holding a flintlock. As the camera zoomed in on the gun, she leaned forward and the gold coin in the massive bezel swung out from her unbuttoned shirt.

Maldias made it a point to keep himself informed, especially when it was likely that there would be a report on the police effort to capture him. He was watching television when the men who had followed Doc returned to the boat.

"Did he see you?" Maldias asked them.

"I don't think so, Captain."

"Then he saw you. The question is, did he see me. We must assume he did. We have our fuel. Cast off the lines. Hurry, we must not stay here."

As the two left the cabin, one reached towards the television to turn it off. "*Espera! Espera!*" Maldias screamed at him, pointing at the screen. "Did you see that coin on her neck? That's the coin I gave my brother! And look, the good doctor is wearing his watch. Leave it on, *compadre*. Television can be very educational."

"You stupid bitch!" Richardson shouted at Karen from the back of the room. All conversation ceased. "I told you not to wear that coin in public."

"You gave it to me and I'm going to wear it. Besides, no one would have seen it if you hadn't unbuttoned my shirt. So screw you!" She ran from the room crying with Jason in hot pursuit.

"Well, isn't this party off to a good start?" Sheri said. Her comment was greeted with strained laughter. "Y'all just let them work it out. Eat the food, drink the booze, barf on the carpets...you know, just like at home. Right, Bob?" More laughter erupted and conversation returned to normal. When the commercials ended, the anchorwoman highlighted the day's top stories and then the piece on the museum's divers and their find began.

Sheri went to the door of Jason's quarters, knocked loudly and called them to come and watch. "We're coming," was the gruff response.

"Oh, making up so soon?" she said and crossed the hallway to return to the party.

She was greeted by Mark who asked, "I wonder where Lisa is. Probably still mad, that's why she's not here."

"See if you can find her," Sheri suggested. "She may not want to attend this gala event, but I'll bet she could use a friendly shoulder about now. Tell her we're on her side, Mark. Try her office in the lab."

Mark went down the stairs, crossed the courtyard and entered the lab as he called loudly for Lisa. There was no response. The offices on the second floor were also empty. She must have gone to her apartment, he thought. Mark found the number and called—still no answer. Perplexed, he went down the hill to the diving locker. Two men with long dark hair, looking very much out of place, passed him on the hill road. He didn't like their looks so he hurried down the rest of the way.

Jason had returned to the party and was leading a toast to their success. "We've won a major victory for science, archaeology and the preservation of wrecks around the world. And I salute you, for without your help and long hours, none of this could have happened. You are the best."

There were cheers and applause. "I want you to stay and enjoy the party. There is enough food and booze even for Bob. And I'll put on my favorite tape, Twenty Thousand Leagues Under the Sea. It was watching this flick too many times as a child that demented my mind and launched my career."

There was laughter and Jason kept the banter coming. "Imagine, our own island base, our own submarine, and finding Mother Ocean's lost treasures. All that, a paycheck and a 401K." The group raised their glasses in a toast and Jason started the tape. He was heading back towards the door when the phone rang.

"It's for you, Dr. Richardson. This guy says he knows who the real thief of the deep is." Jason forced a laugh which ended abruptly when he caught the intensity of Doc's penetrating stare. "I'll take it in my quarters, thanks," he said and hurried from the room.

Jason went to the phone beside the huge bed where Karen lay crying, told her to "shut-up" and picked up the phone. "Got it. You can hang up now."

There was a click, and in a heavy Spanish accent the caller began, "So, Dr. Richardson, you want to catch the thief of the deep? Tell me, Doctor, what would you call a man who kills and then steals from the dead? A scientist? My brother—

he died very mysteriously on a ship that disappeared without a trace. And do you know what? He had a coin, a big gold coin with diamonds all around it, just like the one your woman was wearing. Isn't that an amazing coincidence, Doctor?" There was a pause and Jason said nothing. His hand began shaking again and he reached for the vial in his shirt pocket.

"What do you know about the death of my brother?" Maldias continued. "And where did you get that coin?" Another pause, and Jason bit his lower lip and looked at Karen. She was sitting up on the bed watching him. The vial slipped from his hand and fell to the floor, spilling the contents on the ancient yellow pine. Jason looked panic-stricken.

"What else of mine do you have, señor?" Now Maldias was yelling and Jason held the phone away from his ear. Karen could hear him shouting.

"Two pretty, red life boats perhaps? Some big plastic bags full of nose candy, eh? Did you take my candy, amigo? Or perhaps you helped the big inspector kill my brother and sink his boat? You didn't do that, did you, Doctor?"

"Of course not. I don't know what you are talking about." Jason dropped to the edge of the bed. Karen reached out to him and he took her hand.

"I'm going to kill you, Doctor. I'm watching and I'm waiting and I'm going to kill you—you and your *puta*. There is no hope for you; an eye for an eye. There is only one thing that might save you and you know what that is, don't you?"

Jason stopped biting his lip just long enough to shout into the receiver, "I told you, I don't know what you are talking about. Now leave me alone." He slammed down the phone but missed and hit his thumb. He swore and sank onto the bed beside Karen.

"What's going on?" she asked, wiping her eyes. "What was that about?"

"You may as well know why I was so angry with you. What you've done may get us both killed. I found a new wreck a few weeks ago. The hold was full of grass which we left, but there were lifeboats on the roof, good as new, and I brought them back here for the museum. When I tried to inflate one of them, a seam split and inside was millions of dollars worth of cocaine. The other boat was full too. We went back again and I found your coin and this watch. I...I took them off a body."

She winced and pulled the coin away from her throat, but then closed her hand on it, holding it, protecting it from his grasp. "What else?" she demanded. "Tell me the rest."

"That man on the phone knows. He recognized the coin and says he's going to kill us. He thinks I killed his brother, but I swear to you I didn't."

"If he were going to kill us, he wouldn't warn us first. What does he want? He must want something."

"Obviously the jewelry and the coke. We'll have to do what he says; it's our only hope." He held out his hand for the coin.

"Millions of dollars? You have millions of dollars?" She still held on firmly to the coin. She had no intention of letting it go.

"Yes, in cocaine," Jason answered.

"Millions are millions. You can't give it back...no way." Her face changed. There was a hardness in her, a determination he would never have imagined her capable of.

"I don't want to give it back, but it's dangerous, and we'll have to set a trap for them. I'll need your help. I can't do it alone."

"It's dangerous? And we could be killed?" Her eyes were wide with excitement. His cuddly kitten was emerging as a hungry lioness.

"I'm afraid so."

"What's my share if we make it?"

"What do you want?"

"A million dollars, just for me. One million dollars. And not coke. I want it in cash. You can do it, I know you can."

"Alright, but it won't be easy."

"What do we have to do?"

"First, we have to get out of here unnoticed. This place has a rather unique basement and we'll be safe down there while we make our plans. There's a passage to the stairs in the back of the old stables under the building."

"You mean where the goats are? That's really stinky. Isn't there another way?"

"You could swim three miles," he offered.

"We'll go with the goats."

"The sooner you start, the better. Take your things and go. Try not to be seen. I'll meet you in about twenty minutes." Jason handed her a flashlight from one of his bags. "You'll need this for the stairs. Be careful."

"What are you going to do?"

"There are files here—things I need. Don't worry, I'll be there. Get your things and get started."

Karen put on her backpack and carried her large duffel. He checked the stairs and then sent her down. As soon as she left the room, Richardson pulled an old volume from the bookcase, removed a plastic bag of cocaine and partook generously. Then he watched her from the window. She moved quickly across the courtyard and out the gate towards the goat entrances to the old stables. Two men with long dark hair came out of the shadows and grabbed her. He pulled back from the windows as Karen screamed for help. One of the men covered her mouth with a cloth and she collapsed into limp silence.

Richardson fell back from the window, closed his eyes as the rush hit him, and then shouted, "Yes!" Now wide-eyed and recharged, he returned to his packing. Six minutes later, the phone rang and he answered it.

Jason identified himself and waited until the line was clear of other listeners. It was Maldias again. "That was very foolish, Doctor, but I thank you. Now I have your little playmate and you will do what I say. No more games."

"Please don't hurt her. I'll do whatever you want." Jason's voice sounded terrified, but this time he was pacing beside the bed, listening as if he already knew his next line.

"Now I ask you again. Give me back my cocaine and my brother's jewelry. We'll trade for the girl. You can even keep the grass if there's any left down there—a bonus."

"Listen, I didn't kill your brother. I swear. We were diving and found the wreck by accident. That's all. And your cocaine is not here. I will have to get it."

"Where is it then...at your mother's house? I have no time for foolish games. Where is it?"

"I hid it in an underwater cave near the freighter. I

couldn't risk keeping it here. It's...it's illegal. I'll have to dive for it."

"Tonight. You will dive tonight."

"Not tonight. It's very deep and I'll need help to bring it all up. Trust me, please. You have Karen. Don't hurt her. I'll do whatever you want. Anything, just don't hurt her." He looked at his fingernails, blew on them and buffed them on his shirt.

"That's better. I'll keep her safe for you, Doctor, but just for tonight. She is very pretty, this one, and after tonight, well who knows? You keep your word and I'll keep mine."

"How shall I contact you when we have the bags?"

"Don't worry, Doctor. I'll be easy to find, like your shadow. Good night. Sleep well and tomorrow you will be an honest man again—no more secrets, no more problems. You get your girl back and get rid of all that nasty, illegal coke," Maldias laughed.

"Just a minute," Jason pleaded. "Tell Karen...tell her I...I love her, please." He posed in the mirror and made a sad face like a mime and put his hand over his heart.

"*Si*, I will tell her."

Richardson snapped his fingers when the line went dead, pointed his finger as a pistol at the receiver and slowly pulled the trigger. Then he laughed, looked back in the mirror, winked at himself and dialed. After a brief preliminary conversation, he became angry and then yelled into the phone, "I don't care what they're doing or if they are seen. Bring them in now and give me those torpedoes or we're finished. Do you understand?"

"I'm really worried about Lisa," Mark said to Doc and Sheri when he returned to the party. "There's no answer at her apartment, and she's not in the lab or at the dive locker. I think we should look for her. If she and Richardson got into it, he might have hurt her. I don't trust him. Also, there were two tough-looking guys with long hair on the grounds. Did you see them?"

"No, but they might be from a boat we saw earlier. You may be right. I think we should look for her," Doc answered.

"Sheri, you keep an eye on things here..."

"Not on your life! I'm coming along. I don't trust Richardson either and I'm not staying here without you."

"OK, Mark, we need to keep an eye on Richardson. You wait here and watch his door. If he leaves, you call the lab. Got it?"

"Let's go to the hostel first," Sheri said. "There's something I want in my locker."

They met Inspector Cord coming up the hill. He told them the sportfisherman was gone by the time his men had gotten to the marina, but his boats were searching the north end of the island. Doc told him about Lisa and Richardson's behavior with Karen. Sheri politely excused herself for a moment. When she returned, she was carrying a student backpack.

At the lab, Doc called out for Lisa. His voice boomed off the block walls but went unanswered. Ian went upstairs to check the offices while Doc and Sheri went to the back of the lab. Doc tried the door to the photo file room and then tried the darkroom. The steel door was locked from the inside. He beat on the door and called out again. He heard muffled sobbing inside. He shouted for Ian and put his shoulder into the door. It didn't budge. Ian came running down the stairs.

"She's in here. Sheri, do you know where the keys are?"

"She has a set and Richardson has a set. I'll check her desk."

"Hurry!"

"Shall we get Richardson down here?" Ian asked.

"Yes, but don't go alone. I'm sure he will be armed."

"No keys up here," Sheri shouted and came down the stairs. "Her desk is broken into and stuff is everywhere."

"Let's go get him," Doc said.

"No, you get that door open. I'll take care of Richardson," Ian said and pulled the radio from the holster at his waist. "Don't worry. My lads are on the way. He's not going anywhere."

"Lisa, can you hear us?" Doc shouted at the door. There was a moan from the inside. "We will have you out in a minute, Lisa. Don't worry. If you can, move away from the door, OK?"

Doc motioned Sheri to come into the photo file room and pointed to the drops of fresh blood on the floor leading into the darkroom. He got the lab's acetylene cutting rig and quickly cut through the thin metal. The door swung open. Lisa lay on the floor in the darkness. She was tied and gagged and her head was bleeding.

"What happened? How did you get in the darkroom?" Sheri asked while Doc examined Lisa's head wound.

"After his little show, I confronted him about the guns, and told him to confess or I was going to report it. He hit me and called me a stupid cow. I started crying and he told me to quit my bovine bellowing and hit me again. 'Bovine bellowing', can you believe it? When I came to, I was in the darkroom. He really went nuts this time. Please, don't let him near me again."

Mark came running back into the lab followed by Ian. "He's gone, Doc! He must have taken Karen with him," Mark said between gasps. "I'm sorry, but he never came through that door. I swear it."

Sheri was kneeling beside Lisa holding her hand as Doc began checking her injuries. "This is going to need some stitches," Doc said. "I want you and Mark to take her to the hospital and wait there with her." He wanted Sheri in a safe place and the hospital was as safe as anything he could think of. "I'm going to stay here and help the inspector find Richardson," Doc continued. "And don't you worry, Lisa, we'll find him."

"Count on it, Lisa," Ian said, now kneeling beside her as well. "He'll not get away with this."

Jason made his way carefully down the dark staircase tunnel. He was struggling with two large duffel bags and holding a flashlight. The stairs were damp and steep. They were cut from the soft stone by the convicts who built the dockyard to provide the officers an escape route into the cavern beneath the Commissioner's House. The huge cavern was discovered by accident when two workers digging a well fell through the ceiling and plunged sixty feet to their deaths.

Jason paused at the last step and surveyed the ancient,

hidden fortress. Beneath the dome, a deep pool provided a secure submarine base and was the home of the captured U-boat 505 during World War II. The secret of the cavern had been protected by having the main surface entrance hidden in a large warehouse. At the end of war, the entrance was sealed and mostly forgotten. Dr. Hans Behrmann, however, had learned the secret from Nazi intelligence and he remembered.

The buildings reminded Jason of Hopi Indian pueblos. Living quarters and workshops, constructed with the Bermuda limestone, rose four stories high against the cavern's north wall. The buildings were roofed and beamed with timbers salvaged from old sailing vessels. Now, nearly a century later, the timbers were rotting and the stone was crumbling, making most of the space dangerous and unusable. But enough was reinforced and rebuilt for a crude lab, some living spaces and Bill Roberts's sophisticated computer center. Those spaces were connected by jury-rigged scaffolds and catwalks, cluttered with rotten support cables and power lines and laced with the slippery blue-green algae that thrived in the damp, stale air.

The two generators could not power both the computer center and the lights, so the bare bulbs strung along the catwalks and down to the submarine bays had only a faint orange glow. Fresh air was another problem. Both surface entrances were securely closed most of the time and only limited circulation came through a narrow open crevasse in the ceiling. Historically, the opening had served as a convenient trash dump. And even now an occasional bottle still made the sixty-foot drop as dockyard workmen above could not resist participating in the bottle-tossing tradition begun by their great, great-grandfathers two hundred years before.

Two submarines waited in the bays: first was the *Nautilus*, renamed by Jason and refitted after he stole her from St. Thomas.

Moored next to the *Nautilus* was Dr. Hans Behrmann's dream: the newest, smallest, and most sophisticated of the U-boats. She had been built in America like the early American space vehicles by teams of the best German engineers. She was to be the last sea wolf—the culmination of eighty

years of German submarine technology. Her secrets were
many, but first was her non-detectable, sonar-absorbing plastic hull. Second, and most significant, were her hydrogen
peroxide-burning turbine engines that would deliver unbelievable speed, and produce breathable oxygen as the only
exhaust gas. They were Behrmann's life work.

Behrmann called her the *Black Wolf*. Her 93-foot, blue-
black hull radiated a polished glow even in the low light. She
had the line and style of a supersonic aircraft: a low, swept-
back sail with a command center forward and streamlined
fins aft.

Jason's grandfather and Bill Roberts were at their work
station by the submarine bay. Dr. Hans Behrmann was an
exceedingly fit, barrel-chested, strong-armed man of seventy-
nine. He frequently passed for twenty years younger and preferred women half the age of his daughter Petra. He was a
genius—demanding and short-tempered, especially with his
grandson. Jason clenched his teeth, picked up his heavy bags
and resolutely marched across the catwalk to the older men.

"Now what have you done, Jason?" his grandfather bel-
lowed before he reached the end of the catwalk. "Why do
you need torpedoes? You know we are not ready to leave here.
The *Black Wolf* will not be ready to go back out for at least
two more weeks and still you jeopardize my years of work
with your foolishness. You should have left that freighter
alone as I ordered, but you knew better and now we are all in
danger. Damn you, your defiance and your drugs!"

"Your orders, *Herr Kapitän*? Your orders? You sank that
ship for target practice and killed those strangers as if they
were your mortal enemies. That could have been a hospital
ship bringing home a cure for cancer and you'd have laughed
while she went down. What did that have to do with saving
the world with your damn turbines?

"I won't take orders from a madman or a fool! Just leave
me alone—both of you. I'm going out to solve my little problem and you can get back to playing mad scientist."

"That's enough, Jason. Please. This won't get us anywhere," Roberts pleaded. "You know I can't take your fighting. Now, stop it and tell us what happened."

"The brother of the captain you killed," Jason said glaring at the old man, "knows I have his cocaine. He's threatened to kill us if he doesn't get it back."

"Where is the blonde? I thought she was coming with you," Behrmann snarled, ignoring Jason's story.

"She didn't do as she was told so now the smugglers have her. And as long as they have her, they think they have me. But surprise! I'm going to blow them all to kingdom come, just like my dear old granddaddy would have done." Sarcasm covered his words like an oil slick.

"Jason, you can't sacrifice that girl. We can't do that," Roberts urged.

"Uncle Bill, no one wants to hurt the girl, but she led them to me by not following orders and this plan is brilliant. They'll never know what hit them. All I have to do is get them to follow the dive boat into our trap. As long as they have Karen, they'll feel safe. She's the key."

"He's right, William. It is a good plan. These men are drug dealers. They're a threat to all of us. Perhaps you should go with Jason and make certain things go alright."

"Where is the Holiday girl?" Jason asked. "I want to see her before we go."

"What do you want with her?" Behrmann demanded.

"I'm taking her with us as insurance. If anything goes wrong and we have to deal with the Navy or the Marine Police, they won't risk the life of the girl. And you won't have to worry about the other two as long as I have her. It's just a precaution. And don't worry, I'll bring her back unmolested," he added with a cynical laugh.

"I don't like it. You keep your hands off that girl. That is an order," Behrmann scowled.

"Please, Hans, don't fight," Roberts said. "I'll look after her. Who knows, she might soften some if she thinks what we are doing has real merit."

Jason left the work area and crossed the catwalk to the first level of cells. He climbed the wobbly ladders and walked the scaffold planks to Debbie's cell on the third level. He knocked on the door first, then unlocked it and entered. It was a ten by ten cube with one dim light bulb. Some effort had been made to make it comfortable. In fact it was as comfortable as any of the other living quarters. It had a military

cot, a crude table and a few books. Debbie jumped to the
back of the cell when she heard him coming and stood defiantly facing the door as he entered. The weeks of captivity
had hardened her—not brought her to her knees as he'd
expected.

"I have good news, Debbie. Everything is working just
the way I told you it would. We'll be leaving in a few hours.
Once I get you away from that madman, I'll let you go, just
like I promised. And Uncle Bill is coming with us. Now will
you give me the computer codes?"

"Yes. But what about Tom and Paul?"

"Don't worry, I have that covered too. They'll be safe as
long as you're with me, but you must help me. Come and sit
down, please." He reached out to her but she dodged his
touch by moving to the other side of the table.

"I want to see them. You promised if I helped, you'd let
us be together. Take me to them and then you get the codes."

"I will, Debbie. I know I promised, but my grandfather..."

"I won't help until I'm with Tom."

"Alright, I'll take you. Now come and sit down."

"Not good enough. I want to be with Tom."

"You're an idiot. You could have..."

"You? I could have you? All I have to do is take off my
clothes and show you what little girls are made of. Then you'll
let me go? Tell me another story, Jason. Only next time leave
out the wolf and the grandmother. If you want my help, take
me to Tom and Paul." She stood with her arms folded across
her chest and her obstinate green eyes glaring at him. He
left the damp cell in anger.

Roberts left the work table. He needed fresh air. The
heaviness of the cavern's air was oppressive and he had not
been above ground since his faked suicide. He climbed the
dark steps towards the hidden entrance in the museum warehouse and was nearly gasping when he finally reached the
top. After checking the hidden television monitor, he stepped
into the storeroom and then out into the warehouse. He
opened the sagging warehouse door just a bit, looked out
and breathed deeply.

The night sky was bright with stars, and the openness of it relieved his claustrophobia. He wished he could go up to the ramparts and look out over the ocean, but the risk was too great. He longed for the nights on the *Liebchen*, drifting freely in the cool night air, watching the lights of the island from the comfort of the cockpit with his wife close beside him. He missed Petra terribly.

His solitude was shattered by flashlights. Three men walked across the narrow path between the Treasure Museum and the dive locker. They appeared to be searching the area. He drew back further into the darkness and watched. As they came closer, he could see their uniforms. Why were police searching the museum grounds? He turned and ran back to the hidden stairway in the back of the storeroom. What had Jason done now?

Jason led Debbie to the ammunition bunker that served as a cell for Paul and Tom. As soon as he opened the door, she ran to Tom's embrace. Behrmann had been correct that separating his prisoners would be an effective control technique. Now was the time to take full advantage of it.

"Alright, Debbie, I've kept my word. Now give me the codes and hurry. My grandfather will kill us all if he finds you together."

"Give me something to write on," she said.

He handed her a notebook and she wrote hurriedly. "There, that's all of it." She handed back the notebook.

"What are you doing, girl?" Paul asked. "What are you giving him?"

"The security codes to Roberts's computer. He said he would help us escape if I gave them to him. It's our only chance."

"She's right," Jason said. "It is your only chance, yours and mine too. Now listen carefully; here's my plan. There's been a problem, so in the morning I'm going to use myself as bait to trap a South American drug smuggler. He knows about my grandfather sinking that freighter you found. His brother was the captain and previous owner of this little trinket." He flashed the jeweled Rolex in the light. "This man kidnapped a student from the museum and we're going to try to save her. When that's done, we are not coming back. I'll take Debbie with me and you'll both stay here. And when we're far enough away, I'll let Debbie go. I won't lie to you...this may not work. We'll have to slip Debbie on board the *Nautilus* and then keep my grandfather from coming after us. But as soon as we're safe, I'll call the Navy and tell them where you are. We don't have a lot of time, but if you need to talk it over, I'll be back in an hour. Also, I thought you might like some beer. Here's a six-pack...enjoy."

They waited until he was gone to speak. "Did I understand him?" Tom said. "We are supposed to vote on whether we want to stay in this hole forever or take a shot at trying to escape? His plan sounds workable to me. All in favor say 'aye.' All opposed? What a surprise! The 'ayes' have won the day; it's a unanimous decision...."

"Shut up and kiss me, Tom. I've missed you so much."

"Have you been alright, Debbie?" Paul asked her.

"Yes, Paul, and you?"

"I hope we get out soon. This damp air is taking its toll, but I'm alright for now, girl. How did you ever get those security codes?"

"It really wasn't hard. I spent most of the time sitting in Roberts's computer center. He has full access to NASA's satellite network and the Navy's acoustical tracking grid. He has been building some kind of umbrella to protect the subs. But mostly he just sits at his terminal and laughs—it's real spooky. Anyway, he likes to show off what he's done...how he's fooled the Navy and NASA. I watched, and before long I'd memorized his codes. He's so depressed about what's happened I don't think he cares. He's really sorry that we got involved and I don't think he expects any of us to get out of here. That egomaniac, Jason, brought me some books and then he made an offer. He says he wants to try to make a deal with the government: drop the charges and he'll give them the *Black Wolf* and show them what Bill did to the satellite network."

"Has he...?"

"No. He's made advances, but he's so conceited he thinks he can win me over, so he hasn't tried force. And I'm sure

Roberts is protecting me. He feels responsible for what happened."

"I'll kill Richardson if he touches you," Tom swore.

"Only if you get to him before I do, lad," Paul cut in. "But we can't do anything down in this hole. They'd slice us to ribbons before we found a way out. And frankly, right now I'd say he's our only hope. No, we must wait until we see the sun again, then we'll have a chance.

"Well, let's have one of those beers. It may be awhile before we can have one again. It's good to see that you are alright, Debbie. We have been worried. That old kraut is really something, isn't he? Cold as the North Sea, he is. He didn't sink that freighter for the drugs like we thought. He had no idea what her cargo was. What's more, he didn't care. He did it for target practice—a test for that black devil boat and those torpedoes he's built."

"Jason is the worst," Debbie said almost in a whisper. "He has his grandfather's lust for power and intelligence. But he has no soul—no loyalty even to his family. What a monster! I hate him!"

"And that watch," Tom added. "How could he wear that watch after seeing the body? Every time I looked at it I'd see that face with the bullet hole and the eyes eaten out. What kind of person could do that?"

"The watch is a trophy, Tom," Debbie said. "I heard their men talking. Jason dove the ship to see what the old man had done. Behrmann told him it was a derelict at anchor with no one on board. That was a lie, of course. Behrmann went on board and shot those men himself. Dead men tell no tales, you know. Jason found the bodies and went nuts—he knew there'd be questions. Knew he was finished too if the old man was ever caught. But he couldn't resist bringing back the loot."

"I'd have loved to see his face when he got those boats up and found that coke," Tom said. "Imagine, one of the sub's crew said it's worth twenty million bucks!"

"Yes, but is it worth his career, his freedom, perhaps even his life?" Debbie said.

Jason sat with two of his men in the aft compartment of the *Nautilus*. On the table were two MK XVII recirculators. The canisters had just been refilled with carbon dioxide absorbent, and the oxygen and helium tanks were filled. Jason briefed the others on his plan.

"Chuck and I will take the dive boat. Bobby, you bring the *Nautilus* into position and we'll find you with the sonar. Make sure you have the cocaine and everything else on board before you bring the girl. She's ready and won't be a problem. She thinks we're sneaking her out, so be cool when you bring her on board. The explosion will be hours after we're gone. When she finds out, it will be a terrible shock to all of us, got it?"

"Simply terrible. Hoping to console her, are you?" Bobby said with a sarcastic laugh.

"What a wonderful idea. Wish I'd thought of it first," Jason snickered. "It's too bad about the *Black Wolf*, but once we get her plans, she's too much of a liability. Besides, we can't have dear old grandpa hunting us down over silly little things like hundreds of millions of dollars now, can we? Are the charges set in the tunnel?"

"Just the way you said. We'll activate the timers on the way out. What about your uncle?" Chuck added.

"We'll see. I don't want anything to happen to him until I've downloaded his computer and figured out what he's done to their satellite. I need to know what he does to keep them from being able to track us. The Navy would give the CNO's left nut for that!"

"That's what I like about you, hoss. You got all the bases covered. OK, you get the plans, I'll get the girl and get going. I want to be across the shallows and into deep water before it gets light. See you in the morning, hoss, and have a good swim. Here's to good hunting." Bobby put one hand on Jason's shoulder and gave a thumbs up with the other.

"Good hunting, Bobby. See you," said Jason as he and Chuck picked up the recirculators and left the sub. They carried them to the bottom of the steps and then Jason crept up to the computer center. From his bag he removed a portable computer and connected it to his uncle's large main frame. Reading from his notebook using a red-filtered flashlight, he typed in the codes and began downloading the data. Chuck kept watch in the shadows by the stairs.

It didn't take long to get what he was after, and soon Jason slipped quietly out of the computer room and back to the sub. After final words with his grandfather, he followed Chuck up the rough stone stairs to the back of the storeroom. A hidden surveillance camera showed several policemen searching the warehouse. Then they heard shots and a loud explosion. The officers spoke rapidly into their radios and ran towards the marina.

"Better sit tight until we see what's going on," Jason whispered.

The inspector came running to the back door of the dive shop where Doc was waiting. He pounded on the door and shouted, "Come on! Someone's sunk the *Enterprise.*"

Doc followed him to the car. As they drove towards the stone gates and the Clock Tower building, Ian pointed to the *Enterprise* dock. It was full of men shouting orders, and running with lines and pumps. As they came closer, they could see that the bow of the *Enterprise* was submerged. A large truck crane was brought from the boat yard, but by the time it arrived only a small part of the sub's stern remained visible.

"It was four or five men in a big sportfisherman, like Miami Vice," Captain Johnston began. "They roared in here and opened fire on the sub. Shot out the bow hemisphere with some kind of rocket loud enough to wake the spirits. Who would do this? I can't believe it. The cruise ship's back on Monday, and we're going to lose thousands before we can get another dome from Scotland. We may have to wait for one to be made."

"What about their boat?" Ian demanded.

"Your Marine Patrol boat started after her until the fellows on the big boat opened fire. I think one of your men was hit. Last I saw of your boat, she was headed for town—to the hospital's my guess. The sportfisherman turned back to the cut, towards Teddy Tucker's place. Reckon they're halfway 'cross the Atlantic by now."

Jason and Chuck grew increasingly frustrated as they waited. They heard the sirens, men shouting and the back-up alarm of the big boatyard crane. Jason looked at his watch and decided it was time to go.

Chuck stuffed his long hair up under his hat and walked cautiously out of the supply room and into the boat shed. He slid the big doors open and crossed the Keep yard to the dive locker. Jason crouched in the darkness. He put one recirculator on his back and with the other in his hand, slipped out the doorway. Someone called to him to stop as he ran to the waiting inflatable. The little engine started on the first pull. He was soon away from the dock and headed through the ancient gate into the night sea.

Chuck remained hidden in the dive locker until the police had gone, then climbed the trail to the top of the fortress wall and dropped over the far side to the marina. With all the confusion and attention focused on the *Enterprise,* no one noticed the docile old dive boat chug quietly out of the marina and disappear into the darkness.

The inspector holstered his radio and swore to Doc, "Richardson got away, but he's in an inflatable. He can't get far."

"He may not have far to go," Doc answered. "Not if he's going to meet another boat. No, that's not it—he's headed to that stolen sub! Ask the Navy to get a chopper up on the double or we're going to lose him. Tell them to hurry, Ian. That small boat is fast and we don't have much time."

By the time the helicopter arrived, Jason had made good his escape and was safely on the bottom waiting for the dive boat. The closed circuit recirculator sent no bubbles to the surface to betray him and the empty inflatable was on its way to open sea.

The chopper was also too late to see the *Nautilus* cross the shallow flats and slide silently out of sight into deep water.

Ian pounded the huge desk in Jason's office when he got the message. He put his radio down and crossed to the window overlooking the water. Doc had expected the bad news and only nodded. He continued his search of the spacious office bookcase.

Beside the bookcase was a large oak chest full of shallow drawers for maps. It was locked. Doc found keys in the desk and opened it. Inside were carefully-preserved old charts of Bermuda, including some from both world wars.

Doc studied the World War II chart carefully. "Look at these buoys to the west of the Dockyard. What would they be marking out here in the flats? Could there have been a channel there? Wait a minute. That would be about where we saw that second sub." He put the chart on the desk and continued to look in the map file. In the bottom drawer, he found several sets of computer-generated graphs. They appeared to be some kind of overlays and were covered with hundreds of four-digit numbers and hand-written notes. Some of the numbers were circled in red. But the thing that grabbed him like a boat hook was the handwriting—it was Debbie's.

"Are you certain?" Ian asked.

"Yes, I'm sure. These must be the charts she did on the computer. Look at all these sites. And what about these in red? Could those be the ones not shown on the NASA computer? We need to get these to the base right now and find someone who can tell us what it means."

"I'll radio Mike to get those technicians to Roberts's office and tell him we're on the way," Ian said. "What a night! More fun than a row in a pub with the Royal Marines. Only now it's our turn to start winning. Get your charts, mate. Let's go."

The sky was turning light gray when they arrived at the Naval Air Station and drove to the NASA station at a remote corner of the base.

"There's trouble," Mike told them as he led them inside. "I found out just after you called. About an hour ago the whole network crashed—everything here and at the acoustical sub-tracking network at the annex. They think Roberts did it and the Navy brass is going nuts. Two of the Washington guys will talk to you, but try to keep it short. They're really under the gun. I've got to get back to base. Sorry we missed catching that archaeologist for you, Doc, but he'll have to come up for air sometime."

Two red-eyed NASA technicians met them at the door and ushered them into the plotting and tracking room.

"Will you look at these and see if they mean anything to you?" Doc asked. "We found them hidden in Dr. Richardson's office. He's Dr. Roberts's nephew and I think they are both involved in whatever is going on here." He handed over the charts and as they looked them over, he continued, "Can you tell me if your computer shows anything where those red numbers are? My guess is they are archaeological sites that have somehow been masked. But they could just as easily be..."

"We know what they could be, Dr. Holiday. That's why neither of us have slept in nearly a week." The speaker who interrupted him was a tall, balding man in his late 50's. His sleeves were rolled up to his elbows and his tie pulled down and off center. There were coffee stains on his white oxford shirt and he smelled terribly of cigarette smoke. He said something to his assistant who disappeared and then returned with a portable computer which he set up on the receptionist's desk and hooked up to a large monitor. He brought up the program and explained, "We were able to piece together some of what Roberts destroyed, but without something to compare it to, we had no way of knowing how he was altering the data to hide it from the system. I thought we were finally getting somewhere and then he really threw us a curve. Fortunately, I'd saved what we had so we don't have to start completely from scratch."

He handed Debbie's chart to his assistant who pulled up a side chair and began reading off the numbers back and forth, while the older man's fingers flew as he entered data and compared results. "Shit!" he swore. "That's it! He cloaked the sites alright. How the hell could he do this? He would have had to build this into the original software or we'd have already found it."

"He wrote the original software," the shorter technician reminded him.

"Shit, I forgot. No wonder."

"Can you explain?" Doc asked.

"Here it is, down and dirty. Imagine a checker board and every third or fourth square is elevated. Instead of putting your checker on top of that square, you can hide it under the square and your opponent never knows it's there."

"Connect the squares and you have a tunnel," Doc said picking up the analogy.

"Exactly. A tunnel straight through enemy territory to the king row."

"Can you stop him?"

"Stop him? Oh, of course we'll stop him. All we have to do is tear down the whole network—hardware, software, satellites. Do you have any idea what that will cost?" He fumbled in his coffee-stained shirt pocket for a cigarette. His pack was empty. He crushed it and threw it at the wall, missing the trash can by three feet.

There was a long silence and then the technician looked at Doc. "Well, is that it? Is that what you wanted to know? That Roberts put it to us and we didn't even get kissed?"

"Actually, I was hoping you might be able to help me find a submarine." Doc explained his theory about the second sub, the one stolen from St. Thomas and added the story of the U-505 and its secret base. "If we can find that sub," Doc concluded, "I think we will find Roberts and my daughter as well."

"You really think you could find Roberts?" the technician asked, intrigued with vengeful possibilities.

"I'm sure of it," Doc answered, trying to sound confident.

"Aye, we'll find him," Ian added resolutely.

"Well, I suppose we could scan in these charts and try a negative overlay. If we get the main frame back up, we could use the satellite. It will take awhile...you might as well get comfortable, but I'm willing to give it a shot."

"Thanks," Doc said. "We'll wait."

Sheri stretched out on the couch and fell asleep quickly. Doc sat beside her feeling like an expectant father as he waited for the technicians to deliver the new charts. It took nearly two hours. The large printer fed out the chart and the programmers pulled it to the work table.

"This one looks pretty much like what we had, but on the next one we reversed the print, like a photo negative. It should show only the voids, including the ones your daughter and Morrison found. It'll be ready in a minute."

Soon the printer came to life again. This chart was nearly

blank except for approximately forty small solid ovals. "That's it! That's what we wanted!" the younger man said enthusiastically. "Now we have somewhere to start. Perhaps we can figure out how the hell he did it and plug the holes."

They placed the second chart under the first and held both up to the light. Then they began marking in the sites on the original chart.

Doc moved in to look over their shoulders. "Look at this," he observed. "What's this target right here in the middle of the Dockyard?"

"Let's see if we can enhance that on the computer," said one of the technicians. He sat back at the desk and began manipulating the image. "Let's find something we're familiar with to compare this to. Any suggestions?"

"Yes," Doc answered. "Find the *Enterprise*, that tourist sub in the marina by the big warehouse."

"Got her," the man answered after a dozen key strokes. "OK, let's go hunting. Where was that other target?"

"Dead center under the Maritime Museum," Doc said.

The technician looked in disbelief over the top of his glasses, and then looked back at the screen. Again his fingers moved rapidly over the keys. Then he stopped, looked back at Doc and raised his right eyebrow. "That was more than a good guess, wasn't it?" he asked.

"Perhaps. What have you got?"

"It's an exact match. Don't tell me; let me guess. It's a pre-historic sub buried there since the ice age, and you want to bring it up and thaw it out, right?"

Doc looked at Ian and Sheri rose up on one elbow from the couch.

"You've got it," Doc said excitedly. "The cave under the museum—I've always heard it was flooded, but there must be an air pocket. My friend, you're looking at Bill Roberts's new home. Now, see if you can find me the back door."

The older man stood uneasily by the desk. "I think I should let someone know about this...before we go any further, I mean. Do you mind?"

"Make your calls, do whatever you need to do, but get me that satellite and find me a way into that cave."

The technician disappeared into the main complex and

when he returned just minutes later, his face was red.

"I don't know what this is about, Dr. Holiday, but Washington is real insistent you stay here until Admiral Bartlow and the Secretary of the Navy arrive. It should be less than two hours. They promised to help, but they want to talk to you first." As he spoke, two large marines stepped into the room and stood at parade rest by the door.

Doc's eyes narrowed and his jaws tightened. The damn recirculator, he thought. So it was the Navy after all. His mind raced. He looked at Ian and asked the technician, "Am I under arrest?"

"Oh no, Doctor, you just can't leave, that's all. Sorry."

"May I ask one other question?"

"Of course."

"Assume Roberts is alive and hiding. When you get your system back on line, are you sure you can lock him out?"

The two technicians looked at each other for a moment and then the shorter, older man answered, "Even if we start over like I told you, I'm not sure we can lock him out for long. He built most all of it—we're still learning."

"So it's pretty important that we find him?"

"Listen, depending on how far over the edge he is, he could destroy our national security. Hell, he already has! He could be selling maps of those tunnels we talked about. Yes, it's damned important that we find him."

"Then you've got to help us and let us go."

"Sorry, orders are orders. You know that."

"Who is this Admiral Bartlow?" Doc asked.

"O.N.I., I think—Office of Naval Intelligence. He's the director."

Spooks, I hate spooks, Doc thought.

Ian walked over to the largest marine and looked him square in the eye. "Do you suppose that you can keep this civilian here safe while I go take a whiz, Corporal, or shall I send you some help?"

"No, sir. No help is required, sir."

"Well, that's fine, Corporal. I'll get us some coffee. Be right back." Ian turned to Doc, winked and left the room. The marines remained in place.

Ian returned a few moments later with two large mugs of

steaming Navy coffee. He tapped on the door and asked the corporal to open it for him. When the door opened, Ian poured the first cup down the front of the big marine, relieved him of his weapon, and sent him sprawling on the tile floor. The second found himself looking down the barrel of the lost rifle.

"Trade you, mate," Ian said with a friendly smile. "A good cup of coffee for that weapon. They're not legal here in Bermuda you know. Hand it over before you get in trouble, and then lend your mate a hand. My friend here thinks he knows where your Dr. Roberts is, but there isn't time to wait for social calls now, is there? So tell your mates to give us room and remember, this is my island. Once we leave the base, I'm the law. Understand, boy?"

"Yes, sir."

"Time to go, Doc," he said.

Doc stepped past the downed marine. "We'll try to find Roberts for you," he said to the startled technicians. "The only reason he would take down your system now is that he's ready to run, probably on that sub, and we're the only ones with a chance to stop him. When this is over, I'll be happy to talk to the brass, but not until we find my daughter and learn what the hell is really going on here. Thanks for your help." He grabbed Sheri and they ran from the building to the inspector's car.

"I thought I was the craziest mother on this island. Man, what have you done?" Doc shouted to Ian as they crossed the lawn. He threw the M16s into the back seat and Sheri jumped in after them.

"We all have our days, mate. Regardless of what your Navy boys think, this is still my bloody island and Paul Singleton is one of my best friends. You were right about Roberts. I just hope there's still time. I'll try to keep them off your back while you find the entrance to that cave." He heard sirens coming after them as he sped to the base exit. He turned on the car's siren and blue light, and doubled his speed.

CHAPTER

20

Chuck cut the aging wooden dive boat's throttles and looked around the horizon. He counted six other boats in the pale dawn light: four fishing boats, one large, white sportfisherman, and an unsightly, old steel work boat. He turned on the sonar and rotated the transmitter head. Jason received the signal, and within seconds began following the acoustic trail up to the boat. After a short decompression on oxygen, he surfaced. Chuck lifted the recirculators aboard while the sportfisherman headed towards them at full speed. The work boat lumbered along in its wake.

"Let's go, Watson, the game's afoot," Jason said with a grin and patted Chuck on the back. Jason took the helm and set a course west into deep water to find the sunken freighter, while Chuck began putting on his diving equipment. Ahead in the distance the hydraulic crane of the research vessel *Oceanic Explorer* caught the flash of the morning sun as they launched their sub on its first dive of the day.

After traveling three-quarters of an hour, Jason cut the throttles and activated the sonar again, this time signaling the *Nautilus*. The sub waited one hundred fifty feet beneath them just beyond the rim of the first deep ledge. When the sub returned his signal, Jason eased the throttles forward again and began a slow circle looking for the sunken freighter. As soon as it was visible on the Fathometer, he told Chuck to drop the anchor.

The sportfisherman pulled alongside as Jason was putting on the recirculator.

"No tricks, Doctor," Maldias shouted from the wheelhouse hatchway. He pulled Karen into the sunlight and said, "It's a long swim to the beach. I don't think she would make it."

Jason avoided looking at Karen. He waved from the stern dive platform, and after pulling his mask in place did a forward roll into the water. Chuck quickly followed. They swam down the anchor line to the freighter and beyond it to the waiting sub. Jason went to the aft hatch and banged on it three times. The signal was returned. He opened the hatch and dropped in. There was room for only one at a time so Chuck waited. As soon as air rushed from the dump, he knew the lock was again flooded and ready for him to enter. He got in and waited while the increase in air pressure brought him through a brief safety stop and then to cabin pressure. Bill Roberts was at the controls waiting with Jason when the pressure equalized and the hatch opened.

Jason went forward to the control console and sent the pilot, Bobby, aft to the stern console. Debbie sat in the seat behind the pilot's chair.

"How was your trip?" His tone was friendly, still hopeful.

"How was yours?" she answered dryly.

Jason put on the headset and instructed Bobby to put two plastic bags of flour into the diver lockout and send it to the surface. "Bait," he explained to Debbie. Then using the valves on his right, he vented some ballast and gently raised the sub from the bottom. "It's better than flying; I'll teach you someday."

Maldias watched the surface through powerful binoculars. He saw the large bubbles explode on the surface, and then spotted the plastic bags bobbing in the swells. He ordered the supply boat to pick them up. It didn't feel right, he thought. Where did all that air come from? And then it hit him—there had to be another sub. Divers don't use that much air.

"Bring the girl on deck," he ordered. He wanted Richardson to see her and to know that if he was playing games the girl would surely die. Maldias kept the sportfisherman away from the supply boat. He grabbed Karen when she appeared and ordered her to climb ahead of him up the tall, aluminum tuna tower. He could see much more from the high tower and that lessened his anxiety. He put on a headset, checked the M16 in his gun rack and watched carefully.

Suddenly, sixty yards to starboard, large volumes of bubbles erupted and Maldias saw the outline of a long white hull lurking just beneath the surface. The hunter was now the hunted.

The deck crew of the supply boat was too busy trying to net the cocaine to see the sub or the trail of bubbles left by the torpedo Jason fired at them. From his high tower, Maldias saw it coming and screamed into the headset to warn them, but it was too late.

The explosion ripped a gaping hole in the side of the supply boat and she listed violently to starboard. Maldias watched as her crew jumped into the sea to escape the sinking vessel.

Richardson rotated the remote television camera, which took the place of a periscope, until he found the sportfisherman. Instead of going to the aid of the supply boat, it was coming at him at full speed. There was no time to set up his second shot so he slammed the boat into a power dive. As the sportfisherman approached, Maldias barked orders to his crew. They came running to the deck carrying green metal boxes; as they passed over the sub they dropped a trail of grenades. Several exploded close to her hull, but the *Nautilus* escaped without damage. Richardson took her to the bottom and began looking for a place to hide.

Maldias shouted at one of his men to climb the tower. Angrily, he dragged Karen to the deck and then shoved her aside. He ordered the men to bring him containers of any size, fishing line, rope, hand tools and duct tape. He set them to work taping clusters of grenades to the tools which would serve as weights, and loosening the grenade pins which would be pulled with fishing line.

Jason called Bobby to the bow. The center hatch opened

and Bobby came on a run. "No damage in the stern lock," he reported. "What next?"

They had only one more torpedo loaded, but there were four others in the outside racks. Perhaps he could hide long enough to send his divers out to reload. Then he would set the sportfisherman up for a deep angle bow shot.

Maldias's men stood around the rails of the sportfisherman waiting for his orders. His boat had excellent electronics and he began a patient search of the bottom. He passed over a ship which he correctly identified as the freighter. He circled twice and then extended the circle further west behind the wreck. He increased speed and enlarged his circles. His white-line recorder suddenly etched a profile in mid-water that could only be the sub. He noted the GPS coordinates and made a tight circle. The sportfisherman rolled violently as he cut power and the stern wake caught her. But Maldias was now locked on to his target. He shouted the orders for his men to drop the improvised depth charges. He watched them going down on the Fathometer, and when they were deep enough, he gave the order to pull the pins.

Chuck was taking the first torpedo from the rack when he saw the grenades coming. He watched in horror as the monofilament line jerked and the pins pulled free. He swam away backwards as fast as he could, but he had no chance. The first cluster of grenades went off within feet of him, and concussion crushed his chest and shattered his sinuses. He died instantly.

Bobby had just emerged from the lock. The concussion stunned him and knocked him off the hull. He fell away from the sub holding his head, his eardrums ruptured and bleeding. The cold water entering his middle ears made him dizzy. He clawed his way back along the hull to the lock, dropped in and secured the hatch.

The grenades showering down on the sub had Debbie screaming in terror. Jason filled the ballast tanks with air to rocket them towards the surface. He was on instinct now, doing anything he could to get away. If he couldn't hide, his only chance was to use that last torpedo and get lucky.

On his Fathometer, Maldias could see the sub turn hard to port. Using all the power the twin turbos had to give, he pushed the sportfisherman into a hard 270-degree turn, cut power and waited. He had guessed correctly and was sitting at the sub's stern when she broke the surface. The *Nautilus* lurched upward for blue sky like a breaching whale and then fell back to the surface with a great splash.

Maldias's men rained the sub with heavy-calibre rifle fire. Several rounds chipped the stern hemisphere, but it did not shatter. Richardson dumped the ballast tanks to dive and try again, but before he could get deep enough, Maldias was over him dropping more grenades. An alarm came on as Roberts opened the center hatch and fell into the forward compartment.

Richardson shouted at Debbie to relock it. She pulled her way up the aisle, now a steep incline, as Jason used the bow thrusters to pull the sub into the dive. As she reached the hatch, she heard a sharp crack as a grenade went off against the stern's acrylic hemisphere and it became a latticework of fractures. Roberts helped her slam the dogs on the heavy door just as the stern hemisphere imploded. The lights went out and the stern dropped quickly. Now Debbie was standing on the hatch as the sub plummeted stern first into the deep water.

Bobby was in the lock out chamber with the inner hatch open. As the sub dropped, the water came higher and higher into the chamber. He tried desperately to find his mouthpiece, but it was hung above his head on a valve. He fought frantically to free the hose until the water rose to less than two inches of the upper hatch. He pulled himself up to the rapidly vanishing air pocket and gasped for one last breath before the air was gone.

Maldias's men cheered when they heard the explosion. The captain looked at his Fathometer. The sub was dropping into four hundred feet. He took GPS coordinates and wrote them on his hand. Then one of his men shouted and pointed towards their stern. Two black Navy boats with sailors on the bow guns were rapidly closing from the east. He hit full power and looked for a place to run. The only thing on the horizon was the research vessel.

"They have a submarine," he said to Karen. "Perhaps they would like to loan it to us to bring up my cocaine."

Debbie held on in the darkness as the sub continued to drop. She was terrified and yet she felt a strange, detached calm. But when the sub slammed into the bottom, she was jarred back to reality. The stern stuck deeply in the soft bottom ooze leaving the bow angled towards the surface. The cabin filled with sparks and smoke as radios and navigation equipment ripped from mounting brackets. The cargo boxes snapped free of their tie downs and smashed into the center bulkhead.

"Are you alright?" she called into the darkness. The only answer was the eerie creaking of twisting metal. Red lights were flashing on the instrument panel, and the dim light from the surface silhouetted the pilot chair with blue-green light. Roberts, somewhere on the deck below her, moaned. She crawled towards him.

"It's my legs," he gasped. "I can't feel my legs!" He was trapped under a large wooden crate of artifacts. She couldn't lift it or move him from under it.

"Is there a flashlight?"

"Yes, up forward, port side. Next to the medical locker. See if there's anything for pain," he moaned.

She climbed from the stern towards the bow. Jason lay motionless in the pilot's seat his forehead gashed by a heavy radio which had broken free from its overhead mount. Blood, oozing from the wound, looked green in the eerie light. Debbie climbed up beside him and checked his carotid pulse. It was erratic and weak.

She found the flashlight, got the pain pills and lowered herself back down the aisle to Bill Roberts. He was no longer conscious. With the flashlight, she could see bone sticking through the tear in his left pants leg. She put several gauze pads on the wound and tied them in place with triangular bandages. She tried one last time to move the crate—it was hopeless. His condition was serious, but then so was hers.

Lt. Mike Berry swore at the radio. "Why don't they answer?" He had been trying to warn the research vessel not to let Maldias board. The Navy Swift boats were fast, but it was obvious they would not reach the sportfisherman in time. Berry next placed a call to his commanding officer. "Sir, I think we have a serious situation here. We are going to need some help...."

The sportfisherman pulled to the lee side of the *Oceanic Explorer*. Maldias had two men in the tuna tower with assault rifles. The graduate students on the deck offered no resistance as Maldias jumped aboard with another of his gunmen. They ran up the ladder to the wheelhouse and pulled open the hatch. The mate was at the helm and the captain was below, meeting with the scientific crew. Maldias ordered the captain brought to the bridge, and in three minutes had complete control of the vessel.

Lt. Berry's boat waited near the *Explorer* but stayed out of gun range. He did not want to take fire he could not risk returning. Soon the radio carried the heavily-accented voice of Maldias.

"You have done very well, sailor boys. Now you stay away and no one will be hurt."

"This is Lieutenant Berry. I request permission to come aboard and talk."

"Permission denied. Talk all you want, but if you come within range, you're a target."

"What do you want from that ship, Maldias? If you and your men give her up, we will talk. But I swear to you, if you hurt those people, the only way you'll come off that boat is in a bag."

"You are telling stories, Lieutenant, and just when I was starting to like you. *Que lastima!* You are as bad as that Dr. Richardson. Don't any of you people tell the truth anymore?" Maldias said with a sneer. "This is what I want and I tell the truth. I want these kind amigos to do a little dive for me with their beautiful submarine and find for me what your Dr. Richardson stole. Do you know he would have killed his own senorita? What a fine *mujer.* A gentleman would never do such a thing."

"After they make the dives for you, what then?"

"Then we sail south, far away from you, Lieutenant, far away. And after we have a little fun, I let them go. Don't worry,

Lieutenant."

Inspector Cord's car was parked by the Dockyard marina. They were loading equipment onto the *Mermaid* when a call came through on the radio. He listened for a minute without speaking, then yelled to Doc, "We've got trouble, Doc. Maldias sank Richardson's sub and then boarded the *Oceanic Explorer*. He wants them to dive with their research sub and bring up his cocaine. He has Karen and is holding the crew hostage."

"What about Debbie?"

"She was not mentioned."

"Do we have a position on the downed sub?" Doc asked.

"I don't think so," Ian answered.

"Any chance the Navy will still help us after you decked that marine?"

"It won't hurt to try. I'll call and tell them how sorry I am."

"Maybe Lieutenant Berry can help us again. I'll get Sheri and Mark to help me on the boat. I've got an idea where that entrance might be. Also, where is the best steel-fabrication yard on the island?"

"What do you want?"

"Someone who can make a plug for the stern of the *Enterprise*. We need a sub and that's the only one I know of. A good oil field steelyard could have her welded up in half a day. What can you find for us?"

"I'll get my lads on it. Let you know in a minute."

Ian pulled out his radio and placed the call. After he heard Doc's idea, Captain Johnston responded, "The hull is a titanium alloy. I don't know anyone here who can weld to it. We might try making a steel plug and seal it in place without welding. Your idea might work, but it will take time."

Ian passed the information to Doc who said, "It's still worth a shot. Right now it's our only chance."

Ian stowed the radio and as he handed Doc the last bag, he asked, "Have you thought about some kind of plan? What are we going to do if we can get that sub to work?"

"When I was in dive training learning to use the old Navy

hard hats, another diver and I made a bet that we could exchange Mark V helmets in the bottom of our zero visibility tank, relock the helmets and get to the surface without our tenders figuring out what we'd done until we were back up on the stools."

"Did you make it?"

"Am I still here?"

"So if we could lock out of one sub and into their research sub, the surprise might give us enough of an edge..."

"Exactly!" Doc said. "Maldias will have his guard up this time. If he's smart, he'll keep the *Explorer* moving all night and use the sportfisherman as a scout boat. With her electronics, it would be next to impossible to get in. Their sub would be our best chance."

"Yes, but Captain Johnston sounds less than enthusiastic."

"If it were your sub, would you loan it to us?"

"Good point. Perhaps if the government promised to reimburse him...."

"Are you going to sign that one?" Doc asked.

"Not on your bloody life, mate. That's what the politicians are for—to kiss ugly babies and tell lies."

"Spoken like a true poet."

"I'll call the captain again."

"Good. Mark and Sheri are on the way."

The phone was ringing as Doc walked in the back door of the dive shop. He grabbed it and answered. It was one of the technicians from the NASA base. "Sorry about the trouble, Dr. Holiday. Just following orders. You guys are off the hook, but I wouldn't tour any bases for a while. The brass still wants to chat, and we found something with the satellite. Got a navigation chart handy?"

Doc found a chart and the excited technician began rattling off computer coordinates faster than Doc could write. Doc slowed him down and then began penciling in dots on the chart.

When Doc finished plotting the coordinates, he drew a line through the points which led directly into the west side of the Dockyard's stone walls. "Yes, I've got it," Doc acknowledged. "It's almost in line with Daniel's Head. Good work.

Now give me the GPS coordinates on the downed sub again. OK, got it. You may have just evened the score with Roberts with this info. We'll keep you posted."

Doc hung up the phone trying to remember the technician's name. He could not. Sheri came in the back door with Mark.

"The hospital called," Sheri reported. "Lisa has a mild concussion and they're going to keep her overnight, but she will be OK."

"That bastard Richardson's going to pay for this," Mark swore.

"He may have already written his last check, Mark. If you want to get even for Lisa, I certainly could use your help. You too, Sheri. The base called; we have the coordinates on the tunnel and it's time to go diving."

He pulled the recirculator out from under the cabinet, removed the cover and checked the pressure. The two cannon ball-shaped fiberglass tanks were nearly full. He replaced the cover and put Mark to work carrying equipment to the *Mermaid.*

Ian arrived with the news that Capt. Johnston had become much more agreeable when promised government compensation if the sub were damaged. They were already looking for a welding crew.

Doc told Ian about the call from NASA and showed him the chart. "According to the satellite, there's a tunnel beginning about here," he said, pointing to the line he'd plotted. "It goes back into the hill beneath the museum and the Commissioner's House. We'll start with that tunnel. There must be other entrances. See if you can find them. If there's anyone down there, a distraction could save my tail. I'll take the radio in a drybag and keep you posted."

"I should go with you," Ian suggested. "You still have that bad leg."

"Thanks, but I'll be fine with the scooter. Besides, we've got only one recirculator. Just do your best to get in from up here. Oh, and tell your men to be careful. My guess is Debbie and Paul are down there."

"Of course. Good luck, mate, and watch yourself."

When all the equipment was loaded, Doc climbed to the

fly bridge with Sheri and took the *Mermaid* out of the boat basin. They came over the shallows and headed west towards Daniel's Head. He watched the compass and his watch, and made quick notes on the chart. The boatyard had been unable to repair the GPS so Doc would have to find the position by dead reckoning. Sheri took the wheel and followed Doc's directions while Doc used Paul's sextant to measure angles between landmarks and plot them on the chart.

"This should be about right. Drop the anchor, Mark, and measure the depth."

Mark measured the line with double arm spans and when the anchor touched bottom, he called out, "It's pretty close to sixty feet."

"That's what this chart says we should have. Let's give it a go."

Mark let out more line to increase the scope and then secured the line. Doc was putting on his wet suit when Mark came to the back deck. He frowned when he saw the red seal tattoo and the scars on Doc's upper arm, chest and neck.

"Helicopter shot down in a river," Doc said. "Got a bit messy—I had to make a new door. I'd still be down there without this." He patted the Randall strapped to the inside of his right calf. "Now, you two keep your eyes open. There's enough gas in this recirculator to last four or five hours so don't get anxious in thirty minutes. Ian will send someone to the rampart to call you back in after he hears from me." He picked up the radio and called Ian. "Any word from the welding crew?"

"Sorry, Doc. There's no one on the island who can fabricate what you want in less than a week. Captain Johnston's found another sphere. There was a spare in Grand Cayman. It will be here in the two days. Best we can do, sport. It was a good idea, but it looks like we'll have to try something else. Good luck on your dive. I'll be standing by, over."

"Roger, out," said Doc as he turned off the radio and stowed it in the drybag.

"OK," Sheri said, "remember, no cowboy stuff. If there is trouble, you wait for Ian and his men. Promise. Promise me, damn it, or I'm coming with you."

"I promise I'll be careful."

She kissed him and handed him his mask. He cleaned the lens, put it on, clipped the bag with the radio and Beretta to his harness, and did an easy back roll over the side. Mark lowered the scooter and Doc dropped beneath the surface. He set a course towards the steep cliff wall and squeezed the scooter's trigger. He'd gone about a hundred yards when a natural shelf emerged from the bottom. He followed it until it led to a deep, wide trench. At the end of the trench was the opening to the tunnel. It was fifty feet high and nearly as wide. He pointed the nose of the scooter towards the surface and circled up to control his rate of ascent. Mark spotted him break the surface and began pulling the anchor while Sheri started the engines.

"I found it," Doc told them when the boat was alongside. "Remember to watch the ramparts for Ian's signal."

Sheri gave him the OK sign and yelled, "Be careful!" one last time. He waved back and started down.

Legions of gray Bermuda chub and yellowtail snapper stood guard at the entrance. They parted as he approached and allowed him to pass. Once inside, the scooter's large headlamp was dim in the engulfing darkness, and he could see only what was directly, immediately before him. The walls of the tunnel had the same sawed edges as the Dockyard's stone work, and he had visions of the convicts being crushed by a wall of water when they cut through the last few feet to the sea—their reward for a job well done. He tried to imagine life as a prison laborer. He got as far as the dark stench of a prison ship's bilge—that was enough. He shook it off to concentrate on the job ahead.

Doc ran the scooter just beneath the ceiling. Still near the entrance, curious fish came up to greet him before darting away. As he pushed forward out of the light, he disturbed a large nocturnal nurse shark. It darted ahead in an explosion of bottom silt, seeking the protection and seclusion offered deeper in the tunnel. He watched it go as he continued forward. On the chart, he had estimated the length of the tunnel at just under a half mile—now it seemed endless.

He checked his watch. Eight minutes felt like an hour; he was halfway. At the fringe of his light beam he saw the shark again. It passed beneath him, surrendering its quiet refuge to the noisy, bright-eyed intruder. Distracted by the shark passing, he nearly missed seeing the two thin, plastic-coated wires, one red and one white, running along the ceiling. His brain flashed full alert—those were blasting cap wires, very clean and very new.

He stopped short and used the scooter's light to follow the wires to a long, narrow opening above him. In the light he saw a twenty-foot diameter reel of rusting steel submarine net. He followed the blasting cap wires up over the edge of the reel to a massive set of gears. There the wires ended, in a fifty-five gallon steel drum, wedged in between the support braces of the net's machinery. The drum had several warning stickers pasted on it: Danger EXPLOSIVES, Danger Caustic Material, Danger, Highly Flammable. Then in large, green stenciled letters across the top he read NITROMETHANE. Attached to the top was a square black box with an LED display which read two minutes, then one minute fifty-nine seconds, fifty-eight, fifty-seven, fifty-six. He was mesmerized for only three of those fleeting seconds before he grabbed the wires and followed them to their origin.

Nested in the drum's plug was a booster well—a short, sealed tube protruding down into the clear liquid just far enough to hold a one pound cast pentalite booster with a number eight duPont blasting cap set in its center. He eased the cap out of the booster, cut the wires and looked at the detonator's timer—one minute seven seconds remaining. Then he saw an identical second pair of wires leading back across the ceiling. He swore and looked at the timer—fifty-nine seconds.

Here's why this is a one idiot job, he thought, so only one of us gets blasted into the ozone, and he deserves it. Only an amateur would set one charge or one detonator. A pro would create a closed loop—a redundant system of two charges, two detonators—each capable of initiating both boosters, each self-dependent. He squeezed the scooter's trigger and kicked as hard as he could while following the wires across the ceiling. Again they went up through the machinery to the overhead braces.

The red glow of the detonator's LED quickly came into view. How in the devil had they gotten that drum up there through the maze of gears and chains? he thought. They must have brought both in from the other side. There was no way....He propped the scooter so that the light shone on the drum and peeled out of the recirculator. He hung it quickly on a steel brace and took a deep breath, closed the valve and dropped the mouthpiece.

Doc slowly exhaled as he pulled himself up through the mass of cable and gears. The timer read fifteen seconds when he got close enough to read it. Read it, yes, but not reach it. The big Randall dive knife on his leg was caught on something below him. He kicked and pulled with all his strength until the knife strap gave. He lunged upward and grabbed the wires running from the electronic detonator to the booster well.

It was a bad angle and he had to get the cap out of the booster. He pulled hard on the wires. They cut into his hand as he pulled harder and swore. Finally, the cap pulled clear and a milli-second later, detonated.

Had he been closer, the blasting cap would have mangled his hand. But the small fragments of aluminum and copper were slowed by the water and caused little damage when they hit him. Still, he instinctively jerked backwards, hitting his head on the iron bracing, flooding his mask and kicking the recirculator from its perch. It dropped to the tunnel floor, forty feet below, lost in darkness.

He needed air. He used just enough of what he had left to half-clear his mask. His head buzzed and he swallowed hard, trying to fool his brain and buy a few more seconds. He grabbed the scooter and pointed the light beneath him, but the beam wasn't strong enough to reach the tunnel floor. He squeezed the trigger and started down. At least he hoped it was down, for in mid-water he had lost his reference. His brain screamed for oxygen and he kicked as hard as he could. When at last he saw the recirculator, it was still twenty feet below. He swallowed again, but that trick only works once or twice. He ditched the scooter and kicked to the bottom. Grabbing the recirculator mouthpiece, he exhaled the last of his air and then took a deep breath—nothing. He had forgotten to open the mouthpiece valve. He flipped the lever and tried again. By now the stars he was seeing were exploding like white phosphorus flares. The air came just in time. He pulled long and hard against the rig's big diaphragm. It took a while until his head cleared and his pulse returned to nearly normal.

He unbuckled the remaining strap on the Randall's sheath and slid it beneath his weight belt. By the time he picked up the scooter, he was steady again. He checked his compass heading, squeezed the trigger and lifted off the bottom into the darkness.

Eight more long minutes passed before an air pocket opened up above him. He released the scooter's trigger, turned off the light, and broke the surface silently. The cavern was larger than a football stadium. On the far side, soft orange lights reflected from the hull of a gleaming black submarine. It looked like nothing he had ever seen. Why hadn't the NASA technician told him there was still a sub in the cave? Did that mean his guess, that the Navy was somehow involved, was on target?

He studied the warren of rooms, stacked pueblo-like against the far walls, for any sign of Debbie or Paul. There were men working on the sub and they turned as another man came in shouting. Doc took a compass bearing and slipped back beneath the surface. Soon his hand felt the smooth, plastic hull of the sub and he could hear the whine of a generator inside her. He followed the contour of the hull back to the stern and surfaced again. He was still well-hidden, or so he thought, when a familiar voice said, "Doc, we all know how you love to play in the water, but will you quit screwing around and get up here? We haven't much time." It was Col. Sandy Andrews.

"Hell, I should have known," Doc said as he sat down in the cluttered office and workshop of Dr. Hans Behrmann. Sandy offered him coffee in a standard-issue white Navy mug. Doc looked at it, turned down the corner of his mouth, took it and continued, "Where are Debbie, Paul and the Morrison boy? Are they here?"

"Paul Singleton and Tom Morrison are here and they are fine. I hate to tell you this, Doc, but your daughter is on the sub with Jason. We don't know..."

"That's why you wouldn't give me anything on Roberts

or Richardson—you were in this up to your beady, red eye-balls. And I suppose you didn't know Debbie was here until fifteen minutes ago either. It never changes, does it, Sandy?"

"He did not know," Behrmann interrupted with commanding firmness, "until Jason took the *Nautilus* out last night. I called him this morning." The old man stood and crossed the room to Doc. He stood with hands on his hips, leaning aggressively forward—a man used to absolute authority. He continued his lecture, "Last night Jason stole the plans to the *Black Wolf*, destroyed my computer and all my data, and then tried to sabotage the sub. Of course he was not successful."

"He almost was," Doc countered. "There were a hundred and ten gallons of nitromethane boosted to go high order in the tunnel. It might not have destroyed your sub, but you wouldn't have been going anywhere for a few hundred years. What the hell's going on here?"

Behrmann turned away as if the question did not deserve an answer. Sandy continued the story. "Jason used his sub to sink a freighter hauling grass, the one your daughter and her friends found. It was also carrying cocaine—lots of it, very pure, worth millions. Confronted with the option of staying here and playing dedicated archaeologist, or leaving with the coke and selling the sub plans for many more millions, he and his crew bailed out last night. The plans are worth a lot more if they're the only copy, and grandpa here can't go after him."

"Not millions...my *Black Wolf* is worth billions," the old man added. He ran his fingers through his long white hair and looked about in agony. "This is my life's work, my genius, my soul. That boat could save the environment, save the world..."

"But didn't it belong to the Navy?" Doc asked.

"It did until Behrmann stole her two months ago. The hull is undetectable. The Navy's been going nuts trying to find her. That's when I got involved. And just so you hear it from me, I had no idea this had anything to do with your daughter's disappearance. That's not the way we play, Doc. I hope you believe me."

Doc was silent and Sandy continued, "This sub is really

something—not only is she undetectable but the turbines are really incredible. Dr. Behrmann here is a real genius. He'll be famous one day...."

"Like Wernher von Braun," Behrmann added.

"So what went wrong? Why did you steal her?" Doc asked.

"They left me no choice," Behrmann answered. "The government was scrapping the project. I told them we finally had the answers. After forty years, we could really make it work. Forty years, Doctor, working in obscurity—no money, no recognition. But in spite of all the obstacles, I did it. Do you understand? I, Hans Behrmann, did what the best minds in Germany and in your country said could never be done. And instead of recognizing my genius, they told me they weren't interested. No market they said...no market for an engine that makes its own fuel from raw seawater, solves the problems of carbon dioxide escalation, global warming, and ends your country's dependence on atomic power and foreign oil. No market? They are insane! And they said if I ever went public, they would put me in prison, or turn me over to the Jews as a war criminal. They closed my lab and scattered my staff. I had no choice. The *Black Wolf* is my redemption; she must be saved."

The old man sank to the table, his head in his hands. "I...I was decorated by Donitz and Hitler, I..." His eyes were wet and he began rambling in incoherent German, not realizing that he had lost his audience.

"Can we use this sub to go after Debbie?" Doc asked Sandy.

Sandy shook his head. "There are problems," he said.

"Like?"

"Fixing the turbines. How much do they know up above?"

"They know about the other sub and this base," Doc answered. "So now they must know Behrmann is here as well. That's why the Navy was so anxious to keep us on the base. There's an Admiral Bartlow flying in from D.C. who is real anxious to talk. You know him?"

"He's the head of Naval Intelligence—his neck's in the noose for losing the sub. I imagine he's not real happy."

Behrmann was sitting with his back to them still carrying on a dialogue with an unseen audience. He was drifting between German and English when he turned towards Doc and said, "The turbines were never the problem; it was the fuel consumption rate—twenty-five times higher than a diesel —but I solved that too. Why did they cancel my program?"

"Didn't the Germans originally add small diesels as auxiliary engines to solve that problem?" Doc interrupted him.

"Yes, we did. Very good, Doctor. Are you an engineer?" Behrmann asked, turning to face them and becoming more attentive.

"No; English. I read about it. And as I recall, the advantages of the Walter's turbines were amazing speed, the ability to generate oxygen, and complete independence from surface running. So if I understand you right, you're able to make hydrogen peroxide from seawater and burn it hot, without diesel or any other booster. Is that correct?"

"Yes," Behrmann answered, "but then we started having problems. The perhydrol burns so hot the turbine bearings couldn't take it. They were not the bearings I specified. They were cheap replacements and they failed. The right ones are coming from Germany any day now."

"But could the sub go out as is and rescue my daughter? Is that possible?"

"Not much of a chance, Doc," Sandy interrupted. "Too many problems...too dangerous."

Behrmann looked up quickly, as if surprised at the colonel's response then looked at Doc and said, "I'm afraid he's right. Too many problems." But his hesitation and the tone of his voice didn't sell the line.

Doc studied them, his mind racing to pull together the puzzle's pieces. They were stealing the sub from the government, at least that had been their plan, but what now? What could they hope to do now? The Navy was certain to find the entrance soon and they would never let him take the sub to rescue Debbie. This was no time for diplomacy. Doc's eyes narrowed and he focused on Behrmann. "I see. Well, if what you're telling me is true that this sub can't dive to rescue my daughter, then it's worthless to me and there's no reason I shouldn't call Admiral Bartlow right now, is there?" He pulled the Beretta and the radio out of his bag and laid the radio on the table. Behrmann recoiled from the radio as if it were a snake.

Then Doc turned to Sandy. "So Jason got the plans and all the test data. Any idea who he was in cahoots with? Without those plans, whoever that was is going to be up a creek if the Navy finds this sub, isn't he, old buddy?"

Doc opened Sandy's coat and removed a Glock 9 mm. "I'll keep this one for you, just until we finish choosing up sides. Well, how 'bout it? Can we get this sub underway, or does my daughter just die out there while we sit here and talk politics?"

Sandy glared at Behrmann and backed away from the table. Sandy's trying to hedge his bets, Doc thought. He'll give up the old man and the boat to save his butt. But I don't need him—I need this sub and once I've got it the Navy can wait, at least until we find Debbie. Ball's in my court.

"Dr. Behrmann," Doc began, his voice softer now, "if you stay here, you are going to lose this sub and you will go to prison. We might have a few hours, or we might have five minutes, but I found you and they will too. My only interest is to save my daughter. But there's a ship out there being held hostage by the drug runner who sank Jason's sub. If you could rescue Debbie and the people on that ship, you'd be a real hero. The Navy couldn't touch you after that—the press wouldn't let them. You think about it. It's a chance to redeem yourself and save your sub."

"Don't listen..." Sandy began, but Doc swung the gun under the colonel's chin and glared at him with the intensity of a blast furnace.

"You will help me, Colonel," Doc said very softly, "or by all that's holy I'll feed you to that Admiral. I don't care what kind of deals you made or who you sold out to. Help me, or by heaven you're history."

Col. Andrews glared back, but his resolve could not withstand the heat of Doc's anger and he could only nod in submission.

In the *Nautilus*, Debbie continued to care for Richardson and Roberts. She found an oxygen unit and set the mask on Jason's face. The dressings had slowed his bleeding and his pulse was stronger. She saw a small amount of clear fluid oozing from his left ear. Her diving first aid training had taught her not to do anything to stop the ooze of cerebral fluid and to keep his head slightly elevated. She checked him for other injuries, but found none.

She did the best she could for the two injured men, then climbed on a passenger seat behind Richardson and studied the console until she found the remaining radios. She tried the underwater telephone and the VHF. Neither worked. The oxygen monitors showed less than half, but she had no idea how long that might last. Her first priority was to send some signal to the surface to let someone, anyone, know that she was alive and that she wanted out.

Beside the joystick that controlled the thrusters was a second stick. This one looked like it had been part of a child's toy. There were switches on it labeled in German. She looked at the rest of the console. This second stick was the only thing she saw that could control the torpedoes. But how? There had to be some logical sequence. Germans are logical; this was German. She would figure it out. As she studied the device in the dim, flashing lights, Jason moved for the first time and moaned.

His moan startled her and she fell backward from her precarious perch. As she fell she caught a large cord. She landed hard against one of the seats and the cord pulled out of whatever it had been attached to. She regained her balance and looked at the cord. At its end was a single switch with a red plastic cover. The firing switch for the torpedoes, she thought. She looked at Jason and smiled.

"So you want to go home too? Well, if this works we just might make it. I'm so anxious to introduce you to my father. I'm sure he's been trying to meet you for several weeks now. It will be such fun, watching him teach you some manners. So please don't die yet, you egotistical bastard."

Debbie crawled back to the console and found the control box she was looking for and continued tracing the cord.

An hour passed before a white-uniformed policeman waved to the *Mermaid* from the fortress wall. Sheri cranked the twin diesels and got underway. They were just rounding the point north of the Dockyard when there was a bright flash on the horizon behind them. She looked back over her shoulder and two seconds later, the rifle-sharp crack of high explosives reached them. "That was the same kind of explosion that made me blind for three days—a torpedo. But where could it have come from?" She pushed the throttles full forward and the stout wooden hull climbed on plane and roared towards the marina.

She didn't back the engines down until she was in the mouth of the marina. When she brought the boat to the slip, Ian was waiting and helped Mark walk the boat back between the pilings and secure the lines. He had heard the explosion, but hadn't seen the blast. Yes, it could have been a torpedo, but that was as much as anyone knew. More importantly, however, Doc had called. He knew where Debbie was and she was in trouble.

Ian led them to the boat shed where Col. Andrews was waiting. He took them through the back storeroom and swung open a wide panel of shelves revealing the hidden stairs.

"Where's Doc's daughter?" Sheri asked as they started down the stairs.

"He will tell you all about it," Andrews answered.

When they emerged into the great cavern, Sheri gasped in amazement. "Look at this! Who would believe it? I want to get my camera."

"I'm afraid that won't be possible, miss. This base is top secret. I must have your word..."

"Knock it off, Colonel," Doc interrupted. "She can tell whoever she damn well pleases. We've had enough of your secrets. No more people are going to disappear to protect this one. This is Bermuda, not the U.S. and you..." Doc had come up the stairs to meet them.

"Don't be too hasty, Doc. You don't understand what's at stake here, but that can wait. Sheri thinks she saw a torpedo explode west of Daniel's Head."

"It could be a signal from the sub," Doc said. "Come and look at the chart. See if you can show me where." When they got to the bottom of the stairs, Doc looked for Sandy who was suddenly missing. No time to worry about him now, Doc thought, but I'm certain he's up to no good.

"Too bad your idea to repair the *Enterprise* didn't work," Ian said as they crossed the scaffold and catwalks to the sub. "Can we use this sub to go after Debbie?"

"Yes, I think so, but Andrews is stalling. We have to get this billion-dollar bathtub toy underway before the Navy finds us, or Debbie won't have a chance. He said there was some kind of problem with the turbine bearings, but there's been so much lying you'd think they were writing a government budget. We need to find the old German. Have you heard from Lieutenant Berry?"

"Well, tell me, amigo," Maldias said to Dr. Abrahms, the *Oceanic Explorer*'s senior scientist. "Just how long will it take to fix this thing so that you can make this little dive for me?"

"Mr. Maldias, as I've tried to explain, what you are asking is just not possible. This ship and its equipment were designed for research, not for salvage work. And we have no diving equipment capable of going that deep. Please be reasonable."

"Señor Doctor, my position is reasonable. Come for a walk with me. You two, come with us," he said pointing to two older crew members. Maldias led them from the galley, where his men had gathered the captured crew, out to the crane on the back deck.

"Now, Señor Doctor, explain to me what this does. This big expensive piece of equipment...it must do something, *sí?*"

"It lowers sampling devices to the bottom and..."

"And brings them up again, right, amigo? It brings things up and down. Now all I want you to do is to go down and bring something up for me. How hard can this be for a smart *hombre* like you to understand? Your little sub goes down with a rope and this beautiful crane pulls up that tiny little submarine. Doctor, it is time to go to work—time to get serious. Look at me," he demanded, waving his Uzi. "I'm going to shoot the next person who tells me my brilliant idea won't work. That is serious, *sí?* If there is one thing I can't stand, it's a bad attitude. So we're going to have us some positive thinking. No more negative, negative, negative. No more bullshit."

The torpedo exploded close to the *Oceanic Explorer* and the shock wave hit the research vessel like a heavy hammer. Maldias was knocked to his knees, but kept control of his gun. The pressure wave slammed into the stern and overhead; the crane's boom and block swung violently. Maldias's first thought was that the Navy had fired on them, but he quickly guessed the correct source of the blast.

"So you want to come up? I bring you up, Captain Nemo, and cut out your heart," he said aloud.

"Roberts trusted Debbie and he told her a lot," Paul told Doc as they climbed down the ladder into the *Black Wolf*'s galley. "On paper she's light years ahead of anything in the water. But so much of her is new technology, never tried before—she's still full of bugs. It's basically a steam turbine system with oxygen as the only exhaust gas. Behrmann got her barely shipshape enough for some short sea trials up at New London, then when they pulled the plug on his program he stole her and headed here. That's when they started having problems. Seems the building contractor cut a few corners—critical ones. Like someone didn't want the thing to work. They almost didn't make it and Jason had to tow him the last hundred miles with that tourist sub he stole."

They made their way through the control room to the helm seat which was surrounded by six large screen monitors and another six small ones. "All systems," Tom explained, "including weapons, trim and ballast, were computer controlled with no manual backups. Behrmann didn't think his computer was capable of screwing up. It did and they had to add redundant manual systems. The result was like having a space shuttle redecorated by Ralph, the South Bronx plumber." They moved aft from the galley, past the sick bay and the crew's quarters towards the engine room.

"But why couldn't the Navy locate them?" Doc asked. "And why didn't it show up on that satellite photo?"

"Two reasons," Tom replied. "First, the *Black Wolf*'s hull is plastic. It absorbs sonar the same way the experimental rubber coating on U-1105, the *Black Panther*, did. Second,

Roberts hid the cave with that masking system—the same way he hid the shipwrecks. That's how they got away with keeping the first sub, the *Nautilus*, down here for two years."

"And what you found on the computer could have put an end to their game," Doc said, his first suspicions that there was more at stake than old clay pipes and ballast stones now confirmed.

Tom opened the engine room hatch and Dr. Behrmann climbed up from where he was working on the starboard turbine. The engines looked like jet turbines and were much smaller than Doc had imagined. Behrmann closed the hatch behind them and said quietly, "I've changed the jets so that we can run the turbines on diesel. Not as fast, or as clean, but it will work. Now all we need is fuel—lots of it—and oxygen too. Help me save the boat and we'll rescue your daughter. You have my word, but there are two conditions."

"I'm listening," Doc said.

"Andrews must not be allowed back on board, and I want the plans Jason stole either in my hands or destroyed."

"How much oxygen and diesel, and how soon can we get underway?"

"We can leave now, but we have less than a hundred liters. We won't even get across the flats without more fuel. One other thing, if they lost power on the *Nautilus*, they could be in real trouble. Their Dregger carbon dioxide scrubbers are tied into the air conditioning. Without the blowers cleaning their air, or power to operate the solenoids to feed in fresh oxygen, they can't last long."

"How long?"

"With five people, perhaps three or four hours. No longer."

"Then we may already be too late?" Doc asked.

Behrmann nodded and said nothing.

On board the *Oceanic Explorer*, Dr. Abrahms and the chief engineer worked over a drawing board. "That might work," the chief said and explained. "If we can use the mechanical arm to attach a large hook here, or here, and then add lift bags wherever else they can be attached, we just might be able to bring her up."

"What about the crew? Any possibility they're still alive?"

"Be a miracle if they are. My guess is, that explosion was the battery compartment. I'm betting all we find is one big junk pile."

"For God's sake, don't tell him that! I think we are all alive only as a momentary convenience. Have you thought about taking the research sub and just running for help? At least some of us would survive."

"Of course I've thought about it, but how could you live with yourself after? No, we have to hope the Navy has something going and just do what we can to keep him from going nuts. Let's get the *Deep Ranger* ready and pray that we'll get lucky."

Mike came down the stone stairs and across the catwalk to the sub on a dead run. Ian followed closely behind, gasping to keep up.

"We've got trouble, Doc," Mike said as he braced himself against the galley table to catch his breath. "I just heard on my boat radio that the Navy's sending the marines. Admiral Bartlow gave the order the minute he arrived. They've got choppers and ground troops on the way. Bartlow means business."

"But we still need fuel and oxygen. We can't leave yet," Doc growled. "And then what happens to Debbie? Can't you do something, Ian?" he looked at the inspector in desperation.

"Yes, I jolly well can. They're on my turf now." He grabbed his radio and began barking into it. He paused only long enough to tell Mike, "Call your admiral, Lieutenant. Tell him I've seized this sub as an unregistered pleasure vessel of suspicious nature and he'd best have permission, in writing, from the Premier before he sets foot on this base. If he lands those choppers here, I'll seize them too and arrest the crews."

"Can you do that?" Doc looked in amazement.

"No, but I'm betting that admiral doesn't know I can't and the Premier's on holiday, off the island. Your fuel barge will meet us on the flats. And my patrol boats will meet us with the oxygen. Well, don't just stand there. Let's get going; my plan may not work."

"This isn't your party, Mike," Doc said. "There'll be hell to pay if Bartlow finds out you tipped us off. You'd better go."

"Not a chance, Doc. This is the only way the crew on that research ship have a prayer and I've got a score to settle for two of my men. I'm signed on for the duration. Let's send Sheri topside to call Bartlow. Maybe if he thinks we've already gone, it will get him off our backs."

"Anything's worth a try."

Mike started writing his message as Doc went to find Behrmann. Ian was back on his mobile phone giving orders to his men on the patrol boats who would escort the fuel barge. Doc found Behrmann in his office hurriedly throwing his belongings into cardboard boxes.

"That one is for burning," Behrmann snapped when Doc started to pick it up. Doc saw old photographs of Behrmann's family in the box and a picture of Jason. Behrmann threw a match into the box and ordered, "You get that one," pointing to another full of clothing. They stopped halfway to the sub. They could hear helicopters landing above them.

Sheri was just coming up the ladder with Mike's message as Doc started down. He helped her up and she paused to speak. "Doc, we didn't get time to..."

"I know. Don't worry, I'll be back. Make that call and be careful. Now hurry." He kissed her, handed her his radio and she was gone, across the catwalk and up the stairs on a run.

"So go arrest them," Doc shouted to Ian.

"Don't waste your time," Mike shouted back. "Let's just get the hell out of here." Ian hesitated a moment then followed them down the ladder into the *Black Wolf*'s control room.

Sheri had just slipped out of the warehouse when the first marines came running past her. They went directly into the storeroom and pulled open the hidden door. No one paid attention to her and she walked as calmly as she could until she was out of the museum. As soon as she crossed the drawbridge, she ran to the dive shop.

Debbie sat on the deck by the console. Jason had been silent and Bill moaned occasionally, but there was nothing more she could do for him. She had found the boat's log and in the dim glow of the flashlight, she was busy writing a letter to her father. Debbie's heart was full, but the words wouldn't come. She thumbed through the pages. Stuck in the logbook's back flap was a radio schematic.

She took the diagram and pulled herself up to the radio that had struck Jason. It was hanging from a wiring bundle and some of the wires had broken. The extra length of wire was coiled and held with a tie wrap. She got the scissors from the first aid kit, cut the plastic tie and lowered the unit to the deck beside her. Using adhesive tape, she began splicing the wires. When she was finished, she turned on the power switch. A red light blinked on and the face of the channel selector became visible in white light. She keyed the mike and began, "Mayday, mayday, this is the submarine *Nautilus* calling any station. Mayday, mayday."

Doc froze in mid-sentence as he heard Debbie's voice over the *Black Wolf*'s PA system. He ran to the control room and Dr. Behrmann came in after him. "It's Debbie! Can we answer?"

"Yes, of course. Use this radio." Behrmann handed him the mike.

Doc hesitated. "Could they hear us on the research vessel?"

"Perhaps. It could be the same frequency they use to talk with their sub."

Doc handed him back the mike. "We'd better wait. At least we can thank God she's alive. How soon can we get underway?"

"As soon as you close the hatch. We have company coming," Behrmann said, pointing to the monitors. Marines were running down the stairs. He hit the dive alarm and the *Black Wolf* pulled away from her berth. All that remained when the first marine reached the slip were the ripples of their wake.

A lanky grad student came running into the *Oceanic*

Explorer's scientific center. "Sir," he blurted, "we just received a radio message from the downed sub. There is a girl sending a 'Mayday.' No one else has answered. We've tried, but it doesn't seem like she can hear us. Isn't there something we can do?"

"Not at this range, but if we moved over her we could lower a transponder and use it as a speaker. She would hear that. Have you told him?" Abrahms asked, pointing above them to the wheelhouse.

"He was on the bridge. He gave me permission to ask you."

"Alright, let's see if he will let us move. See how the shop is coming with those hooks for the lift bags. We are about ready to dive."

CHAPTER

21

Capt. Behrmann became a new man the moment they got underway. It was as if he were tapped into the power generated by the sub's turbines. His eyes flashing with enthusiasm, he stood straighter and moved with the agility of a man years younger. The control room was no less sophisticated than a space vehicle command center. Doc stood quietly, trying to learn as much as he could by watching the big screen monitors and studying the old German.

Behrmann ran the boat from a console that rivaled any television studio control room. His monitors provided three-dimensional sonar graphics that reduced bottom profiles to rapidly changing contour lines and interfaced them with the images provided by television cameras in the bow. He piloted the sub with a single joy stick, like a schoolboy playing a video game. Doc was fascinated by the technology. He looked at Ian and Mike who were also transfixed by the monitors. Behrmann was a genius to have created the *Black Wolf*. Now the question was, could they trust him? Would he keep his word and help them rescue Debbie, or would he simply seek vengeance on his renegade grandson, destroy the *Nautilus*, the stolen sub plans and Debbie as well?

Behrmann guided the sub through the long tunnel and soon they passed beneath the steel net into the light at the tunnel's entrance. The legions of yellowtail snapper and Bermuda chub guarding the tunnel entrance scattered as the sub emerged.

As Sheri opened the back door of the dive shop, she could hear Col. Andrews on the phone in the front room. She stepped quietly across the wooden floor and leaned over the counter for her backpack. It was where she had left it, and from its weight, she knew the Smith & Wesson was still inside. She knelt behind the counter and listened as he started shouting. "Admiral, I think that would be a big mistake. You are making a career decision here. If that sub escapes again and becomes public knowledge, you're going to be answering to a mighty pissed-off President. This is not the kind of issue he wants to have to explain in an election year. If your marines don't do the job, I will. We've all had enough trouble from that crazy old Nazi and his plastic submarine. That's all, Admiral. Have a nice day."

Sheri froze and wondered if he had heard her come in. She reached into her pack, found the butt of the pistol and moved slowly towards the door. But as she turned, her knee nudged a chair, which grated on the wooden floor. Abandoning all pretense of stealth, she shoved it aside and ran out through the door. She found Mark in the restaurant and pulled him from his seat.

"But I just ordered!" he protested.

"Forget it. Come on." She grabbed his arm and half pulled, half pushed him towards the *Mermaid* at the dock across the street. She climbed to the fly bridge and hit the preheaters while shouting to Mark to cast off the lines. Then there was a thud behind her and a soft voice with a slight Virginia accent sent her heart into her throat.

"Sorry you couldn't mind your own business, miss. I don't know what you heard, but we can't take any chances now, can we?"

Col. Andrews stood on the fly bridge ladder behind her. He opened his coat, showing Sheri his gun.

She swung her pack with a backhand as hard as she could and hit him square in the face. It stunned him and he fell back from the ladder. By the time he recovered, he was looking up the barrel of the Smith & Wesson.

"Nice gun, but don't you have to cock it or chamber a round before it will fire?" he said, trying to distract her.

"Forget it, asshole. It works just like a Walther PPK. All I have to do is pull the trigger and it fires the first round like an old double action," she said, recalling Doc's description verbatim. "Just keep your hands on the deck and believe me, I'm a country girl and I'll shoot your ass just like I'd shoot an egg-sucking snake, or an old fox in my hen house."

"I am a federal officer. You'd better think twice 'cause you could be in prison a long time for this."

Her hand was shaking badly in spite of her bravado. She shifted to hold the gun with both hands and the shaking moved to her legs and the pit of her stomach. "Listen, mister. You scare me, but you're trying to hurt Doc and that scares me more. So don't you move, or I'll shoot you just like I said. Now take that gun out real slow with just your thumb and your little pinky, and pitch it over the side. We've got to catch a submarine."

When the gun was gone, she marched him to the bow and had Mark tie his wrists and ankles to the bow rail braces. She kept her gun on him even as she climbed back up to the fly bridge.

"Stay away from him, Mark. Come to the bridge with me. I just heard him tell some Navy admiral he was going to keep that German's sub a secret no matter what. The only way he can do that is to kill us all. We have to find that fuel barge before the sub leaves for deep water, and I have to get this message to Admiral Bartlow. Take the wheel—let's go north to the flats."

She shoved the throttles forward and the *Mermaid* left the marina, drawing shouts from other boat owners rocked by her wake. Screw protocol, she thought. She'd just kidnapped a federal officer and Doc's in trouble again.

She picked up the radio, placed the call and relayed Mike's message. She received a polite "Thank you, is that all?" from a woman with a heavy southern accent.

"No," Sheri added. "Tell the admiral we have a Colonel Andrews aboard. He tried to kidnap me and the son-of-a-bitch is now my prisoner. Ask the admiral if he has any suggestions about what we should do with the colonel."

"Just a moment," the professionally polite voice responded. "Honey," the voice began again in a moment, "the admiral says 'Feed the son-of-a-bitch to the sharks' and he wants
to know if you'd like to have lunch next time he's in town."
There was a pause and then the woman returned. "One more
thing, honey. Tell Lieutenant Berry the admiral says to 'Kick
some butt and that SEAL Team 2 is on the way from Norfolk
and will be waiting to hear from you.'"

"Thanks, I'll tell him," Sheri said and turned off the radio. She could see the patrol boats and the fuel barge when
the *Mermaid* rounded the point. Sheri looked anxiously and
didn't see the *Black Wolf*'s swept-back sail until they were much
closer. Then she could see a crew of Ian's men passing oxygen bottles down the main hatch.

"Now, there's a welcome sight," Paul said, seeing the
Mermaid. "She looks as good as new, Doc. Thanks for saving
her." He put his hand up to shade his eyes and looked again.
Her bow was breaking through the waves and it looked as if
someone was tied to the bow rail, taking a real pounding. As
the boat drew closer, they could see Sandy seated on the bow
and tied spread-eagle, catching the full force of the swells.

"Well, look at this," Doc laughed. "I can see the headline
now: 'Ex-Special Forces Officer Abducted by Female PADI
Scuba Instructor.' He must have really pissed her off. Better
get Ian and Mike up here. This has got to be a good story
with all the makings of an international incident."

Sheri brought the *Mermaid* alongside and Mark threw a
stern line over to Doc. She jumped down from the bridge
and into Doc's arms. "Thank God you are still here," she said.
He could feel her trembling. "He was on the phone with some
admiral when I got to the dive shop. Said he was going to
keep the public from ever hearing about the *Black Wolf*. I
tried to get away, but he followed me to the boat. He sounded
like he intended to kill us all."

"Things got so hectic in the cavern I forgot about him

until we were gone," Doc said. "There's only one way he could keep this story quiet. Why don't we invite him below deck and see if he'd like to tell us how he intended to accomplish that?

"Good work, Sheri! I just might have to keep you around." He hugged her again. Ian and Mike escorted their guest below deck.

"I talked to the admiral. They're coming."

"Who?"

"The SEALs from Norfolk. Mike is supposed to call the admiral right now."

Doc looked at his watch. The last of the oxygen tanks were loaded and the fuel lines were being taken off. "It's time," he said.

She held him tighter. "You're coming back in one piece this time?"

"I promise. Now see if you can get back into the cave. Stand by the radios, but don't call until I call you first."

She kissed him and jumped back to the *Mermaid*'s deck. Paul helped cast off the lines and looked longingly after his boat as she pulled away.

Below deck, Mike was on the radio to the base while Ian questioned Andrews. The colonel remained sullen, refusing to talk. Doc listened for a while and then said, "Let's see if we can use a little logic to figure this out.

"What's so important about keeping this sub a secret?" Doc asked Sandy. "National security? Not if you were dumb enough to let this old man steal it. How about our resident genius Captain Behrmann here? Are you protecting him? I doubt that too. He's your scapegoat if the shit hits the fan."

Sandy looked up with an arrogant smile and cocked his head.

"Well, what's left?" Doc asked and scratched his head. "Now, who do we know that would want this sub?" he asked Ian.

"I'd say just about everyone," Ian replied. "The captain's right...she's worth billions."

"Yes, but Colonel Andrews wouldn't do a thing like that, Ian. He's a dedicated American, probably even a Republican. No, he would never commit an act of treason just for a few million dollars."

"Of course not. How could I have ever suggested such a thing?" Ian laughed.

"You're not even close, Doc." Sandy snarled. "You only wish it were that simple. The only chance you've got is to dive this baby as deep as she'll go and stay down about a million years. The Navy will be after you with orders to seek and destroy."

"What about that, Mike?"

"That's not what the admiral said," Mike answered.

"Ha!" snorted Sandy. "That's only because Bartlow hasn't heard from the White House yet. They can't let you go; they're in as deep as you are."

"What? Their own sub?" Paul asked.

"Just think about it. It was a cute little toy until the mad scientist here solved the fuel production problems. Now it's a bigger threat to our economy and the balance of world power than any war. What would happen if Japan or some other non-oil nation got their hands on this technology? The balance of economic power could be turned upside down overnight," explained Sandy.

"But my work—the environment!" Behrmann yelled. His face was flushed and the veins in his thick neck where bulging. "Reverse global warming, stop acid rain and the greenhouse effect," he continued, now on his toes ready to lunge. "Make nuclear power and fossil fuel engines obsolete. The Nobel prize..."

"And put millions of Americans and our friends out of work, render billions of dollars of petro-chemical and automotive plants obsolete. You old fool!" Sandy yelled back. "No one gave you a contract to save the world. All we wanted you to do was build a simple submarine—a nice, safe little killing machine—to preserve the peace and stimulate the economy." Sandy's eyes were cold, steel-gray and his voice had the edge of a razor.

"Then it was true? You were trying to sabotage my work!"

"Yes, but you were too stupid to take the hint, so we had to pull the plug."

"Too stupid!" Behrmann launched himself at Sandy landing a solid right before Doc and Ian pulled him off.

"You'll never get my sub. Never! I'll destroy you and your whole corrupt government. I'll..."

"Captain, we're going to hit the reef!" Mike shouted. "Look at your monitors!"

The monitors showed they were in dangerously shallow water with coral heads dead ahead. The boat had been on autopilot, but it looked as if they had entered a box canyon.

"Let go of me!" Behrmann demanded.

"What's happened?" Doc asked, loosening his grip. The auto pilot reversed the turbines and brought the boat to a dead stop. "Is there a computer problem?"

"My computers don't have problems, Dr. Holiday," Behrmann said stiffly as he raised the red covers on the firing switches for the bow torpedo tubes. He turned his back to them and said, "I'm saving us two hours and probably saving your daughter's life." He hit the plungers and there was a high-pitched whine and then a loud "whoosh" followed closely by a second as the torpedoes flew from the bow tubes.

"Oh, bloody hell, man, you can't blast the reef!" Ian protested. "Oh, bloody hell..." The inspector turned away from the monitors in disgust.

Behrmann watched a digital timer and shouted "Now!" as the last second elapsed. The first torpedo struck the reef with a thunderous roar. Water and coral rock were thrown hundreds of feet into the air. "Now!" Behrmann shouted again. But this time nothing happened.

"The detonator failed," he said calmly. "We will have to fire it manually. Come, Dr. Holiday, back to the torpedo room and I will show you where to place the charge."

They walked through the narrow-carpeted, track-lit passageway between storerooms, past a small sick bay and three small staterooms. All the doors were closed. Behrmann continued to explain that he had used detonators left in the cavern from the war, and that they had been lucky so far to have only one fail to fire. Detonating it would be a simple task.

"They are all exactly alike," Behrmann said as he removed the cover plate of another of his deadly arsenal. He showed Doc the torpedo's firing mechanism and the proper location to place a booster charge.

As Doc studied the wiring, he realized there was nothing

"antique" about the system. The impact detonator was backed up by a sophisticated capacitor-discharge system which could be either fired by timer or radio frequency. Behrmann could fire the torpedo at any time and blame it on faulty hardware. Doc looked up from the torpedo and into the old man's eyes. They were glowing like hot coals and his mouth curled in an evil grin.

"Why the games? Captain, you can fire that torpedo without my help. We don't have time for this." Doc let his anger show.

"*Ja,* I'm glad to see I didn't overestimate you, Dr. Holiday, because you are the only one on board who can appreciate what I have done. I could have destroyed you all and there would have been no questions. Believe me, I still can. There are enough of these torpedoes in the cave under the Dockyard to shorten the island by half a kilometer. The charges are set and the timer is running. Isn't that where your young woman is, waiting patiently by the radio, right on top of the blast?

"This is my show, Dr. Holiday. There is absolutely nothing wrong with this boat. We replaced the bearings weeks ago, but I couldn't risk letting Jason or Andrews know. I was sure Jason was working with Colonel Andrews, but I just couldn't believe that your government would do this. Not after forty years of supporting my work. But now I take no more chances. Don't get in my way, Doctor. Your life means nothing compared to the importance of this sub. That's my insurance. A good policy it is to carry adequate insurance, don't you agree?"

"What about my daughter?" Doc asked.

The old man continued, "I keep my word. We will rescue your daughter, my construction plans and Jason's drugs, but we are not going back to Bermuda. That would be foolish. I will destroy the Dockyard if you try to interfere. Do you understand?"

"I do."

"Good. Now that we've had our little talk, we can get back to business. Put the cover back and we'll put on a show for your friends."

The second blast tore out more of the reef. They could

hear chunks of coral showering the deck, but Behrmann pushed forward even before the visibility cleared. Sonar video imaging told him the course was clear and it was. The sub gained speed. Behrmann had absolute confidence. Suddenly there was scraping against the hull, but his face remained unchanged, his confidence unshaken. He pushed the turbine's revs higher. The scraping grew louder and then there was silence. When the visibility cleared, they were in deep water.

Sandy's nose was broken. He was tied in a chair by the sick bay deep berth and didn't speak while Doc packed his nose with towels and ice to stop the bleeding. Doc's mind raced as he worked. Why would Sandy destroy the sub? Why? Suddenly it came together. Sandy didn't need the sub if he was certain he had the plans. That would have been the safest way—convince the Navy the sub was destroyed and the government could close the files. Now the only remaining set of plans are worth millions, hundreds of millions, thousands of millions.

But what if Jason couldn't deliver them? Then Sandy and whomever he was working with needed to have the sub, and probably Behrmann as well. Especially if Sandy thought there were still problems in the turbines that only Behrmann could fix. That was more of Behrmann's insurance.

Now if I were Sandy, Doc thought, and I doubted that I could recover those plans alone, I'd have to cut a deal with Behrmann or I'd be out of the game. So why the broken nose? Was Behrmann on the level or was that another performance like the one Jason put on in the theater?

Then instead of a single Edison light bulb clicking on in his brain, the realization hit like a Lake Lanier Fourth of July fireworks show.

"Paul, you do the honors and then stay with him in case he suddenly comes down with verbal diarrhea and wants to tell us more about his little games. The rest of you, come with me. We need to search this boat. I haven't forgotten our friend's conversation with that admiral."

Once they were in the passageway, Doc held up his hand and motioned them to follow him to the diving locker. The locker itself was a chamber, large enough for four men to live, or at least subsist, and it contained a diving lock which could also be used as a treatment chamber. Racks of equipment lined the room and narrow bunks were stacked high with boxes of absorbent for the recirculators.

Doc led Tom, Ian and Mike into the equipment locker, grabbed the first recirculator and removed the cover. The wiring and tubing appeared intact. He ran a systems check and read the pressure in the oxygen and helium tanks. They were full. Then he saw it: the third page of Behrmann's insurance policy.

Doc returned to the control room and stood behind Behrmann, watching him dive the boat before moving to the chart table. Only the deep blue of open ocean was visible in the color monitors. The sub slid noiselessly through the clear water as they started down, and the Fathometer read one hundred sixty-five feet when they leveled off and began the run to the *Oceanic Explorer.*

"The position I got from the NASA technicians puts the *Nautilus* at just over four hundred fifty feet. What's the design strength of your hull?" Doc asked.

"I think we will survive," Behrmann answered with a sarcastic snort. "I designed the hull for more than ten times that depth. This alloy, like curved glass, becomes stronger with evenly applied pressure. There are limits, but very deep ones. Did you find any explosives?"

"Nothing, but the men are still looking. Got any ideas?"

"He is bluffing. He has too much to lose. We will go deeper as soon as they finish searching. But your men should ride in the diving locker where they can get to the escape hatch. Up there they could get out just in case. I want you in here with me. If we lose the computer, it will take both of us to operate the manual controls."

They were passing two hundred fifty feet and light was beginning to fade. "As a precaution, we'll go to battle stations. Tell them to secure the watertight doors, and bring back one of the recirculators for yourself."

"What about you?"

"I am the captain," Behrmann said, giving Doc a look which implied only an idiot would have asked that question.

You old wolf, Doc thought, what are you up to? "Right,

I'll see to it," he answered. "Let the games begin," he said softly as he left the control room. He looked in on Sandy as he passed the sick bay. The ice had helped, but not enough to prevent two black eyes and a good bit of swelling. The old man could throw quite a punch. That was something to remember.

He told Paul to follow him, and after checking the colonel's restraints, they moved forward to the diving locker. Doc repeated Behrmann's orders. However, as he spoke, he pointed towards the bitch box and raised an index finger to his lips. Then he pointed to Mike who began writing on a legal pad. When the dual briefing was over, each man gave a thumbs up. They took the recirculators and got as comfortable as they could in the crowded space. Then Doc said loudly to the bitch box, "Everything is ready, Captain. Let's go find that sub."

"*Ja, Ja*, we are ready now. We dive deep now. You come back to the control room please, Doctor. I need your assistance."

When he entered the control room, Sandy moved in behind him, holding a short-barreled Luger. He waved the gun at Doc and told him to close the hatch.

"I'm afraid there will be a slight change in plans, Doc," the colonel said. His voice had a congested nasal resonance and it was apparent that speaking was painful. "We're still going to dive the sub. But your friends don't have a round trip ticket—too bad." He pointed towards a fold-down bench at the radio console and said, "Have a seat. Now, where's your Randall and that Beretta?"

"In the diving locker," Doc answered truthfully. "I thought we were done choosing up sides," he said, glaring at Behrmann.

Behrmann gave no reply. His gaze was fixed on the monitors as he trimmed their dive angle slightly with the joy stick.

"Oh, we chose up sides alright. Too bad you chose the wrong team. Now it's my turn to call the plays and this one's called deep six the losers." Andrews quickly searched him, then taped his hands together behind a pipe.

"Let's get it done," Behrmann snapped. "Open the bypass valve and blow ballast to keep us in trim."

Sandy opened two valves on the ballast control panel and then reached across to a large hand wheel on an eight-inch gate valve.

"Blow more forward ballast," Behrmann ordered as the bow started to drop. Sandy opened the first two valves all the way and turned back the hand wheel on the big gate valve until the bow angle was stable again.

"But they have the recirculators," Doc said. "What good will flooding that compartment do?" Doc asked.

"Wait and see," Sandy sneered. "We took a little precaution just in case you and your friends get lucky."

Behrmann hit the switch on the bitch box, and they could hear the rush of water and the shouts of the men in the diving locker.

Paul could see the open valve. He put on the recirculator and fought his way towards it. The other men shouted in panic as they pulled on the harnesses and fought to hold themselves in place against the blast of water. The compartment was small and filled quickly. The shouting was soon replaced by deathly silence. Doc watched the compartment's digital depth meter drop from one hundred to two hundred then to three hundred feet. The numbers scrolled faster than he could read and then they stopped at three hundred eighty feet. The bottom became visible through the dark water on the other monitors. Behrmann slowed the dive and leveled the boat. The Fathometer now read four hundred and eleven feet.

"I am sorry," Behrmann said when the sub was on the bottom. "Colonel Andrews convinced me I had no choice. I have to have those plans. Now that leaves you two choices. I could destroy the *Nautilus* with one push of this button," he said as he flipped up the red cover on the torpedo firing switches, "or you can rescue your daughter and bring back the plans and the drugs, and you both will live. That's my deal."

"What about after?"

"You will remain with us. Obviously, I can't let you go, but you will be alive, and your daughter as well, if you don't cause trouble."

"And my friends? Why go to all this trouble when you

could have just shot them and dumped the bodies overboard?"

"How unimaginative, Doctor. And if their bodies were found? Oh no. This way it's an unfortunate diving accident, and I'm not to blame. Just a little more insurance, you understand."

"Explosive decompression is no unfortunate accident. How will you explain that?"

"Come on, Doc," Sandy said. "Put that great mind of yours to work. You can be a lot more creative than that. Remember how dangerous closed circuit recirculators are? One simple little mistake and it's oxygen convulsion city. Let's open up this one and see if you can figure it out." He reached down and picked up the backpack.

Doc's heart rate doubled and he tried to remain calm. He had switched back the tanks in all the units including the one Andrews was holding. He closed his eyes as if trying desperately to concentrate and remember, and then blurted, "Oxygen poisoning. You reversed the oxygen and helium tanks. That's a hard way to go, you bastard."

"You're three for three Doc; I knew you could do it," Sandy laughed and set the unit back on the floor—unopened. "And guess who gets credit for setting up the units? Sorry, buddy. It was just too good to resist. We'll have to remember to check that one out before your little dive now, won't we? You do remember, don't you: oxygen on the right...or was it on the left? It's the old shell game, or the lady and the tiger. Which door do you choose?" He laughed again, but it hurt so he stopped, replaced the ice bag and glared at Behrmann.

"What about the others on the sub—Bill Roberts and your grandson?" Doc asked Behrmann.

"They are traitors. Let them die with their toy submarine and their worthless artifacts. Your daughter is the only one who deserves to live. You will deal with it. Those are my terms. You'll need the other recirculators. Start bringing down the chamber pressure," he said to Andrews. "We haven't much time."

Sandy turned back to the console and opened the air valves to blow the water from the diving locker. Green lights flashed on when the chamber was dry. He then secured the gate valve and hit the pump switches to begin pulling down the compartment's pressure. Doc's stomach knotted as he counted the minutes and watched the gauge drop from four hundred eleven to three hundred seventy-five to three hundred fifty. The pressure was dropping much too fast. He swallowed hard and shook his head to clear his vision. At three hundred feet, the gauge had mysteriously stopped and then resumed dropping, but at a much slower rate. He looked to see if Sandy or Behrmann had also seen the gauge stop. Fortunately, they now had something new to worry about.

"It must be from the research vessel," Andrews said, pointing to the top center television monitor. There was no television image, but on the sonar screen a green outline was descending with its range and bearing on the bottom of the screen.

Behrmann typed commands into the computer and the screen analyzed the sonar image. "She doesn't belong to the U.S. Navy. You're right. She must be from the research ship," he said.

As the small sub got closer, the sensitive cameras soon merged the camera image with the one the sonar had first given. Now, through the dark water, they could see the research sub's lights descending ahead of them. She changed course and began moving away off to their port side. When the lights faded to a dim halo, Behrmann blew ballast and lifted the *Black Wolf* up from the bottom, beginning a slow pursuit of the smaller sub. He gained altitude and stalked it like a fighter pilot—above and behind—safely out of visual range.

The pressure in the diving locker continued to slowly drop, and again the gauge stopped. Doc forced himself not to look at it and focused instead on the research sub. It was descending to the *Nautilus*. As they followed, Richardson's sub became visible in the research sub's bright lights. It stood tilted over, its stern lodged deeply in the mud. The faint glow of red and green LED's shone through the bow hemisphere, but there were no signs of life.

Behrmann slowed the *Black Wolf* to a hover, still out of the small sub's range. Sandy glanced at the pressure gauge and noticed it was stuck. He tapped the face of the display and at first nothing happened. He hit it harder and the numbers started scrolling again. "Must be Japanese," he chided. Behrmann's only response was a foul look. Andrews went back to watching the monitors. The needle stuck again.

"Look, someone just moved up in the bow," Doc said. "I think it's Debbie. You can see her in their lights. Turn on your radio."

Behrmann flipped the radio switch. At first there was silence, then they heard Debbie's voice, weak and distant, report that Roberts and Richardson were in bad shape. She wasn't sure how much oxygen was left. The air conditioners and carbon dioxide scrubbers were out. Her breathing was labored and her sentences full of disoriented pauses.

The tiny sub's captain assured her that they would be able to bring the *Nautilus* to the surface, and told her to do everything she could to conserve oxygen. It might take them a while to attach the cables and fill the lift bags.

"We can't let them do that," Andrews said. "We can't risk going to the surface. Do something."

"No," Doc said. "Let me go now. I can get into the main compartment through the center hatch without them seeing me."

"Not yet," Behrmann answered. "Wait until they surface, then you go."

Andrews looked back at the pressure gauge. He tapped it again, but this time it remained stuck. "What's taking so long to pump out that air? This gauge hasn't moved in ten minutes."

"Something could be blocking the valve. Put pressure to it and see if you can clear it," Behrmann ordered.

Sandy opened the valve and sent a blast of air through the line. When he closed the valve, the numbers started scrolling again. "You were right. It's dropping faster now."

Doc watched the needle drop forty feet and then it stopped again. He breathed deeply and flexed against the tape holding his wrists. He succeeded only in cutting off the circulation.

"There is another valve on the outside of the chamber by the hatch. Opening it shouldn't raise our pressure enough to hurt now, and it should save some time. Do it," Behrmann ordered. "Get Dr. Holiday ready to dive.

"Come on, Doc. Let's go feed your friends to the pretty fishes." Sandy motioned for Doc to stand and then cut the tape. Doc moved silently towards the passageway, trying to restore circulation to his hands. Sandy followed at a safe distance, still holding the Luger.

When they reached the diving locker, Sandy ordered Doc to look through the thick view port and report what he saw. Doc said he could see four bodies, all face down. Sandy motioned him away, looked to confirm the report, then opened the exhaust valve. The remaining pressure rumbled through the pipes and moisture blew into the companionway.

"Open it," Sandy ordered and waved the gun at him. Doc opened the hatch and entered the compartment. Paul was closest. Doc gently rolled him over and checked his carotid pulse. It was strong and steady.

"Well?"

"He's dead. What did you think?"

"Get the rigs and we'll put the bodies in the lock."

Doc undid the harness and slid Paul out of it. As he lifted his friend, he saw the 9 mm Beretta hidden in his shirt. Doc dropped to his knees to make certain Andrews didn't see the gun. When Sandy turned away to check on Mike, Paul suddenly shoved Doc clear and put one round neatly through the center of the colonel's chest. The federal agent looked up in astonishment and then dropped without a sound.

"Bloody bastard!" Paul exclaimed. "We should have blown him out a torpedo tube."

"Are you alright?" Doc asked.

"Hell no, I'm not alright. I'm blinkin' dead just like you said. You scared the salt out of me when you said that. Thought I might have popped off and just didn't know it yet." Paul tried to stand again and fell back against the bulkhead. "My feet don't work," he said with a perplexed look.

Doc grabbed the recirculator. "Turn off the helium, breathe oxygen and stay quiet. I'll get you into the chamber in a minute." Mike and Tom were on their feet, but Ian got up more slowly. He was unsteady and disorientated. Mike caught him and helped him back down.

"Take care of them, Mike. Oxygen and all the water they

can hold. I'll be back as soon as I deal with Behrmann."

The stateroom doors were all locked. Doc kicked them open one at a time until he found Behrmann sitting in the captain's cabin, staring down the barrel of a small Luger. Doc lunged at him, pushing the gun away as it fired. "Leave me alone," Behrmann demanded. "Let me die like a warrior. I won't be humiliated like some hoodlum."

"Oh, really? You had plenty of time to use that before I got here. Go ahead, Captain, I'll wait," Doc said as he removed his hand from the Luger. He kept the Beretta leveled at the old man. There was a long silence before Behrmann dropped his gun hand to his lap.

"No, Doctor, go and save your daughter. I'll be here when you return." He handed the Luger to Doc. "The pair of them belonged to Donitz. Hitler gave them to him. He gave them to me."

Doc took the gun and stuck it in his belt. "What about your insurance—your bomb at the Dockyard, Captain?"

"I'm the only one who can disarm it. Let me go or they will all die."

"I'm afraid we can't do that, but I'll make you a promise. If you hurt anyone else, I'll make sure you rot in the worst hell hole on earth. The whole world will know what slime you are and that this boat was a total failure, a worthless toy built by an old fool. That's a promise you can count on. You'll live the rest of your life in public humiliation." He led Behrmann back to the control room and taped him into the chair.

He returned to the diving locker. Paul and Ian were decompressing in the lock out chamber. He looked in through the view port and they looked much better. Mike and Tom were at the external controls breathing from portable oxygen units.

He left Tom at the chamber controls and told Mike to get on the radio to the base. They needed an Explosive Ordinance Disposal team at the Dockyard, on the double. While Mike was making the call, Doc hurried back to the control room to see if the rescue sub was still there. It was still filling the lift bags with its manipulator arm and had a cable hooked to the *Nautilus's* skid frame.

Doc had watched Behrmann closely and had tried to memorize the sub's operation. He opened the air control valve to blow ballast and eased the sub off the bottom. Behrmann stared at him aghast. Doc smiled and pushed the joy stick forward while increasing the power. "How am I doing so far?" Doc asked.

Behrmann looked away, refusing to answer.

"Would you mind telling me where the light switch is? I'm afraid I forgot," Doc asked.

"Try the ones with the red plastic covers," Behrmann sneered.

"Thanks, but I remember what those are," Doc answered. "I'll try these." He reached over his head and hit three toggles. Bright light flooded the area in front of and below the *Black Wolf.* The research sub turned immediately into the lights. Doc hit the switches again, flashing the lights and the smaller sub flashed back. He flipped on the bitch box and asked for a volunteer who still remembered Morse Code. Mike yelled back that he was on the way.

The captain of the research submersible saw the lights flash, grabbed the co-pilot's arm and cautioned him not to speak on the radio. He'd been expecting a visit from the Navy and assumed this was it. He could not see the sub, but the signals were clear. The pilot was ex-Navy and flashed back answers to Mike's instructions without hesitation. Of course they would help. Was there ever any doubt? The *Black Wolf* approached cautiously and dropped rather awkwardly to the bottom. In a moment the lock out chamber opened and the first two divers appeared.

Paul and Ian swam to the smaller sub's diving lock where they could decompress safely at the surface. They swam up to the hatch and left their recirculators where Doc could find them. This was a one-way trip. As soon as Ian and Paul were aboard, the smaller sub returned to the *Nautilus* to check on Debbie. The news they flashed back in Morse wasn't good. Debbie was no longer responding.

Doc hurried back to the diving locker and helped Tom and Mike into the lock out chamber. Mike pulled his mask on and took several deep breaths. "OK, let's go," he said and gave a thumbs up. Doc nodded, closed the inside hatch and opened the valve. He increased the pressure slowly at first, giving them a chance to clear their ears and sinuses. When the gauge read two hundred fifty feet, he opened the valve wider and water flooded the chamber. When it read four hundred eleven feet, Tom spun the hand wheel retracting the dogs and pushed open the hatch. He looked at Mike who gave one more thumbs-up signal and then pulled himself clear of the lock. Tom quickly followed Mike out and they closed and dogged the hatch. Doc wasted no time in joining them.

They swam quickly to the research sub, pausing only long enough to pick up Paul and Ian's recirculators and see their friends wave from inside the cramped diving lock. They crossed the barren silt bottom to the *Nautilus*.

The air inside the *Nautilus* was thick with smoke from shorted circuits and burned wiring. Debbie was struggling to breathe. She sat beside Jason Richardson in the big helm seat looking out into the darkness. She saw lights coming closer and growing brighter until they were nearly blinding. The rescue sub's captain had explained the original plan, but now the oxygen was gone and with it her ability to function.

She watched the lights with disconnected interest. She realized her blouse was wet—warm and sticky. She turned uncomfortably to look at Jason. His dressings had soaked through and fresh blood was seeping onto the seat. She tried to sit up. She intended to find the first aid kit, but a wave of nausea hit her and she sank back to the seat and closed her eyes. She would rest for just a minute, she told herself, just until the nausea passes.

She was drifting now, beyond awareness, beyond caring. Her brain's scream for oxygen was reduced to an impotent whimper. It was over; Jason had won. She would die here beside him, his for eternity—not that it would do him any good. She wanted to curse him, but she had forgotten the words. There were lights—bright lights—and she knew about them. This must be the way then. Why fight it?

She heard someone calling her name, telling her to open

her eyes, telling her to answer the radio. What radio? She opened her eyes and raised her arm to block the glare. Silhouetted by the blinding light were three gigantic creatures dressed in black, descending for her like archangels. There must be some mistake, she thought. They're supposed to be in white. I'm not going anywhere with anyone in black—they must be for Jason.

Doc dropped to the twelve-foot diameter two-inch thick acrylic hemisphere and looked down. He put down the dry pack and dropped to his knees. Debbie was just inches away. He pressed his hand on the hemisphere's smooth surface and its shadow covered her face. She looked up at him confused at first, frightened, and then an awareness tried to pull her back to reality. She tilted her head sideways, smiled, reached up to him and then collapsed. Doc stayed long enough to be certain she was still breathing and then shifted his attention to Jason. "If she dies because of you, I'll chop your heart up for crab bait and then kill the crabs."

Doc signaled Tom and Mike to follow him. He picked up the dry pack and swam down the sub's back to the aft hatch which had been converted to a diving lock. Mike helped him open the hatch and Bobby's body rose slowly up from the darkness. Tom held the body while Doc stripped off the recirculator and then dropped into the lock. He opened its inner hatch into the flooded compartment and then banged on the bulkhead, signaling the others to follow. Tom passed down the body and then helped Mike with the dry packs.

This diving locker was twice the size of the *Black Wolf*'s and extensively equipped . Doc surveyed the tool chests while Mike and Tom checked the pressure of more than a dozen compressed air bottles. There were two Haskel jammers mounted on the bulkhead and all the big storage tanks were full. Four more recirculators had fallen from their racks and had slid to one corner of the room. Doc made circles around them with his light signaling Mike to collect them.

Now they had enough air and mixed gas. The difficult part still lay ahead—to enter the main compartment, and do extensive decompression while bringing the cabin pressure back to normal surface pressure. Then they had to be ready to fight when the sub was eventually raised to the surface.

Doc signaled Tom and Mike to start disconnecting the big compressed air bottles from their manifold rack. He took the brightest light and a handful of tools, and went back out the lock to inspect the hull. Beneath her belly, he found the stainless steel tubing which connected the oxygen bottles to the main compartment.

He took the hacksaw from the tool bag, flicked off the light to save the battery and began cutting. If there were degrees of darkness, he thought, this would be the baseline to which all other levels would be compared. His eyes slowly adjusted, but even after he had cut halfway through the tubing he still could not see the whiteness of the sub's hull, the luminescent dial of his watch or even the inside of his own mask. With his left hand he could feel the cut. There was a strong suction on the hacksaw blade. He removed it carefully and began working the tubing until it broke.

When the first was done, a half-inch stream of water shot into the sub with two hundred pounds of pressure behind it. Soon there was a second, then a third and a fourth. He flicked the light back on and looked for more tubing. All that remained were the lines from the main ballast control tanks and he knew they would be needed. He swam up to the bow again and pointed the bright dive light at Debbie. This time there was no response, but the water level inside the compartment was rising quickly. In the bright lights of the sub, he had seen the large crate against the center hatch and Bill Roberts pinned under it. As the water level rose, the crate floated and Roberts was buoyed up with it. Doc swam to the diving lock to hunt for more tubing in the aft compartment to speed up the process.

Mike had the same idea and was working on opening the medical lock in the center hatch. The external cover had a pressure relief valve, and Mike had found the right wrench and had it nearly removed when Doc dropped beside him. Doc nodded his approval and Mike gave it the last turn it needed. The valve fell from the fitting and Mike could feel the suction as the water rushed past him into the forward compartment. When the suction stopped, they knew the air in the compartment had compressed to the ambient pressure and no more water could enter. With the compartment flooded, they set to work opening the large center hatch between the forward and aft compartments.

The heavy hatch opened inward and was three quarter inch reinforced steel plate. Doc turned the hand wheel to release the dogs and tried to get leverage beneath it to force it up, but couldn't find anything to brace against. Mike worked beside him. He grabbed the hatch combing and brought both feet up against the hatch. With Herculean effort, he managed to open it enough for Tom to shove one of the big air storage bottles into the opening. Mike collapsed and Doc helped him up. It was a start. While they were looking for something larger to wedge into the door, Tom dropped back to the workbench and returned with a lift bag and a scuba tank. He slipped off his recirculator and slid half way into the opening. He attached the bag to the inside handle and spun open the tank valve. Air hammered out, the bag filled and the heavy door lifted open. They were in.

Tom took several long breaths from his recirculator mouthpiece, slipped back into its harness and swam behind Doc, heading for the bow. Each of them carried a spare recirculator and a light.

Tom was the first to reach Debbie. She was still beside Jason in the big pilot's seat which was high enough to be in the air pocket. He opened the valve on the recirculator's mouthpiece, tilted her head back and gently placed it in her mouth. Her skin was grey and cold, and she wasn't breathing. He pulled the mouthpiece out, pinched her nose, and gave her a first long, slow breath and then a second. She coughed and then inhaled. Doc came up and put the recirculator mouthpiece back in her mouth and shouted, "Debbie, breathe!" But the words came out like loud quacks. She opened her eyes, looked up at them both through a confused haze and took a long breath from the recirculator.

Mike surfaced beside them. He took out his mouthpiece and tried to talk. Doc nodded and gave an OK. Debbie was going to make it—if any of them did.

After a few breaths, Debbie recognized Tom and her father, and gave them a feeble smile. Doc took her hand and kissed it. He signaled Tom to stay with her while he checked on Jason and Roberts. Both were still alive. Doc put them on recirculators then signaled Mike to follow him and dropped back beneath the surface. After setting Mike to work loading the big air bottles into the compartment, he went out alone to crimp and seal the tubing he had cut. The rechargeable battery in his dive light was losing power and he flicked it off to save what little remained.

He found the cut tubing, and one by one, crimped them with a pair of channel locks. Mike had loaded all the tanks into the forward compartment by the time Doc returned. They gave the lower compartment one last look with Mike's light. Doc grabbed two large fire extinguishers, pushed them through the forward opening, and then climbed back in. They dogged the hatch behind them and began opening the valves. Air rumbled like a freight train from the tanks and the water level began to drop. It took half an hour to empty the compartment and finally secure the center hatch. Near exhaustion, they began their long hours of decompression.

As planned, the tiny research sub used the last of its spare air to partially fill the lift bags, and then it began its ascent to the surface. Paul and Ian had started their decompression immediately and looked anxiously at each other as the craft was lifted aboard the mother ship. As the power cables and air pressure lines were connected, one of Maldias's men paced beneath them with an assault rifle, asking questions and harassing the students. Cold and tired, Paul huddled at the internal chamber controls with heliox decompression tables and a flashlight. Ian adjusted his oxygen mask and then fingered the Luger's grip in his belt. They were in for a long night.

CHAPTER
22

Doc looked over the instrument panel again with the dive light. He found the cabin pressure exhaust valves and opened them wide. Air rushed out, but then to his surprise the pressure gauge needle stopped suddenly at 197.65psi and water sprayed in through the ports.

"What's wrong?" Tom quacked as Doc quickly closed the valves.

Doc slammed the console with his fist. He started to explain, but remembered no one could understand his helium-distorted words. He ripped a page from the log book which had been high enough to stay dry and wrote, "We're stuck. Can't vent the cabin—outside pressure's too high. Have to wait until we're at the surface to start our decompression or go back to the *Black Wolf*."

Tom read the note, took the pencil and wrote the word "Maldias" followed by a large question mark.

Doc nodded in disgust. How could I be so stupid? he thought and looked away in anger. Now our only chance is to go back to the *Black Wolf*. Richardson and Roberts will never make it and the kids on that research ship won't have a chance.

Doc turned back to get the note pad but Mike was now reading it. When Mike finished, he took the pencil from Tom and wrote "The Haskel jammers!!!" He smiled and handed the pad to Doc.

Doc's face brightened immediately and he slapped Mike on the back. "Let's do it," he quacked.

It took all three of them to lift open the heavy door. Doc put on his mask and dropped through the hatch into the water with Mike following quickly behind. They were down to one working dive light which Doc handed to Mike. The Haskel boosters were bolted to the bulkhead and plumbed to the gas storage bank. Doc found the tools he needed with the fading dive light and set about disconnecting the units. The work space was tight. The angles were bad, and when he could get wrenches on the bolts he could only swing them an inch or two. It was slow going, and to make matters worse, the light soon died. It felt like hours passed before he had the first unit off. Mike collected the tubing and fittings, and carried them back to the hatch. He climbed out and set to work trying to connect them to the sub's plumbing.

Doc's hands took a beating, and the salt water burned each time he smashed his knuckles or cut himself on the sharp metal brackets. But an hour later, the cabin reverberated with the pop-bang, pop-bang, pop-bang of the obnoxious little pneumatically-powered pumps, and the cabin pressure started to drop. He shook his head to clear his eyes, completely exhausted now, and rubbed his temples. He checked the pressure gauges again and looked out into the darkness.

He reached back into the deep recesses of his memory trying to remember the helium/oxygen partial pressure decompression tables he had last used twenty years ago. He turned the slate to catch the dim red LED lights and started writing a long column of depths. The stops would be ten feet apart, that was the easy part. Next he wrote in blocks of stop times, short at first, then longer as the depths became more shallow. How would he care for his crew if one of them got bent on the way up? There was no back-up chamber available on this run. He studied the numbers again and looked back at the gauge.

The pumps had reduced the cabin pressure to two hundred and forty feet, the depth of their first stop. He shut them off and wrote down the time. The quiet was a welcome relief. Now that they had reached the first decompression stop, he could check on the others. Tom was holding Debbie. The boy had earned his wings caring for her—Debbie had chosen well. Doc knelt beside them and stroked her forehead. She opened her eyes and took his hand.

"Hi," she said through the recirculator mouthpiece. Her voice still had the Donald Duck resonance but the shallower depth helped. At least now they could understand each other.

He squeezed her hand. "Sorry it took so long to get here, honey, but the worst is over. We'll be home soon."

He checked on Richardson and Roberts. It was nothing less than miraculous that either of them had survived. Their bleeding was under control, thanks to Tom's efforts, but that wasn't saying much. Doc wondered if the hyperbaric atmosphere, bombarding their wounds with thousands of extra oxygen molecules, was the only reason they were hanging on.

He moved lower to the center hatch and began rearranging furniture. Mike joined him and Doc explained, "We're all going to need some rest. Help me move these bunks and then you can get comfortable." He unhooked the tier of Navy-style bunks and they came crashing down with dozens of bags of cocaine tumbling over him like a waterfall. He fell backward and Mike helped him up.

"You know, as much trouble as this stuff has caused, no matter what happens we have to make certain it gets destroyed. Mike, can I count on you no matter what?"

"Don't worry, Doc. I won't let them get it, no matter what."

When they finished rehanging the bunks, it was time to turn the Haskels back on. Doc climbed back to the console and wearily pulled himself into the captain's seat. He checked his watch and opened the valves. He recorded the time and looked back over his shoulder as Tom helped Debbie into one of the bunks and crawled in beside her. Mike took the berth closest to the helm.

"Man, I'd kill for a cup of coffee," Doc said, but no one was awake to hear him. He sat in the seat like an astronaut staring into the heavens waiting for a pre-dawn launch, listening to the racket of the pumps. He thought about Behrmann tied in the *Black Wolf*'s control room, about the hostages on the research ship above, and about Paul and Ian decompressing in hiding aboard the little sub. And he thought about everything that could possibly go wrong. This was the hardest part—the last watch of the night when your old ghosts come back to haunt you. He checked his Rolex and then turned off the pumps. They were ten feet closer.

Maldias burst through the door from the captain's quarters onto the bridge, pulling on a shirt. He was in a rage. His guard Enrico had fallen asleep and someone had pulled the power cord. Now the night was wasted and the sub's batteries were not charged. She would not be able to dive again for at least five or six more hours. His sergeant, the bearer of the bad news, waited anxiously for Maldias to respond. The one-eyed captain's first order was to have the sub's pilot brought to the bridge immediately.

The *Oceanic Explorer* took a gentle roll and the stateroom door swung open. Karen lay nude across the bed on her stomach. She raised her head and smiled, then collapsed in a narcotic stupor. Miguel, the sergeant, gawked and then grinned when he saw the pillow still beneath her hips. Maldias wondered at his expression and turned around to see the open stateroom door.

Maldias snorted and said, "She's a pretty one, don't you think?"

"*Si, mi Capitan*. She is beautiful."

"Do your job and when we get home, she's yours. She'll love your chickens and pigs. And when you tire of her, you can give her to your brothers. Now what about Enrico?"

"I will shoot him, no problem."

"Yes, but that won't give us back the hours he cost us, will it? Don't kill him yet...later. We may need even his miserable help to get out of this mess. The longer we wait, the tighter the snare. Bring in the pilot." The ship rolled again and the stateroom door swung shut.

"I sent you to do a job and you have failed," Maldias said to the ex-Navy officer standing before him.

"No, sir, we did not fail," the sub's pilot answered. "We

need just one more dive. The batteries on the sub are only good for four hours on a light charge. We told you that before we went down."

Maldias studied the man for a moment and then changed his tactics. "What is your name, amigo?"

"Steven Gonzalez, sir." Gonzalez stared straight ahead, avoiding eye contact.

"Gonzalez? You Hispanic?"

"Cuban, sir."

"And now you have this wonderful gringo job—captain of a submarine! *Muy bueno.* I could make you rich...rich enough to buy this ship and many little submarines, eh? Or...I can kill you and all of your friends. It's up to you. One more dive and no more delays. *Si?* It's up to you. Now go."

Maldias turned back to his sergeant. "What have you heard on the radios, Miguel?"

"Nothing, *mi Capitan.* The little boats are very quiet."

"It is not good, Miguel; we have won too easily. That big policeman is not here. What are they waiting for?"

"I don't know, *Capitan.*"

"And that is why I pay you so well, Miguel. Stay here. Don't let the girl out of the room. I want to go on deck. And Miguel..."

"Si, *Capitan?*"

"The *muchacha* is not yours yet. Keep watch and listen to the radios, *comprende?*" He slapped Miguel playfully and went down the companionway ladder to the galley where his men were holding the crew. His men were arguing over the attractive women and eager to shoot the others, but not until Maldias gave his permission.

The research submersible *Deep Rover* was resting in its cradle. Ian watched the deck through the small, thick port. They had nearly finished their last oxygen decompression stop and Paul was about to open the exhaust valve again when Ian saw Maldias approaching the sub. He leaned back from the port and grabbed Paul's arm. They crouched against the deck, hoping they wouldn't be seen.

Maldias walked directly up to Enrico, his negligent guard,

and back-handed him hard across the mouth. The smaller man reeled and dropped to his knees, pleading for mercy. Ian slipped the Luger from his belt and held his breath. Maldias circled Enrico, yelling at him like a trainer berating a dog. Then Maldias grabbed the terrified man's hair and jerked his head back, forcing him to look up the barrel of an Uzi. Maldias struck him again, kicked him and ordered him to leave the deck. Enrico scrambled to his feet and ran, praising Maldias and thanking him for sparing such an undeserving and worthless life. Maldias yelled and Steven Gonzalez stepped forward.

Maldias again demanded to know when the sub would be ready and was told five to six hours. He nodded and said nothing. Gonzalez remained at attention. Maldias seemed to like that and he walked around the sub, looking her over like an inspecting admiral. Then, without saying a word, he pulled himself up the ladder and threw open the main hatch. Ian held his breath and pointed the Luger up towards the lock out chamber's hatch.

Maldias looked cautiously into the main compartment and then lowered himself inside. He studied the instruments and controls with interest, and then turned the hand wheel to open the hatch into the lower lock out chamber.

On the deck, Gonzalez realized the danger. He looked at the other crewmen in desperation and the co-pilot responded by picking up a heavy wrench and smashing the valve of the closest air storage tank secured to the hull. The brass valve flew off and slammed into the hull before ricocheting across the deck and dropping overboard. Air screamed out through the broken valve, and ice formed on the neck of the tank. Maldias appeared instantly in the hatch, gun in hand. He saw the broken valve and the frightened co-pilot, who threw down the wrench and began backing away.

"It was an acci..."

"Too bad. You're fired," Maldias said in his deadly, calm voice and shot him through the right knee. The co-pilot dropped, screaming in pain, and Gonzalez ran to his side.

"You disappoint me. I thought we had an understanding, you and me." Maldias pointed the Uzi and fired again, walking several rounds towards the pilot.

Gonzalez stood and glared defiantly. "Now I'm the only one who can dive that sub, Captain. Go ahead, shoot another unarmed man. Show us how brave and smart you are."

Maldias ignored the challenge and looked at his gold watch with the diamond bezel. "This little fish goes back down in four hours. For every minute she is late, you lose a shipmate. But don't worry, we kill the captain and the old ugly ones first."

Maldias left the sub and climbed the ladder back to the bridge. When he opened the hatch, the radio was blaring. "*Oceanic Explorer, Oceanic Explorer,* this is the United States Navy PBR-437. Come in, please."

Miguel had a confused look, not knowing which of the three radios to answer. Maldias grabbed the VHF mike and answered, "This is the *Oceanic Explorer.* What can we do for you, Navy?"

"We demand to speak to the captain."

"*Muy bueno.* Today I have the guns and I get to be captain. Go ahead."

There was a pause and then the boyish voice continued, "We heard shots. Explain please, over."

"Target practice, Navy. It is good to practice, yes?"

There was no response.

Debbie opened her eyes. She felt dizzy and sick, and realized the mouthpiece of the recirculator had slipped from her lips while she slept. She put it back in her mouth and soon the narcosis began to clear. From her bunk she could see her father sitting in the pilot seat. His hands were moving in circles, and it took awhile in the dim light for her to realize that he was sharpening the Randall. She felt too tired even to sit up. She watched him for a few moments and then fell back asleep.

The Haskels had pulled the cabin pressure down to one hundred seventy feet and their last stop had been for fourteen minutes. But the pressure gauge on his recirculator's oxygen tank was in the red. It was time to discard the units. He turned his off and took a breath of the stale cabin air. His head began to buzz and his lips felt thick. He knew it was nitrogen narcosis and that it would last until they could lower the cabin pressure further. He was dizzy and had to steady himself as he climbed down from the helm to check on Debbie and the crew, and tell them to turn off their units. He stood beside her, watching her sleep as he had so many times during her childhood, amazed by her, amazed by the whole miracle of children. She opened her eyes and took his hand.

"The recirculators are nearly out of oxygen. It's time to turn them off." Tom, who lay beside Debbie, nodded and removed his mouthpiece.

"How much longer?" he asked.

"Three or four hours," Doc answered.

"Long night," Debbie said and squeezed his hand.

"Yeah," Doc answered. "Will you check on our patients?"

"Sure," she said.

He helped her down from the bunk and then climbed back to the helm to turn on the pumps.

Debbie was soon at his side. "They're doing alright," she reported. "At least they're not any worse."

"I'd have lost that bet," he said. "There are always exceptions, I guess. Some divers claim to never get narked or pee in their suits. Makes you wonder if there are any honest folks left in this world."

She laughed for the first time in weeks and said, "Thanks, Daddy. I knew you'd come. I never doubted that you'd find me."

Doc checked his watch and turned off the pumps. She left him to go back to her bunk and he was alone again with his thoughts.

"Now if I were Maldias..." he began aloud before his mind wandered. The sound of the pumps startled him back to consciousness. Mike stood beside him looking over the decompression schedule. "I've got it, Doc. Get some sleep," Mike said as he checked the gauges, turned off the pumps and wrote down the time.

Debbie was standing beside his bunk when he awoke four hours later. "The research sub is coming, Dad. We need you.

Please wake up." Her voice sounded normal and the pumps were silent. Their long night was finally over.

Mike had opened the drybags and was checking and loading their weapons. Debbie passed around cold C-rations and instant coffee. "If Paul were here," Doc said, "he'd have reminded us that the Royal Navy always sent their men into battle on a full stomach."

"What about their women?" Debbie asked. She was loading a magazine for an MP5.

Soon *Deep Rover* dropped down in front of them, her bright lights flooding the compartment. Steven Gonzalez dimmed them, leaving only his cabin lights on, waved an OK. Paul, in the seat beside him, gave a thumbs up. They could not risk using the radios, but Doc and the desperate crew of the *Nautilus* waved back and cheered. Then Steven went to work. In less than thirty minutes he filled the remaining lift bags, but the sub remained stuck hard and fast in the clay.

Deep Rover backed away and they heard the cable scrape the hull as it tightened. For the first time, the hull moved but only minutely. The cable stretched and scraped, and then parted with the twang of a steel guitar string. The small sub edged very close to the bow of the *Nautilus*. The pilot held up his hands in a football referee's penalty signal for holding. Doc returned the signal and told everyone to find something solid and hang on.

The sub dropped to the top of the *Nautilus's* undercarriage, made contact and began pushing with all its power. The *Nautilus* moved a few inches. The tiny sub pushed again, and again the *Nautilus* responded. Bill Roberts awoke and moaned in pain. The pilot moved to the other side and pushed on the hull. Roberts cried out again. This time they moved nearly a foot. Tom told Roberts to keep quiet. Then the small sub turned and headed back towards the surface.

An hour later *Deep Rover* returned with a new cable and a large air tank attached to its skid frame. Gonzalez painstakingly replaced the cable, and then the sub dropped to the bottom and moved in beside the aft compartment. Soon they heard the rush of air filling the stern compartment.

"That's smart. He's using the stern compartment to gain thousands of pounds of lift. A shame we couldn't have dumped our exhaust in there," Tom said.

The rush of air stopped, but they were still stuck. The tiny sub backed away and again the cable tightened. No luck. Now, like a sergeant major fish defending its eggs, the smaller sub began buzzing the *Nautilus*, pushing and pulling and pushing again. Still they remained stuck.

Doc swung down from the bunk into the pilot's seat. He was humming the Navy hymn as he passed Debbie and she knew that look. He had an idea.

"I want to try something," he told them. "Something risky. First we need to get their attention."

He opened the console valves and blew down the ballast until air came up beside the hemisphere from the tank vents.

On board the research sub, Paul and Steven saw the air escaping. "What the..." Paul blurted out before Steven cut him off with a hand across his mouth. He pointed to the radio and then topside. Paul nodded. Steven maneuvered so they could again see Doc in the helm seat. When Doc knew they could see him, he gave a referee's time out and the sub winked its lights.

"How much of the C-7 have we got?" Doc asked.

"Oh shit! About twenty pounds," Mike answered. "Just how exciting is this going to be?"

"Not as exciting as staying here another night," Doc answered grimly. "Come on, get the demo bag and those fire extinguishers. We're going to build some booster rockets.

"We'll put charges on them and put them in the medical lock. I'll cut the hinges of the lock's back door with small linear-shaped charges. The weight of the extinguishers will force it open. They'll fall to the bottom into the mud, and then poof—their delayed charges go off. All that gas expands in one hell of a hurry and that boost, in combination with the jolt we give the bottom, breaks the suction and we're on our way."

"What happens if the inside hatch blows?" Tom asked.

"That's why we'll use shaped charges," Doc said and explained how shaped charges focus the blast's energy.

Roberts had heard the question and wanted an answer. "But what happens if the damn thing blows?" he demanded.

"Then you won't have to go to jail," Doc answered. "The

way I see it, we've got two chances: this one or a swim for the *Black Wolf* without the recirculators. I doubt that I could make that swim, but if you want to give it a try, we'll be happy to stuff you through the medical lock before we set the charges."

Roberts was silent.

"Alright then if we're agreed, Mike, signal the sub. Tom, find that hacksaw and Debbie, get tape from the first aid kit and find something we can use to make stand-off blocks. Well, how 'bout it?" They were all still frozen in place.

Mike was the first to respond. "There's no future in staying here. This air won't last more than a couple more hours even if we throttle Roberts and Richardson, and Lord knows they deserve it." He looked at Roberts and smiled. Roberts cringed.

"Doc's right about trying to swim for it," Mike went on. "And as long as Maldias is up there holding that ship, the Navy can't help us."

Doc had Debbie cutting plastic coffee mugs in half to make the inch-and-three-quarters stand-off blocks. Then he packed the C-7 on top of the inverted angle iron, made a mock wave generator from a knotted length of thousand grain detonating cord, and taped a number eight blasting cap to the end of the cord. He estimated the thickness of the hatch as half an inch. He remembered the rule for shaped charge penetration—one hundred grains of RDX per tenth of an inch of target. C-7 was new to him, but he guessed it to be at least equal in velocity to RDX, about nine thousand meters per second—fast enough. He worked the plastic explosive like bread dough to remove any air voids and finally wrapped it with the last of the surgical tape.

He was tempted, as an afterthought, to add another fist-sized chunk of the plastic explosive, but remembered how much he disliked the unprofessional attitude of amateurs: if you need a pound, use three; so he added only half the chunk. There would be no way to fire the charges electrically, so he'd use a common fuse cap and pencil detonators. When everything was ready, they secured the medical lock's hatch and covered it with mattresses, more for noise abatement than protection from shrapnel, and gathered behind the wooden crate which had broken Roberts's legs.

"Two minutes," Doc said and winked at Debbie.

"Why so long?" Tom asked.

"To give us time to reconsider all the reasons we shouldn't have tried this. And perhaps a minute to make peace—just in case any of those reasons turn out to be right. And finally, because I've never trusted fuse cord after it's been wet."

The small charge went first as planned. Then there was total silence.

"Fall, damn it, fall!" Doc shouted at the fire extinguishers with the four much larger charges. Then as if on command, they heard the hatch creak open and the extinguishers slide out.

"How long..."

The blast shook the sub, and she creaked and groaned in ecstatic release. Then a shudder passed through the hull as she lifted free of the mud. They rose like a tin can launched by a firecracker, up nearly two hundred feet in less than a minute, like a comet tailing a skyful of burning gas and glowing embers.

"This sure as hell is exciting, Doc," Mike yelled over the roar. Doc shouted back at them to brace themselves; they were nearly at the surface and that could mean a sudden stop.

On the deck of the *Oceanic Explorer,* the crew was cheering. The research sub had radioed that the *Nautilus* was on her way up. On the bridge, Maldias stared at the Fathometer. The sub was surfacing directly beneath them. He hit the starter buttons and the moment the engines fired, he slammed the throttles to the wall. The 300-foot vessel lurched forward awkwardly swinging on her anchor, and in her wake the sub burst through the shimmering water and then fell back on its side, resting in the cradle of lift bags. There were no lights and no life could be seen on the sub. On Maldias's order, the crane operator pulled in the cable and the crew secured the sub along the starboard side of the *Oceanic Explorer.*

In the darkness inside the sub, Lt. Mike Berry turned on his small portable radio and whispered, "We're back. Let's party." On the Navy Swift boats, his men jumped into action.

Word quickly came to the admiral at the base. He smacked his right fist into his left palm and snapped, "Finally! Now let's kick some ass. Send up the choppers. Shoot that drug running son-of-a-bitch, and bring me that pissant Colonel Andrews. Oh, and find out what happened to that girl. I want to meet her."

"Can you see anything?" Tom whispered.

"There are men on the deck with guns," Debbie answered.

"Is one of them wearing an eye patch?" Doc asked.

"No patch. Wait, someone's coming. He's the one; he has the patch."

They had put Jason back at the helm and Debbie lay in the open just behind him. Jason's face was covered with blood-soaked dressings and his skin color was ashen gray. He looked very dead. The others were hidden above the view ports in the Navy racks hung from the ceiling.

"That's the leader, Maldias. He'll send his men, but he won't come himself. So let 'em come. We're ready." Doc stroked the grip of the Randall as he spoke. "I wonder where Ian and Paul are. Can you see the research sub?"

"You're right—only two men are coming. Maldias is waiting by the crane. No, I don't see the sub."

Maldias's men approached cautiously, taking advantage of the deck machinery to give them cover as they tried to see into the sub. When they got to the *Explorer*'s rail they hesitated. Maldias swore impatiently and ordered them to board her. With guns ready, they jumped to the deck and tried the forward hatch. It wouldn't budge. Doc had braced it closed. He wanted them to use the back door. The older man ordered the younger towards the stern. With great reluctance he went aft and lifted open the stern hatch.

The compartment had lost most of its contents during the ascent, but Bobby's body was still in the diving lock. The explosion of the fire extinguishers had not been kind. The flesh of his face had been peeled away and the intruder was greeted by Bobby's toothy, fleshless smile and empty eye sockets.

The gory discovery brought a startled scream. The young man jumped back from the hatch, accidentally firing several rounds as he fell. The bullets slammed into the crane above

Maldias's head and he dove for cover. He expected to be shot at, but not by his own men. He screamed at them and the older man ripped the gun from the other's grasp, then pulled Bobby's body from the hatch. Maldias snorted, but still he remained behind the base of the crane. Inside the sub, Doc breathed in slow, measured breaths. His hand tightened on the black Micarta handle of the Randall.

As Doc watched, the center hatch hand dogs turned slowly one at a time until all six were opened. Doc had his boot against the hatch and braced himself, while Maldias's men pushed from the other side. They pushed again, this time much harder. Doc held, rock solid.

"Once more," he whispered and when they pushed he pulled. The startled men stumbled into the compartment and the waiting arms of Tom and Mike who took their guns and gagged them with strips of towel.

Doc nodded and slipped out through the hatch while Mike removed the shirts from the two prisoners. He and Tom quickly put them on. Mike took one bag of cocaine into the aft compartment. Without showing his face, he held his arm high enough out of the aft hatch that Maldias could see the bag. Mike then laid the bag on the deck and dropped down into the compartment, got a second bag and began a pile on the deck of the sub. Maldias remained hidden behind the crane and yelled for Enrico to get the bags.

Doc slid along the deck of the aft compartment past the bunks and lockers to the open end of the sub. He pulled on his fins and mask, took several deep breaths and slid quietly into the water. With a few strong kicks, he swam under the hull of the *Oceanic Explorer.* He surfaced near the stern and looked for a place to pull himself up on the deck.

Above him, Maldias still crouched behind the base of the crane. Mike tossed out another bag of cocaine. It landed on top of the growing pile. Maldias motioned Enrico forward. The boy moved cautiously as Maldias rose from his cover to watch.

Enrico jumped to the deck and went to the aft hatch. He moved to the edge of the hatch pointing his Uzi into the compartment and called the names of his friends. There was no response. He called their names again and knelt down, trying to get a better look. He could see nothing. He looked up at Maldias for instructions.

"Keep your eye on the ball, son," Mike whispered and grabbed him by the throat and gun arm pulling him head first down the ladder. Maldias saw what happened and ran towards the galley door. Mike came up through the hatch with the Uzi and opened fire. Maldias returned fire and disappeared through the door.

Doc heard the shots but could not see what was happening. As he started to pull himself up on the large tires used as stern bumpers, a hand grabbed his foot and held him. He turned with the Randall, ready to kill. It was Ian with Paul beside him. "Hey, mate," Ian said smiling, obviously pleased with the start he had given Doc. "What's up?"

"There were shots...I couldn't see. Do you know how many there are?"

"The sub's pilot told us he's seen five. Always at least two holding the crew in the galley."

"We got two, maybe three at the sub," Doc added. "That leaves Maldias and the one or two more. Did the pilot tell you how to get in the galley?"

"Three ways: one from the deck, one from the bridge and a ladder that comes up from the engine room storerooms below deck."

"That's what we guessed. Mike is trying for the engine room. I'll take the bridge and you get on top of the crane," he told Paul and Ian. "My guess is they'll use those kids for cover and run for the sportfisherman. You'd have clear shooting from that crane. That leaves only the..."

"I've got it, mate. I just hope that bloody bastard comes my way," Ian said.

"Alright, we'll start our shift in three minutes. Good luck," Doc said as he pulled his dive mask on and slid beneath the surface.

As Paul and Ian climbed up the stern, they heard the sound of helicopters and turned to see the Swift boats approaching. They scrambled onto the deck and ran to the crane.

Doc went hand over hand up the anchor chain, but not as easily as he would have twenty years earlier. He swung a leg over the chain and used the side of the hull to leverage himself into a sitting position. He cautiously looked over the rail and was rewarded with soft-nosed rounds splattering the steel just beneath his face. Maldias had been waiting for him.

He let go of the chain and plunged twenty feet to the sea, his face lacerated by shell fragments. He fought the pain and struggled to keep from losing consciousness. Then Tom caught him and pulled him to the open stern of the *Nautilus*. Tom shouted to Debbie for help. She gasped when she saw her father's wounds, but quickly helped drag him into the forward compartment.

"Help them," Doc told Tom. "Mike will be trapped in the galley...try to get to the bridge." Debbie set to work trying to stop his bleeding.

Tom grabbed an MP5 and jumped to the deck just as Maldias threw open the hatch on the bridge catwalk and shoved Karen out in front of him as a shield. She was wrapped in a sheet and he was pushing her ahead of him, forcing her down the ladder by her hair. He held a pistol to her head and shouted, "Let my men go or I will kill her. Send them out right now, or she dies." Then he glanced quickly at the Swifts making speed runs along both sides of the ship and saw the approaching helicopters.

Doc heard them too and pushed Debbie away. "I have to go, but there's something you have to do right now." He explained quickly while pulling down the folding ladder to the main hatch and then pushed it open. "Let her go, Captain. Let me come and play instead. We didn't get to finish our little game the last time we met."

"*Muy bien*, I thought it was you." Maldias yanked Karen's hair tighter, pulling her head back. "You are always getting hurt, amigo. First your leg, now your face. Perhaps you should get another hobby, eh?" He jerked Karen's hair a second time and pushed her down one more step. She cried out in pain and the sheet dropped away. "*Si*, you may come and play," he said and they descended another step. "Put your hands where I can see them and come slowly."

Doc put his hands slowly the air. The Randall hung from its lanyard on the back of his forearm. Paul stood on the roof of the crane and carefully drew a bead with the laser sight of the MP5.

Maldias saw him and twisted Karen to shield him. As he did, Tom emerged on the bridge roof above him.

"It's over, Captain. Let the girl go. Get on your boat and go," Doc shouted over the roar of the choppers.

"Never! I will kill the crew one by..."

A single, muffled shot echoed in the galley followed by screams. There was a moment of tense silence and then Mike's voice boomed over the PA. "The crew is safe, Doc. Maldias is the only one left. Kill the ugly bastard and let's go home."

Maldias fired three wild shots at Doc and dragging Karen along, ran for the sportfisherman. Doc came out of the hatch after him. Maldias fired again and then tried to pull Karen over the rail to the deck of his boat. She stumbled and fell.

"*Puta!*" Maldias swore and shot her.

Maldias dashed into the cabin and lunged to the console. The keys were missing.

Inspector Ian Cord cleared his throat and said, "I hate to overstate the obvious, but are you looking for these?" He sat in a high-backed leather chair, the Luger in his right hand and the boat keys in his left. He swung the keys in a pendulum arc and said nothing. Maldias turned slowly to face him as Doc landed on the back deck and kicked open the salon door.

Maldias spun towards Doc and then back as he heard Tom drop into the cabin through the forward hatch. Maldias moved first towards Ian who raised the Luger and smiled, and then towards the cabin door and Doc. He saw the knife and stepped back. He stood speechless, glaring at the three of them and then slowly lowered his gun.

"You did this to me," Maldias snarled at Ian as he ripped off the eye patch and exposed the sunken empty socket.

"Want to go double or nothing?" Ian asked coldly. He lowered the Luger and stood up. "I can understand why you would rather have me kill you than go to prison. But I'm not going to kill you yet. That would be too easy. No, I'm going to let you rot for a while and worry about when I'll do it, how I'll do it. You see, I'd give you my eye to have my brother back. Pluck it out myself, I would." Ian moved closer, Maldias stepped back, but there was nowhere else to run. "But since that won't bring Brian back," Ian continued, "I'll just have to amuse myself killing you. An inch at a time it will be. A year at a time with no sleep, months on black water and maggot bread. I've read how the men on those prison ships lived. That will be a holiday compared to what I've got in store for you."

Like a wolf with its leg in a trap and desperate enough to chew it off for another chance at freedom, Maldias glared at each of them with his good eye. Then without warning, he fired the Uzi into the deck and tried to sweep the room with it. But Doc's reaction was lightning fast—the heavy Randall flew from his hand, burying itself in Maldias. At the same instant, Ian fired two rounds from the Luger, which exploded Maldias's skull against the wheelhouse glass in a bloody smear.

Ian stood glaring at the body as the blood pool grew larger and darker on the expensive carpet. He exhaled, put his foot on the dead man's chest and pulled out Doc's deeply-embedded knife. He wiped the blade on a dry part of Maldias's shirt and handed it back to Doc.

"I think he got your point, mate," Ian offered.

"It was a mind-blowing experience," Doc countered. Neither was laughing.

"Holy shit, look at that," Tom said, pointing towards the stern of the sportfisherman.

The gleaming bow of the *Black Wolf* exploded through the swells, thrusting forty feet out of the water before crashing back on her belly and sending a four-foot wake rolling towards the *Oceanic Explorer* and the white sportfisherman. The blue-black hull was thirty yards from the *Explorer* and they watched in awe as the bow torpedo tube doors opened.

Capt. Behrmann's rasping laugh rumbled through the deck speaker. "Surprise, Dr. Holiday. I was hoping you'd swim back to me. It would have been worth the wait to see your face as I suddenly eased away into the void. Now bring me my boat plans, those traitors and the little blonde too, *und* I'll be saying *auf wiedersehen!*" he roared. "And get those helicopters and patrol boats out of my sight. Now, Doctor! Or I'll destroy the Dockyard and roast you all in burning oil. You've seen my torpedoes; you know what I can do."

CHAPTER

23

Doc stepped over Maldias's body and flipped the PA switch on the VHF radio. "Roberts's legs are broken, and your grandson and the girl are both seriously injured, Captain. If they don't get medical attention quickly, they will both die. The others are dead."

"We have a sick bay and medical staff aboard. If they are going to die, they can do it with me just as well as with you," Behrmann answered.

Doc hesitated and, turning to Ian and Tom, asked, "What do you think, do we have any choice?"

"We can't risk this crew or the Dockyard. We'd better do what he says," Ian answered.

At the mention of the Dockyard, Doc winced. "Is Sheri safe?" he asked Ian.

"Yes. Mike got his message through to Navy security and they sent a Navy E.O.D. team. By now my lads will have cleared everyone out."

"Good." Doc picked up the mike again. "Captain, it will take awhile to get the wounded stable enough to move. Tell me what the plans look like and I'll send someone to find them. Enough people have died today; let's leave it at that."

"That is a wise choice, Doctor. You are looking for computer disks. Now get the patients ready. I'll be here."

Doc turned off the radio and said, "Tell the Navy to pull

back and ask them if they've got a couple of small transponders."

"So that we can track him? Good idea. I'll see what's available."

Doc had on surgical gloves and a mask, and was working on Karen's abdominal wound when Debbie found him. Karen was awake and crying softly but was not responsive. The drugs Maldias had given her spared her from the worst of the pain.

"Who is she?" Debbie asked.

"Her name is Karen—a student at the Dockyard. Pretty but not real bright. She was having an affair with Richardson. He got her involved with drugs."

"How bad is it?" Debbie asked. Karen looked up at her and Debbie took her hand, comforting her.

"She was lucky. The slug missed her kidney or the blood would be darker. She won't be running marathons for a while, but in a couple months she'll be good as new."

Karen looked up at him and smiled.

"What kind of luck did you have?" Doc asked Debbie.

"I did what you said. The guys in the computer shack are making the copies now. I told them it was for you and asked them to keep it quiet. No problem."

The ship's doctor came running, followed by two grad students carrying medical supplies. The doctor was an attractive, middle-aged woman in cutoffs and a sweatshirt.

"I was working on your other two. It's amazing either of them made it," she said as she knelt beside Doc and clinically appraised his facial wounds. "You look like hell," she said, reaching towards his face.

He dodged her touch and answered, "Nicked myself shaving. Got a decent set of retractors, some mosquitoes, kelly's and a sponge clamp in that pack? She's going to need an IV—five percent dextrose and water—and an antibiotic drip. She's so full of his drugs I'm afraid to give her anything else for pain. Let's get these bleeders clamped and see if we can find that slug."

"You specialize in bullet wounds?" she asked.

"I teach English. I read about it. How many gunshots have you treated?" he asked in return. "Sponge for me. We haven't got all day. I'm teeing off at two-thirty."

She looked at him distrustfully. Then watching his hands fly as he clamped and tied off a pesky bleeder, she did as he had instructed. Debbie watched and shook her head. It was one of those 'he'll never change' looks. He looked up and winked as if he had read her mind.

"How are Richardson and Roberts?" he asked as he tied the next knot.

The Navy helicopters and patrol boats had pulled back. No one doubted Behrmann was insane enough to keep his threats. An hour passed and most of another. Doc finished closing Karen's wound, dressed it and checked her vital signs. Her blood pressure was low but solid, her heart slow and steady. They lifted her onto the stretcher and carried her to the small inflatable. Ian was waiting and helped ease the Stokes stretcher down, but when Doc started to climb in, Ian stopped him. "Don't give him another chance at you. It's my turn in the barrel. You stay here and take care of Debbie. Besides, your face is so ugly you might scare him. Go get those cuts cleaned up. I'll be back shortly."

Mike put his hand on Doc's shoulder and said, "He's right. I'll go too."

Doc reluctantly agreed. "Don't let him see those transponders. They're not worth getting killed for."

Spray splashed over the inflatable's bow and Mike tried to cover Karen to keep her dry. When they reached the sub, Mike jumped to the deck and pulled the boat in close. Getting the stretcher out of the rocking soft-floored boat was awkward. They were soaked by the time they got her to the main hatch.

Behrmann was waiting. He was at the helm, nervously scanning the monitors and the sonar screens. His right hand rested on the torpedo firing switches. An Erma MP38 submachine gun lay within easy reach.

"Take her to the sick bay, gentlemen, and don't dawdle. I am too vulnerable here on the surface. Anything could happen."

As they carried Karen to the small medical treatment room, they passed the open door of the stateroom across from the captain's quarters. Col. Sandy Andrews was lying on the berth, and there was an IV bottle hanging above him and dressings on his chest. Mike nodded acknowledgement as they passed. They turned the corner into the sick bay and lifted Karen carefully, Ian at her head, Mike at her hips. She moaned when they put her down and she held on to Ian's neck as he tried to pull away. He kissed her forehead, stroked the side of her face and spoke softly. She relaxed, and he placed her arms at her sides and covered her with a light blanket. He looked around the compartment and saw a television camera tracking him from the corner bulkhead. He turned his back to it, bent down and kissed her again, and smoothly slipped the transponder from beneath her blanket and stuck it under his shirt.

"How very sweet of you to be compassionate to that little piece of baggage, Inspector," Behrmann chided over the bitch box. "If she lives, perhaps she'll help me pass away the long, lonely evenings in my kingdom at the bottom of the sea. Cable reception's not the best at nine hundred feet you know."

"You won't be getting away with this, Captain. The whole world will be hunting you down," Ian scowled.

"Your whole world hunted me for years, Inspector. They didn't catch me then and they certainly won't catch me now. But it keeps the game interesting. Now, bring me those computer disks and those two traitors, Roberts and Richardson. I hope you didn't waste too much time patching them back together. My guess is that they will be meeting destiny quite soon now."

"That's enough of that talk," Petra Roberts said from the forward hatch. "Colonel Andrews left them no choice and you know it. You should be thankful they are still alive. I am."

"G'day, Mrs. Roberts. I can't say seeing you here is much of a surprise. That explains a lot of things."

"Good day to you, Inspector. Go and bring me my husband. We'll leave the explanations and amenities for later. I'm sorry I won't be seeing that obnoxious Dr. Holiday again. Did his daughter survive?"

"Yes, mum, she's fine. Shall I pass on your concerns?" His tone was stone cold.

"My husband risked his life for her, Inspector. Tell her that. Tell her he's the only reason any of them are still alive and look what it cost him...what it cost us."

"I'll tell her," Mike intervened. "Come on, Ian, let's go."

"Remember," Behrmann said, "I can blow you all to ashes. No games; bring the others and the disks. Now get out."

Mike followed Ian up the ladder. When they were back in the boat he asked, "Did you hide the transponder?"

"No. The bloody telly cameras are everywhere. We'll try again next trip."

Richardson's stretcher was waiting when they returned. They lowered it into the boat along with the respirator and extra oxygen bottles. As they approached, they could see two Navy divers swimming submerged beside the black hull.

"It's alright, Inspector. I waited for you to return to show you how easily I can deal with them. Watch this," Behrmann's voice blasted out over the speaker. A sonic air blast from the hull stunned the divers and they came to the surface with their ears oozing blood. They swam away holding their heads.

"They are gone," Ian said loudly.

"I know that. They just discovered you can't attach magnetic mines to a non-magnetic hull or were those transponders? It doesn't matter. The fools! Who do they think they are playing with? Bring down my grandson."

They removed the oxygen mask system and carried Jason to the hatch. Mike dropped through first.

Behrmann was waiting. "I'm disappointed in you, Lieutenant. You should have known better than that. I could have just as easily killed your men, and perhaps I should have."

"Those were not my men, Captain. Mine would have succeeded."

Behrmann scowled and waved them towards the sick bay. Petra Roberts was examining Karen when they entered. She was wearing surgical gloves and a mask. She straightened up and pulled down the mask. "Who did this work? Is there a surgeon on that ship?"

"A doctor, but Doc did that. He also kept your husband and Jason alive on the sub."

"Why?"

"I think he knew your husband helped Debbie and Tom, or maybe he just wanted the practice."

"Bring him with you next time; I want to thank him."

"He's in bad shape. His face..."

"Bring him!" she demanded. "And tell me, in what condition is my husband?"

"His legs were broken when the sub crashed," Ian said. "And perhaps his hips. There's no X-ray unit on board. He's in traction and he may have internal injuries. The doctor says he needs tests and lab work—maybe surgery. He needs to be in a real hospital, mum. You are putting him at great risk to bring him here."

She bit her lip, and tears came to her eyes. Perhaps, he thought, perhaps I've got her. Then her face hardened again, and he knew better.

"You mean in a prison hospital, don't you, Inspector? I don't think so. At least now I know what to expect. So much violence...so much pain. My family is destroyed, Inspector. And do you know why? Because my father tried to save your world. Now you had better pray that someone can save it from him, but I doubt it. Go. Bring me my husband and Dr. Holiday."

Ian and Mike rowed back to give Doc the message. He was in the ship's sick bay, growling as the doctor tried to finish a plastic closure on his facial wounds.

"Hold still," she scolded as they burst through the door, "or I'm going to sew you to this damn table. And you two just wait right there until we're done or you'll be next."

"Do you specialize in bedside manner?" he retorted.

"No, I was a marine and then a bio-chemist and we didn't read that book. Now hold still. We're nearly done."

"It's the ultimate proof of a just God," Doc said. "A Navy corpsman being butchered by a marine." They both laughed. "Now tell me what happened." He tried to turn to Ian, but she grabbed his ear and kept him from moving.

"OK," Doc said after hearing what Petra wanted. "Let's get Roberts ready for his homecoming."

"Not yet. Two more," the doctor ordered. "Hold still and listen. Those are some awfully sick patients on that sub. You tell that captain there's a doctor here willing to go with him and take care of them. They need me more than you do and they'll be a damn sight more appreciative." She pulled the monofilament tight and tied it. "Tell him. I'll get ready."

The inflatable was crowded with Roberts's stretcher, Ian,

Dr. Sara Mathews and Doc. Behrmann looked sullen and tired. "Take him to the sick bay," he ordered and waved his submachine gun at them. Petra was changing Karen's dressings when they entered. "You should have left a drain in this," she said. She left Karen and came to her husband's side. She had prepared a berth for him and hovered over them as they moved him from the stretcher. They had sedated Roberts for the move, but perhaps not enough.

His eyes looked around wildly. He had just become aware of his surroundings and he grabbed Doc's arm in panic. "You can't leave me here—not with him, not on this cursed boat. He'll kill us all, man. Don't do this!"

Petra moved to his side and took his hand, "It will be alright. I'm here."

Roberts pulled his hand away from her, "Alright? Are you as mad as he? Don't you know what he intends to do?"

Petra raised a syringe, tapped it with her forefinger to remove any air, and stuck him in the arm. "Demerol—he needs to rest."

After a few moments Roberts's eyes glazed and his jaw went slack. Dr. Mathews put her fingers at his throat and looked at her watch. She said nothing.

Petra moved over to Karen and tossed back the sheet. "Father will be disappointed she's not a real blonde. Hand me some of those dressings," she ordered Dr. Mathews.

"Not again," Dr. Mathews said under her breath. "There are limits."

"You are not needed here, Doctor, nor are you welcome. As you can see, I'm perfectly capable of caring for my family," Petra said as she ripped the tape from Karen's side and wiped the wound with a disinfectant. Karen winced in her sleep.

"Yes, I see—perfectly capable," Dr. Mathews answered. She turned and started unloading the bags of supplies. "I brought them some things. Then I'll be going."

Doc nodded at the camera and Ian stepped in front of it. Doc reached into his pocket and handed Petra a note.

"Can your father hear us?" it said.

She hesitated for a moment, nodded and handed him

her pen. Doc wrote quickly on the pad, and then gave her the note and two transponders. Ian started singing loudly into the speaker as Doc said softly, "This turns it on, and wherever you are we'll be able to find you. I don't know what your father is planning, but now you have a chance to stop it and save your family. Think about it."

"That will never happen!" she shouted at Doc and slapped him. Ian stopped singing mid-word. "I will never betray my father!" She set one of the units on the stainless steel counter and smashed it with a surgical mallet. "Now get off my father's boat. Any debt I owed you for my husband's life has just been canceled."

"Just a moment, Dr. Holiday. You're forgetting something," Behrmann said as they started for the ladder. "The computer disks—I want them."

Doc nodded at Ian who pulled a sealed plastic envelope from a lanyard around his neck and handed it to Behrmann. The old man broke the seal and poured the disks out on the table. He counted them and laughed. "May you all burn in the fires of your own hell. You bought it, you paid for it, now you'll get what you deserve. Goodbye, Dr. Holiday. Give my regrets to the Navy."

"If you intend to live much longer, Captain," Doc said from the ladder, "I'd dive this boat faster than a Georgia rabbit running for cover. I'd dive her deep and stay in that briar patch a long time. And one more thing: if I were you, I'd check real carefully before I tried to fire any more of those torpedoes—capacitor-discharge detonators can be so damned unreliable."

With that, he hoisted himself up the ladder and left Behrmann wondering if he had been bluffing. The hatch closed and locked as Doc hit the deck. Behrmann had already started to dive the sub. "You make a good joke, Dr. Holiday. Have a nice swim." Behrmann's laughter cackled from the deck speakers as the hull dropped from beneath their feet leaving them suddenly swimming.

As the sail rushed towards them, Doc grabbed Dr. Mathews and pulled her clear. They were pulled under in the swirl of the sub's wake. They came back to the surface choking and sputtering. Ian was the first to the boat and helped them in.

"I told you not to get those wet," Dr. Mathews coughed, pointing with a laugh to Doc's stitches.

Their laughter was interrupted by screams from the *Explorer*'s crew as the *Black Wolf* dove straight towards her midsection. The sail dropped just at the last second and cleared the hull by inches.

"What a bloody cowboy," Ian said. "Someone should give that bloke a ticket."

They laughed again, and Ian had just started the outboard when the rumble of a large explosion rolled across the water to meet them like a big train coming through a small mountain tunnel. They spun to the west in time to see debris and water high in the air above the Dockyard.

"Sheri!!" Doc shouted. But his shout was lost in the much louder explosion of a second blast almost beneath them. Just beyond the *Oceanic Explorer*, the ocean split wide and a column of water forty feet in diameter went a hundred feet in the air. The crew were knocked from their feet as the shock wave hit the ship and the bridge windows imploded.

"Doc, did you...?" Ian began. "Not with that poor little lass on board?"

"No, I didn't, I swear. I really was bluffing. Perhaps the Navy...I don't believe this. Why?"

The miniature tidal wave from the blast half-filled the *Nautilus* and she began to sink. Paul and Ian organized a salvage party to save the sub while Mike got on the radio to the Navy.

A Navy patrol boat came alongside the *Explorer* and two of its young officers jumped to the deck yelling orders. Ian rushed at them in anger. "You bloody fools! You killed Roberts and that young girl. How could you?"

"Sir, we had nothing to do with that explosion. We thought perhaps you or Dr. Holiday..."

"Nonsense."

Oil and debris were coming to the surface. Ian turned to them and said, "Call my office. Tell them to get the barricades and clean-up barge out here. Move! Do it now! We can't let this mess get to the reef." One of the young officers gave a snappy "Yes, sir." and ran back to his boat to carry out the order.

"Why can't we ever have a little fight without making such a bloody mess?"

Deep Rover, the research sub, surfaced and motored to the stern of the *Explorer*. The hatch opened and Steven Gonzalez came up into the daylight. Ian went to the *Explorer's* stern and shouted, "Do you have enough power to make another dive?"

"Only a short one."

"Go and see if you can find anything of that black sub. See if you can tell what happened, then report back to me. It's important, man. Hurry!"

A helicopter circled and after dropping a static line, set down on the stern deck. Navy SEALS poured out and began loading the injured on board.

"I'd bet anything you're right, Ian," Doc said as he wrapped a roll of two-inch gauze over a paper drinking cup to protect the eye of a crewman hit by flying glass. "That was nothing but an old U-boat diversion and Behrmann is in deep water headed south."

"If only Mrs. Roberts hadn't smashed that transponder. Now we've no way to follow them."

"Oh, I think we'll be hearing from her. Remember, theatrics run in her family. She made a big deal out of smashing one of those transponders, but I gave her two. Any word about Sheri or the Dockyard?"

"Nothing yet, I'm afraid. Mike is still on the radio."

Mike came running into the galley. "We just got good news. The Dockyard is safe—the big blast was at the mouth of the tunnel. And there was a much smaller one in the stairway going down from the warehouse, but no one was hurt. Ian's men had gotten everyone out.

"The only bad news is Mark and Sheri. They're alright, but they disobeyed orders again. They were on their way out here when the blast went off. I guess they really got a good scare and a bath to boot. Funny, all she asked about you was how many stitches you got this time, Doc. I think that girl's got your number," he kidded. Doc grinned; the Lidocane was wearing off and it hurt.

Paul and Tom had pumps draining the stern of the *Nau-*

tilus and two of the ship's engineers were helping rig a patch on the stern. Paul looked towards the island and smiled—the *Mermaid* was in sight. He went below to tell Doc.

Doc had finished the eye and was debriding a nasty laceration caused by flying glass. A young corpsman who had come aboard with the SEALs offered to take over. "I can handle it, sir."

"Yes, son, I imagine you can," Doc said and handed him the forceps. He found Debbie in the scientific command center, borrowing a computer.

"Well?" he asked her after making certain they would not be overheard.

"I think so," she answered. "Roberts used a lot of the same security he built into the programs at the base. When we crack those, I'll be able to open these too."

"I want to keep quiet about this for a while. For once, we're going to have an edge and I want to keep it that way, at least for now. That OK with you?"

"No problem. I haven't seen anything that looks like plans for a submarine on those disks—not yet at least."

"Thanks." He kissed her temple. "Come topside. There's someone you need to meet."

"What are you telling me, Daddy?"

"Nothing, nothing. I just want you to meet her and let me know what you think. Nothing has happened."

"That's disappointing. I was hoping you had...well, I want you to get to know Tom. Plenty has happened between us, and with luck a lot more will—real soon." She smiled and her green eyes sparkled. When they reached the deck, she squeezed his hand and ran to Tom. She hugged Tom tightly, kissed him and then turned to look again at her father. His expression was one she would always remember. For the first time in her life, she had actually left him speechless.

"What was that about?" Tom asked.

"I just told him we are getting married."

"You what? We are?"

"Remember that big Randall knife? Do you want to be the one to tell him you're not going to make an honest woman of me?"

"I'd be honored to have you as my bride," he said, amazed

that his ears should hear his lips say such words. Then he whispered, "Can we start the honeymoon tonight?"

"Why do you think I want you?" Debbie laughed. "Because you're so good with computers. How 'bout a night on the beach?"

"How 'bout a huge, soft, dry bed at the Southampton Princess with breakfast and a distant, safe ocean view?

"As long as we can go skinny dipping first," she insisted.

"Haven't you had enough water for a while?"

"Never."

Sheri did an excellent job bringing the *Mermaid* alongside the *Explorer*. She came down from the fly bridge dressed in a white cotton blouse and white shorts, once starched and crisp, now soaked like her hair. Still, the white outfit highlighted her perfect tan and was clinging in all the right places. She hadn't seen him for almost two days. She had planned to wait on the boat, cool and aloof, until he came to her. But when she saw his face, and the wreckage and bullet holes across the *Explorer*'s deck, her aloof demeanor melted. She jumped down from the fly bridge and ran to him. "You asshole, look at your face. You promised me you were going to be careful. What the hell happened out here?"

"It's good to see you too," he said as he picked her up and kissed her. It hurt but he did it again anyway. "Come on. I want you to meet Debbie."

"You found her! Thank God it's over."

"I don't think it's over, but yes, thank God we found Debbie."

Two days passed before they all were together again. The gathering took place in Richardson's office. Doc was holding New York and local newspapers, and he was raging.

"Listen to this...'Official government sources today released information regarding the death of Dr. Jason Richardson, Director of the Maritime Museum at the Bermuda Dockyard. According to U.S. military authorities, Dr. Richardson died Friday during the heroic rescue of hostages aboard the American research vessel *Oceanic Explorer.*

'Other casualties included U.S. Government Tactical Task Force Agent, Col. T. Sandifer Andrews; Dr. William Roberts, Bermuda Base NASA Station Director; Karen Wilson, an archaeology summer student from Atlanta, Georgia; and five others yet to be identified.

'Government sources confirmed that Richardson and Roberts had been working in conjunction with an intra-agency drug interdiction task force for several months. Bermuda Marine Police Inspector Ian Cord and U.S. Navy personnel also participated in the rescue effort...' We can't let them get away with this. They are covering up the whole thing and we can't let them do it."

"'They' is your government, Doc," Ian said."'They' can do it and 'they' have done it. There is nothing you or any of us can do about it."

"That can't be right, Ian..."

"It may not be right, mate, but that's how it is. Word came straight from the commissioner to keep a lid on this and that's what I must do. I'm sure Mike got the same. How about it, Mike?"

"We were told they were all killed when the sub exploded and to write it that way in the reports."

"But the sub didn't explode. The research sub never found a single piece...." Doc paced back and forth in front of Jason's antique desk, slamming his fist into his hand.

"Doc, the Navy has its reasons. I do what I'm told, just like you did when you were on active duty. Hell, they'd have a fit if they knew I was here talking about this. You know that."

"Debbie, what have they said to you?"

"The whole thing is under investigation and I'm not to discuss it. With anyone. But I did make Lt. j.g. so now we have two reasons to celebrate."

"Two?"

Debbie looked at Tom. He looked directly at Doc and stood up. "Debbie and I are getting married sometime next month. With your permission, of course." He waited.

Doc smiled, came over and took his hand. "I guess anyone who can handle himself like you did will be able to keep up with her. Congratulations, Tom. Now tell us what happened at the NASA station."

"I was told that the computer has been restored, but until the investigation is over, I no longer have access. I was also told not to discuss any of it. I wouldn't be surprised if they try to transfer me."

"Paul, Janet, anything?"

"We had a visit. Not sure who the chap was. Said there was a big investigation and asked us to keep quiet—hinted we might lose the dive shop's lease at the Dockyard if we went to the press, but he was very polite," Janet answered.

"Lisa, glad to see you up and about. How about it?"

"I've been offered Jason's job on a temporary basis, and of course, contingent on saying nothing that would damage the reputation of the museum. They made the offer while I was still in the hospital. I took it. I need the money and I don't want to leave Bermuda. What I want to know is, where are all the artifacts Jason took from the 1814 site, and how many other sites did he strip?"

"We may find something in the cave. How is the excavation to reopen the stairs going?"

"It's not," Mark said. "They've sealed the tunnel until the investigation is over. I asked when that would be and they said sometime after the investigation starts. I asked when they were going to start and they said when they had money in the budget. Then I got mad and asked when was the last time there was money. They said no one could remember back that far, but that we'd be arrested if we tried to go down there. So I tried to get in last night, but they've put a grate across the entrance and set it in concrete."

"This is a bloody outrage," Paul said. "Next they'll be telling us we weren't kidnapped; Behrmann just forgot to inform us we were on holiday."

"I want to finish the projects we started, Doc," Sheri said. "We still have two weeks. The whole world is telling you to forget this, so forget it and let's get on with our lives. Debbie and Tom are, and you should too. Stay here and help me—the summer's not over yet." She took his hand and kissed it.

Doc squeezed her hand and softened just a bit. He ran his fingers through his thick hair and tried to explain what he was feeling. "It's not that I just want revenge for what they've done. I do, but more than that I want truth. I care about what's happened to all of us and I know what will happen if we don't get to the bottom of this. Behrmann said they were accountable, and I want to know to whom. Who had he sold his soul to that would demand our deaths? And what about his research—his attempt to save the environment? What if that sub could really do all the things he claimed? Do we just pretend we never heard it and let things go on as they are until there's nothing left? I don't know what the next step is, but I can certainly tell you this—it won't be backward. We are not helpless and I'm not quitting until I know the truth. Now you all have to make your own decisions."

Then he looked at Debbie. Her eyes were burning green, an 'I'll be damned if I'll quit now' look she'd inherited from her mother. He winked at her and she winked back.

"I don't need to sleep on it," Tom said. "Just let me know what I can do."

Ian stood and shook his head sadly, "I can retire in a couple of years with a nice pension, Doc. You don't know what you're asking. I'm sorry." He walked to the door.

Mike followed and said nothing, then he paused in the frame. "Ours is not to reason why, Doc. You understand," he said and walked out into the hall. Lisa and Mark also left.

Doc looked at Sheri who shook her head in amazement. "Well, nobody said it was going to be easy. Do I get to keep the Smith & Wesson?"

The tension in the room was broken. Debbie suggested a swim and Paul agreed. They closed the office and walked down to the marina and the *Mermaid*. Paul warmed the diesels and checked the boat while the girls raided the dive shop's refrigerator. Tom and Doc sat alone on the back deck.

"Doc, I just remembered something. Roberts had two sons at Texas A&M. He was there just two weeks ago. He loved those boys and if they had intended to start another base, I can't imagine him leaving without them, or at least letting them know where to find him. If we got there quick enough, perhaps..."

Paul came down from the fly bridge. He saw the seriousness of their faces and guessed the topic. "Doc, I didn't say anything in there. I hope by now you know you don't have to ask. We'll chase 'em to hell if we have to. You were right. This is like the war again. I can't just let it go. I know you can't, and I know Ian won't. He just can't talk about it. Not yet. Here come the girls. Let's go—my tired old soul needs a swim."

They anchored in a moonlit cove to the south of Daniel's Head. Tom and Debbie were the first ones off the boat and were out of their suits as soon as they were discreetly away from the others. Sheri sat beside Doc and waited. He was deep in thought. Paul and Janet were on the fly bridge.

"You are going after Behrmann, aren't you?" Sheri asked Doc.

He pulled her closer. "How could I chase that sub? Swim? No, I'm not going after the sub, but Tom had an idea—a good one. I'm flying to Texas tomorrow. Roberts has two sons..."

She grabbed his ears and kissed him, "That's tomorrow. Let's talk about tonight. Or better yet, let's not waste time talking."

"Have you answered my riddle?"

"No, I haven't answered your damn riddle. And we're not doing riddles tonight either...we're swimming!" She stood and peeled off her shorts and blouse. Only her perfect tan remained. "You don't mind do you? The bikini's at the cleaners."

"I'll bet." He picked her up and dropped her over the side. With his shirt off but shorts securely in place, he followed her in. Janet and Paul were left alone on the fly bridge.

"Doc has changed so much," Janet said. "There is so much sadness in him. He needs that girl. It's as if Nancy found her for him. Do you think at least this drug business is over? I was so afraid for you—for us."

For a moment Paul didn't answer, so she put her head on his shoulder and looked out at the moon's reflection shimmering on the water.

"For us, I think life goes back to business—the boat and the store—but not for him. I'll help him if he asks, of course, but there's a fire smoldering there, like a fire in a coal bunker on an old steamer—and he's never going to be happy until he finds the answers he's looking for. He can't just put it out and forget. He has to see this through, or that fire will eventually burn through his hull and send him to the bottom."

"What happens next?"

"It depends on what he finds in Texas. He's leaving tomorrow."

"What are you going to do?"

"Have a very private chat with Ian Cord. He can't give up his integrity for a bloody pension and he knows it. Not if he's half the man I think he is."

CHAPTER

24

The yellow spinner bait dropped over the submerged log and in a series of slow, low leaps, bumped its way through the branches to deeper water. In the dark tannin-stained water of the lazy Florida river, green eyes the size of quarters, four times more efficient than human eyes at penetrating the darkness, dilated and scanned the fallen cypress tree. She had not fed for two days and her keen predatory senses were fine-tuned by the hunger burning in her belly. Her dorsal fin arched in anticipation as she spotted the lure. She pulled back into the shadows ready to strike.

She waited for it to pass and then took it from behind, not viciously like a walleye or musky, or aggressively with short hits like a sunfish or crappie, but so gently that only the change in the direction his line traveled told Doc of her presence. He raised the rod butt waist high, gripping the cork handle with both hands. In one smooth, straight pull he set the hook and the long brown graphite rod came to life.

It bent double. Line flew from the old red reel. He tightened the drag and began fighting to take back line. The fish was so strong she was pulling the bass boat. The tension on the rod suddenly was gone and he knew the fish was headed for the surface. He kept the rod tip low and reeled as fast as he could. The magnificent bass came two feet out of the water, thrashing her head to throw the lure or break the thin, clear line. He kept the line taut, and gasped at the strength and beauty of the fish.

"Fasten your seat belts, and return your seats and tray tables to their original upright position. We will be landing in Houston in just a few minutes."

"Sir, sir, we will be landing. Will you..."

"Yes, yes of course." He was fully awake now. "Just once, just once, I'm going to catch that fish. I won't eat it. I won't keep it. I just want to catch it, weigh it, measure it, photograph it and let it go. I want to win, just once. Then maybe I can dream about something besides fish."

"I beg your pardon?" said the matron next to him.

"Nothing, nothing at all," he said, embarassed that she had heard.

He was wearing topsiders and his favorite jeans. He had put on a light jacket for the flight. He had only a carry-on and planned to go directly to pick up the rental car for the two-hour drive to College Station.

Tom had gotten him the names of Roberts's sons. Debbie and Sheri had taken him to the airport. When he got on the plane, the girls had their first real chance to talk.

"I've loved the Navy," Debbie told her, "but now I'm being treated like I was the one who did something wrong. And what if Tom gets transferred? I don't like this at all." They were sitting in a small restaurant in St. George's. Sheri's tomboy rough edges melted away as they talked, and Debbie finally asked her about Doc.

"I know I'm not in his league, but I know I love him and that may be all there is to it. I've only known him for a short time, but I know I love him. I just can't figure him out. Most guys are all over you the first time you're alone. Don't laugh, but I've tried everything I can think of and he hasn't made a move. And the crazy thing is, he gives me all the right signals. At least I think he does. And then I started worrying, what if something's wrong? What if he can't?"

"I don't think there was ever a problem with Mom. I used to hear them sometimes, laughing and having a wonderful time. It gave me a good feeling about how it would be for me someday."

"And is it?"

"With Tom?" She blushed and laughed. "Better than I ever imagined. In the ocean, on the beach...the Southampton Princess wasn't bad either!" She paused, enjoying the memories for a moment before focusing again on Sheri's dilemma. "I don't think Dad's been with anyone since Mom died two years ago. He told me in his own funny way that he cares about you, and I think you'd be just great for him. Paul and Janet think so too. I loved it when you gave him hell for getting his face shot to pieces. He did too. Mom would have done the same..." She dropped that thought and finished, "My guess is he's just worried about keeping up with you."

"Do you really think so? Well, what can we do?"

"Would you come and see someone with me? I have a friend I'd like you to meet. I'll go call him."

Debbie found a phone and called the chaplain's office. The assistant put her through to Chaplain Stone. "Hi, Debbie, it's wonderful to hear your voice. I was truly afraid we'd lost you, but your dad never gave up hope. He's a good man. What may I do for you?"

She told him about her engagement to Tom, and then tried to explain about her father and Sheri. She asked if she could bring Sheri to his office.

"I met both of them in the hospital. I was on my way out for the afternoon, but I'd be delighted to see you. Can you come now?"

An hour later they were enjoying tea with the chaplain and Sheri was concluding her story. "Oh, there is one other thing. The riddle. He told me that if I could answer his riddle, like the riddle of the sphinx, I could have whatever I wanted. He meant I could have him."

"And what was the riddle?" Stone asked.

"You won't believe this. The riddle is 'what does sex mean?'"

"That's my dad!" Debbie laughed. "He loves to get to the bottom of things. He wants everything explained, nailed down. He used to drive me crazy asking 'but what does that mean, what does it really mean?' That's what he means by truth. Everything spelled out, no hidden agendas, no double meanings. Read everything three times before you answer!"

"What do you think the answer is, Sheri?" Chaplain Stone

asked, getting the conversation back on track.

"I've thought about it a lot, and about us. I think he is afraid if he opens up to me, if we really go for it, that something will happen and that he can't or at least doesn't want to risk that kind of pain again. So I think he's saying 'don't play unless you are in this for keeps.'

"For me, getting serious always came because of the playing, I mean making love. I guess that's wrong, but after my divorce I was so afraid of being with someone who wouldn't love me the way I wanted. If someone interested me, I wanted to try them out before we even dated. Now I'm in love with him and he hasn't touched me," Sheri said, looking at the floor with tears in her eyes.

Doc left the registrar's office and walked towards the science buildings. He found the office he was looking for and knocked. The light was on but there was no response, so he knocked again. The answer was a gruff "What the hell do you want? I'm busy!"

"Dr. John Holiday to see you for just a minute. The registrar called."

"Yes, you might as well come in. I forgot what I was writing anyway." A robust man in his early seventies with large red eyes and bushy eyebrows glared at him. "I don't know how I can help you, but come in. I have a deadline. Couldn't the registrar help you?"

"I'm inquiring about the Roberts boys. There has been some trouble in their family. Their father..."

"Yes, alright. That's their business, isn't it? I had both those boys as students—brilliant. Randy's the oldest and in his second year of grad school. Martin just finished his undergraduate work. Where'd you say you're from, Doctor?"

"Georgia State, English, but I've just come from Bermuda."

"Oh, yes, Bermuda. Going there myself someday. Hula girls and all that. What did you want to know about those boys?" He rubbed his eyes and squinted at Doc, then reached for a mug of cold coffee. He took a drink, frowned and continued, "Say, you're not recruiting for Georgia, are you? I don't want to lose those boys—they're pure science. Probably never read a poem in their lives. No matter. They both left when school was out, 'bout a month ago. I have no idea for where." He looked away, shuffled through the clutter on his desk and found a large bottle of Murine. He tilted back his head and squirted the drops in his right eye, then his left. The overflow dripped down to his shirt.

"For where...that good grammar?" he continued. "No matter. You say their father's been hurt? You staying 'round here? Somewhere I can call you? I'll ask around a bit if that's what you want, to know where they went. Well, is it?"

"Yes, it's crucial that I find them. The address they left here was their home in Bermuda, but they haven't been there. This is very important. Anything you can find, the names of friends, anything. Here's the number at the motel and my address in Atlanta. Thanks." Doc finished writing and handed over the note. There was nothing left to say and it was obvious his host was anxious for him to leave.

He left the cluttered office and went to the library in search of yearbooks. He found what he was looking for. He took the books to a carrel and discreetly cut the photos out with his pocketknife. From the yearbooks, he learned that the boys were members of the same fraternity. He asked for directions to the frat house and set off across the campus.

The house was nearly empty, but he eventually found one knowledgeable brother willing to talk.

"Marty talked a lot about his diving and living in Bermuda, but he didn't mention his grandfather much. As a matter of fact, all he ever talked about was Brenda. They broke up just before he left. It was pretty sudden, and I don't know where she is. Probably went back to Houston. Randy was an upperclassman—we didn't communicate."

That night Doc sat discouraged in the motel room. He had eaten poorly and was getting ready for bed when the phone rang. He recognized the gruff voice of the old professor.

"Dr. Holiday, if you want to know 'bout the Roberts boys, you need to talk to Ben Travis...used to be one of them grave robbers in the archaeology department. Don't ask questions. Just go up to the University Hospital in Austin. Ben wants to see you. Wouldn't wait too long though...hear he's in pretty bad shape. Serves the old fart right...mean as a snake. 'Night."

In three hours, Doc was in Austin getting a lecture in sickroom protocol from the night nurse on Travis's floor.

"Dr. Holiday, oh yes. He wants to see you. But listen to me. That old man should have been dead three weeks ago after his fourth heart attack. If you get him excited, he'll probably die on the spot. He refused his medication until he could see you so I'm letting you in, but be careful. We didn't bring him back again so that you could kill him, understand? What kind of doctor are you anyway?"

"English, Georgia State."

"Oh," she responded unimpressed.

It was an old and lonely block-walled room, cramped and dimly lit. Stale air hung heavy with hospital smells, both chemical and human. Dark curtains shut out the world and gave the room an oppressive crypt-like feeling. The dried-up old man was sitting with the back of the bed high. The only light was a reading lamp attached to the headboard, which shone like a small flashlight in a great cavern. He was surrounded by hanging bottles and an assortment of life support monitors. A respirator and defibrillator sat in the corner, waiting.

He was reading Homer's <u>Odyssey</u> in Greek through thick glasses and making notes in the margin when Doc knocked and entered.

"Holiday?"

"Yes, Dr. Travis, John Holiday."

Travis rested the book on several file folders on his overbed table. The top folder contained several fax sheets and was labeled "John Holiday, Ph.D., Confidential" in large block letters. Travis made no effort to hide the file or to offer Doc either of the two available chairs.

"Come over here where I can see you, Doctor. You've been asking questions about some friends of mine and I want to know why. What's happened to Bill Roberts? Well, speak up. English professors are supposed to know how to talk."

"He was badly injured in a submarine accident. He was taken aboard another sub by a German, Dr. Behrmann. Do you know the name?"

"The mad scientist? Of course I know Hans Behrmann. The old kraut's probably the most arrogant bastard alive. Go on, what else happened?"

"Behrmann built a sub for the Navy and then stole it. He and his men kidnapped my daughter. I got her back, but they got away. The Navy is very interested in getting that sub back..."

"Screw the Navy. You said Hans kidnapped your daughter and you got her back?" He studied Doc more intently, then continued, "But Hans got away and now you're out for revenge. Well?"

"That's part of it."

"Nothing wrong with revenge, Doctor. It's not one of our higher emotions, but it's certainly an honorable one, held in high regard by ancient cultures. As a matter of fact, I'd like a little of it myself. I can help you, Doctor, but first I need to know if you are worth the effort. I'm a dying man —not much time. I want to know why someone with your ability, your history, is wasting his time as an onion peeler. Why aren't you in science?"

Like a question coming from a good attorney, this one was only rhetorical. He knew the answer from the file and continued, "Early American Literature. Hell, man, those aren't even fresh onions. Been peeled a thousand times. What were you looking for, Doctor? Someplace safe? Somewhere to hide? Don't go snooping 'round after Hans Behrmann if that's what you want."

"How did you get my file, and what does this have to do with finding Behrmann and the Roberts boys?"

"None of your damn business, and it has everything to do with whether or not I help you. And if I don't, you are dead in the water. Now keep quiet and I'll tell you what you need to know."

Doc watched the cardiac monitor. The patterns were arrhythmic. He started to call the nurse.

"If you call her, our meeting is over. What I need is a smoke. Don't suppose you have one? No, of course not—you play it safe, I forgot." He sat back and rested for a few moments, and then in a more subdued voice continued, "Bill Roberts was the best student I ever had, and he became one of my best friends. He was the first to use computers and computer graphics in our archaeological field studies. Saved us hundreds of hours of work. Set up cataloging systems for artifacts and standardized forms for field notes that he then organized better than anyone. Then he heard about satellites. Came into my office all excited one day and said 'What if we could use satellites to find wrecks?' That was the beginning of this mess.

"He designed his doctoral program in computer-satellite interface and I helped him. We kept our intent quiet of course—didn't want the government screwing things up worse. When he got his degree NASA couldn't wait to hire him, and for ten years he got me information no one else even dreamed existed. And then Behrmann entered the picture. The government was backing Behrmann, but word got out about the alternative fuel, the hydrogen peroxide generator, and the politicians went nuts. What about the jobs of our voters back home? What about the Arabs? You get the picture."

"Yes, go on."

"Early last summer, Roberts came to me. He was scared. He was caught in the middle between Jason Richardson and Behrmann and he knew the whole thing was about to blow. He begged for my help. But what could I do? I'd been using bootlegged satellite data for ten years, used it to make the most important finds in the last thousand years. I was trapped just like Roberts and Behrmann."

"Trapped by Jason Richardson?"

"Exactly."

"But why? I don't understand."

"Simple, Doctor. Want to know the lesson of the ages? The one and only true learning from all my inquiry into antiquity is this: greed is the damnation of the masses, and power is the opiate of their leaders. Behrmann wanted to save the world, not because he gave a damn about it, but to get the fame and wealth other Germans got out of the space race—you know, the V-1 rocket boys. And he wanted power. He wanted to be a big shot."

Travis lay back to catch his breath. His eyes were glowing, but his face was ashen gray. Doc had seen that look before—the old man didn't have long. When would he get to the point?

Travis coughed and took a sip of water. Again he stared at Doc as if trying to decide how much to trust him. He put the glass on the bedside table and continued, "Behrmann went nuts when the government threatened to close his lab. Because of the heat the politicians were getting, they demanded he give up work on the new engines and build the sub with atomic power. To keep the project going he agreed, but he lied. He sold everything he owned, borrowed every dime he could get his hands on, and made promises he couldn't keep so he could go on working on the fuel production system. He was a fanatic and so were the people working for him. Going to save the world, you see. Well, one fine Monday morning the Navy woke up and the garage was empty. The *Black Wolf* and Behrmann were gone."

"And they set up shop in Bermuda in the forgotten old sub base under the Dockyard," Doc said.

"Yes, Jason's playpen for that sub he stole in St. Thomas. It was dangerous and there were big problems. They needed money, barrels of it, and Behrmann was about two thirds over the edge. He just couldn't accept what had happened. At times he'd deny what they'd done to him and argue it was his fault—paranoid delusions. They should just say they were sorry, give the sub back and they'd get a ticker tape parade down Fifth Avenue.

"Then in his saner moments, he'd be so full of rage Bill and Jason were terrified of him. He'd flash back on his days as a U-boat captain and only speak German for days. He was in one of those fits when he took the *Black Wolf* out and sank that little freighter—and here's what you don't know—he was looking for a cruise ship full of allied troops on their way to the Normandy invasion."

"Good Lord, have mercy."

"Exactly. Now you're getting a feel for what you're really up against."

"But you said you were trapped by Jason. What did you mean?"

"Right. Remember they needed money. Now they had the locations of thousands of wreck sites because of all those years

Roberts spent collecting data. But there was another problem. His data couldn't tell them the difference between a Manila galleon and a Louisiana shrimper."

"And you could. You had the research—the historical information," Doc said.

Travis smiled a thin, hard smile. "Right. I was the only one who could tell them which of the thousand pins on their charts was worth going after."

"And you wouldn't play," Doc chuckled. "So they were stuck, working worthless sites in Bermuda, hoping to get lucky."

"Hell, no, I wouldn't. Not after spending my life fighting to protect the precious few good sites that are left. Hell no!

"But let me tell you, there were some sleepless nights. Ever hear of the *Verelst*, a Dutchman sunk in 1771 with two million gold florins and seven hundred forty pounds of diamonds? Or the *Grasvenor*, the richest British ship ever lost—two million six hundred thousand gold coins and nineteen chests of diamonds, emeralds and other trinkets? Am I boring you? The list goes on for hours. Name the twenty richest wrecks—I can drop an anchor on any of 'em in less than an hour."

"The stuff dreams are made of. I respect your decision."

"Dreams or nightmares. I knew Jason would come looking for my notes. He'd try to ruin me if I didn't cooperate. My heart gave out just in time. Damn him." He looked away in sadness. "So brilliant and all he cares about is money. Money and drugs, and the women and spotlights they will buy. He'll get what he deserves—they all do, eventually."

"It may have already happened," Doc said. "He was badly injured when the sub crashed—a nasty head wound."

"I knew it. It had to happen. No one who causes that much pain gets away clean." The old man lay back against the pillows and removed his glasses. The cardiac monitor showed steady, uniform spikes and valleys. He pushed the call button for the nurse who appeared almost instantly. "I'll take that pill now. I feel better and now would be a good time to rest." She left the room to get the medication.

"Don't like to go to sleep feeling bad," he told Doc. "'Fraid I won't wake up, I guess. I'd like you to stay, if you don't mind. We haven't gotten to the things you need to know yet. Stick around, I'm feeling better. Maybe we can slip out for a beer," he laughed bitterly.

"I'll stay," Doc answered. "If you're feeling that much better, I'll take you fishing and you can have a whole six-pack."

"Dr. Holiday, there is something you could do for me. Wake me if I do start to croak...dying is the last great adventure I have to look forward to and I don't want to miss it. Thanks."

The nurse returned and was informed that Doc was family, and would be staying. When she smiled and asked how they were related, the old man quipped, "Biologically," and sent her away.

Doc sat in the chair and watched the monitor. The night nurse looked in several times. Each time Doc was awake, waiting in the darkness. She brought him coffee just before dawn and said quietly, "You have been his only visitor. You aren't really related, are you?"

Doc shook his head without speaking.

"Poor old man. So smart, but there's no one left to listen to him. None of the staff can stand him, and not a single call in or out in two weeks—only that package and I think that's what set off his last attack."

"What was it?"

"Some kind of fancy old wine cup. He wouldn't talk about it, but it really upset him. No note, no card. I only saw it for a moment and then he put it away. Well, I'm going off now. Good to meet you. Sorry about all those cuts on your face. That must have hurt. Let me know if I can help. See you."

Travis slept past dawn and on into the early morning. He looked much stronger when he awoke and asked for food. He was given hot cereal and jello, but not the coffee he demanded. Doc excused himself to use the shower in an empty room, shave and quickly eat in the basement cafeteria. When he returned, Travis had just finished eating and was reading.

"Dr. Travis, we were talking about Jason Richardson and the Roberts boys. Do you feel like going on?"

"I know damn well what we were talking about, Doctor. It's my heart that's worn out, not my brain. Come here and get the brown package out of this chest. Don't open it yet. We're going to have a smartness test. You ready?"

Doc placed the package on the overbed table and sat down. The old man's eyes sparkled. He tilted his head, studying Doc in a way that made Doc feel uncomfortable, and asked, "Next to the Holy Grail, taken from Jerusalem to England by Joseph of Arimathea after the crucifixion as the legend goes, what's the second most important cup in history? Take your time and give it your best shot."

"The chalice of hemlock given to Socrates after his trial in 399 B.C."

Travis studied him a while longer without changing his expression, and then slowly a cunning smile, almost evil, changed his entire countenance. "Not bad for an onion peeler, Doctor. Open the package carefully. It contains the chalice you just described."

Doc did as he was told. From the shoe box-sized container came a silver and gold case with Greek figures in bas-relief. He carefully opened the clasp, and raised the silver and gold chalice into the light. It was a magnificently ornate outer shell encasing a ceramic cup. He placed it carefully on the overbed table.

Travis stared at the chalice and anger filled his face. He struck it with his free left hand and it flew across the room, hit the wall and landed, intact, on the carpet. Then he fell back against the bed in silence and stared towards the dark wall. Doc picked up the chalice, replaced it in the case, returned it to the bedside table and waited.

For a moment the monitor was filled with tall spikes close together. Doc asked again if Travis wanted the nurse. He refused. As he rested, his heart slowed and his color slowly returned.

"That came from a ship bound for Alexandria...went down about two hundred years before Christ, and Bill Roberts found her with the satellite. We tried to get several governments to fund the project, but everyone we talked to had better things to do with their money—like buy guns and bombs. So, little by little, most of the treasures like this one were taken by thieves and sold to more thieves and so on, until they ended up in private collections never to be seen again—just as you saw in Bermuda.

"So I decided to do something. I chose my best students and we began a collection and a museum of our own, a place where we could save the great treasures we were finding because of Roberts's work—save them from the private thieves and the government thieves as well. Our intent was to keep our collection hidden, perhaps for generations if necessary, until those treasures could be shown to the world without the greedy bastards destroying everything left on earth worth saving.

"And so that's what we did. We worked that wreck and dozens of others. Not for treasure, but for science. We found a safe place to hide our artifacts, and for ten years we funded our own work and put away the best that was found. Our cannons would not be brought to the surface to crumble in piles of rust in some warehouse; our coin collections would not be turned into pretty necklaces and sold to tourists; our gold, silver and jeweled religious art would not be melted down and sold to avoid taxes or curious eyes. Our sites would not be ground through cutterhead dredges or covered by freeways. No, sir, our treasures would be safe forever.

"Do you remember your Greek history, Doctor? Greece was being destroyed by the greed of bureaucrats and politicians, and Socrates called for a change in the system. He advocated rule by strong philosopher kings, educated men untarnished by that greed. Do away with the money-grubbing, philandering, thieving politicians, and find men of character, strength and vision to rule.

"The politicians told him to keep quiet, but he would not—he could not, and so they had a trial, found him guilty and gave him a choice: his integrity or his life, but not both. He chose integrity and the hemlock.

"That chalice, Doctor, was hidden with my notes. Jason sent it to me because he wants me to know he's won. He thinks with those notes he can have everything. Well, he hasn't won—at least not yet."

Again he fell silent. Exhausted from his tirade, he was soon asleep. Doc kept vigil and made notes while the old man slept. A doctor and a nurse checked Travis that evening and confirmed what Doc already knew. It wouldn't be much longer.

"It's good that you are here. He'll drift in and out like this until...well, who knows how long. I'm sure he would not want to be alone. Can we get you a cot and a decent meal?"

Doc accepted and asked that he be immediately awakened if Travis's condition changed. He slept lightly, frequently getting up to check the monitor and the breathing, now labored, of the dying man.

"Dr. Holiday, wake up," Travis demanded in a gasping voice. "Have to talk...not much time. Help me up so I can breathe."

Doc adjusted the bed, repositioned pillows and reconnected the nasal cannula which had come off while Travis slept. The oxygen helped and soon Travis was breathing more comfortably.

"You have to stop them, Dr. Holiday. Don't let them destroy my work, please. What do you say, Doctor? Oh, I know, I'm an arrogant old bastard. Anna used to tell me the only thing worse than an arrogant old bastard was a tenured arrogant old bastard. But you have to help me, please."

"How? Tell me how. Then I can help you."

"All they want is the money. They don't care about art or science...they'll destroy it all."

"Yes, I know. Now tell me how to stop them and I will." Doc was exasperated and it showed.

"Get the chalice and I'll show you."

After Doc placed it on the overbed table, Travis lifted it with trembling hands. "The case is authentic, done after his death. The Greek inscription here tells it," he said, passing a crooked finger over the writing. "The ceramic cup was gone. I made the replacement out of clay from the region, but that's not important. Did you ever make a test key, one with holes in it?"

"For multiple choice exams, certainly."

"When you remove the clay cup there are stones, tiny ones, in the outer surface. It's a stele. Roll it in soft clay...the pattern it leaves, that's the key. My notes are in Greek and I scrambled them. Jason didn't have the patience for Greek. List the sites on each page alphabetically, the Greek alphabet of course, not chronologically the way I did, and the key will show you which coordinates are the real ones."

"Clever, but where is the list—the notes?"

"Jason...." He fell back exhausted and coughing.

"Jason has them? They weren't in the sub. We would have found them. Have any ideas where else he might have hidden them?"

Travis shook his head, still coughing. Doc lifted his bony shoulders and held the glass for him to drink.

"Is there any way to let them know how important the chalice is so they'll come looking for it? I think I'd rather play this game on my turf."

Travis nodded and flashed an evil smile. "I...I took care of that for you. When you were taking your shower."

Doc eased him back down. "What? You old buzzard! So now I'm sitting here holding a live grenade with no pin. What if I don't want to play?"

"Won't matter. They'll come after you anyway." Travis laughed and started coughing again. Doc hit the call button and tried to help him. There was frothy red blood in the old man's sputum and panic in his eyes.

"Don't worry, Dr. Travis," Doc said, trying to comfort the dying man. "You'll get your revenge, and I promise to enjoy it enough for both of us," Doc said.

The nurse came running in, looked at the monitor and told Doc to leave. She called for help, and as Doc walked down the hall, a cardiac team rushed past him. He went to the washroom and flushed his eyes with cold water. His face looked like hell. Two more nights without sleep and too much coffee had taken its toll. His lacerations were starting to heal enough that the stitches were pulling. He stopped at the nursing station and left word he was going to the cafeteria to wait.

He fell asleep in the booth and the nurse, who the night before had brought him coffee, woke him and said, "It's over, Dr. Holiday, a few minutes ago. There was nothing more we could do. He was stable again for a while, long enough to dictate a sort of will. He wanted you to have everything. There isn't much. He had a small house rented in Galveston where he kept his books and files—that's all, really. He wanted you to make his final arrangements and he tried to write you a

note. Doesn't make much sense to me. Maybe you can figure
it out. Oh, he was insistent that I give you these. Pretty," she
said, referring to the chalice case. Travis's dog-eared copy of
Homer lay beside it in the cardboard box. "But it can't be
worth much, can it? Not enough to cover his funeral...." She
handed Doc the box.

"Anyway, he finished writing and laughed a weird little
laugh, and then his heart just stopped. Just like that. Makes
you wonder...."

Yes, it certainly does make you wonder, Doc thought. Were
Jason and Behrmann the target of his last laugh—or was I?

CHAPTER

25

Three days later, Doc was sitting in his office at Georgia State in Atlanta. Old Ben Travis had been cremated and his ashes scattered in the Gulf. Texas A&M's oceanographic center in Galveston had provided the boat. Now Doc sat proofreading his request for a year's leave of absence on the computer screen. He nodded approval and sent it to the printer. As he waited for the hard copy, he thought about the wild goose chase the old man's will had sent him on. Travis's house in Galveston was empty. Everything had been removed by a professional moving company two days before the old man died. A neighbor said that two nice-looking young men directed the operation. She recognized them as the Roberts boys as soon as Doc showed her the yearbook pictures. But she couldn't quite recall the name on the truck.

In his flight bag were the Greek chalice and the well-worn Greek edition of the <u>Odyssey</u>. The book was filled with Travis's notes, mostly in Greek. Several passages were highlighted and underlined. There were also maps and sets of numbers in Greek which Doc took to be navigational coordinates. There was a lot more in that book than academic footnotes, Doc surmised. Unfortunately, he would either have to learn Greek or find a translator to discover its secrets.

It was the note with the one page transcript of the will and the old man's mysterious final laughter, however, which bothered Doc the most. A shaking hand had written:

> *Greed is your enemy, Doctor. Try KRATOS instead. It's time you learned Greek and <u>Hebrew</u>. Good luck, Onion Peeler.*

When the printer completed the leave request, he signed it and took it to his department head's office. He had a plane to catch.

The lure was a silver shad with an inch-and-a-half clear bill and an internal rattle. His fifty-foot cast dropped it a yard in back of the stump, and the nine-pounder came after it with cautious interest. The monster stopped dead in the water when she saw the boat, looked up at Doc, and made a lazy turn back to her ambush point by the stump.

"That's it," Doc growled. "This is war."

He quickly scanned the horizon. His was the only boat in the dream. With a determined scowl, he pulled out the bottom drawer of the large, black tackle box. There, in neat rows, was an assortment of duPont blasting caps in different colors and sizes. After considering the water's clarity and temperature, the cloud cover and the phase of the moon, he selected a number eight with yellow and green wires.

From the deck compartment next to the built-in cooler came a three-stick bundle of sixty percent Red Cross Extra nitro-glycerine ditching dynamite. He inserted the cap into the bundle and used the trolling motor to quietly guide the boat into position.

"Sir, sir, we are getting ready to land. Will you please put your seat..."

"Not on your life, honey. Not until I blast this damn fish."

He worked frantically to tie the wires to the posts on the blasting machine. The flight attendant shook him gently and he growled at her. She stepped back, frightened.

"It's my dream and I make the rules," he snorted. "Fire in the hole!"

"Sir, you have to wake up; we are landing," she said in her most authoritative voice. Other passengers turned to stare.

The stump left the surface like the cork out of a well-shaken champagne bottle. As it rose in a high arc, it was followed by a large column of water blasting skyward with the force of a broken city water main. Dozens of bass rose high in the column. In their mouths were all the lures he had lost in years of anguished pursuit. He grabbed the large net and maneuvered the boat closer. Water thundered down on the boat. Then came the fish. They were everywhere, and he scooped them in until the boat was in danger of sinking. The heavens rejoiced.

Doc opened one eye and looked at the frustrated attendant.

"Are we there yet, Mom?"

The young woman said something less than complimentary under her breath, turned on her heel and marched to the front of the plane.

"Love those duPont number eight lures," he said with a laugh, but thoughts of fish faded as his eyes tracked her tight skirt working its way to the front of the plane. He smiled and noted that most of the pain from his stitches was gone. He brought the seat back up and looked through the window at the deep blue water below. He was glad Sheri would be there to meet him.

After dinner at the Officer's Club with Debbie and Tom, Doc and Sheri took a cab to the Dockyard. They dropped his luggage at the hostel and walked to the ramparts, stopping at the place where they had watched Richardson and Karen in the water.

"I wonder where they are, or if they're still alive," Sheri said.

"The sub should be deep into the Bahamas by now, perhaps on its way to South America. How have you been?" He put his arm around her, and she leaned comfortably against him, looking out at the water.

"Good. Lisa wants me to stay and be the coordinator for the other groups this summer. I said yes. Now that we have the satellite maps that Tom and Debbie made, we're in for some great diving. I want us to help find and catalog those wrecks. It's the only way to protect them from men like Jason.

"She wants to hire Mark for the rest of the summer, and I really hope you'll help us too. We'll have a great time...."

Doc started to answer, but she put her finger to his lips. "Wait. Before you decide, you need to hear the rest of this. Something happened while you were gone, Doc." He felt the muscles in his abdomen tighten and he swallowed hard to clear his throat.

"While you were in Texas, I had a lot of time to think about us," she continued, "and about your damn riddle. It's really about commitment, isn't it? You want something that will be for keeps, forever, right?"

"Well?" That's it, I've blown it, he thought.

"Damn it, Doc, life doesn't last forever, and I don't know what will happen in the future. I can only promise that I will do my best by you and expect the best from you. But, I can't promise forever. Ask me again after our first fifty years— maybe then.

"But if you want me now, I'll go anywhere with you. I'll live with you. I'll love you like crazy. I'll have your kids. Hell, I'll even marry you, but damn it, I can't promise forever. It's not mine to give. So I hope what I'm offering will be good enough. It's the best I can do."

"That's the answer I was looking for," he said and hoped she wouldn't hear the anxiety in his voice. "You're young, I'm not. If we are going to be together, it needs to be because we chose it, not because we woke up beside each other one morning and didn't know where to go from there."

"I understand that now," she said, turning in his arms until she was looking up into his eyes. "And once I had that figured out, it opened the door to something else—something wonderful that I've never had."

"Yes, what was that?"

"Making love as a celebration of commitment, not as a test to see if we like each other or if we're going to spend another night together. That's what it's supposed to be, isn't it? And that's what I've been missing."

"I think you've got it nailed," he said and kissed her. When they parted, he said, "I did some thinking while I was gone too. Until you, I wasn't thinking about relationships anymore. I had my work and those long night swims, and I was becoming more and more content being alone. Alone in the past, alone to work without interruptions...alone to do exactly what I wanted without having to consider anyone else.

"And then in Texas, in those two days, I saw myself laying in that hospital bed cut off from the world, dying alone. It was like going down the river in <u>Heart of Darkness</u>, Conrad's story. The further you get down-river, the more oppressive the jungle and the story become. Travis said something to me in the first few minutes we were together, and he really had me pegged. He said I was hiding, looking for all the safe answers. He called me an onion peeler and he was right. I've been trying to live in the past—the nice, safe past. But there's no such thing as living without risk, and there's nothing riskier than starting a new relationship."

"But you're not a coward hiding from life. You didn't hide from Behrmann. You put it all on the line to get Debbie back."

"Yes, but I haven't felt alive like this for years. Hell, I haven't even dreamed about a woman since Nancy died—about making love, I mean. I dream about fish. Fish I can't catch. And it would have been safer for me to keep on dreaming about fish than start a relationship with you, so..."

"You asshole! You mean I was competing with a fish? What kind of fish? How big?" She was laughing at the irony of what he'd said.

"Bass, nine pounds, maybe more."

"Largemouth?"

"Yeah, a real beauty." He was grinning now too.

"Tough choice, huh? So who won?"

"That's an answer I can't give you with words."

"Are you serious? This is it?"

"If that's what you want."

"Oh no, the question is, is it what you want? More than a damn fish, even a trophy, a world's record? More than anything?"

He kissed her again and lifted her so that she was sitting in front of him on the stone wall. His hand slid to the buttons on her blouse, but she stopped him.

"Not so fast. First tell me. I want to hear you say it."

"That I love you?"

"No, you jerk, I know that. Tell me that you want me more than a damn fish!"

"More than a fish, more than anything, I love you and I want you."

"Well, it's about time," she laughed and reached for his belt buckle. "Now show me how much."

When Paul came to work the next morning, the *Mermaid* was gone. Doc had left a note with no explanation. None was needed. When they returned the next afternoon, Paul noticed that Sheri was unusually quiet. She just sat in the old rocking chair in the shade of the dive shop's front porch, smiling and looking back at the boat. And there was something different about Doc as well. He was moving slower, more relaxed. The weight of the world didn't seem as heavy on his shoulders, and every time he looked at her he smiled.

CHAPTER
26

Doc went to the Officer's Club to keep his appointment with Chaplain Stone for lunch. He set the Greek chalice on the table between them and told the story of his trip to Texas.

"So you're not the only one who likes riddles, Doc?" Stone said when Doc showed him the note and the worn book with its notes in Greek. "My Greek's a bit rusty, but we'll have a go at that," he said, pointing to the book. "I remember that word *kratos*. When the Old Testament was first translated from Hebrew into Greek, naturally there were problems with semantics. Words which at the surface carried one meaning could have a very different meaning as the context changed. *Kratos* is one of those words. It appears many times in the Old Testament, and it's a classic example of this semantics problem.

"The Hebrew understanding of the word as it relates to the creation story was that Adam, whose name means 'man' in Hebrew, was to be a caretaker in God's garden, fully accountable for his actions, and there to bring to fruition God's plan for the garden. One translation even suggests a sense of bringing something to final perfection. That's a very different concept from the word's most common use in Greek, which meant to have dominion or ownership, as a slave owner had ownership, with absolute power and accountability to no one."

"Quite a difference," Doc said. "That's why Travis underlined Hebrew in his note. He saw himself in a caretaker role
of whatever he'd found, and obviously wanted me to share
that attitude, assuming we ever find anything to be a caretaker of."

"That's it. You're right on target. So what now?" Stone
asked and glanced at his watch.

"I applied for a year's leave from the university. Kind of
short notice, but I think it will be approved. I need to work,
but more than that, I need time.

"And in spite of what everyone wants us to believe, I certainly don't believe our business with Behrmann and his sub
is finished. I want to see that through to the end. My only
hesitation is, I'm not ready to spend the rest of my life joust-
ing with windmills and dodging the government. If we are
going to play to win, great. If this is another war of 'limited
objectives' like Nam, I'm not interested, especially now."

"Especially now?" Stone glanced at his watch again.

"Sheri and I have..."

"I'm happy for you. She is a rare find. Think you'll be
able to keep up?" he asked with a laugh and stood.

"If I die trying, you'll know I went with a smile."

Stone shook his head and excused himself to make a
phone call. When he returned to the table, he remained
standing. "Doc, when you called, I took the liberty of asking
a friend to meet us. He's waiting in my office. Could we go?"

The chaplain's office was paneled in island cedar and
lined with bookcases. It was a large, friendly room with comfortable leather chairs and the smell of fresh coffee. Standing behind Stone's desk, examining a large framed print was
a stocky, fiftyish man in a dark blue three-piece suit and con-
servative red power tie. As they entered, he smiled, and then
looked back at the print.

"Have you seen this?" he asked Doc. "It sends chills up
my spine every time I look at it."

"No, I haven't," Doc answered and moved closer to the
desk.

The print showed a middle-aged executive with his suit
jacket off and his sleeves rolled up, leaning with an out-

stretched arm against the Vietnam Memorial. His head is down, seemingly discouraged. He has come in search of old friends trapped by death within the stone, and they come to its surface to meet him. The ghosts are young, smeared in camo and mud. They carry M16s and wear knives taped to combat harnesses hung with grenades. They reach out to him as a solemn comrade at arms, meeting in spirit if not in flesh. It was a powerful image and Doc was deeply moved by it.

"Every time I get my ass kicked on the Hill, every time I lose to the politicians who worry about where something gets built more than if we need it, or if it will work, I think about this painting and having to face those boys. And I wonder, don't these other guys have ghosts they have to answer to? Boys who died or will die because of the decisions we make? How can you be human and not feel accountable? How can you clean out a savings and loan, or sell drugs to kids, or swindle investors with worthless stock, or build unsafe cars... how can people do things like that and not believe that someday they're going to have to come to this wall? How about you, Dr. Holiday, have you got faces in the stone you'll have to answer to?"

"I was there. I have my ghosts," Doc answered.

"Yes, from what Bill told me, I was sure you did. I do too, and that's why I'm here to apologize to you, Doc. I'm Andy Anderson, Secretary of the Navy."

"Andy was the corpsman who came after me and saved my tail on Operation Arizona. I got shot up a little," Chaplain Stone explained.

"He also got a Congressional Medal of Honor, which he refused."

"I heard a little about that," Doc said.

"Yes, but I didn't fly over here to swap war stories, Doc. You got a raw deal from us and I thought you deserve an explanation."

He confirmed what Doc had learned about Behrmann, Roberts, Richardson and the building of the *Black Wolf.* He added that while they had rebuilt most of the satellite computer surveillance network, there was still no trace of the sub. "Doc, that sub cost us billions to develop, and it could save us billions in the future, plus a lot of Navy lives. We have to protect her and keep her out of the press until we can get her back. You've seen her. You know what a disaster it would be if she fell into the wrong hands."

"Then you believe she's still out there in one piece?"

"Oh, yes, and it's just a matter of time until we find her. I just wanted to explain that to you personally, in case you had any intentions...well, you know."

"Excuse me, sir. You've got a lot bigger problem than keeping me quiet. That sub's already in the wrong hands. Did you know that when Behrmann sank that little freighter, he was really hunting for a cruise ship carrying our troops to the Normandy invasion?"

"What? A cruise ship? I was told Richardson sank that freighter for the drugs."

"That's very convenient. Did you know Behrmann has a boat-load of torpedoes and a very bad attitude towards the U.S. Navy? He intends to use those fish to get even, and when they're gone he'll make more. Oh, you can keep me quiet, sir, but that won't solve your problem. You've got to find that sub and if you can't get it back, you'd sure as hell better destroy it."

"Doc, you're over your head here. That sub cost billions and my team assured me..."

"How are you going to find it, sir? Isn't the sub undetectable? Won't you have to wait until she shows herself again? All Behrmann has to do is have one little relapse, think he's back in his war again, and guess what he's going to do. Or perhaps by now he's crazy enough, or pissed enough, to sink a few thousand tons of our ships just for fun. Then you won't have a bit of trouble finding him, will you?"

Anderson tugged on his tie and looked at Chaplain Stone and then back at Doc.

"If somehow," Doc continued, "you got the chance to talk to Behrmann, is there a chance of getting his turbines and hydrogen peroxide plant built?"

Anderson's jaw tightened. "They won't build it, I can tell you that. They're terrified of the economic implications. Just a minute, Doc. I see where you're headed and I don't like it one bit. We may not be ready to build his engines, but we sure as hell can't let anyone else have that technology. You can see that, can't you?"

"I can see a lot," Doc answered, "and I'd say you've got a big problem." Doc let his defiance hang in the air. Should he tell the secretary about the set of plans Debbie had copied? They were all safe as long as he kept that quiet. They could destroy those disks and no one would know. That's what an onion peeler would do, he thought and scowled. But if he kept quiet, Behrmann could pick any targets he wanted. What then? Screw it! What's the difference between one live grenade in your pocket or two? Play the hand. "Just one more question, Mr. Secretary, if you don't mind."

"Yes?" Anderson answered. He put his hands on his hips like a gunfighter.

"Just suppose there were another set of plans for that sub. How would that change the game?"

"It would make that sub expendable if that's what you mean."

"And...what if Behrmann found out about them?" Doc prompted.

"He or whomever he's working for would certainly want them out of circulation," Anderson said. He was beginning to get the picture and his eyebrow went up like a bad poker player who had just filled an inside straight. "And I'd say that would be very dangerous for the one holding the plans. What are you telling me, Doc? Have you got those plans? If you do..."

"I said just suppose. Now swear to me—swear by everything this picture in front of us means to you, and by everything else you hold sacred—swear that the Navy is clean in this, and that you'll build his turbines and that hydrogen peroxide fuel system. Then we'll talk."

"You're living awfully close to the edge, Dr. Holiday. I'd be real careful."

Anderson straightened his tie and buttoned his jacket. "Good to see you, Bill," he said and headed towards the door. He pulled it open, paused and turned around. "You'll be hearing from me, Doc. I'll do what I can," he said and was gone.

Debbie was wearing an engagement ring. The diamond

was small, but large enough to do the job and her face was glowing. Doc had never seen her more beautiful or more happy. She sat between her father and Tom on the patio of the Squire's Inn overlooking one of the island's most picturesque coves. They were waiting for Janet, Paul and Inspector Cord. Sheri, Lisa and Lt. Berry were seated across the table.

"You mean he'd been in the hospital for weeks and no one had even called? No family or old students? That's terrible," Debbie said when Doc finished telling them about his trip to Texas. "How do you suppose he knew so much about Behrmann and Richardson?"

"I suppose from Roberts. But Travis was pretty adamant that I didn't ask questions."

"I think I know," Lisa offered. "Four years ago, when I worked on San Salvador Island with Jason looking for the Columbus sites, he got a letter that sent him into orbit for two or three days. I'd never seen him so angry. When he finally decided to talk, he told me about his parents. His father had died when he was quite young and his mother, Anna, married a college professor. The professor was away a lot and she got lonely, so she started seeing other men. She left Jason alone, sometimes for days, while she was off on her forays.

"Then when Jason was still pretty young, she left and didn't come back. A few days later he got called by the police—to come identify her body. It was a sailing accident, I think. Anyway, the professor was in Greece or Egypt or somewhere. And little Jason had to take care of the funeral arrangements on his own. It was weeks before the professor returned. Jason lived with foster parents after that, until he was old enough for college. As you've guessed by now, Jason's stepfather was Dr. Ben Travis."

"No wonder the old buzzard didn't want me asking questions; did you ever find out what was in the letter?"

"Only bits and pieces. In spite of what had happened, it was obvious Jason wanted the professor's approval and wanted to work with him. It was as if he would never be a whole person until he had the old man's blessing. So he got scholarships to A&M and set out to be an archaeologist, like Travis. He was brilliant, but there was a terrible scandal his last year of grad school."

"Drugs?" Doc asked.

"Right. Cocaine arrests at the frat house. Jason sold coke and traded it for sex. He never got caught, but he had undergrads working for him, and two of them got busted. One of those boys was the son of Ben Travis's department head. Both boys refused to implicate Jason, but old Ben's boss was certain Jason was guilty. Jason laughed about it when he told me.

"It put old Ben in a very bad light, probably ruined his career. And Jason got away clean. No one ever proved anything so Jason didn't even lose his scholarships. He graduated with honors. But now Travis wanted nothing to do with him. I think that's what the letter was about. Jason was coming to Bermuda and he wanted something. Travis told him where to stuff it."

"What goes around comes around, does it not?" Doc said.

"With parents like that, no wonder he was such a jerk," Sheri said.

"Yes," Doc said. "But before we start feeling too sorry for him, remember what happened to him was the result of his own actions, his own choices."

"And the sins they commit two by two, they shall pay for one by one, aye? Sounds like pretty heavy stuff, Doc," Ian said from behind him. "Welcome back. I understand this party is for Debbie and Tom, so why are you doing all the talking?"

Janet, Paul and Ian joined the table and after an hour of good food and laughter, Ian steered the conversation to a more serious topic.

"Doc, I hate to bring this up, but we have some unfinished business about your private war on Maldias—and the cost to the Bermuda government for the cleanup. But first, I need to tell you I had a visit today—some lads from some government task force in the States. They were hot to know everything we found on the *Nautilus,* wanted to search her themselves. They wanted to know if we found any computer disks. It was my pleasure to tell them no and send them packing.

"We contacted the original owners in St. Thomas. They'll be coming to get the sub and take her home. Now I understand from Paul that you've taken a year's leave and want to stay here on my island. If I worked for Immigration and had a conscience, I'd put in overtime to prevent that. But I don't and overtime isn't authorized, so you are probably safe. However, since you are going to be here, I was able to get the commissioner to agree to a bit of a trade.

"We have this 65-foot sportfisherman we confiscated. Perhaps you remember her? She'll be needing a good bit of upkeep until we sell her, and frankly that's not in the departmental budget. So I suggested that we find someone who knows a little about boats, someone who owes the government, and someone who would rather do a bit of sandin' and paintin' than work on a road crew to pay his debt to society.

"The sad news is that among my other duties as chief inspector is the organizing of government sales. But you know how bloody overworked we civil servants are. It could take years before I even find that paperwork, much less have the motive and opportunity to organize said sale. So I'm afraid you may be stuck with that boat for a long time. However, I was able to authorize a slip at the Dockyard so you won't have to keep her on your front lawn or anything."

Without giving Doc a chance to speak, Ian handed over the keys and two large envelopes of documents. The others applauded and Doc was speechless. Then Ian asked him inside the restaurant for a drink and a private talk.

"Doc, when I had a chance to think about what I said at our meeting at the Commissioner's House, I was not very proud of myself. Then Paul paid me a visit and let me know that he wasn't proud of me either. I don't know what's going to happen officially, but I want you to know that when this heats up again, and it will, I'm in. Pension or no pension. I guess it's 'in for a shilling, in for a pound.' Come by the office when you can. I managed to hang on to most of that illegal hardware we confiscated with the boat. I have a feeling we're going to be needing it again real soon. Enjoy the boat. She's yours for as long as you want her. Just try to keep the bullet holes above the waterline, please."

A fortnight passed with no word of the *Black Wolf.* Doc

took possession of the boat. He and Sheri moved on board and while Sheri worked at the institute, he worked getting the boat shipshape. He equipped her with the recirculators and salvage gear. Mike supplied the ammunition for the hardware Ian contributed. Doc built depth charges and ordered acoustical profiling equipment. If the *Black Wolf* couldn't be seen, perhaps she could be heard.

He lived in anticipation of the call that did not come from the Navy, and by the end of the third week Sheri was asking if it might really be over. And if it was, would she have to give back the Smith & Wesson? At the end of the fourth week, they invited everyone for a meal and an evening cruise. Sheri was below changing when Tom and Debbie arrived. She had spent the day in the water with a new group of students from William and Mary.

Tom came over the transom carrying a large box which he handed down to Doc. They walked into the spacious salon. An area rug covered the bullet holes that were Maldias's epitaph. But the carpet was clean and the cabin window had been replaced.

"Debbie, come and see the master stateroom," Sheri called up to her.

"Mirrors everywhere," Doc explained to Tom. "I was going to take them down, but she threw a fit, so we have mirrors. What's in the box?"

"Better let Debbie tell you."

The girls came up laughing and Debbie gave her father a hug. She picked up the box and explained, "I had insurance on my computer and they got me a new one, but I want to keep the one you put my hard drive in. Now you have no more excuses for not working. We'll call it a boat-warming present, although from what Sheri tells me, it stays plenty warm around here already. Really, Father! I'm shocked!" she teased with a raised eyebrow.

"Come on, I want to show you something before the others get here," she said as she took the computer out of its box. She lifted up the screen, turned it on, and after running through a security sequence, she said, "Behold the *Black Wolf*. I don't understand most of it, and no one's seen this but Tom and I. When we finally cracked the last of Roberts's codes on the programs at work, we were able to open this. Have you heard anything from the Secretary of the Navy?"

"No," Doc said as he scrolled through the pages, examining the elaborate engineering drawings of the sub. "And I'm not holding my breath, but I know he'll be calling. Behrmann won't give him any choice."

Doc turned off the computer as Mark and Lisa stepped down the stern ladder followed by Paul and Janet.

"What are you going to call her?" Paul asked as they came into the salon.

"We've been arguing about that for two weeks," Doc laughed. "I wanted to do something clever with Sheri's name in it, but she refused. So we compromised. The name we chose is from the note Dr. Travis wrote. We'll call her *Kratos*, which means caretaker or guardian. Pretty appropriate, don't you think?"

After dinner Doc brought out the Greek chalice and set it on the table in front of Lisa. Her eyes widened with wonder. "It's beautiful!" she exclaimed. "Just think of the history connected with it."

"And the stories it could tell," Sheri added.

"Or the trouble it could bring to all of us," Doc reminded them.

The phone rang and Sheri answered. "It's Mike," she said, listening intently. Her eyes opened wide and a look of distress came over her face. She leaned back against the bulkhead. "I'll tell him," she said before placing the phone down.

"My God!" she said as she turned to face them. "It's the *Black Wolf*. It's started just like you said, Doc. The Navy's sending a helicopter. They want you to fly to Washington.